RUÍZ WAS HERS.

She was his. Secretly, she had promised herself to him, long ago.

Stroking and caressing, his hands moved through her hair. He lifted his mouth from hers, leaving an aching void, only to salve the hurt by raining tiny kisses over her upturned face.

Julia curled her fingers in the rich, brown waves of his hair while his lips and teeth drove her wild. He nibbled and licked, first her earlobe, then down the column of her throat. She melted into his embrace. Wanting to be closer, needing to be closer . . .

The winery door thudded open.

BOOK YOUR PLACE ON OUR WEBSITE AND MAKE THE READING CONNECTION!

We've created a customized website just for our very special readers, where you can get the inside scoop on everything that's going on with Zebra, Pinnacle and Kensington books.

When you come online, you'll have the exciting opportunity to:

- View covers of upcoming books
- Read sample chapters
- Learn about our future publishing schedule (listed by publication month *and author*)
- Find out when your favorite authors will be visiting a city near you
- Search for and order backlist books from our online catalog
- Check out author bios and background information
- Send e-mail to your favorite authors
- Meet the Kensington staff online
- Join us in weekly chats with authors, readers and other guests
- Get writing guidelines
- AND MUCH MORE!

**Visit our website at
http://www.zebrabooks.com**

MIDNIGHT PROMISE

Hebby Roman

Zebra Books
Kensington Publishing Corp.

http://www.zebrabooks.com

For my friend of over thirty years,
Robin Howard Hill,
whose unflagging support and enthusiasm
gave me the courage to write

ZEBRA BOOKS are published by

Kensington Publishing Corp.
850 Third Avenue
New York, NY 10022

Copyright © 1998 by Hebby Roman

First Printing: October, 1998
10 9 8 7 6 5 4 3 2 1

Printed in the United States of America

Prologue

Coahuila y Tejas, México, 1835

The smoke of burning *copal* filled Ruíz Navarro's nostrils and shrouded the room in a blue haze. Stars of light, from dozens of burning wax tapers, flickered in the aromatic fog.

One entire wall was eclipsed by the elaborate *ofrenda,* composed of a woven arch of greenery, garnished with fruits and flowers. The flowers made brilliant mounds of color, particularly the vivid oranges and yellows of the *cempasúchil,* the flower of the dead.

A table sat in front of the *ofrenda,* laden with tiny dishes bearing delicate foodstuffs. Traditional spun sugar animals cavorted with colorful toys to complete the offering to the souls of dead children.

Tomorrow, the table would be set with an array of sophisticated and spicy dishes. Wine and *mescale* would also be provided for the adult souls' enjoyment.

Las Días de Muertos celebrated a time of reverence and

remembered joy. It evoked the essence of a family reunion, not only for the living but also for the dead, who, for a few brief hours, returned to be with their relatives in this world.

Ruíz's wife and infant son had died last December.

Felipe Flores, understanding Ruíz's loss, had urged him to join the Flores family's celebration. But while Ruíz watched the Flores's simple ceremony, an ugly emptiness rose within him. In his search for solace, his craving for connection, he felt more alone than before.

His son was lost to him forever, nineteen days old when he had died.

But even worse . . . he'd never known Alicia, his wife of five years.

Ruíz closed his eyes in anguish as the realization swept over him. If he hadn't touched their souls when they were living, how could he hope to reach them from beyond the grave?

Shame overwhelmed him. Shame and guilt for the hollowness of his life, for all the missed opportunities. His presence at this celebration was a mockery. It was too painful to remain. He edged along the wall until he reached the front door and slipped silently from the Flores's *casa*. Once outside, he gulped the sharp, chilly air and tried to push the haunting memories away.

His gaze rested on the sprawling *hacienda* of his parents. There would be no similar celebration in the Navarro household. His mother, a *criollo* of noble descent, abhorred Las Días de Muertos as a crude superstition. His family preferred the conventional and sterile blessing of Todos Santos.

Frowning, Ruíz lifted his face to the star-studded autumn sky. They would need every blessing and superstition.

War was coming.

Chapter One

Republic of Texas, 1836

"Look at this, *Papito*," Julia Flores carefully parted the shredded leaves to reveal the battered grapevine.

Felipe Flores ran his hand over the gnarled trunk with quiet reverence. He shook his head. "It's not good."

"We need to prune them . . . now," Julia stated emphatically.

"Mi hija, you overstep yourself. I must counsel with *el patrón.*"

"But Don Federico is away at the war."

"The war is over, and he is expected to return any day. I want to wait for him. It is a serious decision. Pruning will limit this year's crop. That would make two lean years in a row. Last year, it was red spiders. This year, a hailstorm." Felipe's shoulders drooped in weary dejection.

Julia felt a swift stab of sympathy. Her father tried so hard but so many forces were aligned against him. Her own frustration and sense of injustice found voice, "Doña Eugenia is a worse hazard than a thousand hailstorms!"

Her father sucked in his breath, and his voice thundered, "Julia! It is not your place to speak of such things."

"But she's ruining us, *Papito,* with her extravagant spending. She squanders money faster than the vineyard can produce it. The debts are mounting. It's painful for me to keep the ledgers. And no matter how many times I explain the situation to Don Federico, he ignores me."

"Sometimes I think it was a mistake to educate you, Julia. Maybe if we hadn't, you would have married and started a family instead of—"

"*Papito,* how can you say that? Los Montes Verdes is my home. I am content here, but I can't stand by and watch Doña Eugenia destroy everything we work so hard for. Don Federico should control his wife."

Felipe met Julia's gaze. His eyes were troubled. "Because you are unmarried, you do not understand how it is between a man and a woman. Sometimes . . ." His voice faltered, and he cleared his throat. "We will speak no more of this."

"But the pruning, *Papito.* It must be done before the vines produce the new grapes."

His patience obviously at an end, he answered sharply. "*Bastante,* Julia. I know the pruning must be done. Trust me to do what's best."

Instantly contrite for having upset her beloved papa, Julia lowered her eyes and replied, "*Sí, Papito.*"

"*Muy bien.*" His voice softened. "Now I must help Paco. Some of the casks need turning. Shall we start back?"

Hesitating, she glanced at the sky to judge the sun's ascent. In the distance, the whitewashed hacienda compound shimmered in the morning heat. Shaking her head, she replied, "I want to walk among the vines. You go ahead. Tell *Mamá* I'll return to help her prepare the midday meal."

Drawing her into his arms, he gave her a quick hug. With

his hand resting lightly on her shoulder, he counseled, "Don't worry, *mi hija*. It will all turn out for the best."

As she watched him walk away, Julia wished she shared her father's faith. Los Montes Verdes was in her blood. She loved the land and the vines with a fierce possessiveness. And she would fight with every ounce of her strength to save the vineyard.

Ruíz . . .

She had loved him since time before time. Even when he had married a stranger and fathered children, she had gone on loving him. She loved him still, dreaming of a time when . . .

Ruíz flashed by on his distinctive golden stallion, leading his father's black mare.

He lived! Her limbs were like water, gone weak with relief. She sank slowly to the ground. For a moment, she felt joy sweep through her and the blood sang in her veins. Ruíz was alive!

But Don Federico . . .

In the distance, she heard the melancholy jangle of empty, silver-chased stirrups. Grief, that black abyss for which there was no real consolation, sucked her brief joy into its gaping maw, leaving an echoing void inside her.

She lay on the warm earth, sobbing. Despite Don Federico's inadequacies as a *patrón*, Julia had loved him like a favorite uncle. He had been a kind and gentle man. A man who hated strife and confrontations.

How ironic that he'd died in the ugliest confrontation of all . . . war.

San Antonio de Béxar, the oldest settlement in Tejas, lay hushed in the early-morning quiet. The silence was so complete, Julia could hear the doves cooing in the eaves of San Fernando Cathedral. The Flores family had arrived early, expecting to be included in the private, sunrise mass for Don Federico.

Touching her mother's elbow, Julia asked, "Why haven't we gone in? The mass has already begun."

Pilar turned and said, "We will be attending the later mass."

"Why? That mass is the public one. Family and close friends always attend—"

Felipe leaned from the other side of Pilar to answer Julia's question, "We were instructed to wait."

Julia considered her father's answer before realization dawned within her. Recognizing the humiliating truth, she demanded loudly, "What did Doña Eugenia tell you?"

Pilar's wide brown eyes gazed at Julia with obvious disapproval. The empty courtyard in front of the cathedral was beginning to fill. Her mother admonished, "Softly, Julia. Others will hear you."

Julia refused to be hushed. She was no longer a child. Lowering her voice, she persisted, "What did *she* say?"

Lifting one perfectly arched eyebrow, Pilar straightened the black shawl draped over her head. "Doña Eugenia merely suggested we weren't part of the family. She asked us to wait."

Her brother, Paco, flippantly interjected, "Satisfied, *mi hermana?*"

Ignoring Paco, Julia clenched her fists until her nails cut into her palms. She burned with barely suppressed fury. *Not a part of the family,* she thought heatedly.

Her grandfather, Juan Flores, had helped carve Los Montes Verdes from the wilderness alongside Don Federico's father, Don Luis. Although Juan had come to the New World as Don Luis's servant, his loyalty and service had distinguished him. Don Luis had made him his partner, rewarding the Flores family with a quarter interest in the vineyard.

Julia realized the partnership with their common family rankled the aristocratic sensibilities of Doña Eugenia. But there was more to Doña Eugenia's animosity than that. Over the years, her obvious hatred had taken on the shape of a personal vendetta. Julia had often wondered about it.

Voices and shuffling feet interrupted her thoughts. The cathedral courtyard had become crowded. It appeared as if all of San Antonio was here to pay their last respects to Don Federico.

Her gaze snagged on a tall *vaquero*. He stood awkwardly, his wide sombrero crushed between his rough hands. It took her a moment before she recognized him as Señor Soto. She remembered him because she had heard a rumor that he was secretly courting Teresa Navarro, Ruíz's sister.

Studying him, she felt a spontaneous empathy for the man. His expression was expectant, as if he wanted nothing more than a brief glimpse of his beloved's face. His naked longing brought a constriction to Julia's throat, and she turned her gaze away. It was painful to watch him. His face reflected her own secret, unfulfilled longings.

A dull thud reverberated through the courtyard as the massive, carved doors of the cathedral swung open. The mourners solemnly descended the cathedral steps. Her mother and father, and even her brother, lowered their heads in deference to tradition when the Navarros approached them. But Julia kept her head defiantly lifted, her eyes fixed straight ahead.

Ruíz's glance fell on her family. Julia saw a perplexed expression cross his face. She guessed that he was surprised to find the Flores family at the bottom of the cathedral's steps, waiting. But he covered his initial reaction smoothly and stopped to acknowledge them. Shaking hands with her father, he nodded to her mother and then Paco.

His eyes met hers.

Julia felt the breath leave her body. His eyes struck sparks within her, sending scintillating sensations along her nerves. She stared back, mesmerized by his obvious awareness of her.

Ruíz's cocoa-colored eyes boldly lingered. She felt their invisible pull, their tentative awakening. And she gloried in it, experiencing a tiny frisson of pleasure. Almost as if he were touching her.

But it was Doña Eugenia who was touching Ruíz and pulling

him away. Ruíz bent and murmured something to his mother and took her arm.

The Navarros ran the gauntlet of people offering their condolences. When they finally left the cathedral courtyard, Ruíz handed his mother and sister into the carriage. He mounted his palomino stallion, Oro, and signaled the driver to return to the hacienda.

Until he had emerged from the cathedral, Ruíz hadn't realized the Flores family had been excluded from the private mass for his father. He frowned to himself. His father wouldn't have approved. Don Federico had loved Felipe like a brother. He knew that his mother was behind their exclusion. As much as his father had cared for the Flores family, his mother hated them with an equal zeal.

He had barely recognized old Felipe's daughter. When had the lanky, pesky girl he'd played with as a boy turned into such a beauty? Her mother, Pilar, had always been stunning. And Julia possessed her mother's lovely features, further refined to an almost ethereal elegance.

The brief glimpse of her face haunted him: smoldering dark emerald eyes, the color inherited from her father, framed by expressive, arched eyebrows and thick eyelashes. Her heart-shaped face was enhanced by a high brow and glossy, midnight-black hair. A slender aquiline nose exaggerated the wide, ruby curve of her lips.

A full, generous mouth. Perfect for kissing . . .

Ruíz shook himself, startling Oro. The spirited golden stallion danced sideways for a few steps until the authoritative pressure from his knees brought the palomino under control.

He didn't want to think about Julia, but he couldn't help but wonder. Obviously she had never married. If she had, he would have been invited to the wedding, but there had been no wedding for Julia Flores.

Swiftly calculating backward from his own age, he realized she must be over twenty years old. A veritable spinster.

Felipe Flores was a thrifty man. Julia's dowry, combined with her striking beauty, should have won her an army of suitors. The question echoed in his mind like a refrain.

Why hadn't Julia married?

Chapter Two

"Conchita! Not so fast, little one. Wait for me."

Concepción Navarro, nicknamed Conchita, giggled and scampered ahead at an even faster pace.

Julia sighed. Ruíz's four-year-old daughter was irrepressible, full of excited energy. Not comprehending the solemn occasion of her grandfather's funeral, she merely reacted to the unusual commotion at the hacienda with predictable, childish agitation. The steady stream of visitors, some with children her own age, had elicited a frenzy of activity from the high-spirited child.

Recognizing that Luz, Conchita's nurse, was practically at her wit's end, Julia had offered to watch the child for the afternoon. A relieved Luz had readily agreed.

When Conchita disappeared down the slope to the river, Julia picked up her pace. The cane fishing poles banged against her shoulder as she sprinted faster, worrying that Conchita might fall into the water. Topping the slope to the river, she almost fell over the child, who had stopped to gather the pink primroses growing there.

Frowning, Julia admonished, ''If you run off again, I shall be forced to punish you.''

Conchita looked contrite and offered Julia a fistful of flowers.

Suppressing a laugh at the child's obvious bribe, Julia accepted the flowers and repeated, ''Don't wander off. You don't want to be punished.''

With her lower lip trembling, Conchita pleaded, ''No, *Tía* Julia. Don't punish me.''

Unable to remain stern for long, Julia relented, ''I wouldn't hurt you, *mi niña.* But you'll be sorry if you disobey me again.''

The little girl's eyes widened until they eclipsed her face. Laughing, Julia threw down the fishing poles and grabbed for her. Fast as lightning, Conchita eluded her. They raced up and down the slope. Julia purposely let her get away.

''When I catch you, I'll tickle you to death!'' Julia shouted.

At Julia's threat, Conchita burst into giggles and dodged her with surprising agility. Finally, huffing and puffing from the prolonged game of chase, Julia ended it by pouncing on Conchita and holding the child to the ground. She raised her hands and curled her fingers. Hovering over Conchita's ticklish tummy, she teased, ''Tickle, tickle . . . tickle.''

Wriggling and straining, Conchita tried to escape while squealing uncontrollably. After a few moments of spirited play, Julia lifted Conchita to her feet and hugged the child close. Gazing into the little girl's eyes, she admonished, ''I wasn't playing earlier when I said you must stay with me, where I can always see you. *¿Entiende?*''

Nodding, the child wrapped her arms around Julia's neck. Cuddling Conchita close, the sweet smell of sun-warmed child enveloped Julia and tender longings filled her. She loved Conchita and enjoyed spending time with her. She might never have a child of her own. And the child's warm brown eyes reminded her of Ruíz's eyes when he was a boy.

Ruíz, the man, had changed. The expression in his eyes was different now, cold and hooded, except when caught unawares outside the cathedral. He had actually noticed her then, and the usual haughty stamp of his features had been momentarily banished.

Releasing Conchita, Julia rose to her feet, retrieving the fishing poles and flowers. Hand in hand, they ambled down to the old, gnarled live oak on the bank of the Guadalupe River.

The deep green pool beneath the spreading limbs of the oak was their special place to fish. Julia had taught Conchita how to fish, just as Ruíz had taught Julia years before. Fishing was Conchita's favorite activity. The little girl didn't really fish, but she liked to play at it.

Julia baited both the hooks with pieces of bacon. Handing one pole to the child, she urged, "Go ahead, toss it in."

Concentrating intently, Conchita threw her line out. It fell into the water with a soft plunk. Julia tossed her line in beside it. They watched as their lines drifted with the gentle tug of the current through the wide, deep pool.

After a few moments, Conchita lost interest. She bounded off in pursuit of a large orange-and-black butterfly. Julia stayed, watching the poles. Even though they seldom got a bite, Conchita didn't seem to mind. The child was obviously enthralled with the relative freedom of the riverbank.

And it was a joy to watch her run and play in the spring sunshine.

The murmur of voices drifted to Ruíz from beneath the slope. He had unerringly headed for the huge oak by the river. When he was a child, it had been his favorite place.

Pausing at the top of the slope, he surveyed the scene. The tree hadn't changed. Its low, twisted branches spread, like protective arms, embracing both shore and river. The rotted remnants of an old rope swing, high in the branches, caught his eye. As children, he and Julia had spent many hours swinging giddily through the air and plunging into the chilly waters of the Guadalupe. And now Julia was there, playing with his own child.

Their heads were nestled together, Concepción's brown curls next to Julia's thick, black braid. Julia was baiting the lines for them. Seeing his daughter with Julia, Ruíz felt a peculiar constriction in his chest. He was happy his childhood friend was with his daughter, but it raised troubling questions again. Why hadn't Julia married? Why didn't she have her own children?

His daughter threw her line into the river and waited for a few minutes. An orange-and-black butterfly drifted by, and Concepción jumped up to follow it.

Deciding it was time to announce his presence, he called out, "Julia, Concepción, caught anything?"

At the sound of Ruíz's voice, Julia twisted around and looked behind her. Ruíz stood at the top of the slope. He was dressed in formal clothes, a snowy-white linen shirt and black cord pants tucked into glossy, knee-high boots. The clothing emphasized his broad chest and muscular thighs.

With her heart in her throat, Julia stared at his familiar face. His dark-brown, wavy hair lifted off his collar in the breeze. Unlike most men, he wore his hair short, cut off below his ears. He had never possessed the patience to tame its unruly waves.

Cocoa-brown eyes held hers, and she felt the sparks ignite within her all over again. His nose was long and classic but with a bump in the middle, a token of the time he had broken it when he was twelve years old. His mouth, like his eyes, had undergone a transformation over the years. When he was a boy, it had been mobile and inviting. Now, it was set in a thin line.

He was still a handsome man . . . handsome enough to take her breath away.

Conchita ran to Ruíz. The lure of the butterfly was forgotten in her open joy at seeing her father. But Ruíz didn't take his daughter in his arms. He merely bent down and patted her cheek. "Finish your play because soon it will be time for your nap."

The child stared at her toes for a moment, obviously longing for some further sign of affection from him. But Ruíz had already dismissed her. Conchita glanced at Julia, and she nodded to the little girl. Reluctantly, the child returned to the shore and began to gather pebbles, singing softly to herself.

A wave of fury rolled over Julia. Ruíz didn't even know how to be loving toward his own child. Doña Eugenia had trained him well. Julia shook her head. The boy she had loved had become a man she didn't particularly like. Yet, his mere presence still enflamed her senses.

Julia concentrated on the fishing lines as Ruíz approached her. He lowered himself to the ground, sitting uncomfortably close to her. He didn't say anything, he just sat there, watching the river slide past them.

Not able to contain her anger, she observed sharply, "You'll dirty your fine pants, sitting here."

He merely grunted.

An awkward silence grew between them. Julia could feel the warmth emanating from his body, and it made her restless. It filled her with all the old yearnings. Wanting to ignore her runaway feelings, she asked the first thing that came to her mind. "Did Luz send you?"

He shook his head.

Nervous with his mute but disturbing presence, she started to babble. "I would have brought Conchita home in plenty of time for her nap. She needed a place to run off some of her energy. The last few days have been hard on the child. She doesn't understand . . ."

Julia caught herself, not wanting to raise the painful subject of Don Federico's death. Drawing a deep breath, she waited for Ruíz to speak.

His voice was pensive when he replied, "None of us truly

understand. Do we?'' He looked away and cleared his throat. Abruptly, he asked, ''What did you call her?''

''Her?'' Julia searched her mind for his meaning. Realization dawned and she offered tentatively, ''You mean . . . Conchita.''

''I like that. I've never had a pet name for her.'' He unfolded his long legs and stretched them before him.

She tried not to notice the corded strength of the muscles in his thighs as he flexed them. Turning her head, she answered, ''Luz and all my family call her Conchita. I think she likes it.''

''Sí,'' he mused. ''Concepción is quite a mouthful for such a little one. It was her mother's choice.''

''Oh'' was all Julia said. She knew it wasn't charitable of her because Ruíz's wife was dead, but she didn't care to be reminded that he had been intimately linked to another woman. It made her secret longings seem that much more foolish.

''If you don't mind, I think I would like to call her Conchita, too.''

''Ask the child,'' Julia snapped. His complacency, while casually referring to his dead wife and admitting that he'd never bothered to gift his daughter with her own special nickname, infuriated Julia.

Ruíz's eyes, filled with mild curiosity, scanned her face. But he must have decided to overlook her sharp tone because his voice was neutral when he replied, ''Concep— Conchita's nap was an excuse. Like my daughter, I needed a respite. It was all becoming too . . . hard.''

Glancing at him from the corner of her eyes, Julia realized he was obviously hurting. She wished she could retract her earlier words. She opened her mouth to apologize, but before she could get the words out, Conchita ran up, shouting, *''Mira, Papá,* all the pretty stones I gathered.''

Conchita had filled the pockets of her apron with rocks of all shapes, sizes, and colors. Enthusiastically, she began dumping them into her father's lap. Glowing with satisfaction, she asked, *"Papá,* you like pretty stones?"

Ruíz gazed down at his rock-strewn lap. Julia watched while he tried to suppress a grin that tugged at the corners of his mouth. "Conchita, I like them very much. Such a collection! You don't mind if I call you Conchita, like Julia does. Do you?"

Beaming under her father's rare praise, she seemed puzzled by his question. Shrugging one tiny shoulder, she replied, "Everyone calls me that, *Papá.* You don't have to ask."

"Muy bien. I'm glad you approve."

Lowering her head, she scuffed one sandal in the dust. "You haven't thanked me for the stones."

Julia coughed, fighting to hide her amusement. She knew Conchita was parroting Luz's recent lessons on the importance of being polite.

"Muchas gracias," Ruíz said, having the grace to go along with his daughter's suggestion.

"And you like so much, no nap?" Conchita negotiated.

Ruíz appeared bewildered for a moment, then awareness must have dawned because he threw back his head and roared with laughter.

Conchita appeared startled by her father's reaction. Julia knew the child was accustomed to Luz's firm approach to her maneuvering. But Ruíz's laughter was so infectious that Julia and Conchita found themselves joining him.

The laughter bubbling from Ruíz's throat sounded like the sweetest music to Julia's ears. His face relaxed, and the grim lines around his mouth faded. She felt her heart open to him.

Wiping his eyes, he stifled his chuckles and stroked Conchita's thick ringlets, agreeing, "You've convinced me, little one. No nap."

Letting out a whoop of pure joy, the little girl ran along the shore, yelling, *"Papá* like so much. I find more."

Julia's eyes met Ruíz's. He was staring at her with an awakening admiration. Self-consciously, she lowered her eyes. "Conchita's a wonderful child. And you've made her very happy."

His voice was thoughtful, "She's enchanting . . . and so much fun. I guess I've been remiss. I thought that parents don't . . . you know."

"Enjoy their children," Julia ventured softly.

He shook his head. "That wasn't exactly the word I had in mind. I was thinking more along the lines of . . . indulge. I thought parents taught discipline, instilled values. But enjoy is a good word, too."

He paused, hesitating before he asked, *"Dígame,* Julia, why aren't you enjoying your own children? You've never married. Why?"

Heat flooded her face. Caught off guard by his personal question, she cast about for a suitable response. She couldn't possibly tell him the real reason she'd never married, that she had never loved anyone but him.

"Oh, there never seemed time. I had to finish my education and then *Papá* needed help. So . . . I . . ." Her voice faltered. Even to her own ears, her excuses sounded lame.

Ruíz didn't comment. He merely studied her face for several moments. He must have sensed her discomfort, because he changed the subject again. "Still using bacon from the house?"

Julia relaxed. She hadn't realized her entire body had tensed, afraid he would guess her secret. "How did you know?"

"Because you never could stand to hurt the poor worms. I remember."

"Now it's Conchita. She can't stand to hurt the poor worms."

He chuckled. "I'm not surprised, but if you pull those lines in, you'll find the turtles have gotten your bait."

"I know, but Conchita doesn't mind. As much as she loves

to come here and fish, it upsets her even more to hurt the poor fish.''

Smiling, he reached out and playfully tugged the braid draped across her shoulder. ''I remember.'' His voice was unusually husky. ''You were the same way.''

Her skin burned where his fingers had briefly brushed her shoulder. His nearness made her uneasy. Heated awareness streaked between them like the lightning of a summer storm. Julia felt warm all over, and she knew she was blushing, *again.* Every rational thought fled her mind.

Leaning closer to him, she ached for his touch. Her body quivered, yearning to be wrapped in his embrace. Closing her eyes, she willed it. Wanting his closeness, and the taste of his lips upon hers.

He broke the spell by pulling her braid again and admitting, ''I used to yank on your braid until you cried. I guess I was a mean *hombre.*''

With an effort of will, she fought his magnetic pull. Opening her eyes slowly, she forced herself to lean away from him. ''Not so mean. I used to pester you constantly, tagging after . . .''

His voice was husky again, conveying more than he said. ''I didn't mind as much as I pretended.'' At that moment, a small body hurtled itself between the two of them, sobbing loudly. It was Conchita.

Turning instinctively to Julia, Conchita hiccoughed twice, trying to speak. Tears spilled down her chubby cheeks. After a few strangled tries, she managed to point to her knee and cry, ''I fell down. Hurt my knee.''

Julia lifted the child's skirt. Conchita's left knee was scraped raw and bleeding. Wiping away the little girl's tears, she reassured her, ''Don't worry, *mi niña,* it isn't hurt too badly. But we will need to return to the hacienda. You want me to carry you?''

Conchita nodded.

"Esperaté. I'll take her," Ruíz offered. "You gather the fishing things."

In obvious deference to his daughter's feelings, he carefully scooped up the rocks she had given him and put them in his pockets. Julia pulled the lines into shore. Ruíz had been right, the bait was gone.

Rising gracefully to his feet, he stooped over and swept his daughter into his arms. Tenderly, he cradled her against his shoulder and asked if she was comfortable.

Smiling through her tears, Conchita nodded and laid her head on his shoulder. Ruíz kissed his daughter's forehead.

Glimpsing a suspicious brightness in his eyes, Julia felt as if her heart would burst, watching him tenderly hold his daughter.

Maybe there was hope for the boy she had loved.

Raising his eyes from the ledgers scattered on the oak desk before him, Ruíz didn't want to believe their contents. But the figures were there, in black and white.

He glanced at Julia and Felipe. Julia was sitting with her back perfectly straight and her hands folded in her lap. Her eyes were opaque, revealing nothing of her thoughts. Gone was the warm-hearted girl from the riverbank. Her thick, blue-black hair was pulled into a severe bun at the nape of her neck. Her daydress was plain, a dove-gray color that buttoned tightly at her throat.

Ruíz had been surprised to learn that Julia kept the books for Los Montes Verdes, but upon further reflection, it made sense. She had always had a good head for figures. After he had married and moved away, she had completed her education and assumed responsibility for the accounts.

"Did my father review these books?"

"Sí, mi patrón," Felipe replied.

"Felipe, don't call me that. I'm not . . ." Ruíz commanded harshly. He stopped himself and cleared his throat. He hadn't meant to snap at Felipe. It was just that he couldn't believe his father would have allowed such unbridled spending.

Ashamed at taking his frustration out on the man, he apologized, "I'm sorry, Felipe. I didn't mean to be sharp with you, but, *por favor,* don't call me *el patrón.* Those days are over. Father and I fought for independence from the old ways. Now we are partners. Agreed?"

Felipe inclined his head, but Ruíz doubted he really understood. The old traditions died hard.

"How often did my father go over the books?"

"Every month, *mi* . . . ah, Señor Ruíz."

"Every month," Ruíz muttered to himself. His fingers drummed a nervous cadence against the bound calfskin volumes.

He had just come from the reading of his father's will. The Navarros' three-quarter interest in Los Montes Verdes had been split between him and his mother. The hacienda and all its furnishings had been left to his mother. Teresa, his sister, had been bequeathed a handsome dowry. There were no surprises in his father's will. Spanish tradition had been followed to the letter. The surprise was that the vineyard was floundering under a mountain of debt. And there was no money for Teresa's dowry.

¡Perdición! He thought furiously. There wasn't enough money for the workers' wages, much less a dowry!

This year's crop would be crucial to the vineyard's future. He hadn't taken the time to inspect the vines since he'd returned home.

He spoke his fears. "The vineyard, what are the prospects for this year's crop?"

Felipe, obviously tense, fingered the silver cross at his throat. *"Mi* . . . Señor Ruíz, it is, that is—"

Julia's melodious but firm voice rescued her father. "Four

years ago, we had two good years of crops. Unfortunately, expenditures exceeded income even in the good years. Last year, we had an infestation of red spiders. Production went down. This year, just before you returned, the vineyard suffered a hailstorm. Some parts were damaged more than others. Even though it will limit production, we must prune the vines to save them. And we need to prune them before the new grapes appear.''

She spread her slender fingers wide. ''As you know, the vines have already flowered so there isn't much time.''

Jumping to his feet, he demanded, *''Por Dios,* why have you waited?''

Felipe went deathly still and lowered his eyes. His mouth was set in a grim line.

Shame washed over Ruíz again. Why was he terrorizing Felipe? When had he begun to disregard other people's feelings so completely?

Julia's eyes flashed emerald fire as she leapt to her father's defense. '' 'Partner,' you forget yourself. My father didn't prune the vines, despite my warnings, out of deference to your father's authority. He was waiting to consult with Don Federico, but when you returned, and . . . and . . .''

Choking back the words, she rose to her feet, too. ''We didn't want to bother you with this until your father had been properly mourned. Surely you can understand our discretion.''

''Again, I'm forced to apologize. Julia, I bow to your wisdom and to your father's loyalty. *Por favor,* forgive me, but the future of the vineyard is . . .'' He didn't bother to state the obvious as another thought occurred to him. *''Dígame,* has the Flores family received its portion of the profits in good years, before my father's extraordinary expenditures?''

Julia took her seat again and knotted her hands in her lap. ''Your father was an honorable man. The debts he incurred are his own, pledged against the Navarro portion of the vineyard. We received our share of the normal operating profits.''

Ruíz released a sigh of relief and righted his chair. Easing himself into the wide leather armchair, he was gratified to know the Flores family hadn't been directly affected by his father's profligate actions. Not yet. But if he lost the vineyard to his debtors, not only would his mother and sister suffer but the Flores family as well.

At the thought of the Flores's vulnerable position, an idea formed in his mind. The Flores family was capable of running the vineyard. It was obvious they had been operating it for a long time with little supervision from his father. Why not leave the vineyard in their capable hands? After all, it was in their best interests to help him save it. Otherwise, they would need to deal with the new owners, and they would be at a distinct disadvantage. The new owners would not be old family friends, and the Flores family only owned a minority interest. They might even be forced to sell.

By placing the responsibility of the vineyard on Felipe's shoulders, Ruíz could continue to work on his father-in-law's *rancho*. He had no desire to stay at the vineyard and sort out the dismal legacy his father had left him. Don Estéban, his father-in-law, was ill and depended upon Ruíz.

Occasionally, he could ride over to check on the vineyard. It would provide him with an opportunity to visit his daughter, too. Conchita had been staying with his mother since his wife had died. Don Estéban kept a totally male household, unsuitable for raising a small girl.

Feeling the heavy burden of rescuing the vineyard lifted from his shoulders, he was pleased with his plan. Now, all he needed to do was curb his mother's spending and find operating capital to get them through the harvest.

Leaning forward, he decided to use persuasion and flattery to present his plan. ''Felipe, I trust your judgment. You know more about operating the vineyard than I do. I want you to run it. Feel free to ask for my opinion, but you will have the final say. I need your help, partner.'' He rose halfway and extended his hand across the desk. ''Do you accept?''

Felipe's guarded face brightened instantly. His eyes were moist with obvious gratitude for the magnificent compliment he'd been given. Leaping from his seat, he grasped Ruíz's hand and shook it vigorously. ''You won't be sorry, Señor Ruíz. I promise you, we will succeed.''

Ruíz glanced at Julia to gauge her reaction to his proposal, but what he found didn't reassure him. She was sitting stiffly, with her head cocked to one side as if she were studying him. Her moss-green eyes held a knowing look. It was almost as if she had read his thoughts and understood his plan. But that was impossible.

Whether she had guessed his plan or not, she lost no time in returning the conversation to brutal reality. ''You can depend upon my father to move heaven and earth to save this vineyard. But without operating capital, I fear—''

''You needn't worry, Julia. Your father will have the money he needs. Tomorrow, I will—''

It was her turn to cut him short. ''The pruning, Ruíz. After that, the money.''

His muscles tensed at her flat reminder. A coil of anger curled in the pit of his stomach. Julia had always been demanding and stubborn. Sometimes she reminded him of his mother and that disturbed him. He would be damned before he allowed a woman to control him . . . like his mother had controlled his father.

Grinding his teeth, he fought the rising fury. He needed the Flores family's goodwill. He mustn't let Julia's demands bother him. He would do what was necessary to reassure her, but he would retain ultimate control.

With that thought in mind, he nodded and smiled. ''As you say, Julia. The pruning tomorrow.'' He inclined his head to Felipe. ''*Amigo,* we will ride out, first thing in the morning and look at the vines.'' Then, turning back to Julia, he promised, ''The next day, I will get the necessary funds.''

Felipe bobbed his head, but Julia didn't acknowledge his words. Instead, her gaze seemed to penetrate him.

She knew . . . she knew what he was trying to do. And he would stake his life that she would never allow him to forget it.

Chapter Three

The stableyard gate swung shut behind Felipe and Ruíz. Julia felt a sense of relief, watching them ride into the vineyard together. By tomorrow, the pruning would start. And not a moment too soon. Some of the vines on the sunnier slopes were beginning to lose their blossoms, revealing the tiny new grapes. Julia sighed to herself. The pruning was the first necessary task. After that, her father faced a long line of challenges to save the vineyard.

At least Ruíz had been willing to acknowledge the problems, and he seemed to understand the gravity of the situation. But he was unwilling to accept the responsibility. Instead, he had managed to shift the entire burden on to her father's shoulders, even though his family's future was at stake, too.

When had Ruíz become so hard? He was obviously accomplished at using people to further his own ends. He had her father's complete cooperation and loyalty. Felipe was too flattered by Ruíz's confidence to understand he was being manipulated. And even if her father had understood, she knew it wouldn't change anything. Los Montes Verdes mustn't be lost to strangers. If it was, the Flores family would suffer.

Her thoughts strayed to that day on the riverbank. Ruíz had seemed almost like the warm-hearted boy she had known, especially when he had taken Conchita in his arms. But Julia realized that day had been but a brief interlude. Ruíz had seemed vulnerable, mourning his father's death. As soon as the will was read, he resumed his cold, calculating ways.

The sound of high-pitched laughter drifted to Julia from the front of the compound. Conchita must be outside playing in the courtyard. Julia found herself drawn to the laughter.

The layout of Los Montes Verdes resembled a small fortress, with a high adobe wall surrounding the *hacienda,* the winery, her family's *casa,* other homes for the workers, the stable and barns and assorted outbuildings.

Don Luis and her grandfather had built a stronghold when they settled in the wilderness. Over the years, their foresight had been rewarded. The walls had held back Comanche attacks as well as the recent marauding soldiers from both sides of the Tejas war for independence.

The west wall held the front gate, which opened onto the heart of the compound, a huge paved courtyard centered by a multi-tiered fountain. The buildings were arranged, in a horse-shoe shape around the courtyard. The Navarro *hacienda* sprawled along its northern side. Across from the *hacienda* were the chapel, barns and storage sheds, the tannery and blacksmith forge. In the bend of the horseshoe sat the winery. Behind it was the Flores's *casa* and workers' homes. The stables hugged the rear wall of the compound.

Julia skirted her home and the winery, emerging into the courtyard. She spied Luz seated on a bench by the fountain, knitting. Conchita had her sandals off and her skirts knotted up. She was happily wading and splashing in the fountain. As warm as the day was, Julia could easily appreciate the child's delight in the cool water.

Greeting Luz, Julia stepped to the edge of the fountain. Catching Conchita's arm as she streaked by, Julia laughed and asked, "Having fun?"

Conchita giggled and splashed water at her. Julia leaned down to splash water back at the child, but Conchita scampered away and disappeared behind the base of the fountain. Julia shook her head. Most encounters with the little girl inevitably included a spirited game of chase. This time, though, when Julia rounded the fountain's pedestal, Conchita surprised her. The little girl came hurtling from behind the basins and launched herself into Julia's arms.

Startled, she grabbed the slippery, dripping child and clasped her tight. Looking down into Conchita's mischief-filled eyes, she chided, "Give me a little warning, *por favor*. What if I hadn't caught you?"

Conchita's eyes widened at the thought, but she answered with innocent trust, "You always catch me, *Tía* Julia."

Julia smiled, touched by her childish faith. She smoothed Conchita's tousled hair away from her face and retied the ribbon holding the girl's curls. Satisfied, she brushed a kiss on Conchita's forehead.

"Ready to get back into the fountain?" Julia asked. When Conchita nodded, Julia slid her into the water.

Luz had been watching their play. Eyeing Julia, she observed drily, "Señorita Julia, you might as well join *la niña*. You are soaked, too, from holding her."

Glancing down, she realized what Luz said was true. Her sodden blouse clung to her skin. She grinned and agreed, "You're right, Luz. And as hot as it is, I'm sorely tempted to climb into the fountain with her."

The sound of wheels bumping and clacking over the courtyard's paving stones drew her attention away from the cool splash of water. Julia turned to see Paco scooting toward them. His crippled legs were neatly folded on the wheeled platform Felipe had fashioned for his only son.

Paco used his powerful arms and shoulders to propel himself across the uneven surface of the courtyard. As usual, his rumpled brown hair hung over his forehead, falling into his hazel eyes. Julia loved her younger brother with all her heart. From the time he was born with his legs twisted and misshapen, Julia had felt a special bond with Paco.

Two years ago, they had lost Lupita. Lupita had been the middle child, younger than Julia but older than Paco. The same cholera epidemic that had taken Ruíz's wife and infant son had claimed Julia's sister. After Lupita's death, Julia and Paco had grown even closer.

Skidding to a halt next to Julia, Paco tossed the hair from his eyes. *"Buenos días, señoritas.* And what a glorious day it is."

Luz smiled shyly and then dropped her gaze to her knitting. Julia returned his salutation, *"Buenos días, m*i *hermano.* And what brings—"

Before she could finish her sentence, Conchita spotted Paco and demanded, "Ride! Ride! Give me a ride!"

Conchita adored riding on Paco's wheeled platform, especially when Paco indulged her and went fast. Julia lifted Conchita from the fountain. Holding the excited, squirming child, she warned Paco, "If you take her, you'll get wet. She's soaked."

Paco's eyes slid over Julia. His mouth quirked into a grin. "You didn't melt." He held out his strong arms. "Give me *la muchacha.*"

Giggling happily, Conchita went to Paco. He settled her comfortably in his lap. Instructing Conchita to hold on tight, he made several mighty pushes with his arms. Within moments, his platform was spinning in dizzy arcs around the fountain. Conchita clung to Paco, squealing loudly. Her small face was flushed with excitement.

Julia watched her brother. He was always smiling, always carefree, but his entire life centered around the winery. Unable to work the fields, he had honed his vintner skills to a fine art. He had absorbed everything their father and grandfather had taught him about making wines. Now, at the age of eighteen, he had surpassed their skill.

His absorption with wine-making had led him to experiment. Currently, he was blending wine from the European stock, *vitis vinifera,* with the native mustang grapes and testing the use of less expensive pine casks for the aging of white wines. He had developed a tawny port the year before that rivaled México's finest vintages.

As Julia followed Paco's crazy whirling progress, she wondered what would happen to her brother and his talent if they lost Los Montes Vérdes?

Ruíz slammed the heavy oak door of the *hacienda* and strode into the *sala.* Barely contained rage simmered within him.

He had never felt so humiliated in his life.

He went directly to the liquor cabinet and poured himself a large draught of brandy. Bringing the goblet to his lips, he tilted his head back and welcomed the fiery liquid as it slid down his throat. A polite cough startled him. Stopping midswallow, he lowered his glass and turned toward the sound.

In the shadows at the far end of the *sala* sat three black forms. Like buzzards on a fence rail, he thought irreverently. It was the two Hernández sisters. He couldn't remember their maiden name, but the two sisters had married two Hernández brothers. Both of their husbands had died, and the sisters were legendary for their decade of mourning. They were seated beside his mother, who was also garbed in blackest mourning.

Hiding his fury, Ruíz forced a thin veil of civility over his features for the sake of their guests. He placed the goblet on a table and approached his mother and her guests. Taking each of the Hernández sisters' hands in turn, he kissed them and bowed low.

"Señora Hernández y Señora Hernández, *buenas tardes*. How pleasant to see you. *Por favor*, don't let me interrupt your visit—"

María Hernández, the oldest and widest of the two, cut him off by rising to her feet. She inclined her head and said, "Doña Eugenia, it is late. We must leave. *Muchas gracias* for the lovely refreshments. If you need us, just send word."

Turning to Ruíz, she added stiffly, "So good to see you again." Luisa Hernández also rose. In keeping with her taciturn disposition, she merely bowed her head in a gesture of farewell.

"I so enjoyed your visit," Doña Eugenia murmured. "I wish you could have stayed longer." She shot a pointed look at Ruíz and offered, *"Por favor*, come again soon. Don't wait for my summons. Your presence comforts me in this time of distress."

The Hernández sisters puffed up importantly at Doña Eugenia's flattering words, and they acted almost loath to follow José, the Navarro's *mayordomo*. José seemed to have perfect timing, appearing at just that moment to escort the two sisters to their carriage, as if he had been waiting outside the door.

Finding himself alone with his mother, Ruíz's earlier fury returned. It was time to face the dragon. He knew she was angry, too. He waited for her to scold him.

She lifted her heavy black veil and glared at him. "Ruíz, your behavior is deplorable. Slamming into the house. Gulping spirits in the middle of the day. Frightening María and Luisa Hernández. Upsetting my afternoon reception—"

"Mamá, you are lucky you still have a *sala* where you can receive callers."

Doña Eugenia's amber eyes narrowed to slits. "What do you mean?"

"That the vineyard is buried under a mountain of debts. Debts you made, *Mamá.*"

She looked as if he had slapped her. "Ruíz! What an absurd accusation!" Drawing a tiny lace handkerchief from the sleeve of her dress, she dabbed at the moisture on her upper lip.

"I'm a delicately bred lady. I have never involved myself in commerce. Not like that Julia Flores, whom your father allowed to keep the books. If there is anything wrong with the affairs of Los Montes Verdes, it is probably because she and her father are cheating us!"

Ruíz was dumbfounded by his mother's warped point of view. Her machinations and ugly accusations amazed him. He had forgotten just how self-righteous she could be.

"I would never suggest that you might sully your hands with common business. But the winery is heavily mortgaged. The ledger entries tell a very clear tale: trips, carriages, clothes, and parties. The Flores family has not cheated us. But you have, *Mamá*. Cheated Teresa and me of our birthright, by spending more . . . much more than this winery could possibly produce. *Papá* incurred the debts, over time, to keep you in the elegant style to which you are accustomed."

His mother leaned back in her chair and closed her eyes. She sighed deeply. "I didn't want to marry your father. I knew he would never take his rightful place in this world. He didn't have an ambitious bone in his body. My father wanted our marriage. As a dutiful daughter, I did what was required of me."

Ruíz clenched and unclenched his fists. It was all he could do to keep from throttling his own mother. How could she sit, dressed in deep mourning, criticizing his dead father to him? She disdained the very union that had brought him into the world. Her blind selfishness turned his guts, making him choke. He searched for the right words to say to her, to defend his father's memory. To cut her overbearing self-interest to shreds.

"That's why I wanted so much more for you, Ruíz"—she gestured angrily—"than this paltry vineyard. That's why I encouraged you to marry Alicia Estrada. Now, you will inherit the Estrada *rancho*. A property worthy of you."

Ruíz finally found his voice, "That is not the point—"

"But it is the point." She dismissed his words with an airy

wave of her bejeweled hand. "If you're concerned about the winery, borrow the money from your father-in-law. He has plenty of money."

His earlier fury had been replaced by a cold, hard knot inside him. With the abatement of his anger came a certain knowledge. It was useless to argue with her. It had always been useless. All that remained for him was to gather the shredded remnants of his pride and stand on his convictions.

"*Mamá,* I want you to know I have just come from one of the most humiliating experiences of my life."

Doña Eugenia arched her pencil-thin eyebrows and reached for her ornate ivory-and-gold fan. Fanning herself, she waited, giving him her full attention. Ruíz retrieved his abandoned brandy and downed it in one gulp. His mother remained sitting, ramrod straight, fanning and waiting.

Like the spider waiting for the fly, he thought.

"I was humiliated because no one in San Antonio would lend us money. They were polite, but refused to extend our loans. And I can't pay our debts unless I turn a profit this year. And I can't turn a profit without operating capital. Do you know what that means?"

His mother maintained her silence. Her eyes glittered, and she wet her lips with her tongue, but she didn't speak.

He released his breath with a sharp rush. "I will tell you, *Mamá.* The moneylenders will foreclose and take Los Montes Verdes to satisfy their debts."

His bald statement finally forced an answer from her. She abandoned her self-imposed silence and commanded, "No! Sell first!"

Snapping her fan shut, she confessed, "Before you thrust this unseemly discussion upon me, I had decided to sell the winery. I hate living here. I always have. It is too rural. I wanted to go home to México and resume my position in society." She paused, and her eyes held a malevolent light. "But my relatives in Monclovia discouraged me."

Doña Eugenia opened her fan again and examined its graceful folds. Then she raised condemning eyes to Ruíz. "Do you know why I cannot return to México?" Her voice dropped to a hiss, "Because you and your father chose to fight against our homeland." Lifting her fan, she fluttered it rapidly. "So I have decided to join Rolando in New Orleans. My brother has invited me to live there. His business is flourishing, and his social connections are impeccable. I will, of course, observe the customary mourning period of one year before I move."

If his mother's unwavering self-centered stance had shocked Ruíz earlier, it was nothing to what he felt now. Her condemnation of their fight for Tejas independence was nothing new. She had berated him and his father for their stupidity when they had left for the war. What was shocking was her demand that he sell the vineyard. It was all they owned in the world. What was she thinking?

Gritting his teeth, he silently counted to ten. Commanding himself to think, he knew there must be something he could say that would bring her to her senses.

"*Mamá*, with the debts outstanding, we won't get a fraction of the vineyard's worth. There will be no dowry for Teresa. And how will you live? Surely, your brother is not prepared to—"

"Of course not, I would never ask him," she interrupted. "You're my son. It is your duty to care for your mother, now that your father is gone. The vineyard is not important. Your interest in the Estrada *rancho* will be sufficient for my needs and Teresa's dowry."

Duty . . . his responsibility to the family. A cornerstone of his culture, duty to the family had been engraved in his consciousness from the time he was old enough to understand the concept. And he believed in the noble tradition of familial duty. It was what held the fabric of society together. He would never shirk his duty to his mother and sister.

But he would choose how to fulfill that duty.

Shaking his head, he replied, "No, *Mamá,* I will not ask my father-in-law for the money. I groveled and begged today. But no more! I will not ask Don Estéban and that is final. The vineyard must continue to support our family. There will be no sale."

Doña Eugenia's eyes narrowed and hardened. "I own as much of Los Montes Verdes as you do. More, in fact, because I own this *hacienda,* too. If I want to sell, you cannot stop me. I understand your masculine pride and applaud it. You have ambition and drive, unlike your father. Keep the vineyard, but if it interferes with my move to New Orleans, I will sell my portion without you."

"No one would want part of a vineyard."

"Possibly not. But you might be forced to sell, too, to provide Teresa with a dowry. It's your duty."

Duty . . . that word again.

"*Sí, Mamá,* I have a duty to support you and Teresa. But the style in which I am willing to support you . . . is another matter."

"You wouldn't dare to—"

"Oh, wouldn't I? I have already instructed every merchant in San Antonio that any purchase you wish to make must be personally approved by me."

Doña Eugenia gasped. For once, she appeared to be at a loss for words, but he knew her astonishment wouldn't last for long.

Not wanting to linger and engage in more futile arguments with his mother, Ruíz turned to leave.

Doña Eugenia, forgetting her noble antecedents and finding her voice again, hurled imprecations at his retreating back that would have made the lowliest *peón* blush.

"The pruning is finished. I am satisfied with the results," Ruíz declared.

"*Sí,* the vines flourish," Felipe agreed.

Julia and her father were seated across the huge oak desk from Ruíz once again. They were meeting to discuss the future of the vineyard. Julia could sense the tension emanating from Ruíz. She feared his news wouldn't be promising.

The small talk finished, Ruíz cleared his throat and steepled his fingers. His voice was apologetic when he admitted, "I was unable to obtain the operating funds we need." He shook his head, "And to make matters worse, my mother wants to sell Los Montes Verdes and move away."

Julia felt the breath catch in her throat. Without thinking, she blurted out, "Is that what *you* want?"

Ruíz's eyes were muddy with mixed emotions when they locked with hers. "No. It's not what I want, but unless I can get the money we need . . ."

Julia closed her eyes. She wouldn't let him give up now. They must find a way.

"Even if our family had to sell to settle the debts we owe, your family would still retain your interest," Ruíz reminded her.

But Felipe appeared just as upset as she was at Ruíz's news because he said, "*Sí,* we will retain our interest but under what circumstances? Will the new owners be *simpático?* Will we be able to work with them? As the majority owners, they could force us to sell if they wished."

Ruíz released a sigh. His eyes veered away.

His reaction reminded Julia of the old proverb of a man caught between the devil and the deep blue sea. He didn't want to lose the vineyard. But there was a limit to what he would do to save Los Montes Verdes. Julia guessed his lack of commitment involved his conflicting responsibility to his father-in-law and the Estrada *rancho.* The realization was bitter. She wanted Ruíz wholly focused on saving the vineyard. But it was a loyalty that couldn't be forced.

They couldn't depend on him. They must find their own way. She had thought about it since their first meeting to go over the ledgers. She knew of a way to raise the money . . . if her father would agree.

Turning to Felipe, she touched his arm. *"Papito,* we have the money from the dowries you've saved. Lupita won't . . . and I'm willing to use my dowry for this. *Por favor, Papito,* it will be more than enough to see us through the harvest."

Her father appeared surprised by her proposal. For a moment, she was afraid he would dismiss her solution. But he was obviously considering it, turning it over in his mind.

Ruíz's countenance brightened at her suggestion, and he agreed, "A loan from your family is a good idea. That way—"

"Not a loan, Ruíz, it would be a purchase. Part of your share for our money. You would deed us a portion of your interest, enough so the Flores family would own the controlling interest in Los Montes Verdes."

His jaw dropped at her demand. "Part of my interest just so we can operate the vineyard for one year? That doesn't seem fair, Julia."

"The risk, Ruíz. Because of the debts already outstanding, our hard-earned savings would be—"

"Julia! You forget yourself!" Felipe roared angrily. He shook his head and lowered his voice. "We will be pleased to offer Señor Ruíz a *loan."*

She opened her mouth to argue with her father, but his face was closed. She knew that look. Julia shut her mouth. In the heat of the argument, she had been tempted to explain how Ruíz was using them, placing the burden on the Flores family for the success of the vineyard. And now, her father was agreeing to take on the additional risk of adding their savings to the debt Ruíz already owed without asking for anything in return. But she realized her arguments wouldn't reach her father. They would only serve to savage his pride. Saving the vineyard was a direct challenge to his honor and ability.

"Felipe, Julia does have a point." Julia was surprised by Ruíz's response. "It is risky. There may be nothing left to repay you with after I satisfy the other debts falling due this year. Maybe you should reconsider.''

At least Ruíz was giving serious consideration to what she had said, she thought with gratification. But he still hadn't offered them part of his interest in the vineyard.

And her father, for his own reasons, would never demand an extra interest. He merely reiterated, ''Señor Ruíz, we will *lend* you the money.''

Even if she didn't agree with her father, she loved and respected him. She would support him completely. And Paco would help, too. Paco and his devotion to Los Montes Verdes was steadfast. The winery was his life. The winery and . . . his experiments.

Suddenly, a brilliant inspiration seized her. ''I know a way you can repay us, Ruíz. I know how we can turn a higher profit.''

''Mmmm . . .'' Ruíz savored the wine. ''Light and sweet but with a good body.'' He lifted the glass to the candle and twirled it back and forth, openly admiring the wine's clear golden color.

It was nightfall. The day's labors were over. Ruíz had joined Julia in the winery, at her suggestion, to taste Paco's experiments.

''We grow only a few acres of white grapes. But if you think the quality is good enough, we could bottle several cases for shipment.''

Nodding, he reached for one of the red wines on the table. Sipping it, he observed, ''Rich and complex but with a supple texture.'' He studied the ruby-red liquid. ''The color is good, and the wine is clear. Paco has done an excellent job of clarifying this.'' He finished the glass in one swallow.

As much as she was pleased to hear Ruíz praising Paco's expertise, Julia was beginning to worry. Instead of just swishing the wine in his mouth for taste and spitting it out, Ruíz had been steadily drinking the samples. His eyes glittered in the candlelight.

He was watching her. She could feel his gaze burn her skin.

Since she had realized he was manipulating her father, Julia had purposely hardened her heart against him. She didn't want to experience the irresistible cravings his presence aroused. But now that they were alone, surrounded by the heady and evocative aroma of the fermenting wines, she felt her resolve weaken.

Striving to refocus her mind on the business at hand, she inquired, "You like the wines? You believe my idea has merit?"

Ruíz's eyes appeared sleepy. His gaze was casual, open and unguarded for the first time since he'd returned home. But the admiration in the chocolate-colored depths of his eyes was unmistakable. Like a silent caress, they slid over her with glowing warmth. And her body responded immediately, heated awareness growing in her blood, pulsing through her veins.

Ruíz's motions were loose and flowing as he uncorked a bottle of red wine and poured himself another glass. Ignoring her query about the quality of the wines, he asked, "Care to join me?"

Julia considered his offer and then shook her head.

Ruíz shrugged one broad shoulder and sauntered around the table. He stopped a mere breath from her. His own distinctive masculine scent mingled indiscriminately with the earthy aromas of the wines.

Propping one hip on the table next to her, he answered her earlier question. *"Me gustan los vinos.* They are excellent. Paco is a genius."

Mesmerized by his nearness, Julia instinctively moved away from him, but his hand reached out and caught her arm. She stopped, enthralled by his touch. Tentatively, he rubbed his calloused thumb up and down the soft inner flesh of her arm.

The candlelight glowed softly behind him. Reality fell away.

The room seemed to spin around her. Julia was bewitched by his touch. Trailing tendrils of fire followed his fingertips. Gooseflesh rose upon her arm, and the aching pleasure was nearly painful in its intensity, but she was powerless to stop him.

Abruptly, he withdrew his hand, his touch. At the sudden abandonment, she almost cried out in protest. Almost. Catching herself, she took a shaky breath.

She prayed that he wouldn't see she was trembling.

Raising the glass to his lips, a red rivulet trickled down his chin. She was seized with an insane impulse to lick the wine from his skin. He lowered the glass. Her eyes were riveted upon his lips, stained crimson from the wine.

He casually wiped his mouth and chin with the back of his hand. Dazed with longing, Julia forced her gaze away from his mouth. But what she saw in his eyes jolted her to the very core of her being. She saw undisguised lust and something else, too . . . a painful longing. Their eyes locked in silent understanding. An understanding as old as time itself. It was Ruíz who glanced away and broke the spell.

"Your plan is good, Julia." His eyes returned to her, frank respect glowing there. "You've a fine mind. You always did. When I was younger, I often envied you. You were so quick at your studies."

She opened her mouth to protest his extravagant praise, but he stopped her by grasping her braid and tugging gently. He grinned and lightly ran his hand over the plait of her hair. She shivered at his touch. Gently, he worked to release the interwoven strands of her hair.

"We've always sold our wine by the cask in San Antonio. But capitalizing on your brother's skill is a clever idea. I think his wine is ready for a more sophisticated market."

Julia couldn't move or speak. What he was doing to her hair was unspeakably intimate. And when he had freed the coils of it, she felt her body and heart soar free, too. Her hair fell about her face, unfettered, like a thick curtain. It caressed her shoulders and bare arms. A blind craving rose within her. Melting slowly, she leaned closer to him.

Burying his hands in her hair, he drew her even closer. His voice was velvety when he promised, "I will write to Rolando, my uncle in New Orleans. He will send us the necessary bottles. We will send them back, filled with our wines, to be sold at a premium price. Are you satisfied, Julia?"

Rational thought had fled as she savored his hands stroking her hair. She heard his words, but she couldn't understand their meaning. His touch was soft, gentle. The sound of his voice was deep and reassuring. Trusting blindly, she nodded and flowed, like molten fire into his embrace.

His hands stroked through her unbound hair, and he murmured, "This midnight veil. How I've longed to . . . Julia. You are beautiful. So very, very beautiful."

And then his mouth burned on hers.

Julia had dreamed of this moment. Ruíz's lips on hers, his compelling, muscular body pressed against hers. She dug her fingers into the coiled strength of his shoulders. The hard planes of his chest crushed her breasts. The powerful sinew of his thighs molded themselves about her legs, making a mockery of the flimsy protection of her skirts.

And she felt, with a glorious wonder, the intimate thrust of his burgeoning manhood.

His mouth moved over hers, testing, tasting, teasing. She grew drunk on the pungent, earthy taste of wine on his lips. And she thrilled as he deepened his kiss, insinuating the hot tip of his tongue between her lips. She met and responded to each sensual thrust of his tongue. They explored each other's mouth and lips, learning the intimate promise there.

Tiny shivers of pure pleasure chased up and down her spine. She clung to him fiercely, her body perfectly fitted to his. And then the tender aching, craving started. From the pit of her stomach it wove itself through her veins, setting her very being on fire, consuming her with long denied, secret needs. Needs of the flesh, needs of the heart, needs of the soul.

His mouth devoured hers, and she responded with an equally fierce passion. The passion she'd felt for him since time began. The passion she had freely bequeathed him. Ruíz was hers. She was his. Secretly, she had promised herself to him, long ago.

Stroking and caressing, his hands moved through her hair. He lifted his mouth from hers, leaving an aching void, only to salve the hurt by raining tiny kisses over her upturned face.

Julia curled her fingers in the rich brown waves of his hair while his lips and teeth drove her wild. He nibbled and licked, first her earlobe, then down the column of her throat. She melted into his embrace. Wanting to be closer, needing to be closer . . .

The winery door thudded open. Cool night air washed over her feverish body. Ruíz tensed immediately and released her. Dazed, she looked up at him, silently protesting his sudden abandonment.

Felipe and Paco burst into the room, and her father declared, ''I see you've been sampling Paco's wines. How do you like them?''

Ruíz's gaze snagged hers, and for one split second, she read the desire there. And then his eyes were hooded again. With his features set in a mask of polite civility, he turned and greeted her father and brother.

Slapping Felipe on the back, he congratulated him. ''The wines are excellent. Your son is a master vintner.'' He beamed at Paco and promised, ''With a bit of luck, your wines will save Los Montes Verdes.''

Chapter Four

Teresa Navarro opened the heavy wooden gate just a crack. The sleeping guard didn't stir. Slipping quietly through the small space, she found herself outside the hacienda compound.

The night was dark. The thin fingernail of a new moon provided no light. Teresa made her way to the river by memory. As she approached the old, gnarled live oak, she strained her eyes.

A darker shape detached itself from the bulk of the tree, and in the next moment, she was swept into Allende Soto's strong arms. His mouth crashed down on hers, feverishly seeking, pushing her head back.

Savoring their intimacy, she melted into his embrace. The heady scent of man tinged with the lingering smell of horseflesh filled her nostrils. She pressed closer to Allende, lacing her hands behind his neck, reveling in his blatant masculinity.

It was Allende who finally broke off their passionate kiss. He tucked her head beneath his chin and stroked Teresa's back.

Nestled close to him, she could hear the rapid beating of his heart.

She smiled to herself. Her heart was beating fast, too. She knew he wanted her, but she trusted him implicitly. He treated her like a princess, always deferring to her wishes.

Allende murmured into her hair, "I'm sorry, Teresa, so sorry about your father. I wish I could have been by your side to comfort you."

His concern for her grief almost undid her. She felt hot tears rise in her throat. His gentleness and caring reminded her of her own sweet *Papá*. But she was also drawn to Allende's silent strength, the hard core of him that she intuitively sensed. It was his iron will that had attracted Teresa in the beginning. She had learned about his tenderness later.

"*Gracias,* Allende, for thinking of me. Even though we couldn't be together, I carried you in my heart. Knowing you were near, waiting to come to me, is the only . . ." She choked, and the tears seeped from the corners of her eyes. "I loved *Papá* a great deal. I will miss him. If I didn't have you, I don't know what I would do."

Allende bent and kissed her tears away, one by one. "I will always be here for you, *mi princesa.* You have my solemn oath. And one day, we will be together forever. One day, I will make you *mi esposa.*"

"*Sí,* Allende, I want you for my husband." As she spoke the words, Teresa knew that for the very first time, she really meant it.

Since she had become a woman, she had engaged in flirtations to amuse herself. Flirtations with men that were wholly unsuited to her. Men who lived by their wits, without a *peso* to their names. At the same time, Teresa had dismissed every proper suitor her mother had chosen for her. Landed men, arrogant and cold in their power, didn't interest Teresa. Or maybe she wasn't interested because her mother was so domineering, so certain she knew what was best for her daughter.

Allende was different from all the other men, rich or poor.

At first, she had thought he was just like the others, another exciting interlude in her life, another way to upset her mother. He was only a poor *vaquero*. He driffed from job to job. But as she grew to know him, she came to learn the man beneath his rough surface. And unlike her other suitors, Allende had never disappointed her. Teresa had found that she could rely upon his strength and his gentleness.

Allende's voice interrupted her thoughts. "We cannot marry for at least a year. You're in mourning."

Lifting her head, she gazed at Allende's shadowed face. "What do the social proprieties matter, Allende, when you know my mother won't allow us to marry at any time. She won't even let you court me. We will have to run away."

"I don't want to sneak away with you, Teresa. I would never forgive myself if I took you from your family. I grew up an orphan, and I know what it is to be without a family. I won't deprive you of that." A hint of steel crept into his voice. "We will observe the proprieties, Teresa."

Teresa was surprised Allende was being so firm with her. Before, he had always yielded to her wishes. But this time, she could sense something was different. They were talking about her future, and he obviously had strong ideas about what was best for her. It warmed her to know that he cared so much. She preferred to have her family's blessing, too, but she refused to let them stop her from loving and marrying Allende.

"What if my mother refuses again? I don't want to lose my family, either, Allende. But what about us? I couldn't bear to lose you." She grasped him tighter, burrowing into the sanctuary of his arms.

He sighed deeply and held her closer. "I won't let you go, *mi princesa*. If everything else fails, we will run away together. But for now, your family needs you. When a year has passed, then—"

"A year is such a long time, Allende," she cut him off. "It

isn't that I don't want to honor my father's memory, I do, but . . .
I'm afraid, Allende. I'm afraid my mother will find a way to
tear us apart. You don't know her.''

His strong hands massaged the taut muscles of her neck, and
he murmured low nonsense words to her. When she had relaxed
in his arms again, he said, ''Your brother is the head of the
family now. Do you think he could convince your mother to
let me court you?''

Teresa considered his suggestion for a moment before replying, ''I don't know, Allende. Sometimes my brother can be
just as cold and proper as my mother. I can try. I will approach
him tomorrow before supper.''

''Muy bien. Tell him I would like to meet with him and pay
my respects.''

''Allende, if my family accepts your suit, I can help us to
get started. *Papá* left me a generous dowry, enough to buy a
small *rancho* where you can breed and train horses.''

''I don't want your money, Teresa. I only want you. I have
plans of my own. This year will give me time to save and
prepare a home for you.''

A warm glow suffused her at Allende's words. All of her
other unsuitable attachments had been deeply interested in her
dowry. But Allende was different.

''Te amo,'' Teresa whispered.

''And I love you, Teresa.''

Their lips met and they clung fiercely to each other, savoring
their stolen moments before Teresa had to return to the hacienda.

It felt good to be riding Oro across the rugged hills again.
Ruíz enjoyed his brief freedom. He was leaving behind the
worries of the vineyard, only to exchange them for a new set
of headaches at the Estrada *rancho.*

He had been away from his father-in-law's domain for many

weeks. He hated to think of how much work had accumulated during his absence to fight for Tejas independence and . . . mourn his father.

His father-in-law, Don Estéban, was a shrewd businessman. In a few short years, he had built the largest *rancho* outside of San Antonio de Béxar. It was his father-in-law's business acumen that had attracted Ruíz to Don Estéban in the first place. He was so different from Ruíz's father, and Ruíz was ambitious. Ruíz wanted to leave his mark on Tejas. He wanted to expand and grow, both at the *rancho* and the winery. If he were able to save Los Montes Verdes, he believed Julia's scheme for selling premium wines could bring them new prosperity.

Ruíz didn't like thinking about Julia, but he couldn't seem to erase her from his thoughts. He had told himself he was rushing to the Estrada *rancho* because Don Estéban needed him, but the real reason he'd left Los Montes Verdes in such a hurry was . . . Julia.

What had driven him to kiss her last night?

He shook his head. He could blame his behavior on the wine he'd freely imbibed, but that would only be an excuse. If the truth were known, he'd used the wine to give him the courage to kiss her. He had wanted to kiss her since that first day outside the cathedral.

And she had responded to his kiss with a passion he had never experienced before. Her response had shaken him to the very core of his being. Shaken and confused him. What did he want from his childhood friend, Julia Flores? He wasn't ready to marry again, and his mother would bitterly oppose such an alliance. Julia was a respectable woman. He couldn't expect to take her as his mistress.

He shook his head again. Julia should have married long ago.

* * *

Oro topped a rise, and Ruíz gazed at the Estrada *rancho,* nestled in the green valley below. Don Estéban's sprawling empire encompassed so many buildings that his headquarters resembled a small town.

Guiding his stallion through the outlying structures, he greeted some of the workers. It was his policy to know all of Don Estéban's employees by name. At the gate to the hacienda, he was warmly welcomed and told that Don Estéban was in the central barn. Ruíz's heart lightened at the news. If Don Estéban was in his office in the barn, it must mean his father-in-law's condition hadn't worsened.

Pulling up before the huge barn, he dismounted and tossed Oro's reins to a stableboy. "Pedro, give Oro a good rubdown and don't let him drink too much water too fast."

"Sí, Señor Ruíz." The boy's white teeth flashed in his dark face. *"Bienvenida.* It is good to have you back. Don Estéban awaits within."

"Gracias, Pedro."

Ruíz slipped inside the barn and walked between the stalls. The Estrada *rancho* boasted several barns, but this particular barn held Don Estéban's prize stock. The stalls were filled with Arabian mares, Andalusian stallions, and English Hereford cattle. Don Estéban took great pride in his stock as well as relishing the fat breeding fees they earned for him.

The tack room door at the back of the barn stood open. It was a small, grimy cupboard of a room, but it was where Don Estéban preferred to keep his office. He had a magnificent study in the hacienda, beautifully appointed with furniture.

Alicia, Ruíz's late wife, had refurnished the entire hacienda shortly after their marriage. Alicia had spent vast sums of money, and waited for months for furnishings, draperies, and decorative pieces to be shipped from New Orleans. Despite Alicia's best efforts, Don Estéban had never seemed to take pleasure in his refurbished home.

Through the open door, Ruíz glimpsed Don Estéban seated

at his desk, shuffling papers. The faint sunlight filtering through one dirty window was augmented by a lantern hanging over the desk. The tiny, austere room was exactly as Ruíz remembered it, with one exception. A bare cot had been placed in one corner, probably as an accommodation to his father-in-law's illness.

Don Estéban suffered from a disease of the lungs, and despite Ruíz's earlier hope, it was obvious his father-in-law's condition had worsened. His hoarse breathing seemed to fill the room, shaking the very walls.

Upon Ruíz's entrance, Don Estéban half rose from his seat and extended his hand. "Ruíz, welcome home. It has been a long time."

Ruíz returned his father-in-law's handshake. Don Estéban's grip was still firm, but Ruíz could see the decline in the older man. Despite his prodigious girth, folds of skin hung from the older man's jaw, and his face was the color of *masa*.

Don Estéban wheezed as he lowered his bulk into the chair. *"Por favor,* be seated." He coughed once into a wadded handkerchief and added, "I want to personally extend my sympathy for the death of your father. I would have attended the funeral mass, but I find the shortest trip fatiguing."

"Of course, Don Estéban, *yo entiendo.* I appreciate your condolences."

"I sent a note to your mother."

"Sí, she mentioned it." Ruíz replied.

"Muy bien. I've missed you these past weeks, Ruíz. I won't pretend that I haven't. There is much to be done." Don Estéban pinned Ruíz with his small black eyes. "I hope your time was well spent, playing the patriot."

Ruíz bridled at the older man's veiled mockery. Don Estéban had been vehemently opposed to Ruíz going to fight in the war. His father-in-law had remained neutral during the conflict, not wanting to gamble the future of his *rancho* on uncertain political events. Ruíz respected the older man's position, but he deplored Don Estéban's belittling of his own beliefs. Ruíz's own father had given his life for those same beliefs.

"You know my position, Don Estéban. I fought for freedom from the tyranny and centralism of Santa Ana's government."

"You're lucky the marauding troops from both sides didn't find any value in your grapevines. Had your grapes been ripe, they would have been stripped."

Frowning, Ruíz replied, "I heard there was some raiding during the war, mostly for provisions, but—"

Don Estéban slapped his open palm against the scarred oak desk and bellowed, "Some raiding! Whole farms and *ranchos* were wiped out, women raped and children butchered. Despite my neutrality, this rancho wasn't spared, either. We suffered no violence because I've enough men to protect my interests, but I lost over three hundred head of cattle and at least fifty horses." He leaned forward, his breathing a dry rattle. "That's war for you, Ruíz, nothing but sanctioned thievery." A spasm of coughing seized Don Estéban, and he doubled over, gasping like a beached fish.

Ruíz watched helplessly as his father-in-law struggled for air. Desperate to aid Don Estéban but not knowing what to do, he rose to his feet and moved around the desk.

Between gasps and hacking coughs, Don Estéban pointed to his collar and a brown glass bottle on the desk. Moving quickly, Ruíz opened the older man's collar and uncorked the bottle. Catching a whiff of its contents, he was surprised to find that the smell was so strong. The bottle obviously held some type of medicine. Gently, Ruíz cradled his father-in-law's head and held the bottle to his lips.

Don Estéban gulped greedily at the syrupy liquid. After a few swallows, he waved it away. Ruíz lowered the bottle, and Don Estéban drew a labored breath. A few moments passed. The only sound was the raspy noise of the older man's hoarse breathing. The medicine had stopped his coughing fit.

"Do you want me to help you to the cot?" Ruíz offered.

"No," Don Estéban croaked, and gestured for Ruíz to resume his seat. "Just give me a . . ."

Regaining his seat, Ruíz averted his eyes. It was painful to watch the pitiful spectacle of Don Estéban struggling for every breath. He felt sorry for his father-in-law, but he also realized that talking about his lost livestock was what had thrown the older man into a paroxysm of coughing. It wasn't the brutality of the war that had upset Don Estéban; it was the loss of his livestock.

"I'm better now," Don Estéban declared. "Thank you for helping me. I don't want to lie down just yet. We've much to discuss."

"*Sí.*"

"Not only do I need you to help me replace the livestock I lost, but I want you to find me a new horse trainer."

"What happened to Señor Ramos?"

"I've promoted him. He's the new foreman."

"And Señor Carrillo, the old foreman?"

"I caught him stealing, had him whipped and my men left him ten leagues west of San Antonio."

Ruíz winced at Don Estéban's recital of his brutal punishment. "That's Comanche country. He'll be lucky to survive."

Nodding, Don Estéban's raisin-black eyes glittered with malevolence. Ruíz studied his father-in-law covertly. He had heard the old rumors surrounding Don Estéban before he married his daughter, but Ruíz had discounted most of them as spawned by envy of Don Estéban's success.

Don Estéban had founded his *rancho* some twenty years before, taking the virgin land from the Indians and anyone else who stood in his way. His background was clouded in mystery, and his manners were rough, suggesting a humble birth. His wife had died suddenly, ten years ago, leaving Don Estéban to raise their two children alone.

Lázaro, Don Estéban's only son, had run away soon after Ruíz had married Alicia and come to the *rancho* to live. It was whispered Don Estéban had brutally beaten his son all of his life, but Ruíz had seen no signs of cruelty during the time Lázaro had been at the *rancho*.

Alicia had maintained a polite but distant relationship with her father. She and Ruíz had never been close, either. Even though Ruíz had seldom paid attention to his former wife's vaporings, he could remember several occasions when Don Estéban had spoken sharply to Alicia. On those few occasions, Ruíz had seen abject fear in his wife's eyes. Now, he silently berated himself for not having been more attentive to her feelings.

Ruíz didn't know if his absence from Don Estéban had enabled him to see the older man in a more objective light, but he suddenly felt disturbed by his father-in-law's blatant greed and brutality.

"I'll find you a new horse trainer, but I don't believe in whipping employees. I won't help you run the *rancho* that way. If I catch anyone else stealing, I'll turn him over to the authorities in San Antonio."

It was Don Estéban's turn to study Ruíz. His father-in-law's eyes narrowed, and he frowned, as if he didn't like what he saw. The tone of his voice was filled with acid. "You mean the *gringo* authorities. The same people you so 'wisely' fought for so they could take this land from our people. They'll do worse than whip any of our men. The proper *gringo* authorities will hang Tejanos."

"It would depend upon what was stolen. Some stealing doesn't carry—"

"It won't matter *what* was stolen," Don Estéban cut him off and jerked back the sleeve of his shirt. Brandishing his dark arm, he said, "Tejanos will be hung for the color of their skin."

"Don Estéban, I disagree! I fought beside Anglos at San Jacinto to win freedom for all of Tejas. There are many Anglos I would call my friends."

"You fought beside the Anglos?"

"*Sí.*"

"I thought you were with the other Tejanos under Captain Seguín."

"That's right," Ruíz admitted, already guessing where his father-in-law was heading.

"Then they kept you separate from the Anglos, didn't they? Wouldn't want us greasers mixing with them." Don Estéban shook his head, and his voice was barely a hiss. "Don't be such an innocent, Ruíz. I realize you've been distracted by your father's death, but the groundswell against Tejanos is already starting. Especially against the ones, like myself, who remained neutral. The *gringos* in power are denouncing us as traitors."

"Tempers remain high after a war, Don Estéban. People are still burying their dead. I admit it's hard for some Anglos to make a distinction between the Mexicans they just fought and Tejanos, but you need to give the situation time."

"Time," Don Estéban repeated, drumming his stubby fingers on the desk. "*Sí,* time might cool tempers, but I've never known the passage of time to mitigate greed."

Ruíz thought it ironic that Don Estéban condemned Anglos for the very trait that was the guiding force of his life.

"What do you mean by . . . greed?"

"Many of the *gringos* who fought for Tejas were promised land. They were given scrips, redeemable for unclaimed land, in lieu of pay. All of the choice land is taken. The only unclaimed land lies to the north and west. And you just mentioned that it—"

"Is in Comanche territory."

"*Sí,* and very few men will be willing to settle among the hostiles. But the *gringos* are resourceful at stirring up old hatreds from the war. They might be able to obtain good land without fighting the Indians."

"How?"

"They are examining the old Spanish land deeds for irregularities."

"You mean they're trying to steal our lands under the cloak of some obscure legality?" Ruíz tried to keep his voice calm, but, inside, he burned with righteous indignation against this new injustice.

Don Estéban leaned back in his chair. A look of satisfaction crossed his face. Ruíz hadn't fooled him, and his father-in-law was obviously glad to have shaken him up.

"I wouldn't be too concerned about your lands. Your father gave his life for the Republic. They won't go after your family until their other options are exhausted. But I've already had a letter about my title." Don Estéban paused and coughed into his handkerchief. "That's where you can be of service to me, Ruíz. Are you still friends with that Anglo attorney in San Antonio? What was his name?"

"Peter Meredith is his name and we're still friends."

"*Muy bien.* I don't have an attorney. I've never felt the need for their shady dealings." Don Estéban's voice conveyed his contempt. "But I need one now, and I want him to be an Anglo. He'll know better how to deal with his own kind. Do you think you can retain him for me?"

"Certainly. Peter will welcome the business."

Don Estéban grunted and shifted his bulk. "I've told you the most pressing matters." His father-in-law's face softened, and he asked, "Did you bring Concepción with you?"

It was Don Estéban's one soft spot, Ruíz knew, the love he felt for his grandchild. The only open tenderness he had ever seen Don Estéban display had been for her.

"Not this time. I was afraid I'd be too busy." Ruíz smiled ruefully. "And it seems I was right. I'll get started on the livestock and horse trainer. I'll go into San Antonio in the next few days and visit with Peter. The next time I return home, I'll bring Concepción for a visit." Ruíz hesitated, knowing what he was about to say wouldn't please his father-in-law. "I'll be visiting Los Montes Verdes more often now because my father isn't there . . . And this harvest is critical."

Don Estéban waved his hand, as if dismissing Ruíz's responsibilities to the winery. "I've heard of your difficulties. How much do you need?" He opened a desk drawer and pulled out a strongbox. Ruíz knew the strongbox held ready cash for the daily operation of the *rancho*.

Not entirely surprised that the Navarro family's misfortunes had reached the older man's ears, Ruíz hadn't tried to keep it a secret. After all, he had begged money from every lending establishment in San Antonio.

"*Gracias,* Don Estéban, for your generous offer. But I've found other funds to carry me through."

Shrugging, his father-in-law pushed the strongbox to one side. "I wish you good fortune, although I can't help but agree with your mother. You should seriously consider selling the vineyard. Your duty and future lie here. You're the only son I have now, and Concepción is my only living grandchild. Soon, the *rancho* will be yours."

That word again . . . duty. And this time, Ruíz *was* surprised Don Estéban knew about his mother's intentions. Had his mother enlisted Don Estéban to put pressure on him, too? And if she had, Ruíz felt as if he were being backed into a corner. He didn't like the feeling. At first, he wasn't certain about his level of commitment for saving the vineyard. With every attempt to convince him to give up, rebellion blossomed in his heart.

Stopping his runaway thoughts, he returned to their conversation. "There is still your son, Lázaro. In time, you and he will be reconciled and—"

"No!" Don Estéban thundered and slammed his fist against the desk for the second time, making the strongbox jump. "I will never be reconciled with Lázaro. Spawn of his mother, weak and whining and lazy. *He is no longer my son.*" Don Estéban's eyes were feverish, and Ruíz felt as if they were burning a hole into his brain. "You must be prepared to take over the *rancho*. The vineyard is unimportant."

Ruíz bristled at his father-in-law's casual dismissal of the land and vines that had been his family's life for three generations. The more Don Estéban and his mother tried to discourage him, the more committed he became to saving the vineyard.

Thinking about Los Montes Verdes brought Julia to mind, and her beautiful face rose before him. Beautiful but filled with determination, she was willing to sacrifice everything to keep the vineyard and winery. Julia and her family were depending upon him. His decision was made. No more wavering. He would do everything in his power to keep Los Montes Verdes.

"Los Montes Verdes is important to me, Don Estéban. I will help you with the *rancho,* but I also need to look after the vineyard."

Julia savagely attacked the weeds in the vineyard. Pulling up a clump of milkweed, she tossed it onto the pile of wilting weeds behind her. She stopped and mopped the perspiration from her brow with the back of her hand.

The hot sun felt good, burning through her thin cotton blouse. And the hard labor was helping to purge her mind of her most venomous thoughts.

Ruíz had kissed her last night. Kissed her with so much passion she had thought he meant it. Now he was gone. He had left without a word to her, returning to the Estrada *rancho.*

He only kissed me because he was drunk, she thought furiously. *And because I was so damned willing,* a nagging voice in the back of her head added. Ruíz had become a man who took what he wanted, without considering the consequences.

Julia had sought the hardest work she could find to erase the shame from her soul. The accounts for Los Montes Verdes were her responsibility. But the land was what she really cared about, and it never disappointed her.

She was pleased with how well the pruning had gone. Her father had made certain each vine was individually pruned to yield its maximum potential. Ruíz had appeared satisfied with the results, too, but only in an abstract way. It was clear he didn't care about the venerable vines, only the harvest and money they brought.

Throwing down her hoe in exasperation, she straightened up. All her thoughts centered around Ruíz. She couldn't seem to rid him from her mind. And he was a user, beneath her thoughts. He had used her last night to steal a meaningless kiss. And he was using her father to save the vineyard while he spent his energies on the Estrada *rancho*. It wasn't right or fair. And the next time she saw him, she vowed she would tell him.

Out of deference for her father's feelings, she had kept her mouth shut. But no more. She couldn't bear to think Ruíz believed she was a witless ninny as well as a mindless wanton.

Chapter Five

The wench kneeled before him with her hands behind her back, making her breasts thrust forward. She was wearing a red, lacy shift that barely covered her nipples or the tops of her thighs.

Grasping the red-gold fire of her hair, Lázaro Estrada cupped her head and firmly shoved her lips over his distended member. He closed his eyes and allowed the exquisite hot suction of her mouth to envelop him. Lost in dark lust, he reached down and squeezed one taut nipple while his other hand, tangled in her hair, guided her mouth up and down.

When he'd found his release, Lázaro sent the whore back to Madame Plaisance's Pleasure Palace. Languishing on the heavily draped bed in his quarters off Rampart Street, he reached for the bottle of absinthe and poured himself a glass.

Raising the crystal glass to his lips, he gave a mock salute and addressed the canopy above his bed. "To Ruíz Navarro's destruction and a tortured death for my father."

Tonight was a celebration of sorts. Word had reached him

in New Orleans that Ruíz's father was dead and that his own father, Don Estéban, was weakening fast.

Events were proceeding to his satisfaction.

Ruíz managed to settle most of his father-in-law's pressing needs, with one exception. He hadn't been able to find a qualified horse trainer. Don Estéban possessed some very fine horseflesh, and he was especially particular about who handled his pedigreed horses.

After being at the *rancho* for just one week, Ruíz found himself rushing to finish. His haste surprised him. He had never felt the need to hurry in the past. Before, the running of the *rancho* had been a challenge he enjoyed. Now, despite his best intentions, his thoughts kept turning to home. At the first opportunity, he pointed Oro's nose south in the direction of Los Montes Verdes.

He tried to tell himself he was anxious to see his daughter, but that was only part of the truth. If he were honest with himself, what had driven him to leave for the Estrada *rancho* was the same thing drawing him back . . . Julia.

When he reached Los Montes Verdes, he found her working in the Flores's herb garden. Pilar, Julia's mother, was renown as a *curandera,* an herb healer. The Flores family maintained a large plot of medicinal plants growing behind their *casa.*

Silently and without moving, Ruíz watched Julia tend the herb garden. His blood warmed, following her graceful movements. She seemed to be attuned to the soil, in perfect harmony with all growing things. Even from a distance, he could sense her tranquility as she moved among the plants.

Stepping from the shadow of the stables, he approached her. She must have heard his footsteps because she paused while patting the dirt around a fern-leafed sprig of rosemary. After a moment's hesitation, she rose and faced him.

Her nose had a wide smudge of dirt on it, making her look

like a little girl. A beautiful little girl. But her hands were balled into fists, resting on her hips. Ruíz had the sudden premonition their encounter wasn't going to be a pleasant one.

"Buenas tardes, Julia. I don't want to interrupt your gardening, but I feel I owe you an apology."

Her dark moss-green eyes widened at his words, and she appeared to relax a fraction. Raising her arms, she crossed them on her chest. Looking him directly in the eye, she nodded.

"I . . . I wanted to say . . . that night in the winery. It shouldn't have happened. Paco's wine . . . *Perdición!"* Ruíz snatched the hat from his head and slapped it on his thigh. He shook his head. "I won't blame the wine. It was my fault." His eyes searched hers for understanding. "What happened . . . shouldn't have . . . I apologize," he finished lamely.

Julia inclined her head. Her voice was brusque when she offered one word. "Accepted." Unfolding her arms, she dusted her hands. Pulling the kerchief from her head, her jet-black braid swung free. She used the kerchief to mop the perspiration from her face, smearing the dirt from her nose across her forehead.

With dirt spread across her face, the youthfulness of her features struck him again. She looked scarcely older than Concepción, Ruíz thought. So tender and young and . . .

"Ruíz, I've another unpleasant matter to discuss with you." Her words interrupted his thoughts.

"¿Sí?"

"The . . . ah . . . arrangement you've forged with my father concerning Los Montes Verdes. I don't like it."

"I don't understand, Julia. What are you talking about?"

"That you are using my father and my family's money to rescue Los Montes Verdes without offering us anything in return. It isn't fair."

Ruíz sighed. So this was the cause of the tension he had detected when he greeted her. He felt strangely cheated. He had hoped she was as discomfited by the kiss in the winery as he had been. But not Julia. Los Montes Verdes and her family took precedence over everything else.

"Julia, we've been over this before. Your father agreed to help me. He not only agreed, he was eager to do so."

"I know. You manipulated my father."

Her ugly accusation hung in the air between them. He knew what she said was partially true, but he had done it as a matter of expediency. He couldn't be everywhere at once. He needed Felipe's help with the vineyard.

"If you feel I'm manipulating your father, why don't you tell him?"

"My father would never listen. You know that. He's a proud man. You've issued him a personal challenge to turn the vineyard around. He would never dream of backing down."

"Then it must be what your father wants to do. It shouldn't matter why. And I don't intend to leave all the work on your father's shoulders, either. I intend to help him."

Julia's eyes burned, a crucible of emerald fire. She stared hard at him and then looked away. Her voice was sharp. "A part of Los Montes Verdes belongs to my family. We don't want to be bought out or turned out."

"Julia, why is the vineyard so important to *you?*" Ruíz asked abruptly.

She glanced back at him for a moment, but then, her eyes veered away and dropped to the ground. White teeth worried her bottom lip. Her voice was barely a whisper when she replied, "It's because of Paco . . . it's his life."

Ruíz felt suddenly hollow and very small inside, like the shriveled remnants of an old pecan rattling around in its too large shell. Julia was worried about her younger brother—that there wouldn't be any place for him. He had been a fool not to have guessed her real concern earlier.

He took a step toward her with his hand outstretched as if to draw her close and offer comfort. "Julia, *lo siento.* I didn't think. I can see how you would be worried. But certainly, your father is concerned, too. That's why I trust him to turn the winery around.''

Her eyes were suspiciously bright, and there was a raspy tone to her voice. "Even if my father succeeds, there are no guarantees that . . .'' She moved away and turned her back to him.

When she faced him again, her features were composed. Her voice was cold. "Ruíz, I believe your first loyalty is to your father-in-law's *rancho*. That's where you spend most of your time. And you told us your mother wants to sell Los Montes Verdes. With the passing of your father, I don't believe your family is committed to the winery. But my family is. That's why I asked you to deed us the controlling interest. Then my father's efforts would bring security for our family.''

"Don't be so certain of my motives, Julia,'' Ruíz countered. "It's true the Estrada *rancho* is demanding but that doesn't mean I'm not committed to the winery, too. As to deeding your family the controlling interest in Los Montes Verdes, that's impossible, Julia. I've explained it before. I also have responsibilities and duties to my family.''

"*Sí*, responsibilities you're only too willing to share with my father,'' she retorted sharply.

"That's not fair.''

"Neither is your arrangement with my father.''

Ruíz expelled his breath and clenched his teeth. "We're talking in circles, Julia. You must trust your father's judgment. The winery will prosper, you'll see. And I promise to work alongside your family. I can't do more than that.''

"You mean you *won't* do more.''

"Julia—''

"When did you become so cold and unfeeling, Ruíz? You're using your 'noble' position to bludgeon my family into submissiveness. We've put everything at risk, and all you do is spout empty promises.''

Fury almost choked him, and he felt the bitter bile of his

anger rise in his throat. She had pushed him beyond the limits of reasonableness with her tenacious demands. When Julia sunk her teeth into something, she bore a disturbing resemblance to his domineering mother and it never failed to enrage him.

Wanting to silence her once and for all, he observed cruelly, "If I'm not mistaken, Julia, you were the one who was so eager to risk your own dowry. Am I the one who is cold, Julia? Or is it you? You're so cold you would squander your dowry on a vineyard rather than finding a husband."

How dare she! Ruíz thought as he entered the hacienda. How dare Julia try to dictate to him about his family's vineyard. He almost regretted the last cruel words he'd thrown at her. Almost. But when he remembered her not so subtle efforts to dominate him, he shook with impotent fury.

"*Papá,* you've come home." Concepción appeared in the foyer and flew at him, hugging his legs. "I've missed you, *Papá.*"

Ruíz bent down, trying to control the anger still boiling in his veins. He gave Conchita a brief hug and kissed her forehead. Holding his daughter at arm's length, he exclaimed, "*¡Que bonita!* I like the red ribbon in your hair. And I've missed you, too, little one."

Conchita ducked her head at his compliment. Tentatively, she reached out and placed her hand in his. "Can we go fishing, *Papá*? I liked it when you came fishing with me and Julia. *Por favor,* ask *Tía* Julia, too."

Shaking his head, he tried to explain. "I've been away, Conchita. I have a great deal of work to catch up. Maybe later."

The expectant glow suffusing her face disappeared. She lowered her eyes and thrust out her bottom lip. Releasing his hand, she drew back a step.

Ruíz had his mouth open to call for Luz to come and take his daughter, but Conchita's blatant disappointment stopped him. Staring at the thick sweep of her eyelashes fanning her chubby cheeks, a lump rose to his throat. He remembered her snuggling in his arms when he'd carried her from the riverbank.

Squatting down, he opened his arms and coaxed her back to him, promising, "*Mañana* we'll go fishing. Right after breakfast."

Conchita leaned into his arms, and he hugged her again. But this time, he took the time to enjoy their embrace. Closing his eyes, he savored the warmth of her tiny body and inhaled the fresh scent of her. He kissed the top of her head. It felt so good to be holding his daughter.

"You promise, *Papá?* Right after breakfast?"

"I promise."

"And *Tía* Julia?"

Ruíz had almost forgotten that Conchita had requested Julia's presence, too. But when he thought of Julia, their acrimonious encounter returned in a rush, and he murmured, "Let's just you and me go fishing this time. We've never been fishing by ourselves. We'll take, ah . . . *Tía* Julia next time."

With her head bent, his daughter seemed to be gravely considering his offer. After a moment, her face lit up, and she giggled. "I like that . . . just me and my *Papá.*" She kissed him on the cheek and confessed, "I want tomorrow right now."

Ruíz laughed.

Luz appeared and exclaimed, "*¡Ahí estas!* Conchita, how many times must I tell you not to run off?"

"But *Papá* came."

"*Sí.*" Luz's eyes took in their embrace, and her features softened. "Señor Ruíz, it's time for Conchita's supper."

Giving her a final squeeze, he told her, "Run along with Luz now." Addressing Luz, he said, "I'm taking Conchita fishing tomorrow after breakfast. Can you have her ready for me?"

"*Sí,* Señor Ruíz."

"*Muy bien.*"

Conchita ran to Luz and then turned around. "*Papá*, will you come to tell me goodnight when I'm ready for bed?"

Ruíz winked at his daughter. "I'll be there."

He looked forward to tucking his daughter into bed. He seldom had the opportunity. On the *rancho*, even when Conchita was with him, he usually didn't return to the hacienda until after she was asleep. There was always so much work to be done. Work. He had work to do here, too. That was where he had been headed when Conchita found him.

Striding across the foyer, he opened the door to his study. The room was stuffy and shadowed. He opened a window and lit the fat tallow candle on his desk. Pulling open a drawer, he retrieved the ledgers and spread them across the top of his desk. Seating himself in the leather armchair, he studied the rows of figures. The entries were precise and scrupulously annotated. All in Julia's flowing hand.

The figures blurred and ran together. He rubbed his eyes, and rose from the chair. Pacing in front of the desk, he admitted to himself that his mind wasn't focused on the operating expenses of the vineyard. A brief glance had affirmed that Felipe was managing quite well, just as Ruíz had known he would.

His mind was on Julia, not the vineyard.

He still hadn't gotten over being angry with her, but he couldn't fault her motivations. She was worried about her family's future and especially Paco's.

Ruíz shook his head and stopped pacing. He had responsibilities to his family, too. He *couldn't* deed away the controlling interest to Julia's family by giving them part of his interest. It wouldn't be fair to his family. What Julia wanted from him was impossible.

And what he wanted from Julia was just as impossible.

He wanted her, warm and willing, in his embrace. He wanted to crush her mouth to his and taste her sweetness again, even though he had apologized to her for doing just that. He wanted to take her in his arms and revel in her soft curves again, even though she sometimes drove him to a frenzy of rage. Passion or anger, Julia stirred him deeply.

She was like a bright flame, filled with light and warmth. He needed her fire in his cold and empty life. He had lied when he had told her she was cold. It was he who was cold.

Already, her tender example had helped him to overcome his earlier reticence with his daughter. For the first time in his life, he was enjoying Conchita and wanted to spend time with her.

All because of Julia and that day on the riverbank.

Perdición take the vineyard and duty be damned!

He wanted Julia . . . like he'd never wanted anything else in his life.

By the time Ruíz returned to the study, he had managed to put Julia from his mind. After tucking Conchita in for the night, he ate a quick supper in the *cocina*. He had purposely avoided eating a formal dinner with his mother. Tomorrow, after fishing with Conchita, would be soon enough to hear his mother's latest complaints.

Night had fallen, and the study was completely dark. The tallow candle had burnt itself out. Ruíz replaced it with a candelabra of fine wax candles for better light. He returned the ledger books to the desk drawer and pulled out a clean piece of parchment. Taking a fresh quill from the bundle on the desk, he sharpened its point and opened the inkwell.

Ruíz massaged his neck muscles and rubbed his temples. It had been a long day, but he had one more task to complete. He needed to compose a letter to his uncle, *Tío* Rolando.

Rolando Montemayor, his mother's youngest brother, was a successful merchant in New Orleans. Ruíz hoped to enlist his uncle's support to sell Los Montes Verdes's bottled wines in his establishment. He also needed his uncle to ship him some sturdy glass bottles for the wine. Ruíz wanted to send the letter as soon as possible so they would receive the bottles before the fall harvest.

Halfway through his letter, there was a light rapping on the study door. Ruíz looked up from the letter and laid his pen down. *"Entra."*

His sister, Teresa, entered the room.

A part of Ruíz begrudged her unexpected interruption, for he was tired and wanted to finish the letter, but another part of him was glad she had sought him out.

He hadn't been close to his sister while they were growing up. Doña Eugenia and her strictures on the proper conduct for a "noble" girl child had kept them apart. By the time Teresa was old enough to join Ruíz's play, their mother had forbidden Teresa from rough pursuits.

His younger sister had been relegated to a strict existence of needlework, music, and social graces, besides her academic studies. Her skin was zealously guarded against the harsh Tejas sun. The only acceptable form of exercise for Teresa was riding, but Ruíz hadn't possessed the patience to canter tamely beside his sister when she rode sidesaddle.

While they were growing up, he hadn't stopped to consider how Teresa had felt about her circumscribed childhood. He had merely accepted it as the way all proper Spanish girls were reared.

Julia hadn't been raised like Teresa. As soon as she was able, Julia tagged after him, courageously partaking in every rough and tumble adventure he could devise. His mind started to drift dangerously, thinking of Julia again.

Stopping himself, he turned his attention to his sister. Regret washed over him, thinking of all the fun she had missed as a child. He wondered if her rigid upbringing had contributed to her rebellious nature. It was certainly a possibility. Now Doña Eugenia was in charge of his daughter's upbringing. But he wouldn't allow his mother to subject Conchita to such an unhappy childhood, even if he had to fight her every step of the way.

Teresa wasn't looking rebellious tonight. She looked quite lovely in a blue muslin dress with her nutmeg-colored hair pulled into a sleek chignon. Teresa had become more serious since the death of their father. Her rebellious spark had dimmed some, and she appeared to be more self-possessed. Along with her newfound poise, Ruíz noticed something else, too. The unmistakable look of determination was boldly stamped on her features.

"*Buenas noches,* Teresa." Ruíz half rose and indicated a chair to the left of the desk. "*Por favor,* be seated."

"*Buenas noches, mi hermano.*" Teresa moved to the indicated chair and gripped the back of it. Her knuckles shone white against the chair's dark wood.

Involuntarily, Ruíz tensed, sensing the agitation in his sister and realizing her visit wasn't just a courteous gesture.

"I'd prefer to stand, Ruíz, because what I have to say is . . ." Teresa hesitated, and she lifted her eyes to his. He thought he could read a silent plea in her gaze.

"*¿Sí?*" Ruíz prompted her.

Drawing herself up, she released her grip on the chair and knotted her hands together. "Since father's gone . . ." Teresa paused again, and a shadow crossed her face. She began once more, and, this time, there were no hesitations. "Since our father's gone, you are the head of our family and I need your permission. I want to marry. *Mi novio* is willing to speak with you, to ask for my hand. But our mother will be against it, and I will need your help. I heard father's will. He left me a sizable dowry. I don't care if I have a big wedding. Padre Carrasco in San Antonio can marry us and then we'll go away. But I need my dowry."

Stunned, Ruíz just stared at his sister. Her declaration was completely unexpected and ill-timed . . . and determined-sounding. With a sinking feeling, he knew this was going to turn into a very delicate situation.

He lifted his hands and spread them wide, imploring, "Teresa, could you slow down a bit. My first thought is, I'm surprised you would consider marrying so soon after Father's death. It's customary to wait at least one year."

"Allende said we should wait a year, but I'm afraid to wait. And it won't matter whether we observe the social proprieties or not, *Mamá* will never allow us to marry. I love Allende and want to be with him. We'll have to go away." She lifted her eyes and remarked, with a touch of her old rebellious nature, "Wouldn't you prefer I be married in the sight of God rather than just running off?"

"Of course I don't want you to run off, Teresa. But why must you marry *now.*"

"Because *Mamá* will find out, and she'll stop me. I know it. *Por favor, mi hermano,* help me to find my happiness."

Ruíz ignored her plea and asked, "Do I know the man you want to marry?"

"No."

"Who is he?"

"His name is Allende Soto."

"Why will our mother be against him?"

"Because he is a poor *vaquero.*"

Ruíz sighed, and his shoulders drooped. His voice was filled with exasperation. "*Mi hermana, mi hermana,* when will you quit becoming infatuated with unsuitable men? I fear you do it just to challenge our mother."

Although she blushed at his blunt words, her embarrassment didn't keep her from protesting, "It's not like that . . . this time. I love Allende and he loves me. I admit that, in the past, I've taken pains to find men that *Mamá* thought were unsuitable. But I've never wanted to marry any of them."

"Teresa, stop to consider, your attachment to another unsuitable man has only moved a step further this time . . . to marriage.

Which is not surprising, given the circumstances. We're all feeling a bit empty without . . . because of Father's passing. *Yo entiendo.* I feel the same way, I—''

"That isn't it, Ruíz,'' she interrupted him. "Allende is different. I loved him before I knew about Father. I was waiting for Father to come home to ask if he would meet with Allende and consider his suit. But *Papá* . . . is gone, and he left me a dowry. All I want is—''

"And I'm certain Allende wants your dowry, too,'' Ruíz interjected harshly.

Teresa's eyes blazed. The golden flecks in her sienna-tinted eyes glittered. Her voice was filled with hurt. "How dare you? Allende told me he didn't want my dowry, just me, but that's not fair to him. Allende is very skilled at what he does, which is to break and train horses. I've watched him. He's like an artist. A touch here, a word there, and the wildest mustang will eat from his hand. He . . . we deserve a start. I want my dowry so we can buy a small *rancho* where Allende can raise and train horses. Is that so much to want?''

"No, Teresa, it's not, but you were raised for so much more. Running a *rancho*, even a small one, is backbreaking work. At first, I doubt if you'll be able to afford servants. And then the children will come, one after another. You'll be an old woman before your time, Teresa. You were reared to expect much more. Noble blood runs through your veins, *mi hermana.* Both our father and mother are descended from nobility. How can you forget that?''

His sister's eyes widened until they seemed to fill her face. She took a step backward and muttered, "I can't believe you're talking like that. I never thought you were a snob. I knew you married Alicia because you were ambitious, but her background wasn't noble.'' Her voice filled with contempt, and she accused him, "You're just like our mother . . . a snob.''

"Snobbery has nothing to do with this. I am merely trying to protect you from—''

Her sobs stopped him. Tears were pouring down her face. Her voice was a ragged whisper, "You fought beside *Papá* to bring freedom to Tejas. I thought you believed, like the Anglos, that class doesn't count. It's what you make of yourself . . . with your own hands."

"It's not that simple, Teresa. I fought for a lot of reasons. The old judicial system was a horror, and the new taxes México proposed were outrageous. But I do believe in freedom and . . ." Ruíz stopped.

Did he really believe in those things? He had told Felipe he was no longer his *patrón*, just his partner. But according to Julia, he had exercised his rights as a *patrón* by taking what the Flores family gave him without just recompense. Was he a snob and a hypocrite?

Teresa's tearstained face had turned to stone. Her eyes were muddy with emotions. Distrust emanated from her, and she was slowly backing toward the door. Ruíz wanted to stop her, to say something reassuring, but his mind was a blank. He felt hollow and unsure of himself.

Retreating to the door, she placed her hand on the latch. Her voice sounded loud from across the room. "If you won't help me, it doesn't matter. I will go away with Allende. After we're married and settled, I hope you will come to your senses and give me my dowry."

The door behind his sister opened suddenly, causing her to jump in surprise. Doña Eugenia stood on the threshold. She glanced at Ruíz and then turned her gaze to Teresa.

"You're not going anywhere. *Su hermano* was wise to refuse you the dowry. He and I must protect you from your baser instincts. If it weren't for us, you would gladly wallow in the gutter with the first man who—"

Teresa's hand shot out and landed with a sharp crack. Her mother's head jerked back from the impact. The red imprint of Teresa's hand blazed on Doña Eugenia's cheek.

Whirling around, his sister ran from the room.

Ruíz, appalled at what had happened, moved to his mother's side.

Doña Eugenia's features were distorted with fury, and she screamed, "José!"

José appeared and his mother commanded, "Señorita Teresa isn't herself. I want her locked in her rooms until she comes to her senses."

Bowing, the *mayordomo* scurried away to do Doña Eugenia's bidding.

"Mamá, I deplore Teresa's behavior, but she's too old to be locked in her rooms. *Por favor,* can't we—"

"Now you sound like your father. He was always too soft on Teresa." Doña Eugenia stroked her reddened cheek and observed, "You can see the result of his spoiling her. She's not responsible for her actions and if I don't lock her up, she'll run away. She said so herself."

Ruíz closed his eyes for a moment. His temples were throbbing, and his stomach was in knots. What an ugly mess. Since his father had died, his family seemed to be splintering into pieces.

"I suppose you're right, *Mamá.*" But even as he said the necessary words to calm her, he wondered about Teresa. So much of what his sister had said made sense. He regretted deeply that she had slapped their mother. There was no excuse for her behavior, but it underscored the unshakable determination he had sensed in her.

Maybe this time was different. Maybe his sister really was in love or maybe her behavior was a result of her grief over their father's death. Either way, Teresa needed understanding, not imprisonment in her rooms.

He silently vowed to do everything in his power to help his sister.

Chapter Six

Julia watched Paco wrestle with the wine casks. He rolled a new, empty cask into place and opened the spigot on the full cask, draining it into the empty one. Drawing the wine off into new casks was a process called racking, and it cleansed the maturing wine of lees. Lees were particles in the wine that remained from the original pressing, such as stems, skins, or seeds.

Paco's powerful arms were more than a match for the heavy wine casks, but he relied upon Julia to reach objects beyond his grasp. Unfortunately, Julia's mind wasn't on their work. She couldn't erase Ruíz's angry words from her mind. She suspected he had lashed out because he knew what he was doing wasn't fair, and he hated to face his own guilt. Even worse, he had known where to strike, too. At the most vulnerable part of her . . . her spinsterhood. The irony of his blow made it all the more bitter. The reason she had never married was . . . Ruíz.

Paco disrupted her unhappy reflections by declaring, "I think that finishes the reds.'' He dusted his hands and rinsed out the silver tasting cup dangling from a chain around his neck.

"What about those casks, Paco?" Julia pointed to a row of untouched barrels in the corner. "We haven't racked those."

Shaking his head, he scooted over to the casks. He placed his hand on one of the spigots and filled his tasting cup. He sipped the wine and swished it in his mouth. Spitting it on the hard-packed earth floor, he observed, "The wine in these casks is mature, ready for bottling. There's hardly any sediment left in them." He held out the cup to Julia and asked, "Care for a taste?''

"No, thanks, I trust your judgment."

He laughed, and his hazel eyes gleamed. "And so you should, *mi hermana,* so you should."

His cocksure attitude didn't surprise Julia. Her brother knew the age of each cask of wine, the number of times it had been racked, and when the wine would be mature enough to drink.

"Do you have the eggs I asked you to bring? We need to clarify that new batch from last year."

"*Sí,* I brought the eggs from Mother's hens. I'll fetch the basket and separator from the tasting room."

Julia returned and joined Paco in front of a new set of oaken wine casks. Carefully, she broke open and separated several eggs, retaining the yolks for cooking in one dish and filling another dish with the egg whites.

One by one, Julia lifted the bung from the top of each cask and poured some of the egg whites into the wine. Paco watched, instructing her as to the amount to put into each cask. The egg whites served as a magnet to attract and coagulate the unwanted, floating particles in new wine, causing them to settle to the bottom as lees to be drawn off at a later time.

When they had finished applying the egg whites, Paco reached up and patted one of the casks, remarking, "I'll check these next week to see if they're ready for their first racking." He wiped his brow with the back of his hand. For an early summer day, it was cool in the thick-walled winery, but Paco had been handling the heavy casks for several hours and his face was coated with perspiration. Julia laid aside the eggs and offered, "Care to rest for a while?"

"No, we're almost done. I just want to have a look at the whites in the cellar. It shouldn't take long."

"Are you sure?"

Paco grinned at her and replied, "I'm fine, *mi hermana*. A little honest sweat never hurt anyone."

Julia nodded. She knew better than to press her brother about his stamina. He hated any reference, no matter how oblique, to the fact that his body was different.

"Besides, Julia, it's cooler in the cellar. It should be a welcome change. Did you bring the paste of crushed fish bone?"

"Sí," Julia answered, digging in the pockets of her apron. She pulled out a flat packet and a candle. *"Mamá* made it last night." Julia had never understood the chemistry, but egg whites didn't work well as a coagulating agent for the white wines. Crushed fish bones were used for the whites.

"Muy bien, vengase."

Together they opened the heavy oak doors leading to the cellar. Julia lit the candle and descended the stairs while Paco pulled himself down a specially constructed ramp with the aid of a rope strung between two posts at each end of the incline.

When they reached the bottom, Julia could feel the temperature change Paco had mentioned. It was cool and humid in the wine cellar, a perfect environment for white wines. The cellar backed up to the main well of the hacienda compound and droplets of water from the well clung to the cellar walls. The drops of water caught the candlelight, reflecting the light like a skein of glittering jewels.

Los Montes Verdes produced only a few casks of white wine each year. Red wine was a common staple, but white wine was considered a luxury for sophisticated wine drinkers. The grapes for whites were more delicate, and easy prey to disease. And the maturing white wines had to be kept cool, lest they spoil. Julia was certain there would be a market for them in New Orleans, but she wondered if they would be able to transport the fragile wines.

Even the casks they used for the whites were different, made from pine rather than oak. Whereas the oaken casks imparted a body to the rich red wines, Paco believed oak casks left a residue that overpowered the gentle white wines. It had been his idea, two years before, to try pine instead. Based on the results so far, Julia had to admit Paco's vision had proven flawless.

Paco moved from cask to cask, sampling the wines. She helped him top off some of the casks with wine of a similar maturity. White wines were extremely susceptible to air, even more so than the reds, making it imperative to keep the casks full and as airtight as possible.

After they had finished, he declared, "None of the whites need to be racked, but these two casks should be clarified."

Julia wasn't surprised that the whites didn't require racking. White wines went through a careful initial crushing. All stems, seeds, and skins were removed, as far as was humanly possible. Particles in white wines were kept to a minimum lest they sour the wine. It was another reason they kept their production of the whites to small batches. Proper crushing of the white grapes was particularly laborious.

"Let me have the fish paste, Julia."

She handed him the packet, and he measured two half-fingers of paste, instructing her, "Drop one into each cask."

Gingerly, she accepted the fish paste and averted her head as she applied it to the casks. The paste possessed a particularly distinctive smell.

He laughed at her obvious distaste and teased, "It's not just the paste that has your nose out of joint, *mi hermana.*"

Replacing the bungs, she wiped her hands on her apron. "What do you mean by that?"

"The way you just snapped at me, that's what I'm talking about. My teasing has never bothered you before. You've been in a fine temper for some time now." He pursed his lips and cocked his head. "Let me think, could it have anything to do with Señor Ruíz?"

Julia blushed to the roots of her hair and retreated several steps. Her mouth worked, but no sound came out except a strangled gurgle.

"Hey, don't take the candle away. I can't see what I'm doing."

Thrusting the candle at him, she said, "Put it on the shelf. You're almost done. You don't need me anymore."

"Temper, temper, *mi hermana.*" He took the candle from her and placed it on the low shelf under the wine casks. "Are you certain you don't want to talk about it. I'm all ears." His eyes twinkled with mischief in the glow of the candlelight. "It wouldn't have anything to do with the night Señor Ruíz was tasting the wines, would it? I thought *Papá* and I burst in at a most inopportune time."

If Julia had been blushing before now her face felt as it were on fire. She had no idea Paco and her father might have suspected what had happened that night.

"It's . . . it isn't what you think. That night we weren't . . . That is . . ." Throwing her hands into the air, she purposely changed the subject, hoping to deflect her brother's acute insight. "I'm upset because of the arrangement Ruíz made with *Papá*. It isn't fair to risk our money and our time to save the winery for the Navarro family."

"We'll be saving it for our family, too."

"*Sí*, but the Navarros still own the controlling interest. It isn't fair." She stamped her foot on the hard dirt floor, needing an outlet for her pent-up anger and resentment.

He shrugged. "You shouldn't expect a man like Señor Ruíz to be fair. He's used to getting his own way, being fair has nothing to do with it."

"How can you not care, Paco?"

"I care, *mi hermana,* but I'm wise enough to know I can't change how the world is. And I have faith in our family." Paco reached out and grasped her hand, giving it a reassuring squeeze. "Don't worry, we'll survive. If Los Montes Verdes can't be saved, we will sell our interest and start our own vineyard and winery."

"But all the best land is taken, Paco. Scripted to the soldiers of the Republic or sold to settlers by the *empresarios.* Where would we go?"

"There's plenty of land left, north and west of here."

"That's Comanche country, and the southern border of Tejas is still in dispute. Mexico says it's the Nueces River, and our new government says it's the Río Grande."

"You're well informed, but there's always opportunities if you have the courage. This was a wilderness when our grandfather settled here."

"*Sí,* but our grandfather was . . ." Julia stopped herself and bit her lip. Shame washed over her, and she turned away. In her frustration, she had almost made reference to Paco's condition.

"You worry too much, Julia." Paco's usual bantering tone was gone, and his voice held a warning note, "In particular, you worry too much about me. I'm not a child to be cozened for the rest of my life . . . despite my limitations. It's time you worried about yourself, Julia. Time you thought of having a family of your own. *Papá* has other savings. He's too canny to risk it all. A suitable dowry could be found for you."

Julia went hot and then cold. She hadn't meant to hurt Paco. The last thing she wanted was for her brother to know she was concerned about his future. But he had seen through her. Seen to the very heart of her worry about the vineyard.

And he was telling her, in the plainest terms, that he didn't want or need her concern. He wanted her to realize he was capable of taking care of himself. And she would try, by the

Blessed Virgin Mary, she would try to honor Paco's independent spirit.

But the other part . . . the part about her starting her own family was another matter. How could she explain to Paco the only man she had ever loved, the only man she had ever wanted was Ruíz.

She couldn't.

Whirling around, she abandoned him. Running from the cellar as if all the demons of the underworld were pursuing her.

Julia emerged from the dark winery into the brilliant summer sun. Temporarily blinded, she ran headlong into Ruíz.

He caught and steadied her, his hand lingering on her waist. The light touch of his fingers burned through the cotton of her blouse and sent a sudden warmth streaming through her body. Standing toe to toe with him, her eyes were focused on his open collar. A sprinkle of brown hair peeped from beneath his shirt, coated by a thin sheen of perspiration.

Against all logic, she longed to bury her face against his chest, to taste the salty essence of him, to stroke his corded muscles. To hold him in her arms and run her fingers through the wavy silk of his air.

"Where were you running to, Julia? Is something amiss?"

Licking her dry lips, she swallowed. Backing up a few steps, he was forced to release her waist. "I . . . ah, I wasn't really running. The sun blinded me. I didn't see you coming. Nothing's wrong. I've been helping Paco in the winery."

He smiled at her. The flash of white teeth in his bronzed face almost took her breath away. "I've been working, too, in the vineyard. The new grapes are thriving. I think we'll have a good crop this year despite the hailstorm." Raising his hand in a dismissive gesture, he said, "Enough about the vineyard. I was looking for you. Your father told me you would be in the winery." Grasping her elbow, he directed, *"Vengase,* let's sit on the bench where we can talk."

He led her to a rough stone bench beneath the drooping branches of a venerable pecan tree that stood next to the winery. Dressed in its summer foliage, the pecan tree provided a private haven under its low-hanging branches. Julia could remember playing hide-and-go-seek under this very tree with Ruíz when they were children.

Ruíz seated her on the bench, but he remained standing with one leg bent and braced against the bench. Julia averted her eyes from the tensile strength of his flexed thigh. Staring down at his dusty, booted feet, she wondered at Ruíz's demeanor and what he wanted to talk with her about.

She knew she should still be angry with him. But as hard as she tried, she couldn't seem to summon forth her righteous indignation over the way he had spoken to her the day before. It was as if her exchange with Paco had washed her clean of emotion, leaving her empty.

Leaning forward, he cupped her chin in his hand and raised her head so her eyes met his. As soon as he'd gotten her attention, he removed his hand. Her face tingled from his brief touch, and she wished . . .

"I went fishing with Conchita this morning, and she sends her love. She made me promise the next time we go fishing, I'd bring her *Tía* Julia."

Julia felt a warm coil of some indefinable emotion spread through her body at his words, banishing the empty feeling. She was happy he had taken his daughter fishing and even happier to learn that Conchita had missed her. The thought of them as a threesome was a dream Julia cherished, late at night in her solitary bed.

"I . . . I would like that."

He smiled again. "I'm glad you agree. I think you and I need to call a truce." Julia opened her mouth to speak, but he forestalled her by raising his hand and imploring, *"Por favor,* just hear me out. We're going to be working side by side, especially when it's time to harvest. And Conchita is very attached to you. Will you consider putting the bitterness behind us?''

Julia nodded, afraid to speak. What he was asking made sense. It didn't mitigate the injustice of his actions, but if they wanted the winery to succeed, she knew they must all pull together.

''There's more, Julia. I'm sorry for what I said yesterday, and I'm asking you to trust me. If we don't save Los Montes Verdes, I will find the money to help your family start their own winery. I don't know where I'll find it, but I promise you I will. I won't take Paco's future from him.''

''That won't be necessary.''

''What do you mean?''

She gulped hard, fighting the sobs rising in her throat. ''We can't take your charity, Ruíz.''

''But it's not charity, Julia, it's . . . just added security.''

The sobs crowding her throat spilled out, and she covered her face with her hands. She could feel her shoulders shaking, and she was ashamed to let Ruíz see her this way. But she couldn't seem to help herself. Paco was so precious to her, and, inadvertently, she had wounded him.

Seating himself beside her, he drew her into his arms without saying a word. Holding her close, he stroked her tense back. Julia wanted nothing more than to relax in the protection of his comforting arms, but she felt like a blubbering fool. What must he think of her?

''I'm sorry I lost control, Ruíz, but I've just hurt Paco. He realized I was worried about his future because . . . because . . . he's a . . .'' She couldn't bring herself to say the awful word. ''And I'm afraid if we lose Los Montes Verdes, he'll do something foolish just to prove he's a man.'' Fresh tears sprang to her eyes, and she twisted away from him, worrying, ''Will Paco ever forgive me? What if I've driven him to—?''

Ruíz placed two fingers over her lips and commanded, "Don't say it, Julia. I know Paco will forgive you. You've been devoted to him since the day he was born. I remember."

Removing his fingers, he gazed into her eyes. "We won't fail, Julia. We won't lose Los Montes Verdes. I'm with you." Pausing, he admitted, "After my father died and I saw the debts, and my mother wanted to sell . . ." He shook his head and confessed, "I wasn't certain that I . . . that we could . . . But now, I'm committed to saving *our* vineyard. I won't allow us to fail."

Dabbing at her eyes with the hem of her apron, she nodded, silently extending her trust.

He pulled her into his arms again and murmured low, soothing words to her as if she were a child. Reveling in the protection of his embrace, she savored the earthy masculine smell of him. Her head fit perfectly into the hollow of his shoulder, and she wondered anew at this gentler Ruíz. This man who listened to her fears and tried to comfort her was the boy she remembered.

He hasn't changed, her heart counseled. *He has just lost his way for a while.* And now, she was falling even deeper in love with the man he had become.

There was a knock on her door, and Teresa listlessly called out, *"Entra."*

She had been a prisoner in her rooms for a week now, and no one had been allowed to visit except her mother and personal maid. Since her maid had just left to fetch supper, Teresa assumed it must be her mother at the door. She hoped not; she was weary from arguing with her mother about Allende.

Allende . . . what must he be thinking? She hadn't been able to meet him at their accustomed place, and she hadn't been allowed to send word. Both her maid and José had flatly refused to help her, fearing Doña Eugenia's wrath.

The door opened and Teresa was surprised to see her brother

standing there. He entered her small *sala* and greeted her. *"Buenas tardes, mi hermana.* I hope you are well."

"As well as can be expected," Teresa replied with bitter sarcasm. Ruíz had sided with their mother. He wanted her to forget Allende, too. No one wanted to help her.

But her brother's next words belied her bitter thoughts when Ruíz announced, "I've brought some good news. You're no longer a prisoner. I managed to convince our mother."

Her eyebrows lifted and she studied Ruíz closely, afraid this was some cruel jest, or, even worse, that he was going to extract a promise from her to never see Allende again.

"Muchas gracias, mi hermano. But how did you convince *Mamá* to—?"

"Esperaté, there's more, Teresa. I met with your young man, and I was impressed by him. I also made some inquiries. It would appear that Allende Soto has quite a reputation as a horse handler. Don Estéban—"

"You mean you liked Allende?" Teresa interrupted Ruíz. His kind words were music to her ears. A heavy weight lifted from her heart, and a tiny flicker of hope ignited within her. Could it be possible her snobbish brother was willing to give Allende a chance to prove himself a worthy suitor?

Ruíz's mouth quirked at the corners, as if he were trying to suppress a smile. He advanced a step closer and spread his hands.

"I can't say if I *liked* him, Teresa, but I was favorably impressed with him. And I'm trying to tell you that I want to get to know Allende better. Since Don Estéban is in need of a horse trainer, I offered Allende the position. It will give me a chance to work with him, and the wages are good. There's even a small *casa* that goes along with the position. I hope you're pleased."

"Pleased!" Teresa squealed as she hurled herself into her brother's arms. "I'm so happy I don't know what to say." She hugged Ruíz with joyous abandon and promised, "You're not making a mistake, Ruíz. Allende is a hard worker and a good man.''

Ruíz returned her hug and then held her at arm's length. His eyes reflected her happiness, but his features were stern. ''There's some conditions to be met, Teresa.''

Teresa nodded and held her breath. Surely her brother wouldn't be willing to help Allende, only to forbid her from seeing him, would he?

''I want to make certain you and Allende really care for one another, so I'm offering you a trial period. You may visit me at the *rancho,* and Allende will court you under my supervision. I know you've been sneaking out to see him and that kind of situation can be . . . seductive. An open courtship should prove if you're suited to each other.''

''But what about *Mamá?* How did you get her to agree to this?''

''Our mother knows nothing of it. She would never agree to such an arrangement. This is between you and me, Teresa. Remember you said I'm the head of the family now, and I mean to take that responsibility seriously. While you're at Los Montes Verdes, you will obey our mother without question. You'll only see Allende at the Estrada *rancho.* Do you agree?''

Did she agree? How could she not agree. Ruíz's proposition was beyond anything she had hoped for. To be able to see Allende openly and have her brother's blessing was too wonderful for words.

Smiling at her brother, she said, ''*Sí,* I agree. I want to prove to you my feelings are deep and strong for Allende. This is not just another passing fancy.''

Returning her smile, he admitted, ''I'm beginning to believe you do care for him, which is why I want to give you this chance. But I have another reason, too.''

''*¿Qué?*''

''I don't want you to think I'm a snob.''

Teresa dropped her head and studied the mosaic pattern on

the tile floor. Her voice was a whisper. "I'm sorry I said that, Ruíz, truly sorry."

"And I'm sorry I didn't take you seriously . . . at first. Is it settled then?"

She raised her eyes and replied, "I have one question."

"*¿Sí?*"

"You mentioned a trial period . . . For how long?"

"One year."

Teresa's heart stopped, and she felt her brief joy drain away. Disappointed at having to wait so long, she wanted to argue with her brother. But her gratitude for what he was willing to do stopped her. She realized he was only trying to protect her from doing something rash that would affect the rest of her life. It would be hard to abide by his condition, but she and Allende would prove their steadfast love for each other by waiting. And she wouldn't be estranged from her family, at least not from her brother. Lifting her chin, she nodded her acquiescence.

"I know it seems like a long time to wait, but I have my reasons," he admitted. "As I mentioned before, I think we should honor the period of mourning for our father's passing." Ruíz paused and reached out to squeeze her shoulder. "But there's an even more pressing reason, Teresa. I don't have the money for your dowry. In a year's time, I should be able to raise the funds."

"Is it because of *Mamá* and her spending?"

It was Ruíz's turn to study the pattern in the tiled floor. He nodded.

"Oh, poor Ruíz. I didn't know. *Por favor,* forgive me. You must have so many worries on your shoulders now." She blinked back the tears that had started in her eyes. "But you're willing to help me." She hugged him again and promised, "*Mi hermano,* you won't regret it."

Chapter Seven

Julia averted her eyes from the nasty cut on Señor Alberty's leg. He had accidentally sliced his shin with a sharp-edged machete while clearing some underbrush from the edge of the vineyard

Pilar's expert touch was gentle as she examined the wound. As a well-respected herb healer, Pilar took care of all the workers on Los Montes Verdes as well as anyone else who requested her help. And many others did come, some from as far away as Nacogdoches.

Her mother's voice broke Julia's reverie, "Get me some clean cotton strips from the cupboard, Julia." Then Pilar turned back to the wounded man and said, "Señor Alberty, I won't need to take stitches. The wound is ragged but shallow. Keep it bound and use this salve for a week." Pilar handed him a pottery jar. "Have Señora Alberty apply the salve twice a day and change the dressing each time. Be certain your *esposa* boils and dries the cotton strips. The wound must be kept clean and dry. Return in a week's time, and I'll see how it's healing."

Returning with the cotton strips, she handed them to her mother. Taking them from her, Pilar requested, *"Gracias, mi hija. Por favor,* put the kettle to boil."

Julia hurried to do her mother's bidding. If she couldn't help with the actual healing, she like*d* to assist her mother in other small ways.

When she finished with the bandaging, Pilar asked, "You understand what to do, Señor Alberty?"

"Sí, Señora Flores *y muchas gracias.* I will bring you a token of my thanks when I return."

"It isn't necessary."

"I insist."

"Muy bien, hasta la vista."

Pilar joined Julia at the hearth and instructed, "As soon as the water boils, put in the soiled linens and clear away my medicines. The table needs washing down, too, Julia, if you don't mind. I need to finish mending a torn shirt for your father."

Pilar washed and dried her hands carefully in a porcelain basin and then seated herself in the rocking chair beside the hearth. Taking up the shirt and needle and thread, she announced, "There's a *fandango* in San Antonio on Saturday night."

Her mother's unexpected announcement caught Julia by surprise. She finished placing the bloody cloths in the boiling water and stirred them with a long-handled ladle while adding a sliver of lye soap.

"There's always a *fandango* in San Antonio on Saturday night," Julia responded, wondering where her mother was leading.

"Sí, and we haven't been in months. The Losoyas have been kind enough to invite us to visit them and stay overnight. I think we should go."

"I'd rather not, *Mamita.* Can't I stay at home with Paco?"

Julia moved from the hearth to gather her mother's jars of medicines, returning them to their place in the cupboard.

"Julia, you can't bury yourself forever at Los Montes Verdes." Pilar's voice carried a note of exasperation. "Your father and I have been patient, but—"

"I won't go without an escort, *Mamita*." Julia purposely interrupted, afraid of what her mother was about to say. "It's so humiliating to stand in the corner and wait to be asked to dance."

"But your father and Luis Losoya will be there. They'll dance with you, and you've never lacked for partners when we've gone before."

Julia closed the cupboard door and sighed softly. Had Paco said something to her mother about it being time for her to find a husband or was her entire family suddenly conspiring against her? Her mother's veiled urgings made her think of that day, several weeks before, when she had hurt Paco and then cried in Ruíz's arms.

Gracias Dios, her relationship with Paco hadn't suffered from her blundering. With his usual aplomb, he had put the incident behind him and not referred to it again.

But shortly thereafter, Ruíz had gone to the Estrada *rancho,* taking his sister and Conchita with him. Teresa and his daughter had returned after a week, but Ruíz had remained at his father-in-law's *rancho*. Despite his promises, he had deserted Los Montes Verdes again, leaving the Flores family to cope with the vineyard.

Bitterly, Julia realized Ruíz had extracted a truce from her so she wouldn't upset his plans. He hadn't meant his promises; he just wanted to obtain her cooperation. She had been naive enough to believe him, and she had even humiliated herself by crying in his arms and revealing what had passed between herself and Paco.

When would she learn that she could no longer trust Ruíz?

He was not the open-hearted friend of her childhood. He was cold and manipulative . . . like his mother.

Thinking of Doña Eugenia made Julia wonder why Ruíz's mother despised her family. It was a question that had troubled Julia for a long time.

Hoping to divert her mother's attention from the proposed *fandango,* Julia asked, "Why does Doña Eugenia dislike our family so much?"

There was a rustle of fabric, and Julia glanced up from sponging the table to find that Pilar had dropped the shirt she was mending. Her mother's eyes were thoughtful as if she were considering Julia's question, but her voice sounded impatient. "What does Doña Eugenia have to do with the *fandango?*"

"Nothing, *Mamita.* It was just a thought I had. I've asked you before, and you always said I was too young to understand. I'm grown now, *Mamita,* and I wish you would answer me."

"*¿Por qué,* Julia?"

"Because . . . I . . . because . . ." Julia stopped herself. She had almost admitted that the knowledge might help her to better understand Ruíz. But she didn't dare tell her mother that.

"Doña Eugenia wants to sell Los Montes Verdes. I wondered if it had anything to do with her animosity toward our family."

Pilar retrieved the shirt from her lap and dropped her eyes, returning her attention to the sewing. Her usually smooth brow was creased in a frown.

"Doña Eugenia wants to sell the vineyard to satisfy her greed, pure and simple. As to the other," her mother paused and tied off the thread, biting it in two with her teeth, "it is a private matter and none of your concern."

Julia shooed aside the flock of imported geese. The geese, brought at great expense from France, had been one of Don Federico's ideas. The long-necked fowls were specially bred to eat insects that plagued vineyards.

She stopped to inspect the grapes. The results of the pruning were evident. The grapes were fewer but appeared to be stronger and healthier. Julia pulled up an errant weed, glorying in the warm sun upon her arms and shoulders.

After she had crossed the length of the vineyard, the sun grew hot and she grew tired. The woods bordering the rows of vines beckoned. She found a grassy spot beneath a tall cypress and flung herself onto the ground. Drawing her knees up and placing her chin upon them, she stared across the vineyard.

Heat waves shimmered and shifted between the vines, creating mirages that disappeared when she shut her eyes and reopened them. But one of the mirages proved to be stubborn. It took shape, moving slowly toward her. And as it approached, she realized it wasn't a heat-induced fantasy. The figure was a man, and the man was Ruíz. He was stopping to inspect the vines as she had done, moments before.

It's about time he came home, Julia thought to herself. With that thought, her resentment simmered.

Shifting on the hard ground, she brought her legs down into a more conventional position. After smoothing her skirt over her legs, she realized her movements must have caught his attention, because he waved at her and called out, "Julia, may I join you?"

Hesitating to answer, she realized she had nothing to say to him. She still felt he had manipulated her the last time. Weeks had passed without a word from him. She didn't care to hear any more of his empty promises. The drowsy solitude of the vineyard was ruined for her. She rose and dusted off the back of her skirt.

When she turned around, he was there, smiling at her. His shirt was soaked through with perspiration. The thin cotton clung to his muscled torso, revealing the washboard flatness of his stomach and the sculpted swell of his chest.

Julia licked her dry lips. It was a hot day . . . and getting hotter by the second.

Ruíz reached out and took her hand. *"Cómo está?"*

Jerking her hand free, she replied, *"Muy bien.* I was just leaving. There are some accounts I need to go over, but I wanted to check on the grapes."

"Sí," Ruíz agreed, removing his hat and wiping his face with a bandana. "I wanted to inspect the vineyard first, too. We can go over the books later. Don't rush off."

"But—"

"I'm pleased at what I saw," he interrupted her. His voice was enthusiastic, "The crop looks good. I don't know when I've seen the vineyard looking healthier."

No thanks to you, Julia thought darkly, but, aloud, she murmured, "I'm glad you're pleased. *Con permiso,* I'll go now."

Before she could move, his hand shot out, and he grasped her arm. Gazing into her face, he seemed to be studying her features as if searching for a clue to her feelings. Her eyes met his, and she stared back, unwilling to flinch before his steady gaze.

"You're angry with me, aren't you? I can see it in your face. I thought the last time we spoke that we agreed upon a truce. Didn't we?"

"Sí, but that wasn't all we agreed upon," she flung back at him and wrenched her arm free of his disturbing touch.

"What do you mean?" He paused, still searching her face. And then his caramel-colored eyes widened, and he inclined his head. *"Yo entiendo.* You're angry because I've been away for so long, and I haven't been helping with the vineyard, aren't you?"

Julia stared straight ahead, her gaze trained past his broad shoulders. She refused to meet his eyes or admit her anger.

Ruíz ran his hand in obvious agitation through his wavy brown hair. *"Por favor,* Julia, be reasonable. This is the growing season at Los Montes Verdes. There is little enough to do in the vineyard. I plan on being here when it counts." He paused and reached out as if he wanted to touch her again, but he must have changed his mind because he drew his hand back.

Stony silence was his only answer.

"I did stay away longer than I had planned," he admitted. "But you must understand, I have a new horse handler to train, and it was calving time on the *rancho*. And ... and ..." He paused, as if choosing his words with care, "There's been some rustling at the Estrada spread. We almost caught the thieves. I hope we got close enough to make them think twice about coming back."

"Not Indians or Comancheros?" Julia asked, dreading the answer. At the mention of rustlers, her hands had begun to perspire, and her heart beat double-time. The precincts around San Antonio de Bexar had been relatively free from Indian attacks in the past few years, but the fear was always there, just below the surface.

"No, Julia, they weren't Indians or Comancheros. Not based on the signs we found."

Relieved to hear Indians weren't behind the rustling, her pounding heart slowed. She thought over the reasons he had given for his long absence. Maybe she had jumped to conclusions about why he had stayed away. Studying him closely, she was able to see past her anger.

His usually short-cropped hair was long, and there was a stubble of beard on his face. His cocoa-brown eyes were rimmed by dark shadows, and the creases in his forehead had deepened. He looked exhausted.

Julia's heart squeezed, and the barrier she had erected against him crumbled. He must have been working very hard at the *rancho* if his unkempt appearance was any indication. And he was right about the vineyard; it didn't require much care during the growing season.

Was it his absence from the vineyard that had made her bitter and resentful? Or was it because she felt his absence, personally? She knew she had missed him and looked forward to working beside him.

And if she were honest with herself, no matter how angry she was while he was away, his mere presence banished her wrath . . . only to be replaced by yearning. A yearning that had lived so long in her soul it had become a part of her. And try as she might, she couldn't purge him from her heart.

"Am I forgiven then?" Ruíz interrupted her thoughts. "It seems I'm always begging your forgiveness, Julia. I wish—"

"Don't. I understand you have other commitments. I just—"

"Worry too much."

Julia couldn't suppress her chuckle. "Now you sound like my family."

"Why not? I've known you as long as they have." His warm brown eyes twinkled.

Why not indeed?

Ruíz had known her for all of her life. And maybe that was the problem. She must seem like a sister to him. Had he ever noticed she was a woman . . . someone he might desire? He had kissed her that one time, in the winery, but then he'd apologized and said it shouldn't have happened. Why? Because it had been like kissing his own sister?

Long past, almost forgotten images flooded her mind. Ruíz and she playing and rolling in the mud together, swimming as naked, innocent children in the river, and fighting like cats and dogs. Did he still think of her as a child? How could she change his mind?

As if he'd been reading her thoughts, his next words provided the opening she sought, "Our grapes are thriving. I think a small celebration is in order, and it has been a long time since I've done anything but work. Your father mentioned that you're going to the *fandango* tomorrow night. I would be honored if you would allow me to escort you."

Julia's heart leapt at his offer. Ruíz was asking to escort her! Her hopes soared. Maybe he had already begun to see her in a different light. Or maybe he was just being polite. Either way, it didn't matter. The *fandango* would be an ideal opportunity, and she owned the perfect dress to convince Ruíz she was no longer a child.

Clenching his jaw, Ruíz ground his teeth painfully, watching Julia twirl by in the arms of David Treviño. Treviño had hounded them since they'd arrived at the *fandango,* demanding every other dance with Julia.

He had struggled to remain polite with Treviño, but it was getting increasingly difficult by the minute. David Treviño's family owned the most reliable freighting business in San Antonio. Los Montes Verdes's bottled wine, upon which the future of the vineyard depended, would be transported to New Orleans by his wagons. Ruíz couldn't afford to antagonize the man.

And he couldn't blame Treviño for his obvious interest in Julia, either.

Gone was the familiar Julia that Ruíz knew, to be replaced by a sultry temptress. She was a study in seductive contrasts. Red against black ... black against red. Her rich ebony hair was plaited and wrapped around her head in a regal crown. Bloodred roses were woven among her jet tresses, echoing the crimson satin of her dress. Her red gown was edged in black lace at the throat and hem, and the tops of her high breasts swelled provocatively against the lace-trimmed, scooped neckline of the dress. When she twirled through the steps of the *fandango,* the bottom of her skirt billowed, revealing her dainty ankles and slender legs. The scarlet satin dress fit Julia like a second skin ... like an open invitation to sin, accenting her tiny waist and molding to the soft swell of her hips.

The faintest trace of her perfume assailed his nostrils when she whirled past, the heady fragrance of gardenias.

Ruíz clenched his teeth again, following Julia's progress across the smoky *taverna.* The strumming of the Spanish guitar pounded in his blood, the screech of the fiddle grated at his nerves, and the whine of the accordion made his temples throb. He couldn't take much more of watching Julia in another man's arms.

She belonged to Los Montes Verdes and to . . . Ruíz shook his head. Julia didn't *belong* to him. If anything, she was a constant thorn in his side, a daily reminder to do his duty to the vineyard. And an unwanted reminder of his cold, empty life.

He had wanted her since that first day outside the cathedral, but he ignored his own desires, replacing them with a round of duties and responsibilities, throwing himself into his work at the *rancho* and vineyard. Spending time with his daughter, playing cupid for his sister, and pacifying his mother—they were all worthwhile pursuits, but they weren't Julia.

His loins tightened painfully when he spied Julia tilting her head back and laughing at something Treviño whispered in her ear.

No!

He couldn't stand to watch her and Treviño together any longer, not for another moment. For once, he wouldn't deny *his* desires. The *fandango* ended, and Ruíz strode purposefully across the dance floor.

"Gracias, David." Julia fanned herself and added, "I enjoyed our dance."

A warm and familiar hand grasped her elbow, making her flesh tingle. Ruíz's voice was a hot caress against the flesh of her neck. *"Con permisso."*

Before she could respond, he propelled her across the uneven brick floor. Bewildered by his abrupt abduction, she glanced over her shoulder. Her parents, standing beside the Losoyas, were staring at her and Ruíz with their mouths open.

David Treviño was staring, too, but his mouth was clamped

firmly shut. And his eyes were narrowed. Fury and resentment were plainly etched on his handsome features.

She thought of struggling against Ruíz's rude intrusion, but it was what she had set out to do ... to make him want her. And David had, unwittingly, aided her plan.

They stepped outside, and she felt the cool night air on her flushed face. There were knots of people standing outside the *taverna,* also enjoying the night air or playing endless games of *monte.* Ruíz threaded their way through the people without speaking a word or looking back. He led her across the street and down a flight of carved steps to the narrow ribbon of the San Antonio River winding through the center of town. At the top of a curved stone bridge, he stopped abruptly and drew her into his arms.

His mouth covered hers with unexpected strength. Her response was instantaneous. Molding her lips to his, she kissed him back with all the pent-up passion she possessed.

With his mouth pressed against hers, she tasted the sweet brandy on his breath, and the taste intermingled with the starchy smell of his ruffled shirt. His lips were warm and supple. They moved like a song over her mouth, tasting and savoring.

Julia rose on her toes and curled her arms around Ruíz's neck, pulling him closer, melding her body against his. They flowed together, her breasts against the hard planes of his chest, their legs entwined.

Ruíz's kiss grew bolder, and he pushed past the barrier of her teeth. His tongue felt like hot velvet with the nap turned the wrong way. She slid her tongue along his, shivering in pure ecstasy at the sensual feel of his tongue against hers. Their tongues swirled together, dancing and mating.

Every nerve in Julia's body strained with life. Her blood heated, throbbing through her veins with a pulsating pleasure-pain. The very air seemed to singe her flesh, charged with lightning, spinning her away to a private place where only she and Ruíz existed.

The hot core of him pressed against her abdomen. Julia melted closer, drawing the heat of him nearer, absorbing it into her body and . . . craving more.

Ruíz groaned deep in his throat, and his mouth left hers to travel down her throat. He plundered a path, licking and nipping, leaving a shivery trail of caresses. Julia arched her back, baring her throat to him, silently begging for his touch . . . his lips . . . his tongue.

His mouth moved lower, brushing across the tops of her breasts, insinuating his tongue tip between the deep cleft of her bosom. Julia's heart stopped and the breath left her body. His scintillatingly intimate exploration coursed through her like a spark igniting dry kindling. She felt her stomach muscles clench, and lower . . . a burning throbbing began between her thighs.

Instinctively, she rotated her hips, cupping the hard evidence of his desire, needing something, wanting something deep and . . . something she could not name, a closeness that would assuage the ache between her thighs, that would quench the conflagration in her blood.

She felt a rush of cool air on her heated bosom and, glancing down, she saw the full orbs of her naked breasts cupped in Ruíz's hands. For a brief moment, uncertainty filled her, but when his mouth captured her nipple and suckled, her reticence fled.

The warm adhesion of his mouth on her breast was like magic. Heat shimmered through her. The ache between her thighs crested, becoming almost painful in its intensity. Exquisite ecstasy pulsed from her breasts, spreading streamers of pleasure lower and lower, making her knees weak, melting the very marrow of her bones.

Julia swayed against Ruíz. All rational thought had disappeared, only to be replaced by the fragile, crystal-brilliant sensations of passion. And when she thought she would shatter from the sheer intensity of her desire, he lifted his head from her breasts and cradled her in his arms.

His words were a husky whisper. "Julia, I want you. More than anything in the world. I need you and your fire . . . and your caring."

She heard his words as if they echoed from across a deep canyon. Her body was a riot of tumultuous feelings, all so new and unexpected, begging for a release that she didn't understand. She wanted to focus on the words he'd said, but it was almost impossible. Breathing deeply, she tried to still the erratic beating of her heart.

"Julia . . .?"

"*Sí.*"

"I want you."

His unadorned statement doused the lingering fire in her blood. The reality of what he meant reared its ugly head. Her plan to make him see her as a woman had worked . . . all too well. He wanted her as a woman. But his passion for her hadn't included a declaration of love.

Trembling inwardly, she extricated herself from his embrace and turned her back to him. With a steadiness that belied her inner turmoil, she adjusted her low-cut gown to cover her breasts.

Taking several deep breaths, she prayed for composure. She gazed down at the dark, eddying waters of the river. The sweet smell of honeysuckle lay heavy in the air. She wondered that she hadn't noticed before. She loved the scent of honeysuckle, which embodied the sultry promise of summer.

Ruíz broke her self-imposed reverie by grasping her shoulders and gently pulling her around to face him. She didn't resist. Their confrontation was inevitable.

"I thought you wanted me, too, Julia."

"I do."

He released her shoulders and clasped her hands. Bending his head, he rained tiny kisses over her upturned palms.

She shivered and pulled her hands away. "Don't."

"*¿Por qué?*"

"I want you, Ruíz, but not like this."

"Of course, Julia, I understand. I didn't mean we would . . ." He hesitated, his brows drawn together in frustration. He expelled his breath in a ragged sigh. "The waiting will be torture, but will you come to me tomorrow night by the river under the old oak?"

Her heart stopped in her chest. Nausea filled her stomach, bringing the bitter taste of bile to her throat. All he wanted from her was a quick tumble. He didn't have one shred of respect for her . . . or her family.

"You want me to lie with you."

Even in the black night, she could see his face darken with embarrassment at her bald words. But it didn't keep him from admitting his desire in soft tones. "*Sí.*"

"Ruíz, you dishonor me." And even as she said the ugly words, she knew he was only partially to blame. In her desperation for his love, she had flaunted herself and allowed him to caress her where no other man had touched her before.

His features had turned to stone, and the tone of his voice was now harsh. "We want each another, Julia. You're a grown woman, and you haven't married. I thought . . ."

The guilt she had so readily shared with him only a moment before curdled into a burning resentment at his nasty presumption that she was so shameless or so needy as to . . .

"You thought I'd rather be your *puta* than a dried-up spinster, didn't you?"

"Julia! I didn't mean it like that I . . . I didn't think past—"

"Your lust."

"*Sí.*" He lowered his eyes.

"Just because I haven't married doesn't mean I don't want a husband and children."

"I see."

Julia bit her lip. Her pride was already in tatters. Why not risk everything? She blurted out, "You won't offer me marriage?"

Ruíz lifted his head slowly. His eyes met hers. She could see the cords of his throat working, and it seemed like an eternity before he had the courage to answer.

"I can't."

Chapter Eight

Lázaro leaned forward, neatly fitting his eye to the peephole. The lissome brunette was using her most practiced skills to bring the old, gouty planter to erection.

Stepping back from the tiny hole, Lázaro strategically placed some snuff in one nostril, snorting softly. With his eyes watering from the strong tobacco, he pinched the bridge of his nose to forestall sneezing. It wouldn't do to attract attention to his presence. The peepholes in each room were to ensure the customers at Madame Plaisance's received full satisfaction, but he always tried to carry out his duties discreetly. The prostitutes knew he watched, but the customers didn't.

Raising a lacy handkerchief to his nostrils, he blew gently. Taking a sip of absinthe, he fitted his eye to the peephole and was gratified to see that the ancient Creole planter had finally attained an erection. Matters were drawing to a satisfactory close. The customer was engaging in intercourse. The assignation would be over in a matter of moments.

Watching his customers getting their money's worth wasn't

all business. It also provided Lázaro with titillating pleasure and a sense of power.

His manhood strained against the placket of his pants. He needed to find his own release. As part owner of the finest bordello in New Orleans, there was an intriguing variety of ways he could satisfy his urges.

Reflecting on how he would take his own pleasure, Lázaro walked along the dark passageway. He touched a button in the wall. and a wooden panel swung open. Ducking through the narrow opening, he stepped into the roomy office he shared with Madame Plaisance. At this time of night, the office was empty. Madame Plaisance was in the parlor, overseeing her "girls." He walked to the liquor cabinet and poured himself another glass of absinthe.

There was a knock on the door, and he called out, "Enter."

The door cracked open and a short, wiry man slipped into the room.

"It is good to see you, Chivato. What news do you bring me?" Lázaro hid his displeasure at being abruptly interrupted from contemplating his pressing needs. Chivato never bothered him unless it was important.

Chivato's eyes darted to the bottle of absinthe, and he licked his lips. Lázaro smiled inwardly. Chivato was an absinthe addict. Working for Lázaro provided him with the means to indulge his addiction. It also made Chivato very loyal.

The small, nondescript man was perfect for Lázaro's purposes. His hair was a muddy brown, and his eyes were an odd mixture of colors. He possessed yellow, feral teeth. His physical appearance had earned him the nickname of weasel—Chivato. Lázaro didn't know his real name.

"I have news from the men you hired to rustle cattle on your father's *rancho*," Chivato declared.

"You mean the men *you* hired," Lázaro corrected. He didn't intend for anything to be traced back to him. "What's your news?"

Lázaro took a long sip of absinthe, purposely letting the liquor slide slowly down his throat. From the corner of his eyes, he watched Chivato's reaction. The man's eyes were glazed, and his nose twitched like a rabbit's. Lázaro enjoyed torturing the addict before he allowed him access to the absinthe.

Chivato dragged his eyes away from the liquor with obvious effort. "The men sent word that it's getting too dangerous. Ruíz Navarro almost caught them this time."

"*Muy bien.* Pay off those men and wait a few weeks. Then hire some more men. I want to keep the pressure on my father and Ruíz, and I want to keep them guessing." Lázaro took a key from his pocket and opened a strongbox. While he was counting the money for Chivato, a thought occurred to him. He snapped his fingers. "Better yet, Chivato, try to find a family instead of more men."

"A family, Don Lázaro, what do you mean? A family wouldn't make good rustlers. I don't think—"

"I don't pay you to think," Lázaro hissed at him. "I'll do the thinking and give the orders." Lázaro slammed the gold coins onto the desk.

The small man jumped and agreed quickly, "*Sí*, Don Lázaro, as you wish."

"*Mira,* times are hard in Tejas after the war. Whole families have been displaced and many are searching for land. I've learned from some of my Tejas customers that many of the old Spanish land grants are in question."

Chivato tugged on his ear, and his narrow brow creased in frustration. It was obvious he didn't follow Lázaro's line of reasoning, but he rushed to obey, offering, "I'll find a family, Don Lázaro, just as you require."

"Not just *any* family. They must be *gringos,* and if possible, they must think they have some right to my father's lands."

"Don Lázaro, begging your pardon, but how—?"

"The old man has always feared the *gringos*. He is certain

they want his precious land. If we can find a *gringo* family to squat and rustle cattle, my father's discomfort will increase greatly.'' Lázaro chuckled and bragged, ''A clever plan, no? As to *how* to find this family, advertise in one of those handbills that are always circulating. The new Republic of Tejas has been handing out scrip for land to hundreds of its *patriots*. You could have some scrip counterfeited. I will leave those details to you, but you'll need to go to Tejas.''

Lázaro emptied additional coins into a bag and handed it to him. ''This should more than compensate your trouble and expenses. And get a supply of absinthe from Pierre, *mi mayordomo*, to take with you. They don't have absinthe in Tejas.''

Hefting the bag of coins, Chivato's beady eyes gleamed at the mention of the absinthe. ''I will do my best, Don Lázaro.''

''*Just do it.* And as soon as you've found a family, return to New Orleans. *¿Comprehende?*''

Marriage. Marriage to Julia Flores. Marriage was the last thing on Ruíz's mind. Marriage meant additional responsibilities, additional duties.

Ruíz kicked Oro into a gallop and headed north to the Estrada *rancho.* He couldn't bear to return to Los Montes Verdes and face Julia in the morning. His stallion's fast pace helped to soothe his tumultuous feelings, but it didn't rid him of the vision of Julia's stricken face when he had said he couldn't marry her.

Tonight had been the one time in his adult life that he'd abandoned his customary caution and desired something for himself. He hadn't stopped to consider the consequences.

¡Perdición! He hadn't *cared* about the consequences. His desire for Julia had consumed him, emptying his mind of all rational thought. But Julia hadn't forgotten about the consequences, and she had been more than willing to remind him of his responsibility to her . . . and her family.

How long had it been since he had been with a woman? He couldn't remember. After his wife had died, and he realized the emptiness of their arranged marriage, he hadn't wanted a woman. It was as if the passion within him had withered, drying up like a grape left too long on the vine. By pouring himself into work and then the war, he had held his natural desires at bay.

But Julia had stripped away the dried husk of his feelings and touched the kernel of desire within him. And *Madre de Dios,* he wanted her with every fiber of his being. His need for her was so strong, he had been eager to dishonor the daughter of his life-long friend and business partner.

But not eager enough to make Julia his wife.

A wife would be an additional responsibility, and he already possessed more than enough obligations. His mother and sister were completely dependent upon him, as well as his daughter. The prosperity of both Los Montes Verdes and the Estrada *rancho* weighed on his shoulders.

Ruíz shook his head. He couldn't face marriage again . . . especially not with Julia.

His mother despised the Flores family and considered them beneath the Navarro's position in society. Doña Eugenia wouldn't approve of his marrying Julia. If he knew his mother, she would have a screaming fit if he so much as mentioned the possibility. But his mother's displeasure wasn't what concerned him. Ironically, the similarities between the two women was what disturbed him. Julia was strong-willed and tenacious, just like his mother.

With Julia, he knew there would be no danger of repeating the sterile desert of his past marriage. She was passionate and responsive, but she was also headstrong. He had no desire to enter into a marriage that would degenerate into a struggle for dominance, like his parents' marriage.

He had known her all of his life, and he admired her courage and perseverance. But those same traits could prove disastrous in a wife.

Julia moved through each day in a daze. It was as if she were outside of her body, watching herself go through the motions of living. All of her senses had died. The musky richness of the winery didn't register. She found no pleasure in the fertile bounty of the earth. Sounds were muffled, distant, and everyday conversation was a dull buzz. Her food was tasteless, unappealing. Her limbs felt weak, and her eyes glazed, unfocused.

The pain was real. It was all that was left. It lived inside her, like a trapped animal, tearing and devouring her from within.

Ruíz had wanted her as a woman ... but not enough to marry her.

She had gambled that night in San Antonio. Gambled and lost, or won, depending upon how you looked at it. She had accomplished her objective—to make Ruíz realize she wasn't the unruly tomboy of his youth. She was a woman.

And by the Blessed Virgin Mary, he had responded to her as a woman, beyond her wildest dreams.

But not enough to marry her.

Now that he was gone again and the constant pain was her only companion, she wondered why she had refused him that night. She loved Ruíz with all her heart and soul. Why had she withheld her body from him? If she lived to be ninety years old, she would never desire another man. Wasn't a part of Ruíz better than nothing?

Her dreams for marriage were shattered, but her consuming desire for Ruíz remained.

* * *

Ruíz hooked his arm over the top of the corral fence and watched Allende in action. Teresa's suitor had proved to be more of an asset to the *rancho* than he had expected. The man was a wizard with horses, from gentling the wildest mustang into a dependable mount to teaching the high-spirited and spoiled pedigree horses to mind their manners.

And Allende knew how to charm prospective horse buyers, too. He adapted his wide knowledge of equine confirmation into a rhythmic, almost singsong pitch that extolled each horse's attributes. His delivery mesmerized and reassured buyers at the same time.

Ruíz watched as Allende convinced Señor Gonzáles that the dun they were examining would be a perfect addition to the man's *remuda*. Allende had already sold Señor Gonzáles fifteen horses, and Señor Peña had purchased thirty horses this morning. Señor Medina stood beside Ruíz, impatiently waiting for his turn.

Allende was definitely earning his keep, and his attentions to Teresa had been above reproach. Teresa had visited Ruíz several times at the *rancho,* and Ruíz had watched them together. They appeared to be completely in love with each other. The way they exchanged heated glances had filled Ruíz with a dangerous longing ... and his own vision of wide, emerald eyes.

Willing Julia's face from his mind, he concentrated on Allende and Señor Gonzáles's spirited negotiations. Ruíz hadn't returned to Los Montes Verdes since the night of the *fandango*. He told himself he was too busy at the *rancho*.

The hot, dry summer had hastened Don Estéban's declining health. His hacking cough was unrelenting; no medicine soothed it. In his weakened state, Ruíz's father-in-law was unable to spend more than a day or two each week in his tack room office. Ruíz was running the ranch on his own, and there was a great deal to be done.

But his duties at the *rancho* weren't the real reason he avoided the vineyard. Julia was the reason. He still wanted her, but he couldn't offer marriage. As long as he stayed away, he wouldn't make a fool of himself. But he couldn't hide forever, either. Conchita had visited briefly with Teresa two times. Don Estéban, as much as his health would allow, had delighted in seeing his granddaughter. Unfortunately, the business of the *rancho* was so pressing, Ruíz had spent very little time with his daughter. He missed her sorely.

"Don Ruíz, I have a message from Señor Flores."

Startled by the voice behind him, he turned from the corral to find himself face-to-face with one of the workers from Los Montes Verdes. He recognized the man; his name was Alberty.

Señor Alberty bowed and handed him a slip of folded paper. Ruíz took the paper and said, *"Gracias."* Scanning the brief contents, he found an urgent message from Felipe to return home at once. No explanation was given.

A dozen reasons for the summons danced through his head. The crop could be threatened by root rot. But he dismissed root rot as soon as it crossed his mind. It had been too hot and dry, but there were a variety of grape molds that could thrive in this weather while destroying the crop.

And there were any number of insects, such as aphids, that could pose a problem. Some of the insects were quite deadly; in particular, there was a root louse that attacked only the *vitis vinifera* stock, the vines his grandfather had obtained from the missions' vineyards in San Antonio. The original mission root stock constituted one-third of the vineyard. The remainder of the vineyard was comprised of indigenous vines and hybrids. Inexplicably, the indigenous and hybrid vines were impervious to the deadly root louse.

With Los Montes Verdes in its present precarious financial position, Ruíz could ill afford to lose one vine, much less one-third of the vineyard.

"Don Ruíz, do you want me to return with a message," Señor Alberty inquired.

Señor Alberty's words snapped Ruíz from his panicked thoughts. He took several deep breaths and told himself he didn't know why Felipe had sent for him. Worrying about all the disasters that could befall the vineyard wouldn't serve any purpose. He must return to Los Montes Verdes to find the answer.

"Señor Alberty, I'll return with you."

Ruíz called out to Miguel Vega who was assisting Allende. "Miguel, saddle Oro for me and a fresh mount for Señor Alberty."

Turning to Señor Medina, who was still waiting at the corral fence, he bowed and explained, "I've been called away, but Señor Soto is more than capable of helping you with your selection. I know I'll be leaving you in good hands. *Con permiso,* Señor Medina."

Señor Medina returned his bow and murmured, *"Yo entiendo. Hasta la vista."*

Ruíz faced the corral and caught Allende's eye. When he motioned to Allende, the *vaquero* nodded and begged Señor Gonzáles's indulgence.

"I've an urgent message to return to Los Montes Verdes," Ruíz explained. *"Por favor,* inform Don Estéban and tell him I'm not certain how long I'll be gone. I'll send him a note as soon as I know. You're capable of concluding the sales with Señor Gonzáles and Señor Medina. Hold the monies for me until I return."

Allende inclined his head. "I'll handle everything, Don Ruíz, don't worry." Hesitating, he added softly, "I hope all is well with your family. *Por favor,* give Teresa my regards."

"I will."

"Vaya con Dios."

The courtyard of Los Montes Verdes was crowded with a heavily laden caravan of mules and three wagons. The mules were piled high with bundles and valises. The wagons contained a collection of trunks and odds and ends of furniture from the hacienda. At least twenty mounted men milled about the courtyard, mingling with the mule and wagon drivers. The mounted men were all heavily armed, with pistols on their hips and carbines lashed to their saddles.

"*Por Dios!* What is happening?" Ruíz muttered aloud.

He didn't have long to wait for his answer. Felipe materialized from the shadows near the winery and approached Oro. His partner's features conveyed an odd combination of uncertainty and resignation.

Vaulting from Oro's back, he greeted Felipe with the bald question, "What is all of this?"

Felipe held his straw hat in front of him. His fingers were clenched so tightly on the hat's brim, Ruíz feared he would shred it. A sudden foreboding filled Ruíz.

"Don . . . ah, Señor Ruíz . . ." Felipe loosened his grip on the hat with one hand and gestured at the crowded courtyard. "All of this is why I sent the note. Your mother is leaving for New Orleans immediately, and she is taking your sister with her. I thought you should know."

Ruíz realized his mouth was gaping open. He shut it firmly, but he knew that the astonishment he felt must be stamped upon his features. Why would his mother leave suddenly, during her year of mourning, without telling him? And a more practical voice wondered where she had obtained the funds to do so?

"*Gracias,* Felipe, you did the right thing. I'm grateful that you sent for me. I'll speak with you later."

Felipe nodded and withdrew. Ruíz strode into the *hacienda,* anger simmering beneath his carefully composed features.

Ruíz found his mother in her rooms, directing the packing of more trunks. He didn't bother with polite greetings; instead, he demanded, "What are you doing, *Mamá?*"

Doña Eugenia stopped directing her maid and turned. She crossed the room and stood before him. She was dressed in a black broadcloth traveling suit. His mother's attire, combined with the mounted men outside, indicated that her departure was imminent.

Extending her hand, she admonished, *"Mi hijo,* where are your manners? Is this any way to greet your mother?"

Clenching his teeth, he accepted her hand and bowed formally. *"Buenas tardes, Mamá."*

"That's better, Ruíz. Now, what was your question?"

Ruíz ground his clenched teeth. His mother never tired of her little games. She knew damn well what he had asked. Even if he hadn't asked it, the question would be obvious considering the chaotic confusion of trunks and valises, both packed and half packed, and stacks of clothing waiting to be packed.

"You're going to New Orleans," he stated flatly.

"Sí."

"And you were going without telling me."

His mother's eyebrows drew together, and her lips thinned. "Two can play at deceit as well as one, Ruíz."

"What do you mean by that?"

"Why don't you tell me, Ruíz."

"Mamá, enough games!" he ground out.

Patting an imaginary strand of hair, she smoothed her perfect coiffure and replied, "I'm referring to the things you've neglected to tell me, such as contacting *my* brother behind my back to obtain bottles and sell Los Montes Verdes's wine in New Orleans. The bottles arrived three days ago, along with two letters. One of the letters was for me, and the other one," she strode to her dressing table, picked up a folded piece of parchment and brought it to him, "is for you."

Ruíz accepted the letter and tucked it inside his vest pocket. *"Gracias.* I wasn't trying to deceive you, *Mamá.* I thought you weren't interested in 'filthy' commerce."

"I don't want you to save the winery, Ruíz. I told you before. I want to sell."

"And I told you before that Los Montes Verdes won't bring

a handful of *pesos* while it's awash in debt. The steps I took were necessary.''

Doña Eugenia waved her hand, dismissing both his argument and good intentions. The tone of her voice was acerbic when she threw his earlier words back at him, ''And did you also think I wouldn't be *interested* that you were aiding your sister in a totally unsuitable relationship?''

Ruíz sucked in his breath. Here it was; the confrontation he had dreaded. He should have known his mother would find out. He remembered Don Estéban had known his mother wanted to sell the winery. Probably, his mother and Don Estéban communicated frequently, and he didn't like it. It made him feel as if he had no life of his own ... as if his every action was being monitored.

''At a loss for words, *mi hijo?* I can understand your embarrassment. Playing with your sister's future without my consent was wretched of you. I don't know what you were thinking of—a common *vaquero* with nothing to commend him. Really, Ruíz.''

''I was thinking of Teresa's happiness. Allende isn't common, he's—''

''Por favor, spare me,'' Doña Eugenia interrupted, holding up her hand as if to deflect his words. ''I knew you would be unreasonable and that's why I'm leaving for New Orleans. Before any more damage is done to Teresa's reputation. Your uncle will be able to introduce Teresa to men suitable for her station in life. And I'll be rid of this awful, boring place. That's why your father and I traveled, so we could expand our horizons. It's time for Teresa to expand *her* horizons.''

''What does Teresa have to say about this?''

Ruíz didn't know if their angry voices had attracted Teresa's attention or if his sister had been waiting outside the open door until the conversation turned to her, because Teresa chose that moment to step into the room and answer him, ''I've agreed to go with *Mamá.''*

Teresa's eyes were red-rimmed and swollen as if she'd been crying for a long time. But outwardly, she appeared calm when she explained, "I've agreed to go to New Orleans. *Mamá* has promised I could return next spring after Mardi Gras, if I still desired it. I know Allende will wait for me. I will rely upon you, *mi hermano,* to explain to Allende and assure him that I'll write."

"But why, Teresa, after all you've risked—?"

She shrugged. "I won't be waiting any longer than you asked, *mi hermano.* It will be harder . . . not being able to see Allende, but—"

"Now that *Mamá* knows, you wouldn't be allowed to see Allende even if you remained here, would you?"

Dropping her eyes, Teresa knotted her fingers together. *"Mamá* is merely trying to protect me, like you, Ruíz." She lifted her chin. "I want to—"

"Prove to our mother this isn't another one of your passing infatuations," Ruíz finished for her.

"Sí."

Pride. The Navarro pride mixed with a youthful naiveté was responsible for Teresa's acquiescence. He glanced at his mother's cold face. And something else, too, had driven Teresa to her decision. Ruíz recognized Teresa's unspoken motivation because he had struggled with it himself.

Teresa wanted to win her mother's approval.

Ruíz felt a frisson of some indefinable emotion crawl up his spine. Teresa would never be able to prove anything to their mother. He had walked that path himself, and it had led to a dead-end existence of empty and pressing duties.

But it was his sister's life, and she would need to find her own way. He had done what he could to help Teresa and Allende. Teresa had made her decision.

Clasping his sister in his arms, he hugged her tightly. "I'll miss you, Teresa. We've grown closer since—" He stopped himself. He had been about to say they had grown closer since their father had been killed. "I'll have your dowry for you when you return."

Returning his hug, she kissed his cheek. *"Gracias, mi hermano,* for everything. I'll count the days until I come home."

"Have you finished packing?"

She shook her head.

"Go and finish. I'll come to your rooms before you leave."

"Mamá, con permiso?" Teresa inquired.

Doña Eugenia inclined her head and said, "Do as your brother asks. I want to leave within the hour."

Ruíz watched his sister until she had closed the door behind her. Turning to his mother, he noticed her usually composed features were distorted with something that resembled jealousy.

"Mamá, I have accepted that you are leaving. I doubt anything I say will stop you. But I would like to raise two questions. First, what about my daughter?"

"She has her nurse, Luz."

"But she will be alone here with just Luz most of the time. I have responsibilities at the *rancho.* It won't be the same as having her *abuela* to care for her."

"I thought you disapproved of the way I've raised Teresa. Why would you want me to raise your daughter?"

"I never said that." Even as Ruíz denied his mother's accusation, he admitted to himself that the prospect of Conchita being raised like Teresa wasn't what he wanted. But the thought of his daughter with no female guidance or companionship beyond a servant was also troubling.

"No, but you obviously thought it, or you wouldn't have conspired with Teresa against me," his mother observed with unerring accuracy. "And if the welfare of your daughter concerns you, it's just one more reason to sell this blighted place and take Concepción to the *rancho."*

"There are no women, except servants, at the *rancho,* either. Besides, I can't sell Los Montes Verdes."

"You mean you *won't*. But I'm through arguing with you. I'm leaving, and the winery is of no importance."

"And is your granddaughter also of no importance, *Mamá?*"

"Of course Concepción is important to me. Don't try to put me on the defensive. It's *you* who has rebuffed my efforts to find a suitable wife and mother to Concepción. I've tried, but you haven't cooperated. I wash my hands of your predicament. Concepción is your daughter and your responsibility."

"It would seem everything is my responsibility, *Mamá*— which brings me to my next question. What are you using for money? In particular, who's paying for this caravan to New Orleans? My uncle perhaps?"

"Of course not, it's your—"

"Responsibility."

"And *duty, mi hijo,* don't forget it. Since you've asked, I need two hundred gold *pesos* to pay for my escort. And don't try to give me any of that worthless Republic paper money. I'll also need an allowance for rent and expenses for my town house in New Orleans."

"I thought you would stay with your brother in New Orleans."

"I wouldn't dream of imposing upon my brother's hospitality. How will it appear to Teresa's prospective suitors if we—"

"I don't have the money, *Mamá*, for your own town house," Ruíz interrupted, his voice firm. "And I would think that it would appear highly irregular for two women to live alone."

His mother's brow creased in consternation, and, for once, she seemed to be giving his objection consideration. There was a grudging note in her voice when she admitted, "Perhaps you're right . . . about Teresa and me living alone. But we will need money for our . . . needs. One hundred gold *pesos* each month should be sufficient."

"I can't pay that."

"But you must. We have to buy clothes and other necessities. I won't live off the charity of my brother when I have a son that is bound by *duty* to care for his mother and sister."

Duty. That word again. Ruíz felt trapped, torn between responsibilities to his mother and sister and the vineyard ... and the Flores family. *Por Dios,* how could he free Los Montes Verdes from its debt while maintaining two households?

He had no idea of what would constitute a fair living allowance in New Orleans, but knowing his mother's extravagance, he guessed half the amount she expected would probably be more than fair. In the meantime, he needed to raise two hundred gold *pesos* immediately, but he had very little cash on hand. The furnishings of the *hacienda* belonged to his mother. What did he own that would bring two hundred *pesos?*

The only precious item he possessed was the diamond signet ring he had inherited, emblazoned with his grandfather's coat of arms. Jerking it from the middle finger of his right hand, he offered it to his mother.

"Sell this when you reach New Orleans. It will pay for your journey."

"Ruíz—"

"It's all I have, *Mamá,* on such short notice, and I can only give you fifty gold *pesos* each month for an allowance." As the words left his mouth, Ruíz cringed inwardly. What had his mother brought him to? He sounded like a fish wife haggling over the price of day-old fish.

His mother refused to take his ring, protesting, "Don Estéban can cover your expenses. I don't understand why you won't go to him for money. He considers you his heir and son."

"I won't ask Don Estéban for money and that's final."

"Then you're a fool, and the paltry allowance you're offering will beggar us."

"But it will fulfill my *duty*." Ruíz couldn't keep the scorn from his voice.

Doña Eugenia snatched the ring from his outstretched hand and muttered savagely, "You're an ungrateful son, Ruíz. I will never forgive you for this."

Chapter Nine

Julia stood by the winery door. She took advantage of the partial cover provided by the branches of the drooping pecan tree. From her vantage point, she could watch without being noticed. And there was a great deal to see.

Her gaze encompassed the spectacle unfolding in the courtyard. The milling men and masses of luggage were worthy of a sultan's caravan. Doña Eugenia and Teresa were leaving for New Orleans.

She had heard the gossip from Luz. Doña Eugenia was angry with Ruíz for aiding his sister with an illicit love affair. Teresa was being taken away to be presented to more worthy suitors.

Ruíz and his mother emerged from the *hacienda* with Teresa and Conchita trailing behind them. Ruíz broke away from his mother to speak with a broad-shouldered man who stood beside his sorrel mount. Julia didn't recognize the man, but she guessed he must be the leader of Doña Eugenia's escort. Julia had watched while the broad-shouldered man barked orders at the other men.

Ruíz and the leader exchanged brief words before Ruíz left the man to rejoin his family. The leader mounted his sorrel and began issuing orders in a tone of command. The caravan shifted, writhing like a beheaded snake to form a cohesive unit.

When Ruíz returned to his family, he embraced his mother and sister. Doña Eugenia lifted Conchita in her arms and awarded the child with a perfunctory peck on the cheek and a quick squeeze. Teresa took the child and held her for a long time, kissing and hugging the little girl repeatedly. Julia's eyes swung to Ruíz while he watched his sister and the child together. His face was an abject study of misery.

A lump rose to her throat, and her chest constricted. Her heart went out to Teresa and . . . Conchita . . . and Ruíz.

She had never been close to Teresa. Doña Eugenia hadn't been able to prevent her adventuresome son from playing with her, but Teresa had been carefully supervised as a child. Doña Eugenia's animosity toward the Flores family had also served to poison the possibility of Julia and Teresa establishing a relationship with each another.

Despite their lack of intimacy, Julia felt the deepest empathy for her. Teresa was a woman in love, who was doomed to be separated from her beloved. Julia knew exactly how Teresa must feel.

Conchita's plight was even worse.

Ruíz's daughter was barely more than a baby, and she had no mother. What would happen to the child, left alone without her *abuela* or *Tía* Teresa? Ruíz never remained at Los Montes Verdes for long. He could drag Conchita back and forth with him to the Estrada *rancho* or leave the child with servants. Neither option seemed satisfactory to Julia.

As much as Luz loved Conchita, the little girl needed the semblance of a family. Her grandfather had disappeared from her life only a few weeks ago. Now her grandmother and aunt were leaving, too. Tears sprang to Julia's eyes, and she wondered how Conchita would endure the loss of her family.

Julia realized even Ruíz would be affected by the departure of his mother and sister. Despite his constant clashes with his domineering mother, he cared deeply about his family. She felt certain their absence would leave an empty place in his life.

The wide compound gates opened, and the mounted party filed through with the wagons rattling along at the rear.

Conchita, perched in her father's arms, waved bravely to the departing caravan until the gates swung shut behind the last wagon and its guard. When the gates closed, Conchita buried her head in her father's shoulder. Julia could see the sobs wracking her small frame. Ruíz held his daughter close, stroking her hair. His features appeared to be chiseled from stone.

Watching their desolation, Julia came to several decisions.

Ruíz sat in his study in the wide leather armchair rocking his daughter back and forth in his arms . . . back and forth. With his voice pitched low, he murmured soothing endearments under his breath. He didn't know what else to do for her. He wished there was some way he could absorb his daughter's pain into himself.

His body and mind sagged with weariness. Weary of coping . . . tired of struggling . . . broken-hearted over Conchita's desolation at losing the only family she had ever known.

The shadows of the lengthening day strayed across the floor, encroaching steadily, blanketing his despair in a welcome darkness. His daughter's sobs finally ceased. Her small body was limp, cuddled in his arms. Blessed sleep had taken her.

But still he sat there, wondering what to do next. How could he properly care for Conchita and oversee both the *rancho* and vineyard? The prospect was overwhelming . . . daunting. And the money? Where would he get the money to send to his mother and sister?

If the plan to sell their premium wines in New Orleans succeeded, he had calculated the vineyard would be able to meet his father's outstanding notes that were due this year. But he also hoped for a profit, above and beyond his most pressing obligations. With that profit, he meant to repay the Flores family and have operating cash for the next year.

Now the monthly allowance for his mother and sister would swallow every excess *peso* he might earn. All this back-breaking labor for nothing. How would be ever explain to Felipe . . . and Julia?

He buried his face in the downy softness of his daughter's hair. What could he do? Turn to Don Estéban? He shuddered at the thought. His mother had already entangled him in a web of obligations. The last thing he needed was to be further indebted to Don Estéban as well.

Ruíz heard the scrape of a shoe across the tiled floor outside the half-open door of the study. Raising his head, he gazed at the door and waited, not wanting to call out and disturb his sleeping daughter.

Luz slipped through the doorway, and her gaze swept over them, huddled together in the chair. Approaching until she was close enough to reach for Conchita, Luz asked softly, "She's sleeping?"

"*Sí,*" Ruíz whispered in response.

Nodding, she held out her arms. "Let me take her, Señor Ruíz. I'll put her to bed."

"But she's had no supper."

"It won't matter. She needs sleep more than food. I'll make certain she eats a large breakfast."

He hesitated. He felt so alone and . . . empty. All he had was his daughter. He hated to relinquish her comforting sweetness, but he knew Luz was right. Conchita needed to rest. Gently, he transferred his daughter to her waiting arms. The child jerked in her sleep and mumbled some unintelligible words, but she didn't awaken.

Cradling the sleeping child against her shoulder, Luz said,

"Julia is outside. She's been waiting to speak with you. She said she didn't want to disturb you until—"

"*Yo entiendo.* Send her in. I'll see you in the morning, Luz."

"*Sí, Señor, buenas noches.*"

Ruíz bent toward Luz and kissed the top of Conchita's head. "*Buenas noches.*"

Luz left the room, and Julia entered.

Julia closed the door behind her. She leaned against it for what seemed like a long time. Finally, her eyes lifted and met his. Their gazes locked. Neither one of them moved a muscle, but heated awareness streaked between them . . . as vibrant and alive as if their flesh had touched.

He couldn't stand the intensity. It had been a long and exasperating day. His eyes veered from Julia's, and he observed, "It's grown dark." Reaching for the tinderbox, he said, "I'll light the candle." He scraped a spark, and the wick of the candle caught.

Light pooled in the room. Julia's eyes shone in the flickering candlelight. Their dark-green color reminded him of the mossy depths of the Guadalupe River.

She moved toward him, her hand outstretched, her silken throat working, "Ruíz, I wanted to tell you I'm sorry that—"

"Don't."

"But Conchita, where will she live?"

"I don't know."

"I want to help you . . . and especially Conchita. With Lupita gone, we have room at our *casa* for both Conchita and Luz. *Por favor,* let your daughter stay with us. I want her to have . . . a family."

Lifting his eyes to hers, his voice was rough with emotion, "Why do you want to do this?"

"Because I love Conchita, and I know my family loves her, too. A loving family is very important to a child."

A loving family was important. He had dreamed about having a loving family. He had wanted one for himself.

It wasn't that he hadn't known love within his family. His father had loved him deeply and without condition. And he and Teresa had grown close since their father's death. But his mother . . . his mother had always broken the circle, making it impossible to have a loving family. Her wants and needs had taken precedence over loving. If there was anything Ruíz had learned over the past few years, it was that every member of a family had to *want* to share their love.

Growing up in his divided household, he had envied the constant love that surrounded Julia and her family. Despite their hardships, Lupita's passing and Paco's crippled legs, Julia's family had persevered and continued to love one another.

What better upbringing could he possibly offer his daughter?

He dropped his head and covered his face with his hands. Even as he accepted the wisdom of his decision to allow the Flores family to foster his daughter, bitter resentment choked him. Where had he failed?

Julia's soft touch on his shoulder startled him. He looked up. Her face was a breath away; her full, carmine-colored lips were slightly parted. The candlelight was behind her, shining through the thin cotton of her blouse, illuminating her dark nipples against the gauzy fabric.

Tight bands stretched across his chest, and his heart banged like a hammer against the constriction. His manhood rose, hot and aching, straining against the placket of his pants.

He wanted her so badly, he could taste it. But what did he have to offer her in return? Everything he touched turned to ashes. Failure and shame covered him. Shame at allowing Julia to see him like this . . . his desolation and defeat worn, like a badge, on his shirtsleeve.

Taking a deep breath, he raised his arm and knocked her hand from his shoulder. "I don't want your pity, Julia."

Thrown off balance by his rejection, Julia stepped back and argued, "It's not pity, Ruíz."

"Then what the hell is it?" He clenched his jaw. He could

feel the muscles jerking in his face. Grudgingly, he admitted, "You're right. Conchita should stay with you. She needs a family, I agree. But don't worry about me, Julia. I'll survive. We'll discuss the arrangements for her *mañana*. It's late. *Por favor,* leave me in peace."

"No, I won't leave you."

"I'm warning you, Julia. I don't want to be cozened like Paco. I'm not—"

"It isn't that."

"Then what is it, Julia? I thought we reached an understanding that night in San Antonio . . . remember?"

"I remember, Ruíz," she answered softly, her melodious voice like a caress.

"You refused me and said I had dishonored you."

"I was wrong."

Ruíz expelled his breath in a harsh rush. He shook his head. "Julia—"

His next words never left his mouth. They disappeared, lost forever . . . unimportant.

Julia removed her blouse. She stood before him, naked to the waist, her golden, coral-tipped breasts thrust forward, uptilted and pointed, begging for his touch. He remembered how soft her breasts felt, like silken velvet.

Against his better judgment, he stretched out his hand. His fingers uncurled tentatively, brushing the tops of her warm breasts. Before he could savor her wondrous offering, he was distracted by the whisper of fabric. She had loosened her skirt. It pooled at her feet. She kicked her sandals off.

Ruíz caught his breath. His eyes flicked over her. She stood naked before him. Naked and perfect. From the pouting coral points of her breasts to the tiny indentation of her waist and the soft swell of her hips . . . naked and perfect.

He released his breath with a groan.

His gaze dropped to the juncture of her long, lean legs . . .

to the velvet midnight of her woman's mound. His throat went dry, and his heart pounded in his ears.

"Julia, I hope you know what you're doing. There's no turning back."

"Yo entiendo."

"Are you certain, Julia. I can't offer you—"

"Te amo, Ruíz."

"Dios help you then," he grated out. "I can't." He rose and clasped her face between the palms of his hands and pulled her to him.

Lowering his mouth to hers, he twined his hands in her hair. He forced his tongue past her teeth. When he touched the warm, honeyed essence of her mouth with his tongue, he shuddered from the intensity of feeling. Feverishly, he mated his mouth with hers while he tore the pins and combs from her hair.

Her hair swung loose, falling in an ebony curtain to her hips. The smell of her gardenia perfume wafted through the still air, filling his nostrils with its heady, sensual scent. He stroked his hands through her thick, straight mane, pulling her hair forward to veil her bared breasts.

He caressed her breasts with soft tendrils of her own hair until her nipples hardened into tight buds. Lowering his mouth, he took one breast into his mouth. His tongue and teeth savored the puckered flesh of her aureole while his hands kneaded the mounded softness of her breasts.

Julia sighed and arched into his caresses. Her fingers raced down his shirt, bursting the buttons open. She splayed her fingers across his chest, weaving her fingertips through the mat of his chest hair and tentatively circling his sensitive male paps.

Somewhere in a corner of his mind, Ruíz was surprised by her boldness. Surprised, but also pleased. *Por Dios,* he wanted her so badly, he ached with it.

Lost in the pure sensation of his burning need, he clutched her hands in his and forced them from his chest. Lower and lower still . . . until her fingers closed over the buttons on his pants.

Straining against the blissful pressure of her touch, he implored, *"Por favor,* Julia, take me."

Her eyelids fluttered. The luxuriant sweep of her inky eyelashes fanned her high cheekbones. A small gasp escaped her lips as his engorged manhood sprang forth into her hand.

He heard the swift intake of her breath.

Her silken touch closed around him.

He throbbed, hard and hot, against her gentle touch. Bucking his hips, he surged forward into the warm cup of her hands.

Julia moaned and gyrated her hips against him in response. He understood her need and reached down, cradling the nub of her passion against his hand. Circling it with his thumb and pressing his manhood against her mound, he felt her hot, slick desire spill over his fingers.

Pounding ecstasy flowed through his body at her response. Their hearts thundered in his ears, racing together, heartbeat for heartbeat. He suckled her breast and explored the soft folds of her femininity. Julia molded her body to his. With her hand kneading his manhood, he felt crazed with desire.

When he couldn't stand the sweet torture any longer, he lifted her in his arms and lowered her to the rug. Kneeling beside her, he spread her thighs apart. Stroking the swollen bud of her passion, he gloried in his intimate possession of her. She was his! Warm and willing, wanting him.

Moaning and thrashing beneath his caresses, she bucked her hips off the floor and begged, "Ruíz, Ruíz, *por favor, por favor . . ."*

Through eyelids drugged with passion, he watched as his touch enflamed her. Never had a woman so entranced him. Never had his passion mounted to such heights. She was a woman . . . desirable and enticing . . . and she was his childhood friend . . . soul of his soul.

Her breath was hot upon his cheek, pleading her need, *"Por favor,* I want to ... I want ..."

"I know." He cupped her buttocks, raising her hips to meet his. Thrusting inside her, the hard length of his desire plunged past the thin membrane of her maidenhood.

Julia went still and cried out, "Ruíz, I don't understand ... the pain."

He rained kisses over her brow, her cheeks, and the pulse at her temple. Whispering against her parted lips, he tried to reassure her, *"Esperaté,* Julia, it will be better."

Slowly and with infinite patience, he withdrew from the glove-tight heat of her sheath. Tenderly, he entered her again, stroking slowly and carefully. He ground his teeth, desperately trying to control himself. He had waited so long for this moment, so very long.

Pleasure exploded within him, followed by ecstasy, searing his flesh, bursting through his throbbing veins. The pleasurable pulsations rippled outward from the core of his sex, spreading in exquisite circles of sensation throughout his body.

He drifted downward into a soft nest, a warm sense of belonging. A feeling of coming home. Closing his eyes, he nuzzled her breasts, thanking God with each breath for the wondrous gift of her.

When the pleasure had ebbed into satiated completion, he rolled to his side, still sheathed within her. They lay together bathed in contentment. Her full breasts were crushed against his chest, their loins were joined intimately, and their legs entwined.

Ruíz bent his head and breathed a caress across the hollow of her throat. Julia's eyelids fluttered open. The jewel-green depths of her eyes met his.

"Did the pleasure take the pain away?"

She hesitated before answering, "Partly, I'm not certain. It was wonderful, but I'm not ..." She shook her head.

Ruíz's heart expanded at her innocent response. She had

favored him with the most beautiful gift he had ever received. Her innocent passion. He needed to offer her something in return. He kissed her swollen mouth and murmured, "Not good enough. I'll do better next time." And then he drew her head down against his chest. His hands moved, with a profound tenderness, through her hair, over her shoulders and back, stroking and caressing.

She sighed against his chest, cuddling closer, falling asleep in his arms.

Julia felt the scratchy nap of the rug against her bare skin. The musky, unfamiliar but unmistakable scent of spent passion filled her nostrils. She shifted in Ruíz's arms, only to be brought up against the thick cushion of brown hair on his chest. Her slight movement must have awakened him because he opened his eyes and smiled at her.

She returned his smile. A slow, comforting warmth suffused her. He was happy and so was she. It felt so good to be close to him, to have his naked body stretched beside hers. Julia felt no regrets about what had passed between them. It had been inevitable . . . and wonderful.

Ruíz lifted his hand and tenderly traced the contours of her face. She could remember falling asleep earlier while his hands stroked over her. How long had it been? She glanced at the half-burned candle. They must have slept for one or two hours.

His fingers paused at her lips. His mouth replaced the gentle exploration of his fingertips. His warm lips covered hers, firing her blood. Starting the scintillating streamers of pleasure in her body again. She responded with a fierce hunger, clasping his shoulders and melting into his embrace.

After long moments of feverish kissing, Ruíz pulled away. His voice was gruff with desire as he said, "I want you to be comfortable." With those words, he rose and bent to scoop her into his arms.

The hallway was dark and deserted. Clasping her tightly, Ruíz took her to his bedroom and lowered her onto his bed. When he lit a candle, Julia gazed, for the first time, at the masculine chamber that belonged to him.

It was sparsely furnished. The canopied bed where he had placed her, a table with a bowl and ewer of water, an armoire, and a ladder-backed chair comprised the furniture. One corner of the room held a reliquary niche with a simple cross and several flickering votive candles.

The tinkle of water caught her attention. Ruíz suddenly loomed over her with a damp cloth in his hands. The sight of him stopped the breath in her lungs. A tiny shiver of pleasure shot through her while she gazed at his chiseled male body and remembered, in vivid detail, their previous intimacies. His broad, dark-sprinkled chest had been her pillow. His muscular thighs had been entangled with hers. And his powerful loins had thrust . . .

Her undisguised admiration of his body must have acted as an aphrodisiac on Ruíz. With a sense of wonder, Julia watched as his manhood thickened and rose, springing from the brown nest of his loins. A warm flush crept over her, and she looked away. All the sensations were so new, so exciting . . . and sometimes, so frightening.

Julia felt the bed shift beneath her. Was he coming to her again? Her heart thudded against her ribs in rapt anticipation. She turned toward Ruíz to find him bending over her.

"I want to cleanse you."

She gasped when he gently spread her thighs and began to sponge the most intimate part of her. At first, she felt embarrassed, and she turned her head away again. He must think her the most callow of women . . . so unsure of her own body. It was a miracle she had summoned the courage to seduce him, earlier in his study. But his need had been great, and she had felt so close to him.

Now, with the knowledge of passion and all that it encompassed, she felt more tentative, like a newborn lamb taking its first wobbly steps.

Despite her uncertainty, she had to admit that the warm sensation of the cloth between her legs felt marvelous. As the water cleansed away her virgin's blood and Ruíz's seed, she relaxed, enjoying his tender ministrations.

Her eyelids drifted shut. She gave herself over to the unfamiliar sensation. Her body felt both languorous and strangely titillated at the same time. A deep, pulsing ache began between her thighs, and, unconsciously, she pressed herself against the cloth.

When she did so, there was a pause and a rustle. And then the sensation began again between her thighs. But this time, it changed dramatically. Gone was the rough abrasion of the cloth, to be replaced by the warm molding of flesh. It felt as if Ruíz were kissing her again, but not on the lips . . .

Julia's eyes flew open, and she lurched up. Ruíz's dark head was nestled between her thighs and . . . *and he was kissing her there.* The exquisite ecstasy of his tongue and mouth exploring that very private place washed over her.

Shamed to the core of her being at his intimate lovemaking, she tried to jerk away from him, crying out, "Ruíz, no, no . . ."

When he lifted his head, an unruly lock of his sable hair lay slanted across his forehead. She had the most absurd impulse to brush the shock of hair from his eyes.

He smiled at her, his white teeth gleaming in the shadowed room. His voice was low and full of tenderness. *"Por favor,* Julia, let me pleasure *you.* You've given me heaven tonight. I want to take you to paradise."

Without waiting for her answer, he dropped his head and took the swollen, sensitive nub of her desire into his mouth. She fell against the bed with a moan of pure pleasure. Her hands knotted in the sheets as his mouth suckled her, rolling her enflamed flesh between his lips. His hands drifted upward and cupped her breasts. His thumbs made lazy circles over her nipples, stimulating them to pucker into strutted points.

Julia gasped again as streamers of sensation coursed through her body. The blood rushed through her veins, hot and molten with desire. Every nerve she possessed strained toward the shimmering promise of his magical touch.

She arched her hips in desperate need, straining against his mouth. Wanting something . . . reaching toward some tantalizing pinnacle that hovered just beyond her reach. And when she thrashed and moaned and couldn't stand any more of the maddening pleasure-pain, Ruíz mounted her in one swift thrust.

The explosion rocked her body. Her senses shattered into a million, jewellike stars of ecstasy. The pleasure went on and on . . . building and building until she soared to the top of that elusive pinnacle. And when she reached it, her body seemed to melt . . . to flow molten . . . surrounding and encompassing Ruíz's rock-hard manhood.

Groaning, he called out, "Julia, Julia," before she felt his release break over him. The hot, wet glory of his seed spilled into her.

They lay together, still joined in the sweet aftermath of their love. Ruíz rose on one elbow and feathered kisses over her face and neck. His voice was heavy with spent passion when he asked, "Did you feel the pleasure this time?"

"*Sí*, Ruíz, I never knew how it could be . . . between a man and woman."

His warm brown eyes locked with hers, and he admitted softly, "I didn't know either, Julia."

His response surprised her. Ruíz had been married and sired two children. He must know how it was between a man and a woman. What was he trying to tell her? That their joining had been as special and magical for him as it had been for her?

The pleasure had been beyond her comprehension, but their intimacy was even more wonderful. Julia snuggled in his arms, savoring their closeness. She felt languid and fulfilled and blissfully drowsy again. Her eyelids started to close, but Ruíz abruptly brought her back to consciousness by rolling to his side.

"Don't go to sleep again, Julia. You must go home. Dawn will be here in an hour. I'm surprised your family hasn't come looking for you already."

"I told them I was going to stay with Conchita for the night."

"Were you going to stay with her?"

"*Sí*, but when I came, Conchita was already asleep and . . . I wanted you."

"To comfort me." His voice was sharp.

"No, Ruíz, before I knew your mother and sister were leaving, I had made up my mind. Ruíz, I love you. I always have."

The silence her declaration brought filled the room. Julia held her breath, hoping and praying he would say he loved her, too. But her words echoed in the hollow stillness. Her heart constricted, and a hurt so deep she couldn't name it rose within her, bringing tears to her eyes.

He broke the awful stillness. "You must return home, Julia. Tell your parents I'll be joining them tonight for supper. I don't usually invite myself to share someone else's table, but there's much to discuss. You don't think your parents will mind, do you?"

"No, they won't mind." She lifted her arm and smoothed the errant forelock from his brow.

He bent his head and kissed her with a fierce possessiveness.

Julia clung to him, wanting his kiss to go on forever, forgetting, in the sweet surrender of her senses, that he hadn't told her he loved her.

Chapter Ten

Leaning forward into the mirror, Julia pinched her cheeks to give them color. She had taken special care with her appearance that night. She wore one of her best gowns, dyed a deep-green color that matched her eyes. Her mother had helped to braid her long hair. It lay in two flat coils behind her ears.

Ruíz was coming to supper.

She was giddy with excitement. And when she remembered the intimacies they had shared last night, she didn't need to pinch her cheeks again to coax forth their color. Her face grew hot and flushed just thinking about it.

He had told her there was much to discuss with her family. She knew they would talk about Conchita and the future of Los Montes Verdes. But would he ask for her hand, too?

Last night had been magic. As much as she had yearned for and loved Ruíz all of her life, she hadn't been prepared for the intensity of their joining.

The joy they had shared was beyond anything she could have imagined. They had explored their passion and it had been more wonderful than any fantasy she had ever woven in her mind. Perfect. Their night of passion had been perfect . . . with one exception.

Ruíz hadn't told her he loved her.

"Señora Flores, *por favor,* could I have a second helping of the *carne guisada?*" Ruíz asked politely while passing his empty plate to Pilar. "Your stew is excellent."

"Of course." Pilar accepted his plate and said, *"Gracias* for your kind words. I'm glad you like it." She ladled another helping of stew and added a rolled *tortilla* to Ruíz's plate.

Pilar was happy to see he had retained his appetite after yesterday, and she was touched by his courtesy to her family. The courtesy that had brought him, personally, to their table to ask a favor of them.

"Have you unpacked the bottles my uncle sent?" Ruíz inquired of Felipe. "I haven't had an opportunity to inspect them for breakage."

"Sí, Señor Ruíz, we have unpacked and inspected them. They are sturdily made, only half a dozen were broken," Felipe answered.

Laying his half-eaten *tortilla* to the side, Ruíz replied, "I'm pleased to hear the bottles are well made." Turning to Paco, he asked, "Are they suitable for the wine, Paco?"

Paco swallowed a mouthful of stew. *"Sí,* they will do. When do you want to ship the wine?"

Ruíz leaned forward, pushing his plate to one side. "As soon as possible, preferably before the harvest begins. Once we start harvesting, we won't be able to spare the men. Can it be done, Paco?"

Paco nodded. "I can have the red wines bottled and ready for shipment in two weeks' time. But I won't bottle the white wines now. They need to be packed in sawdust and shipped during the winter to limit spoilage. The freight costs will be higher if you wait and make a separate shipment, but—"

"I agree, Paco," Ruíz interrupted enthusiastically. "Every precaution should be taken with the delicate white wines. I received a letter from my uncle, and he's hopeful about our scheme. He says he will be able to sell everything we send him at better prices than I had hoped. We can easily price our wines lower than European bottled wine while earning a hefty profit." Ruíz caught Paco's gaze and added, "But my uncle stressed the quality must be high."

Paco met his gaze and promised, "Don't worry, Señor Ruíz, each bottle will contain quality wine. I also intend to bottle some of the reds that will mature next year so the wine can age in the bottle. I believe early bottling will enhance the flavor. You might want to send to your uncle for more bottles." Pausing, he said, "I'm glad to hear your uncle believes our wines will sell at a good price." Paco winked and chuckled, "We will all look forward to the increased profits."

Felipe smiled and clapped Ruíz on the shoulder. "Indeed we will, Señor Ruíz. You've made our family very happy."

Pilar raised her head and caught her husband's eye. She gifted Felipe with a small, triumphant smile, gratified to know that the vineyard's future was virtually assured. It would give Paco security and Julia a place to live if she never married. Felipe returned her secret smile and reached across the table to squeeze her hand.

Pilar silently thanked the Blessed Virgin Mary for this good news and for her understanding husband. It was comforting to know Felipe shared the same goals she did. They both wanted to see their children happy and secure before they quit this earth.

Ruíz interrupted her private thoughts by making a dismissive gesture with his hand and declaring, "Don't thank me, Felipe. It was Julia's idea, and Paco's wine that made this plan possible. No, it is I who should be thanking all of you." Ruíz's gaze swept the Flores family, and Pilar noticed that Julia didn't lift her head to meet his eyes.

Julia's behavior throughout supper had been strange. Her daughter had dressed with care and she was looking very beautiful, but she'd been uncharacteristically quiet. Every time she happened to glance in Ruíz's direction, she blushed deeply. Even more unusual, Julia, who had been desperate to save the vineyard, didn't act jubilant at Ruíz's hopeful news. Instead, she seemed distant and tense, wrapped in her own private thoughts.

Pilar knew that her daughter had been in love with Ruíz since she'd been old enough to toddle after him. Pilar had secretly grieved for Julia, wishing she could spare her daughter the heartbreak of caring for a man whose family disapproved of her. When Ruíz had married Alicia Estrada and moved away, Pilar had breathed a sigh of relief. She had hoped that, in time, Julia would find someone else to love her.

But Julia hadn't been interested in other men, and Alicia Estrada had died, leaving Ruíz without a wife.

"I have another favor to ask of your family, Felipe," Ruíz ventured. "And what I am about to ask means more to me than anything else in this world."

Lifting her chin, Pilar gazed directly at Ruíz. This was the reason for his personal visit, not the vineyard or the shipment of wine. All those things could be discussed in Ruíz's study. Julia had already broached the idea to her family before she had made the offer to Ruíz. They had all agreed to Julia's idea. Ruíz's formal request was merely a matter of courtesy. He was going to ask if Conchita and Luz could live with them.

A small one was such a joy to have around the house, especially one as delightful as Conchita. The only problem Pilar foresaw was when Ruíz remarried and reclaimed his daughter. Breaking the attachment would be difficult. They would all mourn the loss when that time came. But it was a small price to pay for Conchita's security and happiness.

"I would be most humbly grateful if you would allow Conchita and her nurse to live with you. My daughter needs a family, and I can't think of a finer family than yours."

"We will be honored to have Conchita as part of our family," Felipe declared without hesitation, speaking for all of them. "And I can assure you, Señor Ruíz, we will love her as our own."

Ruíz bowed his head and murmured, *"Muchas gracias,* I cannot thank you enough. I will be forever in your debt." Slowly, Ruíz lifted his head, and his eyes snagged Julia's gaze. This time, Julia didn't look away.

Pilar sensed the intensity of feeling passing between Ruíz and her daughter. The very air seemed to vibrate with their unspoken feelings. It was as if they were completely alone and totally absorbed in each other.

Felipe must have sensed the awkward moment, too, because he cleared his throat and pushed his chair back from the table.

Julia dropped her eyes, and Ruíz's head jerked up. His gaze swept the table, and he blinked several times as if returning from a trance. Composed again, Ruíz leaned toward Felipe.

"Con permiso, I have other business to discuss. I must beg your family's indulgence as these are private matters. I wish to speak with you alone, Felipe. If everyone has finished their supper, and it won't be too much of an imposition, I need a few minutes of your time."

Pilar's heart lurched at Ruíz's unexpected request. She glanced quickly at Julia. Her daughter's face was flushed again.

The look Julia and Ruíz had exchanged. Ruíz wanting to speak privately with Felipe. Was Ruíz about to defy his mother and make all of Julia's dreams come true?

If her suspicion was correct, Pilar wasn't certain whether she should be happy or concerned for her daughter.

* * *

Julia lingered in the kitchen long after the dishes had been washed and dried. Long after she'd served Ruíz and her father some of Paco's special port. Even after her mother had pressed one of her herbal remedies upon Ruíz to soothe Don Estéban's coughing and after Paco and her mother had retired for the night, Julia waited.

Her nerves were stretched taut with waiting . . . with hoping. Her stomach was tied in knots, and she found it difficult to breathe. Pacing softly, she clenched her fists so hard that her nails bit into the tender skin of her palms.

At any moment, she expected to be summoned, but as the moments dragged by, her hope died slowly, painfully.

By the Blessed Virgin Mary, she must have misunderstood Ruíz's penetrating gaze. But why else would he need to speak privately with her father? He must be asking for her hand in marriage. There could be no other possible explanation.

Could there?

When she had relinquished all hope and was prepared to hide in her room and weep in frustration, her father called out, "Julia, *mi hija,* are you there?" A chair scraped, and she heard her father mutter that he would see if Julia had retired for the night.

Julia wanted to leap for joy at the summons, but, instead, she forced herself to take several deep breaths, willing the erratic beating of her heart to subside. With shaking hands, she smoothed her hair and adjusted her skirts. Crossing the kitchen, she pulled aside the curtain separating the dining area.

Her first glance settled on her father. His eyes twinkled, and his usually weary countenance was wreathed in a broad smile. Her heart skipped a beat. Felipe's pleased face confirmed her fondest wish.

Carefully, she peeked at Ruíz from beneath her eyelashes, feeling inexplicably shy that he had declared for her. But Ruíz must have seen her surreptitious glance because he met her eyes and nodded his head slightly as if in silent acknowledgment. His mouth was also curved in a smile, but the expression was merely polite, not filled with triumph like her father's.

His casual demeanor wounded her. She craved to see the joy in Ruíz's face. After all, he was going to ask her to marry him, wasn't he? She had thought so, but now, she wasn't certain.

"*Papito,* you called me?"

"*Sí,* Julia, and I'm glad you haven't gone to bed for the night. Señor Ruíz wishes to speak with you."

"*Sí.*"

Ruíz rose and stretched out his arm, offering her his hand. She clasped his warm fingers, reveling in the feel of his flesh and remembering the sweet magic of his touch upon her body.

Ruíz bowed formally, first to her father and then to her, requesting, "*Con permiso,* if I may take Julia for a short walk. I promise we won't be long."

Felipe's demeanor was expansive when he urged them, "Go, children, and have your walk. Don't worry about how long it will take." He beamed at them. "*Dios te bendiga.*"

Tucking Julia's hand in his arm, Ruíz nodded to her father. They slipped through the front door, and he led her to the hacienda courtyard. He took a seat on the rim of the fountain and pulled her down beside him.

Julia closed her eyes. The tinkle of the cascading water sounded in her ears, the warm night breeze caressed her flushed face, and the rich perfume of blooming roses filled her nostrils. Savoring each moment as if it were a precious keepsake, she waited, vibrating with so much happiness she felt her heart would burst. Years of dreaming were about to be fulfilled.

He was going to ask her to marry him.

His deep voice wove reality into her fantasy, "Julia, will you marry me?"

Her eyes flew open, and she launched herself into his arms, babbling with excitement, "Of course I'll marry you, Ruíz. I love you. I've always wanted to marry you." She paused and took a shaky breath. "But you couldn't know that. I've tried

to hide my feelings for you ... afraid that you wouldn't ..."
She hugged him and whispered, "Last night I stopped hiding.
I wanted you to know how much I love you."

He returned her hug, and Julia expected him to kiss her, like
he'd kissed her last night ... transporting her to a realm of
sensual promise. But instead, he chastely pecked the crown of
her head and pulled away, breaking their embrace. Leaning
back, she searched his shadowed face, wondering at his reticence.

"I'm glad you agree to marry me, Julia. And I'm pleased
my proposal makes you so happy."

Ruíz's lack of emotion recalled Julia's earlier foreboding.
She remembered the night in San Antonio when he had said
he couldn't marry her. Their intimacy last night had pushed
his earlier reluctance from her mind. She had given freely of
herself, out of her love for him. Innocently, she believed the
power of their joining had changed him. But now, she wasn't
sure.

Why was Ruíz suddenly willing to marry her?

"Julia, I want you to know that your father and I spoke of
several matters, not just our marriage."

"*¿Sí?*"

"I'm going to deed your family the controlling interest in
Los Montes Verdes. I'll retain a fifth ownership as well as look
after my mother's interest unless she chooses to sell. I don't
think she'll find a buyer easily, and even if she does, your
family will have control."

Julia sucked in her breath at Ruíz's surprising admission.
Her heart flooded with love for him. He cared so much for her
that he was willing to relinquish his birthright because she had
asked him. *Asked* him? She had badgered him unmercifully,
believing that it was the right thing to do! And he wanted to
marry her, too! Julia shook her head in stunned disbelief. It
was a dream come true. Paco's future assured and Ruíz as her
husband.

She grasped his hands. "Ruíz, I can't thank you enough for this. It means so much to my family."

He squeezed her hands and lowered his head, seemingly embarrassed by her open gratitude.

"I should have listened to you sooner, Julia. Deeding your family the controlling interest is only fair. I thought I had to save the vineyard for my family, but when my mother left, I realized . . ."

"Yo entiendo."

His eyes met hers. Motes of color in the depths of his caramel-colored eyes reflected the faint moonlight. Releasing her hands, he shook his head slowly.

"No, Julia, you can't understand all of it, and I don't want you to believe my reasons for deeding the vineyard are completely unselfish and noble. I'm trapped, cornered by my mother's unswerving selfishness . . . and my duty to take care of her. I cannot hope to maintain two households, repay my father's debts, and your family's loan. I've even promised to have Teresa's dowry for her next spring."

His shoulders slumped, and he sighed. "I couldn't ask your family to wait for repayment, especially after what you've done for Conchita. It's all too much. The only honorable solution was to give your family the controlling interest."

"But you mustn't feel indebted about Conchita, Ruíz. When we're married, I'll be her new mother, and I already love your daughter."

"No, it isn't that. I know your family loves her, and you'll make a wonderful mother, Julia. I only mentioned Conchita because I wanted you to understand how much I value your family. Your family is all Conchita and I have. Your family's interests are my interests, and the Flores family should control the vineyard. My mother has turned her back on Los Montes Verdes, and she shouldn't be allowed to decide its fate." He paused, before continuing. "As for Teresa, I will make certain she receives her dowry." Ruíz gave Julia a lopsided smile and admitted, "That was another issue your father and I decided . . . your dowry to me."

She turned her head and bit her lip. Was her dowry so important to him, especially after what they had shared last night? It was obvious Doña Eugenia's abrupt departure had put further strain on Ruíz's finances. But surely her modest dowry wouldn't be enough to entice him to change his mind about marrying her. Would it?

"Don't scowl like that." He reached out his hand and brushed his fingertips across her creased forehead. "It's not what you're thinking. I didn't even want a dowry for you. But you and I both know your father's pride would have been crushed if—"

"He couldn't offer a dowry for me," Julia finished for him.

"I hope to use your dowry to build a suitable house for us." Ruíz combed his fingers through his hair and observed wryly, "I wonder at your enthusiasm to marry me, Julia. I don't even own a proper house to start our marriage. The hacienda belongs to my mother, and I don't think it would be wise to . . .

"I can't take you to the *rancho*. I don't want you living in the shadow of my first wife." His gaze snagged hers. "Haven't you thought why I wanted Conchita to live with your family if we were to be wed and start our own family?"

Julia dropped her eyes. She felt foolish for not having put the two things together. It hadn't crossed her mind. Everything had happened so fast. Where Ruíz was concerned, she wasn't always practical. His bald admission made her wonder. Where *would* they live?

Drawing her into his arms, he kissed her forehead. "Now you understand all of it, and it's a tangled web." He sighed again. "Promise me you'll be patient. Your father understands. We may have to wait to marry."

Julia burrowed into the sanctuary of his arms. She didn't want to wait. She had already waited all of her life to be with Ruíz. But she possessed no ready answer to their predicament.

Needing his physical reassurance, she lifted her mouth and their lips fused together in searing abandon.

When they broke off the kiss, Julia murmured, "I'll wait to marry, but I need you so, Ruíz. Can't we . . . can't we . . .?" She felt the warmth climb the column of her throat when she asked, "Be together like we were . . . last night?"

Ruíz appeared startled by her question. He turned his gaze from her, almost as if she had embarrassed him and replied, "No, Julia, that's not wise."

"*¿Por qué?*"

"Last night was a mistake, Julia. Even now, you may be with child. If that's the case, we won't be able to wait. We'll need to marry as soon as possible."

His matter-of-fact tone was eerily familiar. When he had first kissed her, he apologized by telling her it had been a mistake. And he had dismissed their passion in San Antonio as a mistake, too. Did he feel everything about their relationship was a mistake . . . a mistake he was forced to rectify?

She hadn't stopped to consider that she might be pregnant, but he obviously had. Was that the reason he had proposed to her? Was his waiting to build a house just a ploy to give him time to see if she was carrying his child? And if she wasn't pregnant . . . would he conveniently dismiss tonight as another mistake?

She had to know the truth.

"Would it be so awful if I were pregnant? I don't care where we live as long as we're together. We can live in one of the worker's houses, and, in time, you'll build us a home. Ruíz, it doesn't matter where we live."

"But it does matter."

Julia could feel him slipping away. She clutched his arm. "But we want to marry. We love each other. Where we live shouldn't—"

"It's not that simple, Julia."

Her heart plummeted, and all of her earlier forebodings

returned with a rush. She was swamped by doubts. The bright promise of tomorrow darkened, tarnished by her suspicions.

Every word he had spoken to her in the last two days flew through her mind. And she realized his words were hollow . . . without feeling. Despite the fact she had proclaimed her love for him, he had never said he loved her . . . Not once.

The realization pierced her. Disillusionment sucked at her, twisting her stomach and stopping the breath in her lungs. Her temples throbbed, and her throat filled with bitter gall.

"You don't love me." It was not a question, but a statement of fact.

"Julia—"

"¡Dígame!"

She watched his jaw clench in the wan moonlight, the tense muscles quivering beneath his flesh. She heard the concern in his voice, but his words were brutal. "You came to me a virgin, Julia. Remember San Antonio . . . when you spoke of dishonor? I told you before, Conchita and I have no one . . . just your family. It is my—"

"Duty!" Julia spat at him. The word started low, tearing upward, ripping from her guts. She had known Ruíz all of her life, and she understood his unfailing devotion to duty. The truth cut her. He was offering to marry her, not from love, but from *dut*y.

Pain exploded in her brain, numbing her limbs. And with the numbness came sorrow. A sorrow so deep, so black, she couldn't name it. She thought of Lupita's passing and Don Federico's untimely death.

It was the same black despair.

He reached for her. "Julia, it's not so awful. I do care—"

With an effort of will, she twisted away from him, forcing her limbs to obey. "Duty, Ruíz? I don't want your *duty* or your *guilt*. By deeding the vineyard to my family and marrying me, *if I do carry your child,* you'll absolve yourself of everything. Won't you?

"It's not that simple, Ruíz. Life is not a tidy package you can tie up with a ribbon." She stopped, gasping for air. The constriction around her chest tightened. For a moment, she felt as if she were going to faint, but she refused herself that easy surrender.

"As for the vineyard, I agree, it's the only honorable solution. But I'm a person, Ruíz, not an honorable solution. And I don't want your obligation or your precious duty."

He opened his mouth to speak, but Julia held up her hand to stop his words. "Don't try to convince me, Ruíz. I *know* you. Sometimes I think I know you better than you know yourself." She dropped her hand and rose to her feet.

"Nothing I've said changes what you should do for Conchita. She belongs with my family." She added spitefully, "It may be the *only* love she'll receive without strings attached."

"Julia—" Ruíz stood up, too, and reached for her again.

"No!" she cried out and retreated a step. "Don't try to touch me. I want your *love,* Ruíz, not your *duty.*"

Ruíz sat beside the gurgling fountain for a long time after Julia left, thinking. He knew what she wanted from him . . . words of love. But they choked in his throat. He couldn't say them.

Julia was strong and willful like his mother. If he admitted he loved her, he feared she would use his love against him. He was prepared to fulfill his duty to her, but love carried such a heavy burden. Love was a trap. If a man loved a woman, it was a weakness that could be exploited by the woman to gain domination over the man. He had seen his mother use that weapon, over and over, to her advantage.

It wasn't that he was a coward, unable to protect himself. He could face anything . . . anything but losing a part of himself. And he had been losing bits and pieces of himself with every demand his mother made of him.

He buried his face in his hands.

Responsibility, obligation, duty ... marriage encompassed all of these things and more. He wasn't ready to take a wife. His lust for Julia had compromised him. Already, she had learned to wield her power over him. Her innocent offering had seduced him. Taking Julia had been a mistake.

With marriage, trust should come, but he didn't trust Julia. He didn't trust her to consider his wishes, to compromise and be willing to give. Marriage to Julia would be an armed battle-field, a constant jockeying for power.

And he didn't want that.

He knew he must eventually remarry, especially for Con-chita's sake. He wanted to have more children, too. But there would be time later when he had straightened out his life. His choice would be a young and malleable woman whose only desire was to give him children.

Ruíz raised his head.

Julia had spurned his offer of marriage, and he should be relieved. It was better this way. If she wasn't carrying his child and she had refused his offer, he didn't owe her anything.

But he needed to be careful when he was near her because she made the blood boil in his veins. Never had he desired a woman so completely. And last night hadn't sated him, either.

Chapter Eleven

Julia pulled the brush through her hair with unthinking precision. Staring at her image in the mirror, she was amazed at how normal she looked. Scrubbed and dressed in her nightgown for bed, she doubted anyone would guess the torment she had undergone since that night with Ruíz.

Her feelings had swung from one extreme to another. After she had turned down Ruíz's marriage proposal, she had been filled with rage. Rage at his unfeeling betrayal. She had hated him for taking her freely given passion and then turning it into a trap. How could he have shown her the heights of pleasure and remained so uncaring of her as a person?

She had asked herself that question over and over, but she hadn't found an answer.

When her rage was spent, she had plunged into despair. Nothing touched her. She moved through each day automatically, doing her best not to think, not to question, not to feel.

Despair had given way to grieving for what she had gambled

and lost. She had cried until there was no moisture left in her body. And with her grief came regret.

A thousand times she had regretted her decision to turn down Ruíz's offer of marriage. If she loved him so much, why had she refused? After they were married, she reasoned, he might have learned to love her.

She lifted her a chin a notch. Pride. Pride had stopped her from accepting his dutiful proposal. Pride and perhaps a touch of fear. It was common knowledge he hadn't learned to love his wife, Alicia Estrada. Their marriage had been one of convenience and polite distance.

Dropping the brush, she buried her face in her hands. She didn't want that kind of marriage, especially with Ruíz.

Her troubled thoughts were broken by the sound of her mother's voice. Julia raised her head and retrieved the brush. Pilar knocked and then entered her room.

"Sí, Mamita."

Pilar crossed the room and placed her hands on Julia's shoulders. Giving them a gentle squeeze, she stepped back.

"Por favor, mi hija, continue to brush your hair. I just wanted to ask about Conchita. Does she seem happy in our home? You spend more time with her than I do. What do you think?"

"I think she's happy. She occasionally asks for her *abuela* and *Tía* Teresa, but that's only to be expected. She's so young; she doesn't really understand. But sometimes I think her youth is an advantage."

Her mother seated herself on the foot of Julia's bed.

"I agree her youth is an advantage, but she won't always be so young. I had one reservation when Ruíz asked us to foster Conchita—that our attachment would be difficult to break when he remarried and took Conchita away. When your father told me Ruíz wanted to marry you, I was relieved. The attachment wouldn't be broken. But you haven't mentioned Ruíz's proposal. I thought you would be pleased, but I can see you're not happy."

Julia's heart wrenched at her mother's gentle probing. She had been expecting her parents to question her about Ruíz's proposal. It had only been matter of time.

I haven't spoken of it because I refused him.''

"¿Por qué? You've loved Ruíz Navarro since you were younger than Conchita.''

Julia drew in a quick breath and asked, ''Am I that obvious?''

"Sí, hija mía, but only to your family, because we love you so much. And you didn't answer my question,'' her mother pointed out. ''Why did you refuse him?''

Julia dropped her arm and laid the hairbrush aside. Her family had given her plenty of time to invent a plausible excuse, but all she could think of was the painful truth.

''Ruíz doesn't return my love. His proposal was an obligation, a fulfillment of his duty.''

''Why would Ruíz feel obligated to propose, Julia?''

It was the question she had been dreading. Intuitively, she knew her mother would be understanding about her intimacy with Ruíz, but her father would not share that understanding. In typical male fashion, he would demand she marry him. There were no secrets between her parents, and Julia didn't want to impose the burden of duplicity upon her mother. Although she wanted to confide in her mother, she dared not to.

''I think Ruíz felt obligated to us for taking Conchita. He wants to secure a permanent home for her, but I don't think he's eager to marry again. He would have married me for Conchita's sake.''

Pilar's eyes searched Julia's face. Her mother knew her so well that she was certain Pilar knew she wasn't telling the whole truth. But her mother didn't challenge the veracity of her statement. Instead, she merely remarked, ''Is what Ruíz wanted to do so terrible? Many marriages have been founded on a great deal less.''

''I know, *Mamita.* If I didn't love him so desperately, it might have been enough. But since Ruíz became betrothed to

Alicia Estrada, he's changed. He's become cold and unfeeling . . . like his mother. And without love to soften him, I was afraid . . .''

"I think I understand, Julia, but you could have asked him to wait. To court you and see if—''

"He wanted to wait," Julia interjected. "That was part of the problem. I didn't feel his proposal was genuine, that it was only a gesture. He was more concerned about where we would live than anything else." A lump rose to Julia's throat, and there was a catch in her voice. "It all seemed so calculated, as if . . . as if . . ." She dropped her head, unable to continue.

Julia heard the rustle of Pilar's skirts, and then she was drawn into the comforting embrace of her mother's arms. Pilar stroked her hair, reassuring her softly, "Don't fret. You did what you thought best. I could upbraid you about your romantic notions, but I would be the last person to underestimate the power of the human heart."

Releasing her, Pilar returned to her perch on the foot of Julia's bed. Clasping her hands in her lap, her mother's voice was thoughtful when she offered, "You've wanted to know for a long time about Doña Eugenia's animosity toward our family. I think it's time you know the truth. Maybe my experience will serve to help you."

Julia raised her head. She hadn't expected this, that her mother would confide in her. Her mother's understanding and empathy touched her heart, making tears well in her eyes.

"Your experience? What do you mean?"

"It was a very long time ago, *mi hija*. I was younger than you are now. Don Federico noticed me at a *fandango* in San Antonio, and he paid me court. My family was respectable, as you know. My father was the *alcalde* then, but we weren't descended from nobility, like the Navarros. Don Federico's parents were against the match." Her mother paused and sighed. "I was young and impressionable, awed by Don Federico's position and excited by the adventure of an illicit love."

"But you love *Papá,* don't you?"

"Of course, but that came later."

"What do you mean?"

"The Navarros left Los Montes Verdes on an extended business trip to Monclovia, México. The reason given for their journey was to bring back new vines, but that was only a convenient excuse. The real purpose for their trip was to find a suitable match for Don Federico, and his parents were successful. Doña Eugenia was the daughter of a Spanish grandee, a *marqués,* who owned rich properties in Monclovia. Don Federico didn't know what his parents had planned for him, so before he left, he asked me to wait for him." Pilar shrugged and admitted, "I promised I would wait, but I didn't."

"*¡Mamita!*" Julia gasped.

There was a mischievous twinkle in her mother's eyes that reminded Julia of Paco. "I had a good reason for not waiting. I met your father while Don Federico was away and fell in love with him."

"And Don Federico?" Julia prompted.

"As a dutiful son, he fulfilled his parents' wishes and returned with Doña Eugenia as his bride. But when he returned, he made it clear he still loved me. I was betrothed to your father and he was married, so we parted as friends. Don Federico was the perfect gentleman, never allowing his true feelings to show. It was a sad irony I fell in love with a man whose home was Los Montes Verdes, where I would be faced with the Navarros for the rest of my life."

"If Don Federico was already married and he was such a gentleman, why does Doña Eugenia—"

"Hate me so?" Pilar finished the question for her. "Maybe she heard the gossip about our courtship or maybe she guessed. Don Federico never said or did anything unseemly after his marriage, but just the way someone looks at a person can give the secret away." Pausing, she added, "It doesn't matter how Doña Eugenia found out. She never forgave Don Federico for loving me. And she has never stopped hating our family because of it.''

''*Mamita,* it must have been such a trial for you.''

''Not really. I told your father everything before we married. Since he was a partner with the Navarros, he needed to know what an awkward situation he was getting himself into.'' Her mother's eyes glistened with moisture. ''Bless him, he stood by me and didn't allow it to interfere with our love for each other. And, of course, Don Federico was a fair man. He never let the past prejudice him against Felipe. It was only Doña Eugenia's animosity we had to bear.''

Julia's thoughts were racing. Her mother's story explained so many things . . . past and present.

''Sometimes I think our present difficulties with the vineyard were brought about because Don Federico felt he had to indulge his wife to assure her he cared. When I think of it, I feel guilty. But then I remind myself that Don Federico was a grown man. He made his own decisions. I cannot accept the responsibility for his unwise actions.''

''Of course not, *Mamita.* It all happened so long ago.'' Julia hesitated. She had another question to ask, but she didn't know if her mother's answer would shed any light on her present predicament. ''Do you think Ruíz knows?''

Pilar met Julia's eyes and smiled wistfully. ''And so we return to the present . . . enough of the past. No, I don't think Ruíz knows. Doña Eugenia would never admit it. Her pride is too strong. But pride is a lonely thing, which brings me to the reason for my confession.''

The reason . . . Julia had been so engrossed in her mother's story, she had forgotten the reason for her mother's unexpected confession.

''Always follow your heart, Julia. I did, and it was the right thing to do. I believed Don Federico would come back to me, but when I fell in love with your father, I didn't hesitate. I followed my heart. You should, too.''

"But *Papá* loved you. Ruíz doesn't love me."

"That remains to be seen. I've watched him look at you, Julia. I believe he cares."

Her heart leapt at her mother's words, soaring like a bird that had been caged for too long. But reality intruded swiftly, snaring her heart and returning it to earth, laden by doubts.

She shook her head. "I would like to believe it, but . . ."

"Remember what I said about giving it time. You've loved Ruíz for so long, what are a few more weeks or months?"

"I suppose it couldn't hurt . . ."

Rising from the bed, Pilar put her arm around Julia's shoulders. Drawing a piece of folded parchment from the pocket of her apron, she offered it to Julia, saying, "This invitation came today. Our family will go, but the other is a personal invitation. You'll need to decide for yourself."

Her mother kissed the top of her head and said, "Try to get some sleep."

"I will."

Pilar moved to the door. On its threshold, she turned and remarked, "I know you've loved Ruíz for a long time. But sometimes, when love isn't reciprocated, it can begin to whither and die . . . or change. Do you still love him, Julia? Or is it that you're infatuated with the concept of loving him? You need to listen to your heart and get on with your life, either way. Don't grow old waiting for something that won't come. But if the love is really there, you will know it if you'll listen . . . to your heart."

After her mother had left, Julia sat as still as a statue for a very long time, thinking. Sighing to herself, she didn't know how she felt. It was all so confusing.

Opening the invitation and scanning its contents, her confusion mounted. It was really two invitations. One, inviting her family to the *quinceanera* of Carmen Treviño, David's sister. The second invitation was a personal note from David, asking to be her escort to the party following the *quinceanera*.

Her mother had told her it was her decision. She had spurned Ruíz's loveless marriage proposal, but in her heart, she still felt bound to him. Yet she couldn't go on indefinitely loving a man who didn't return her love. Could she? She didn't know the answer, despite her mother's advice, and the present question remained.

Should she accept David Treviño's invitation?

The summer had been dry and hot. Ruíz found he had his hands full at the *rancho,* moving the horses and cattle from pasture to pasture, seeking green grass and fresh water. Each time they moved the herds, they lost a few cattle or some horses, particularly in the northern pastures. It was difficult to know whether the rustling had begun again or if the Comanches were helping themselves to a few strays.

Ruíz closed the barn door behind him. He'd left Oro with Pedro to be rubbed down and fed. It was already dark. As he strode toward the hacienda, he caught sight of the lantern shining in Allende's two-room *casa.* Ruíz had come to value Allende a great deal. The *vaquero* was loyal and trustworthy, efficient and shrewd. And he worshipped Teresa.

Every night, no matter how long and difficult his day had been, Allende wrote to Teresa in New Orleans. Ruíz understood the monumental effort this took on Allende's part.

When Teresa departed for New Orleans and asked Allende to write to her, he had confessed to Ruíz that he couldn't. He knew enough to sign his own name and he knew the alphabet, but he had never learned to read and write.

Ruíz had given him a few rudimentary lessons and loaned him his old primer books. Allende had thanked Ruíz, and now he struggled manfully to correspond with Teresa.

His heart squeezed at the thought of Allende's devotion, and he felt the tiniest twinge of envy. Would he ever love a woman like that? Love her enough to be willing to transform himself to please her? He didn't know.

The next morning, Ruíz was working in Don Estéban's unused study, going over his correspondence and the papers pertaining to the business of the *rancho*. The first packet of letters from his sister had arrived the day before. Placing the letters to one side to read at his leisure, he felt certain Allende had received a similar packet of letters.

As if the thought of Allende had conjured the man, Ruíz glanced up to find him standing in the doorway of the study.

"Buenos días, Allende. Come in and be seated."

Allende nodded and returned his greeting. *"Buenos días,* Don Ruíz." He moved to a chair facing the wide desk and gingerly sat down on the edge of its seat. Removing his wide hat, he balanced it in his lap.

Ruíz couldn't help but smile at Allende when he pointed to the pile of letters from his sister. "I would guess you received letters from Teresa, too."

"Sí, Don Ruíz," Allende admitted. But instead of appearing pleased, he looked uncomfortable. Nervously, he plucked at the hat on his lap and refused to meet Ruíz's eyes.

The smile slid from Ruíz's face, and he was suddenly worried that something might be amiss with his mother and sister.

"Por favor, Allende, tell me what has brought you here, looking so concerned? I haven't had time to read the letters. I hope my mother and sister are well."

"I didn't mean to cause you alarm, Don Ruíz. Your family arrived safely in New Orleans, and they are in fine health. I spent most of last night reading Teresa's letters and . . ." He paused and shook his head. "I'm afraid this isn't going to work. Teresa is miserable and so am I."

Expelling the breath he had been holding, Ruíz observed, "You knew this separation wouldn't be easy on either one of you. But isn't waiting—?"

"I feel helpless and used, Don Ruíz," Allende cut him off.

"As if I were a sweetmeat your mother dangles before Teresa's lips." He stopped and bobbed his head, apologizing immediately. "Forgive me for my uncouth reference to your mother, Don Ruíz. But it isn't a pleasant situation, and my pride suffers."

His eyes were troubled, and his brow was pleated. He appeared to be searching for just the right words to explain himself.

"When you offered me a job and allowed Teresa and me to see one another, I didn't mind waiting. I wanted to earn your family's trust. I didn't want to marry Teresa against her family's wishes. But now that her mother has taken Teresa away and is throwing every eligible bachelor in New Orleans at her, I'm not so certain . . ."

"Allende," Ruíz reassured him, "Teresa loves you. You mustn't despair. I'm certain my sister will return to you."

The *vaquero* hunched forward in his chair. His shoulders were slumped. Ruíz could hear the dejection in his voice. "It's not only that, Don Ruíz. I feel like a puppet. I have this job because of Teresa, and it's as if we are just waiting for her dowry, too. I told Teresa before, I don't want her money. I can provide for her, but I didn't want to take her away from her family." His voice cracked when he admitted, "I know what it feels like to be without a family."

Leaning back in his chair, Ruíz considered Allende's words. It was obvious he had done a great deal of soul searching. Ruíz understood the man's pride was bruised, and he empathized with him. But he also didn't want Allende to underestimate his own value.

"Allende, one of the best decisions I ever made was to hire you. And it has nothing to do with my sister. You're a valuable employee, so valuable I'm willing to give you a raise to prove my point."

"*Por favor,* no raise. I appreciate your kind words, but—"

"I mean those words."

Straightening his posture in the chair, Allende lifted his chin. "This is very difficult for me, Don Ruíz. I came to you to quit my job. I had a plan, before I came to work for you, that would earn me the money to buy a place of my own. I think I should go now and earn that money. When Teresa returns, I will have a home for her."

Ruíz opened his mouth to dissuade him but thought better of it. His curiosity was piqued, and he reasoned the more he knew about Allende's plan, the more effectively he could argue against it.

"Would you mind sharing your plan with me?"

A look of surprise crossed Allende's face. He appeared startled by Ruíz's interest. Recovering quickly, he spread his broad, calloused hands.

"It's a simple plan, Don Ruíz. There are many bands of wild mustangs roaming the Llano Estacado. I will go there and capture a large herd of horses. Then I will break and train each horse. It will only take my time and a few supplies. The profits should be good."

Ruíz couldn't stop from gasping at the boldness of Allende's plan. Boldness? It was incredibly dangerous.

"The Llano Estacado is Comanche country, and the Comanches look upon those wild herds as theirs. What you are proposing to do is—"

"There is no gain without danger," Allende interjected. "It is better than being a . . . a lapdog!" he declared fiercely.

"Allende, you wound me! You're not a lapdog." Ruíz's voice dropped, "What if you don't come back? Who will console Teresa? What difference will the money make then?"

Allende dropped his head. His hands fidgeted with the straw brim of his hat. Ruíz could see that he was considering the consequences.

"I need you, Allende, especially now. Don Estéban is much weaker. He cannot leave his bed. The doctor says it's only a matter of weeks." Ruíz paused and waited until Allende lifted his head and met his eyes. "I understand your pride, but I also know you're loyal. Can I appeal to your loyalty? If you're careful and save your wages, you could strike out on your own, too, and with much less danger."

Gazing straight into Ruíz's eyes, he nodded his acquiescence.

"*Muy bien.* I'm glad that's settled. And you must accept a raise or a portion of the profits from the horses you sell for the *rancho.* Under your expert guidance, our profits have doubled. What do you say?"

"The profits, Don Ruíz. That way, I would feel I had *earned* the money."

Ruíz rose from his chair and extended his hand across the desk. "Is it a deal?"

Allende lifted one hand and rubbed his jaw. He rose, too, and after a moment's hesitation, clasped Ruíz's hand and agreed. "It's a deal."

Lázaro scowled as he scanned the operating expenses of the bordello for the past month. Laundry, cosmetics, lingerie, french pastries, beefsteaks . . . the amounts were staggering. Madame Plaisance, in his opinion, was too soft on the whores. They lived like queens, spoiled like royalty.

He slammed the ledger shut with a thud. The bordello made a great deal of money, but not nearly enough to suit his expectations. When he became the sole owner, things would change. The whores would learn their place and do without their luxuries. Then the bordello would be capable of supporting him in the style to which he aspired.

First, he would need to buy out Madame Plaisance's share. And to do that, he would need his father's treasure.

The door creaked and Chivato's pointed face pressed through the opening. He wasted no time explaining his intrusion, "Madame Plaisance said I could find you here."

Lázaro disguised his annoyance at Chivato for not knocking

by greeting him with a mocking welcome, "*¿Cómo está, mi amigo?* You've returned from Tejas. I hope your journey was pleasant and . . . successful."

Chivato slipped into the room and bobbed his head. "*Gracias,* Don Lázaro, my journey was successful, but also very hot." He licked his lips and darted his eyes to the open bottle of absinthe sitting on the liquor cabinet.

Lázaro followed Chivato's hopeful glance. Normally, he would torment the man for a time, but tonight he was feeling uncommonly irritable. He didn't want to play games. The old sport with Chivato didn't interest him.

"Help yourself."

Scurrying to the bottle, Chivato poured himself a glass. He downed the liquor in one gulp and smacked his lips.

Lázaro winced at his crude manners. He would be glad when Chivato's use was at an end. It would be a pleasure to rid himself of the man . . . once and for all.

"What news do you bring me?"

"I found a family for you, Don Lázaro, and, believe me, it wasn't easy. I had to—"

Raising his hand, he brought it down with a loud smack on the desk. "I don't want the details of what you had to do. You were well paid for your efforts. Just the results, Chivato, just tell me your results."

The small man jumped and gulped, his Adam's apple bobbing in his stringy throat. "I beg your pardon, Don Lázaro." Gulping, he rushed into what sounded like a memorized speech, "The man's name is MacGregor, and he's got a mangy crew of kids and a wife. They were all starving. I bribed a clerk to counterfeit some scrip. The MacGregors are squatting and rustling on your father's *rancho.*"

"*Muy bien.* You did well. Anything else?"

"*Sí.* Your father is confined to his bed. Word has it that he won't last the summer."

Lázaro felt a thrill of joy and anticipation at the imminent demise of his father. He wouldn't have to wait much longer. With his father alive, he had no hope of gaining access to his childhood home. But when his father died, it would be another matter. And he needed to get inside the hacienda compound, because that was where the treasure was hidden.

"I've already paid you, but here's a little bonus." He flipped him a single gold coin, offering sarcastically, "Don't spend it all in one place."

Chivato snatched the coin from the air. Swiftly scrutinizing its value, his face fell. He raised his eyes. Panic swam in their murky depths.

Guessing Chivato had already spent the money he had been given to go to Tejas, Lázaro knew the coin would purchase one bottle of absinthe but no more. His irritation had lifted at the thought of his father's death. He was enjoying baiting Chivato again.

"Find me five trustworthy men who are good with knives and pistols. Men who are willing to do anything for a price. And I want them to remain close by, ready to leave at a moment's notice for Tejas. ¿*Entiende?*"

"*Sí,* Don Lázaro, y*o entiendo,* but I'll need . . . some gold to buy drinks and . . . look for them. If you could just . . ." His voice had dropped to an ingratiating whine.

"Here." Lázaro tossed him two more coins. "Return when you've found the men."

Chapter Twelve

Julia stepped from the *casa* and wiped her hands on her apron. The freight wagon had arrived. It stood before the entrance to the winery. She and Paco had carefully packed the newly bottled red wines in crates the day before. All that remained was to load the crates on the wagon. It would be their first shipment to New Orleans.

Two figures emerged from the winery. Julia was surprised to see Ruíz. He was carrying a crate of wine. Paco rolled along beside him, gesticulating and laughing. She had intended to see the shipment off, but she hadn't counted on Ruíz's presence. Since the night she had refused his proposal, she had only caught glimpses of him when he visited Conchita or took his daughter to see her grandfather.

Conchita's grandfather, Don Estéban, would be another loss in the child's life. Last week, Ruíz had taken his daughter to say good-bye to her grandfather. Don Estéban was dying, but the child didn't understand. Julia wondered how much more Conchita could bear.

Could Julia bear facing Ruíz?

As much as she wanted to be present to see the fulfillment of her plan to save the vineyard, she realized she didn't want to see him, even at this triumphant moment. Having made her decision, she turned to reenter the *casa*.

Before she had gained the door, Conchita came hurtling from the house and wrapped her arms around Julia's knees. The little girl's sobbing pleas were garbled. "No! *Tía* Julia, *por favor,* don't let her! I'm sah . . . sah . . . sorry."

Lifting the wailing child, she held Conchita in her arms. She hoped her touch would calm the little girl enough so she could find out what was wrong. Before she could speak, she saw Luz rushing toward them with Conchita's favorite doll in her hands. Stopping in front of Julia, Luz shook the doll at Conchita.

"See what your temper has done! You should be ashamed, Concepción María Navarro y Estrada." When Luz was really angry with Conchita, she used the child's full name.

Julia looked at the doll Luz waved and was appalled to see that its beautiful china face had been shattered. One glass eyeball clung obscenely to the broken remnants, and the caved-in features were surrounded by a tangled web of silken tresses. Julia opened her mouth to speak, but Ruíz forestalled her by joining their unhappy circle.

"Luz, what has happened?"

"Perdóneme, Señor Ruíz, but Conchita had a temper tantrum. She didn't want to take her nap, so she threw her doll against the wall." Luz lifted the sadly damaged doll for Ruíz's inspection. "This doll, the one you brought her from San Antonio. Now it's ruined."

Ruíz took the doll from Luz's hands and examined it. *"Sí,* it's ruined. Throw it away."

"No!" Conchita screamed, and almost lunged from Julia's arms. "It's mine."

"No longer is it yours, Conchita. You must learn when you

destroy something you care about in a fit of temper that you may lose it forever," Ruíz observed gravely.

Conchita slumped in Julia's arms, sobbing in utter desolation. Julia's heart went out to the child, and she wondered if Ruíz's daughter hadn't been acting out the losses she had faced these past few weeks.

"Must you take it away from her? Isn't it punishment enough that she's broken the doll."

Ruíz's eyes met hers, and Julia read the silent challenge in his gaze. As if he had spoken, she understood he was trying to do what he thought best for his daughter, and he didn't want her interference.

Julia lowered Conchita to the ground. The little girl clung to her leg with her eyes screwed shut and her bottom lip sticking out. It was obvious Conchita was milking her for sympathy. She wavered. It was so difficult to know how best to raise a child.

Even if Conchita had unconsciously broken the doll because she *was* acting out the losses in her life, was it right to condone her inappropriate behavior? Julia asked herself. What if it had been just a fit of temper, nothing deeper than that? Julia shook her head. Maybe she was making this too complicated. The doll was ruined, beyond repair. Conchita had only herself to thank. Perhaps Ruíz was right to try and control his daughter's bad temper.

Before, when Ruíz seldom paid attention to her, Julia would have challenged his right to discipline the child he so often ignored. But the situation was different now, and he consistently made it a point to spend time with her.

"You're right, Ruíz. I'm sorry I interfered. Conchita needs to learn to control her temper." Julia reached down and cupped the child's face in her hands, asking, "Do you understand, *mi niña?*"

The child's bottom lip quivered, and her liquid eyes darted back and forth between Ruíz and Julia. Their unified front must have made an impression on her, because she stopped sobbing and held her arms out to her father.

Ruíz bent and lifted her, murmuring, "It's a hard lesson to learn, little one, but you'll remember next time. Won't you?"

Conchita nodded. Contrition was stamped on her young features.

He kissed her forehead. *"Muy bien.* Now, I believe it's time for your nap. No more fussing. After you wake up, I'll take you for a riding lesson." He handed her to Luz's waiting arms.

"Really, *Papá,* you'll take me for a riding lesson?"

"Really, *hija mía."*

Conchita peeked at Ruíz and Julia from Luz's shoulder. Her tentative smile was like a rainbow after the storm. "I'm sorry for my bad temper."

"You're forgiven," Ruíz and Julia responded in unison.

Startled by their simultaneous answer, they laughed. Ruíz took Julia's arm and tucked it beneath his. The tone of his voice was gentle when he said, "Thank you for supporting me. I know you don't like to be . . . harsh with her, but she has to learn. It's important to start early before she gets out of control."

Julia barely took in his words. His touch had galvanized her. Warmth suffused her body, and tingling sensations chased along her nerves. Unconsciously, she leaned into him. It seemed like an eternity since they had touched. She had tried to harden her heart against him, but his mere touch crumbled her best efforts. She remembered her mother's advice to follow her heart. But how could she? She had waited so long for Ruíz to return her love.

"I want you to see the shipment off," Ruíz interrupted her churning thoughts. "It was your idea to send the wine to New Orleans, and you should share in our success."

Julia felt a lump rise to her throat. She was moved by his

consideration for her feelings. She nodded and said, *"Gracias,* I would like that."

Withdrawing his arm from hers, he stated, "I need to help with the loading. *¿Con permiso?"*

"Of course."

Ruíz flashed a grin at her and rolled up his sleeves. It was as if that night beside the fountain had never happened. How could he be so casual when her heart was shattered? Didn't he care?

Julia purposely stopped her errant thoughts. Wondering if Ruíz cared . . . or how much . . . would lead to madness. She closed her eyes and took several deep breaths, trying to chase the distressing questions from her mind.

When she opened her eyes, she felt in control again. She watched the loading of the freight wagon, gratified to witness the reality of her dream. And once the wagon was full and lashed down, Julia watched it rumble away, across the cobblestone courtyard and through the front gates. She offered a brief prayer to the Virgin Mary, asking that their wine reach New Orleans safely.

Ruíz raised his arm and wiped the perspiration from his brow. "That's done." He winked at Paco and said, "I feel a toast is in order. Don't you? Do you have some of that delicious port on hand?" Ruíz turned to Julia and offered, *"Por favor,* join us in a toast."

Julia inclined her head in acceptance of his offer.

Her brother nodded also and declared, *"Sí,* I'll fetch the port, but I'm looking forward to doing some serious celebrating tomorrow night."

"Tomorrow night?" Ruíz sounded puzzled.

"Our family's been invited to Carmen Treviño's *quinceanera,"* Paco explained. "The entire population of San Antonio will probably attend the *fiesta* afterward. You must have received an invitation, Señor Ruíz."

Ruíz rubbed his jaw, obviously trying to remember. After a few moments, his face cleared and he agreed, "You're right, Paco, I did receive an invitation. I hadn't planned on going . . ." He turned his head and stared at Julia.

She flushed with embarrassment. Ruíz had caught her shaking her head at Paco and putting her finger to her lips, silently urging her brother to keep quiet about the Treviño *quinceanera*. From the look in Ruíz's eyes, it was already too late.

Perdición take her brother! He had obviously alerted Ruíz on purpose, because, at this very moment, her brother was grinning smugly and his eyes were alight with mischief. She would have cheerfully throttled him if they had been alone.

"I think I've changed my mind, Paco. Sounds like I shouldn't miss this *quinceanera.*" Ruíz's eyes seemed to bore straight through Julia, exposing her innermost thoughts. "It could prove interesting," he added.

"Muy bien, Señor Ruíz, I'll look forward to seeing you." Paco propelled himself toward the winery, calling over his shoulder, "I'll fetch the port for our toast."

Julia looked down at her hands. They were clenched into fists, the knuckles strained white. She shouldn't care what Ruíz might suspect. She had every right to get on with her life. Didn't she? But as hard as she tried to reassure herself, the question kept echoing in her mind.

How will he react when he discovers my escort is David Treviño?

"Carmen Treviño y Galindo, the Church welcomes you and your parents, grandparents, godparents and friends to celebrate with you your fifteenth birthday, your *quinceanos.* This celebration is to rejoice and give thanks to God and renew your baptism, communion, and confirmation of becoming a young lady." Padre Carrasco opened Carmen Treviño's *Quinceanera* Mass with the traditional words.

Julia studied the birthday girl. Carmen looked like a young

swan in her white lace dress. Slender and elegant and so achingly tender.

She wondered if she had looked as innocent and fresh at her own *quinceanera*. Over the years, she seldom thought about her fifteenth birthday celebration. Instead of it being a joyous occasion with her trembling on the brink of womanhood, Julia's memories were bittersweet and tainted.

The week before her *quinceanera*, Ruíz had become officially betrothed to Alicia Estrada. Instead of the happy anticipation of life that was gleaming in Carmen's eyes today, Julia's future had been steeped in bleakness. So much had happened since that far-off day . . . and so little had changed.

Ruíz still didn't love her.

It was if she'd come full circle and accomplished nothing. On that night she spent with Ruíz, she had truly become a woman. He had entered her flesh and consecrated her to womanhood. But the confirmation had proven hollow. A passion of the flesh, nothing more. How could she follow her heart, as her mother had advised, when her heart recognized no one but Ruíz? Coming with David Treviño today had already proven to be a sham. She felt less than nothing for him.

Tears welled in her eyes. Would she ever be free of Ruíz Navarro?

The priest genuflected and kneeled before the altar. The congregation kneeled, too. There was a long prayer for Carmen and her life as a Christian. Padre Carrasco rose and offered the kneeling girl communion. Carmen took the sacramental wafer and wine, and the priest blessed her. The altar boys swung heavy metal vessels with smoking incense in them. Padre Carrasco made the sign of the cross over Carmen's bent head, and the congregation rose to their feet.

Julia's eyes strayed around the cathedral. She and her family had found a place toward the back of the sanctuary. David had offered for Julia to sit up front with his family, but Julia had demurred, saying it wouldn't be proper. Only if she were betrothed to David would it be acceptable to sit with the Treviños.

She shut her eyes. Surely David's invitation hadn't meant anything beyond a polite gesture. She didn't think she could stand it if it did. As it was, the night to come stretched interminably before her.

While she gazed about the crowded sanctuary, she silently agreed with Paco. It appeared as if all of San Antonio was present today. And the *fiesta* would be even more crowded. But Ruíz wasn't there. Maybe pressing business had kept him away after all. His absence would make tonight infinitely easier.

Her attention was drawn back to the ceremony. The *Quinceanera* Mass was drawing to a close. The presentation of the ritual gifts to the birthday girl from her family and godparents had begun.

First, a crown for eternal life with God had been placed on Carmen's head, followed by a ring with her birthstone to remind her of the month of her birth. The priest handed her a new Bible to symbolize the word of God and a rosary for devotion to Our Blessed Mother, with a crucifix attached for faith. A gold bracelet was slid upon Carmen's slender arm as a remembrance of this day. Carmen knelt on the final gift, a *cojon*, or cushion, that symbolized the comfort of friendship in this life.

Padre Carrasco intoned the closing prayer over Carmen's kneeling form and a choir of young boys sweetly sang "Ave Maria." Carmen rose and offered the *abrazo* of peace to her parents, grandparents, and godparents.

The ceremony was at an end, and well-wishers swarmed to greet and congratulate Carmen. Julia accompanied her family and waited patiently for their turn to reach the birthday girl. Pilar had knitted Carmen a beautiful shawl as their gift.

When Julia took Carmen in her arms and hugged the young

girl, Carmen whispered in her ear, "I hope we'll be celebrating your wedding next, Julia . . . to my brother. I've always admired you, and, when you marry David, we will be sisters."

Julia went stiff with shock at Carmen's innocent words. David's earlier offer for her to sit with his family had been serious. Breaking off their embrace, she managed a frozen smile. A huge lump formed in her throat. Her lips moved, and she tried to frame a polite answer but no words came forth.

Smiling shyly, Carmen patted Julia's arm. "I know I shouldn't have said anything to you. David hasn't spoken to you or your parents yet. But I'm so happy today, I want everyone around me to be just as happy!"

"I . . . I understand," Julia croaked.

Julia felt trapped. She didn't want David Treviño to propose to her. If she had known his intention, she wouldn't have come today. She knotted her fingers in the handkerchief she held. It was all so unexpected. She hadn't seen David since the *fandango*. If he was so interested in her, why hadn't he come calling?

She knew he was busy with the freight business, but how could he want to marry someone he barely knew? Even as she tried to deny the possibility that he could be seriously interested in her, she realized such a proposal was not that unusual. She was available and suited to his social standing. That he also seemed to find her attractive was an added benefit. Being with her and getting to know her wasn't important. And love seldom entered into most marriages.

Her parents' marriage, based on love, was the exception. And it was what Julia wanted, too. A marriage based on love . . . not convenience.

Julia didn't love David, and she doubted he loved her. She shuddered at the thought of having to turn down another loveless proposal.

She tried to think of ways to avoid David. She could plead

sickness and have her father take her to the Losoyas' home, where they were staying for the night. But she hated to spoil her parents' fun. They so seldom got away from the vineyard.

Before she could formulate a viable alternative, a strong hand grasped her elbow and spun her around. It was David, and he was smiling at her when he confessed, "Santa María, am I glad the mass is over. Let the *fiesta* begin!"

He turned toward her father and bowed, "*Con permiso*, may I take Julia now? I need to get outside so I can dance with my sister after my father opens the dancing with her. After that, I want to dance with Julia."

"You have my permission," Felipe agreed. "We'll join you shortly."

The sun was setting in tones of deepest coral and mauve when Julia and David left the cathedral. Carmen's father had already begun the traditional opening dance with his daughter. The birthday girl then shared a dance with David and her other two brothers in splendid isolation. All eyes were trained on the lovely young girl in the virginal white dress. After Carmen had danced with her male relatives, the dancing was opened to everyone.

The street was full of people. All of them were eating and drinking, dancing and laughing. Flickering torches lit the *fiesta* and long trundle tables swayed under the weight of platters of food. *Mescale, tequila*, and *cerveza* flowed freely. The Flores family had donated one of their casks of red wine to the festivities.

Julia danced with David and tried to make pleasant conversation. They talked about the vineyard and the Treviño shipping business. David thought shipping their wine to New Orleans was an innovative idea. Julia explained they would be shipping the white wine during the winter months when the weather was more moderate.

Whenever the conversation veered toward personal issues, Julia carefully steered it back to safe topics. When they rested, she made certain they joined a group of people. She undertook every precaution so that David wouldn't have the opportunity to propose.

After an hour or two of cautious maneuvering, Julia began to feel the strain. Her nerves were stretched taut and she felt exhausted from the effort. And David never left her side. He was the perfect gentleman, solicitous of her welfare, urging her to eat and drink.

She drank some fruit punch to quench her thirst, but she wasn't the least bit hungry. All she wanted to do was escape. Despite her lack of appetite, David prevailed upon her to try his mother's special *tamales*.

The *tamales* proved to be very tasty, but Julia's mind wasn't on the food. With her mouth full of *tamale*, she was unable to carry on a conversation. She used the opportunity to search the shifting, shadowed crowd for her parents or the Losoyas. She wanted to leave the *fiesta* and retire to the Losoyas' *casa*. But she couldn't find her parents or their hosts.

She did spot Paco, sitting on the adobe wall in front of the cathedral. Luz stood beside him. They had their heads together, talking and laughing. Julia wondered who was taking care of Conchita, and if Paco might know where her parents were.

Swallowing a mouthful of *tamale*, she started to excuse herself so she could speak with her brother.

Ruíz sauntered into view. He joined Paco and Luz, and the two men chatted for several moments. Ruíz raised his head and looked directly at her. Their gazes snagged and held. Golden glints reflected from the torches dancing in his caramel-colored eyes. He stared pointedly at David's arm encircling her waist. Compressing his mouth into a thin line, he made a mocking bow to her.

Julia recoiled from his thinly veiled insolence. What right did he have to pass judgment on her actions? Fuming, she turned away from Ruíz and faced David.

"These *tamales* are delicious."

"I'm glad you like them. I know my mother would be pleased to share her recipe. Would you care for some more?" David asked.

"Maybe she could eat *tamales* later, David," Ruíz interrupted smoothly. "Right now, she's going to dance with me."

David arched his eyebrows at the unexpected intrusion and turned to Ruíz, greeting him with, *"Buenas noches,* Ruíz. What a pleasant surprise. I was afraid you wouldn't be able to join us."

"I almost didn't—business at the *rancho.*" Ruíz slapped David on the back and said, "But I couldn't miss such an auspicious occasion. *Por favor,* convey my regards to your sister. I spoke with your mother and added my token to Carmen's gifts."

"Sí, gracias, Ruíz," David's voice sounded wary, and he shrugged off Ruíz's hand on his shoulder.

Ruíz let his hand fall and bowed to David, renewing his offer. "I'd like to dance with Julia if I may."

David's tone of voice went from wary to almost hostile, "Ask her." He shrugged again, a shade too elaborately, and said, "It's her decision."

Julia was appalled at Ruíz's high-handed tactics. He hadn't even bothered to ask *her* if she wanted to dance. Despite David saying it was her decision, he still hadn't asked her. Instead, he stood before her with his hands on his hips and his eyes narrowed.

She felt cornered again. How she longed for the quiet solitude of her own bedroom. She was eager to get away from David, but dancing with Ruíz would be like leaping from the frying pan into the fire. And Ruíz's cocksure attitude was grating on her nerves.

Without speaking any words, he offered his arm to her. Julia hesitated. Her mind told her to turn him down, but her body longed for his touch. Tonight had been so trying, and now . . . this. She longed again to leave the *fiesta.*

With that thought in mind, she decided to accept Ruíz's invitation, hoping to spot her parents while they twirled through the street. She linked her arm with Ruíz and nodded. If he wasn't going to speak to her, she didn't have to talk to him, either. She was merely using his invitation to try to locate her parents.

When she glanced at David, she couldn't help but notice how crestfallen he looked. His eyes were cold and his mouth appeared set in stone. He gave Julia and Ruíz a curt nod and stalked off into the crowd.

Julia was furious. Both David and Ruíz were acting like idiots, and bad-mannered idiots at that! She hadn't meant to make David jealous by accepting Ruíz's invitation, but she had. David had no right to feel that way. She had lavished her undivided attention on him all night. Ruíz was just as bad . . . acting as if he owned her. It made her want to scream at both of them.

Instead of screaming, she placed her half-empty plate on a nearby table and moved into Ruíz's waiting arms.

When Ruíz touched her, her fury drained away. She forgot about David's reaction and looking for her parents. The only reality for her existed in Ruíz's strong embrace. She melted against him. Just the touch of him fired her blood, sending sensations sizzling through her body.

Embarrassed by her strong reaction, she closed her eyes and let him spin her about the street. Images played against her closed eyelids, images of them together, clasped intimately, their naked bodies pressed together, flesh against flesh. Trying to eradicate the disturbing scene from her mind, her eyes flew open.

Ruíz was staring at her. His cocoa-colored eyes were opaque, his own thoughts hidden from her. His close scrutiny unnerved her. It was as if he were trying to divine her thoughts, while keeping his own thoughts secret.

Wanting to bridge their tense silence, she murmured, "I saw you with Paco and Luz. Who's watching Conchita?"

"The Losoyas' housekeeper."

"I'm glad. Luz doesn't have many chances to enjoy herself. She and Paco seemed—"

"I didn't ask you to dance to discuss your brother's romantic trysts," Ruíz cut her off. "I wanted to talk with *you.*"

Julia's heart skipped a beat at Ruíz's pointed words. Hope surged within her, only to be checked by the wall she had carefully constructed around her heart. Refusing to rise to the insult of his curt words, she waited for him to speak.

His voice was low and harsh. "Rumor has it that David Treviño is going to ask you to marry him."

"Perhaps." Julia purposely gave him an oblique answer, reveling in this newfound power she wielded over him. Could it be that he cared . . . that he was jealous? Was jealousy the catalyst he needed to admit his feelings? Feelings her mother believed he possessed for her.

"Is that all you have to say?"

She tossed her head. A touch of jealousy was one thing, but Ruíz was fast becoming overbearing. What right did he have to question her if he wasn't ready to commit himself?

"Julia?" He practically growled at her.

"I don't think it's any of your affair, Ruíz, whether David asks me to marry him or not," she shot back.

"Does he *love* you?"

"You have no right to ask that."

Suddenly, in the middle of the street, in the midst of other whirling couples, Ruíz stopped. He grasped her shoulders and gave her a shake. She sensed the curious eyes of their fellow dancers trained on them. When she tried to wrench herself from Ruíz's grasp, he only held her closer.

With a tight smile that seemed to mock himself for creating a scene, he resumed dancing. She stumbled after him, her face flaming. If Ruíz felt embarrassed for drawing attention to their acrimonious confrontation, it didn't deter him from his goal.

"Does he love you, Julia?"

"I don't think so."

"Do you love him?"

"Ruíz, I fail to see—"

"Do you?"

"Of course not." She lowered her voice and cursed him. *"Perdición* take you, Ruíz, for this ugliness."

"It would be even uglier if David married you, only to find you're carrying another man's child," Ruíz struck back. "Or maybe that's your plan, to marry David quickly so he'll never know."

"Oh!" Julia exclaimed. Fury burned within her. It was her turn to abruptly stop their dance, digging her heels into the cobblestones. She raised her hand to strike him, but thought better of fueling the inevitable gossip such a public display would cause. She let her hand drop to her side.

He ignored her aborted attempt to chastise him. Facing her squarely, his eyes glittered a challenge. His voice was a hiss. "Are you with child, Julia?"

Rage battled with shame at his question. Her face must be almost purple, judging from the way she felt. She wished herself a million leagues away . . . anywhere but here, facing Ruíz and his insults. She wished she could hurl words at his head that would wound him as much as he had hurt her. But nothing sufficiently nasty came to mind, nothing but the bleak truth.

"No, Ruíz, I'm not with child."

Ruíz studied her face for a long moment, obviously trying to assess the truth of her statement. She met his eyes bravely. He had known her for all of her life. She wasn't a liar.

He must have reached that same conclusion because he nodded and muttered, "Then I have no further hold on you, Julia."

His eyes clung to hers for a flicker of time, and she thought she detected something there. Something that looked suspiciously akin to regret.

But he turned without another word and left her standing, conspicuously alone among the swirling eddy of the dancers.

Chapter Thirteen

Allende and his five men crept quietly through the *mesquite* thicket, swatting at mosquitos as they advanced. They had tethered their horses at the far side of the thorny woods. The tracks and droppings they followed were fresh. They had left the horses behind so they could get close to their quarry without any unnecessary noise.

The occasional missing stray had increased to seventy head of cattle and ten horses. The rustling had started again, in the far northwest corner of the *rancho*. Don Ruíz had sent Allende with several men to capture the rustlers. For two days, they had been following a trail of churned earth from livestock being driven and half-butchered carcasses of cattle. The rustlers were obviously living off the livestock of the *rancho* as well as stealing it.

All the signs led Allende to believe they were getting close to the rustlers. When they reached the edge of the thicket, he was gratified to see his suspicions confirmed. A stranger stood over a freshly killed calf, gutting it.

The cocking of carbines sounded behind Allende. He held up his hand and whispered, "We won't rush him. Tomás, go back and bring the horses around the southwest corner of the thicket." Pointing to a nearby ravine, he directed, "Hide the horses in that gully until we come for them. The rest of us will wait. I want this one to lead us to the rest of his *amigos.*"

Tomás bobbed his head and faded into the brush.

"There are ways to make him lead us after we catch him," Miguel noted harshly.

"Perhaps, but I say we wait," Allende responded.

The men murmured softly among themselves but settled to wait. The rustler finished butchering the calf, taking only the choicest cuts of meat and leaving the remainder to rot. Such profligate waste sickened Allende.

Sweat trickled between Allende's shoulder blades, and the mosquitos were a constant torment. Each time he twisted away from the blood-sucking insects, he found himself impaled on a *mesquite* thorn. Swearing under his breath, he knew his men were just as uncomfortable. He wished the rustler would finish and move on.

To take his mind off his discomfort, he studied the stranger carefully, storing the memory of his face and form, in case they lost him.

The man was an Anglo of medium height and lanky build. The clothes covering him were little better than rags, and his boots were cracked and riddled with holes. He had sandy-colored hair that might have been even lighter if it weren't so greasy. It hung down in limp strands to his collarless shirt. His face had a low brow and bushy eyebrows. Allende was too far away to see the color of his eyes, but his nose was fleshy and red, in direct contrast to his thin, colorless lips.

Finally, the stranger seemed satisfied with his butchering job. He tied the meat to the back of his mule and mounted a bay mare Allende recognized as belonging to the *rancho.*

When the rustler disappeared over a hill, Allende said, "*Vámonos, amigos,* let's get our horses and follow him."

The men scrambled after him. They found Tomás and the horses waiting in the bottom of the ravine. Within seconds, they were mounted and trailing the rustler. Allende took his time, making his men hang back. The rustler was in no particular hurry. Allende didn't want to overtake him.

Afternoon shadows were lengthening when Allende heard a strange noise coming from beyond the next hill. At first it sounded like the wailing of the wind, but there was no real wind today, just a gentle southerly breeze. When he edged closer to the top of the hill, the sound became stronger and more distinct. Allende cocked his ear toward the noise, listening carefully.

Anglo hymns.

Someone on the other side of the hill was singing church songs. He listened, bewildered. It wasn't exactly what he had expected to hear from a rustler camp.

Allende's eyes swept his men. They had heard the sound, too, and they all had puzzled expressions on their faces. None of them spoke English. Having worked on Anglo ranches, he was the only one who spoke the language.

Shaking his head, he shrugged for the benefit of his men. What could he say? Rustlers singing church songs was mighty peculiar.

When Allende and his men topped the rise, the sound was loud enough for him to make out the words: "Shall we gather at the river, the beautiful, beeeutiful river . . ." Ignoring the singing, his eyes scanned the small valley below. These rustlers were indeed puzzling. Singing hymns without a lookout, and their dwelling built in plain sight.

He scratched his head. This was where the man they had followed had gone. There could be no mistake. Allende recognized the bay mare and mule tethered outside the dwelling, but the camp below didn't look as if it belonged to rustlers.

The dwelling was a lean-to, built against the limestone wall of an overhanging cliff. The lean-to was what could barely be described as shelter, consisting of the trunks of live oak trees lashed upright and with no filler between their twisted trunks. Some of the gaps were at least a handspan wide, and Allende could detect movement inside the hut. The roof was a crude thatch fashioned from prairie grass. A curl of smoke rose from an open hole in the thatch. A tattered quilt served as the door covering.

To the west of the lean-to was a corral, also constructed from live oak trees. Several horses and one or two cows milled about the corral. Grazing in the far end of the valley was a herd of about fifty or sixty cattle. It was obvious they had found the right place. This must be the rustlers' home camp, but the unguarded arrangement didn't make the least bit of sense to Allende.

It was almost as if they were daring someone to catch them.

Allende shrugged again. It was none of his business if the rustlers believed they were safe from justice. His job was to capture them. Since there didn't seem to be a lookout to warn of their approach, he had surprise on his side.

Turning to his men, he instructed them, ''Ready your pistols and carbines. This looks too easy. I just hope it's not a trap. We'll ride down and surround the lean-to. Quickly now.''

Moments later, they pulled up their mounts in front of the hut. A few chickens scratched at the doorway, yet another incongruous sight, but Allende also noticed a large, rock-rimmed pit with several branding irons propped against the rocks. It was the only thing that identified the place as a rustlers' camp.

Motioning for his men to dismount, he swung down, too. He held a pistol, primed and cocked, in each hand. His carbine was also loaded and lashed to his saddle, within arm's reach.

Allende and his men had made no attempt to hide their arrival. The noise of their approach brought out the unkempt man they had tracked. He held a carbine in his hands. It, too, was cocked and pointed straight at Allende's heart.

Not bothering with polite greetings, Allende drove straight to the point, phrasing his question in English. "Do you know you are trespassing?"

The rustler hawked and spat a dirty stream of tobacco juice at Allende's feet, revealing black and rotten teeth. The man's voice was a nasal sneer. "You're the ones trespassing, you dirty greasers."

He stiffened at the man's words, relieved his men didn't understand English. They might react without thinking to the rustler's insult. Allende preferred to handle the situation, if possible, without bloodshed. To that end, he didn't allow the rustler's words to affect him.

"You are mistaken, Señor. This is Don Estéban Estrada's land."

"I ain't no Señor. Name's MacGregor, and this Estrada you're talking about sounds like a dirty greaser, too." MacGregor guffawed loudly, "Ain't you Mexs heard there was a war? We don't want your kind on this side of the border." MacGregor's eyes narrowed, and he spat again. "This here's my land. I earned it in the war."

"And the livestock, Mr. MacGregor, did you also earn it?"

A feral gleam lit MacGregor's watery blue eyes. "No law against rounding up strays. Them's strays I got."

Allende jerked his head in the direction of the fire pit and asked, "Strays with brands? What about the calf you butchered a few miles back? Was that a stray, too?"

MacGregor's hands tightened on his carbine. He raised his voice and declared, "It were a stray 'cause I says so. No one in authority is gonna take a spic's word over a white man's."

"Can you prove you own this land?"

MacGregor's eyes darted from Allende to his men and back again. They all had their firearms pointed at him. After a moment of studying the odds ranged against him, he appeared to shrink in the face of their numbers.

His nasal voice flattened into a whine. "Can't parlay with so many guns stuck in my face. If you'll lower yer guns, I'll get the paper to prove it's my land."

"No," Allende countered, "stay here where I can see you. Have someone bring out the paper." Switching to Spanish, he said, "*Caballeros,* lower your weapons." There was a murmur of resistance, but without turning to look, he knew the men had followed his orders.

"Obadiah, fetch me that paper, son. The one about the land that we got from that feller," MacGregor called out.

And then everything exploded. MacGregor dived for the doorway, shooting his carbine, using up his one bullet. Allende felt the impact in his left shoulder, but there was no pain as he rushed the lean-to.

"Ma, toss me that loaded pistol!" MacGregor screamed. "Boy, git yer firearms and back me up."

Allende didn't stop to consider the danger. MacGregor had already shot him. Rage and instinct took over. He hit the dirt floor of the lean-to and fired point blank into MacGregor's chest before the man could aim the loaded pistol.

MacGregor dropped to the ground, the crimson stain of his blood blossoming on his chest. Allende's men rushed in behind him. The red haze of Allende's killing rage drained away as the other occupants of the lean-to voluntarily dropped their weapons. The other occupants, "Ma" and the "boys," were just that—a wizened, white-haired woman with six male children of varying ages standing around her.

Ignoring his throbbing shoulder, he blinked his eyes. Instead of uncovering a nest of hard-bitten rustlers, he had found a family. The man he had shot must have been their husband and father. Suddenly, the unusual camp made sense . . . a twisted sort of sense.

Allende shook his head. How could a man, even a man like

MacGregor, involve his family in such a dangerous undertaking? Wanting to avert any further bloodshed, he cautioned his men, *"Amigos,* stay alert but holster your weapons."

The small woman threw herself onto MacGregor's lifeless form, weeping loudly. The boys stood by helplessly. Huddled in a corner were four girls of different ages. The oldest girl was holding a baby in her arms. The children, like their mother and father, were dressed in rags. Their frightened eyes peered at Allende from faces covered in grime mixed with the livid hues of multi-colored bruises. All of the children were skinny with protruding bellies. Allende knew what that meant. They had been starving until they started feasting on Estrada beef.

A wave of nausea washed over him, and he wasn't certain whether it was due to his wound or the unwanted memories crowding his mind. Orphaned at an early age, he knew what it felt like to starve. Thinking about it made him feel faint. He didn't want to remember; it was too painful. Instead, he concentrated on the situation at hand.

"Tomás, help me with my shoulder. Then we need to get to the bottom of this."

Untying the kerchief at his throat, Tomás fashioned a make-shift bandage, murmuring, "I don't think I can stop the bleeding, but I can slow it some. You'll need to see a *curandera.*"

"Gracias, Tomás, but the *curandera* will have to wait. We've unfinished business."

Returning his attention to the family before him, Allende noticed Señora MacGregor had stopped weeping. She sat on her heels, beside her dead husband, her hands clasped in prayer. The woman sported a livid yellow-and-purple bruise that ran from her prominent cheekbone to her jaw.

Allende recognized physical abuse as readily as he did starvation. All of the children, with the exception of the oldest boy and the baby, carried the evidence of their father's brutality.

Even realizing the kind of man he had killed, Allende couldn't ignore the burning guilt he felt. He had never killed a man before. The killing had been instinctual, blind self-preservation, but that knowledge didn't erase the guilt . . . or his responsibility to the MacGregor family.

Speaking slowly in English, he said, "Mrs. MacGregor, I'm sorry for what I had to do. I know it's a bad time, but could you answer some questions for me?"

The tallest boy stepped between his mother and Allende, speaking up, "Mister, Ma don't talk much. She's been knocked around some. She sings hymns like an angel and she prays, but Ma don't talk much."

"I understand."

"My name's Obadiah. I'm sixteen and the oldest. I can answer your questions."

"Thank you, Obadiah. I . . . I don't know what to say about your father. He shot first, and I didn't expect to find one man and a family. I thought I was going up against several men."

"Pa was mean, 'specially when he was liquored up. I don't think we'll miss him much. Doc done told Ma she would die if'n she had another kid, but Pa couldn't keep clear. We could've backed Pa up like he asked, but we didn't want to." Obadiah's light blue eyes stared guilelessly at Allende when he repeated, "We won't miss Pa much."

Allende shuddered at the boy's chilling reassurance that he had done the family a favor by killing MacGregor. The admission didn't alleviate Allende's remorse over the unnecessary killing, but it did make him realize what a nightmare their lives must have been. Although he felt a bone-deep sympathy for the remaining MacGregors, he still had a job to do for Don Ruíz. And he still needed answers.

"Obadiah, what brought your family here?"

"We lost our farm in East Texas, and Pa met a man in a saloon. The man gave him this." Obadiah handed Allende a greasy, creased piece of paper. "It was what Pa was calling for when he gunned you."

He stared at the paper. It was written in what must be English with an official-looking seal stamped on it. He could speak English, but he couldn't read the language. He was just learning how to read and write Spanish. He would keep the paper and show it to Don Ruíz.

"Obadiah, I'll need to keep this for my boss."

The boy shrugged. "I don't guess we'd want to stay now, anyway."

"But why did you come here in the first place?"

"The man Pa met said that paper gave us this land. That's all I know. I can't read neither, mister."

"The livestock, Obadiah, what about the cattle and horses your pa stole?"

"Pa hated . . . ah, begging your pardon, Mex's. He believed that 'cause we won the war, he had a right to the animals. When Pa was liquored up, he even bragged that the man who gave him the paper also gave him money to take the livestock." The boy shrugged again and said, "But I never knew whether to believe Pa when he was drinking."

"I see."

But Allende didn't see. He couldn't begin to understand the boy's story. It was too fantastic. A mysterious man had given MacGregor a paper and money so MacGregor could help himself to Estrada land and livestock? It just didn't make sense. And MacGregor must have been an idiot to believe he could get away with it.

"Wasn't your father afraid he might get caught?"

"Mister, I don't want to rile you none but . . . that is, Pa didn't think you Mex's would dare. He said the law would . . ."

"There's no law out here, Obadiah."

The boy dropped his head and stared at his bare feet. "I know, mister. I think that's why Pa kinda got scared and shot you."

He nodded and gazed around the pitiful shelter. The dirt floor was pockmarked, and because there wasn't a proper chimney, just a hole in the thatched roof, the hut was half full of smoke. There wasn't a stick of furniture in the place, just some filthy blankets thrown on the ground. One corner was stacked high with corn liquor jugs. If there really had been a man who gave MacGregor money, Allende suspected it had gone to purchase the stash of corn liquor.

If the brutal surroundings weren't enough to wrench his heart, the vacant-eyed stares of the children were enough to turn his guts inside out. The fate of this family hung in the balance . . . dependent upon his decision.

His eyes flicked to MacGregor's wife. She had remained in the same posture, kneeling and praying over her husband's stiffening body. The woman's skeletal face was creased and furrowed with deep lines. She looked to be at least sixty years old.

"How old is your mother, Obadiah?"

The boy appeared to be startled by the personal question. He scratched his head.

"I don't rightly know, mister. Never did learn my figgers right." Counting out loud on his fingers, he stopped after he had counted his fingers three times, answering, "About that old, I reckon."

Allende shuddered again. The woman was probably in her early thirties. He knew what having large families could do to a woman, but he had never seen anything like this before. He vowed to himself Teresa wouldn't suffer the same fate as Señora MacGregor. He would find some way to limit the size of their family.

Just thinking about Teresa and how much he loved her had a calming effect on him. For the first time since he had entered the lean-to, his mind seemed to be working clearly. He made his decision.

"Obadiah, do you know enough about herding cattle to move those cows in the valley?"

The boy blinked hard and his eyes narrowed. He licked his lips and appeared to be afraid to answer the question.

With the calmness he now felt came the realization of how fast he was weakening. His shoulder was still seeping blood. He had to get the situation settled once and for all.

"Just get behind the cattle and push them in the direction you want to go. The bay mare your father was riding is a good cow pony. You can string the extra horses together with rope hackamores and lead them." Allende nodded at two of the older boys and said, "Your brothers could help."

Obadiah's eyes widened and his voice filled with awe, "You're letting us go, mister?"

"Yes."

"And you want us to take the animals with us?"

"Yes."

The boy sucked in his breath and gulped. His brow was creased in obvious concentration as he turned the startling information over in his mind. "Where would we go, mister?"

Allende considered quickly. For a long time he had had his eye on a prime parcel of land that was still unclaimed. This family needed the land far more than he did.

"Head southwest until you come to the Guadalupe River, turn west and follow the river. You'll come to a creek after . . . how do you call them . . ."

"Miles?" the boy supplied.

"Yes, that's it. After about ten miles, you'll come to a creek. That's Mustang Creek. Follow it north to the source, an underground spring feeds it. There's a real nice valley there. No one owns it."

Obadiah raised his hands above his head and whooped for joy, dancing a jig. Flinging himself to the ground, he grabbed his mother and rocked her in his arms.

"Did you hear that, Ma? He's letting us go, and with the cows and horses and even our own piece of land. I'll work real hard and build us a good cabin, Ma. It'll be warm in the winter with a real chimney. I promise."

Señora MacGregor's eyelids fluttered, and she ceased praying, but her eyes were still staring . . . vacant and empty. Allende doubted she understood. Obadiah's mother had obviously escaped to a place, long ago, where nothing else could harm her. But her son's enthusiasm must have struck some buried chord of response deep within her, because she patted Obadiah's face and murmured, "Good boy, Obadiah, good son."

Obadiah gave his mother one final squeeze and leapt to his feet. He stared at Allende and then dropped his eyes.

"I don't know how to rightly thank you, mister . . . I don't even know your name."

Allende managed a stiff smile. He had done what he thought best, given the circumstances. But he didn't want the MacGregors to know his name . . . for a variety of reasons.

"My name's not important, and I don't need to be thanked. It's the least I can do. We can't stay and help you, not even to bury your father. You'll need to do that yourself. And there are two other conditions: take good care of your family and be off Estrada land by sundown tomorrow. If you linger, there could be trouble."

"Yes, sir! We'll be gone. And we'll do fine. I just know it."

Allende wished he shared the boy's unbridled enthusiasm, but he was well aware of the privations and hardships this sixteen-year-old would need to endure to make a home for his family. At least he had given Obadiah a start.

"Then I'll leave you to it." He had an overpowering urge to take Obadiah in his arms or at least shake his hand, but he held back. He had killed the boy's father . . . nothing would change that.

Turning to his men, he spoke in Spanish. "It's finished. We'll go now."

As they filed from the crude shelter, Obadiah's voice followed them, reaching past prejudice, saluting them in their own language. *"Gracias, mis amigos."*

Later, when they stopped to water their mounts, Allende

explained his actions to the bewildered men. Because they spoke no English, his men hadn't understood why they had abandoned the stolen livestock.

Assuring them he would take full responsibility, he admitted Don Estéban would probably skin him alive when he found out. But he believed Don Ruíz would understand his reasons. But whether Don Ruíz understood or not didn't matter.

He couldn't have done anything else.

The long, dry summer ended abruptly. The first chill of autumn came and, with it, rain. But not a gentle rain. The sky opened up and poured buckets for days on end. Ruíz knew the rain was good for the *rancho*. It would strengthen the winter forage for the herds. But the same rain could ruin the ripening grapes at Los Montes Verdes.

After six days of solid rain, Ruíz couldn't wait any longer to see how the vineyard was faring. He donned his thickest *poncho* and his widest leather *sombrero*.

The grapes would be ready to harvest soon, but the continuing rain posed a serious threat to the crop. At this stage of the grapes' maturation, too much rain would cause mold. Mold could ruin this year's crop.

Galloping over the hills on Oro's back provided Ruíz with the leisure to ponder some perplexing matters. He had been surprised by Allende's tale of the MacGregors. The story was so bizarre. He had examined the paper Allende brought back and found it was Republic of Texas scrip awarding the Mac-Gregors two hundred and forty acres of Estrada land. But when he showed the scrip to his friend and attorney, Peter Meredith, Peter declared it to be counterfeit.

Ruíz shook his head, sending the accumulated water on his *sombrero* flying. If the son of MacGregor had spoken the truth, who would have initiated such an elaborate scheme just to rustle from Don Estéban's *rancho?* And why would someone involve a family instead of a group of men?

None of it made any sense, except what Allende had done to help the MacGregors.

After hearing Allende's description of MacGregor's wife and children, Ruíz would have done the same thing. Allende had offered to pay for the livestock, over time, from his wages but Ruíz refused him.

And for the first time in his association with Don Estéban, Ruíz had kept the truth from him. Don Estéban was very ill, and Allende's actions would have enraged him, further endangering the older man's health. To even hint to Don Estéban that someone might have purposely engineered the rustling on his *rancho* would worry the dying man needlessly. Ruíz hated being less than honest with him, but he couldn't see the value of upsetting the dying man.

His father-in-law already had plenty on his mind. Don Estéban never stopped worrying about the land grant work Peter was doing for the *rancho.* It had become almost an obsession with the older man, and Ruíz feared the constant strain was worsening Don Estéban's illness.

Peter's petitions had, so far, gone nowhere. The new government of Tejas was still in disarray and the land office, which would oversee all new as well as old surveys in question, wasn't open yet. Don Estéban fretted daily about the legal stalemate, obviously wanting to know the *rancho* would survive intact after his death.

With the burdens of the *rancho,* Don Estéban's advancing illness, and this new concern for the vineyard, Ruíz felt weary from all of his responsibilities. When he felt weary, he let his guard down . . . and when he let his guard down, his thoughts inevitably turned to Julia.

Although he had been home several times to see Conchita since the night of Carmen Treviño's *quinceanera,* he hadn't seen Julia. He had surmised she was purposely avoiding him, and he couldn't blame her. He had hurt her that night . . . and he hadn't meant to.

He didn't understand why he had acted the way he had. He had thought he didn't want to marry her, but it was a sad testimony to his confused feelings that he didn't want anyone else to marry her, either.

When he had heard the rumors about Julia and Treviño and then seen them together, blind jealousy had taken over and he had lashed out at Julia. He hadn't heard any new rumors, but he expected Julia would marry Treviño when David returned with his freight wagons from New Orleans.

With that disturbing thought troubling his mind, Ruíz didn't realize how far he had come. Oro knew the way home without guidance. When he glanced up, through the driving rain, the hacienda compound loomed in front of him. There was a group of men standing, hunch-shouldered against the downpour, just outside the gate.

Guiding Oro to the knot of rain-drenched men, he recognized Felipe and several of the workers. There were other faces he didn't recognize. Felipe was issuing orders and dividing the men into work details.

Ruíz slid from his wet saddle and held out his hand in greeting. *"Buenas tardes,* Felipe. I came as soon as I could. We needed rain, but not this much," he observed wryly.

"My same thought, Señor Ruíz. I'm glad you came. I would like to explain what we're doing and see what you think."

Ruíz nodded. Felipe was very capable, but Ruíz realized the new responsibility of primary ownership of the vineyard still made Felipe uneasy. He felt better when Ruíz agreed with his decisions.

"I've got men cutting back all the leaves surrounding the grapes so when the sun does return, the grapes will dry quickly. And I have other men digging trenches from the vines to carry off the water so it doesn't pool at the roots. I don't want any of the vines sitting in standing water."

Ruíz clapped Felipe on the back and said, "That's exactly what I would have done. Short of a miracle that would stop the rain, we can do no more."

"I'm glad you approve . . . er, agree, Señor Ruíz. In order to cover the entire vineyard quickly, I had to hire extra, temporary workers. It is an added expense you should be aware of."

Ruíz remembered the unfamiliar faces he had noticed when he first rode up. They must have been the temporary workers. The welfare of the entire crop hung in the balance, and Felipe was usually frugal. Ruíz knew Felipe wouldn't have hired the extra men unless it was absolutely necessary.

"I understand about the additional expense, but I feel we should do everything possible to save the crop."

"I had hoped you would see it that way."

"You're the boss now, Felipe," Ruíz reminded him.

Felipe ducked his head, sending a curtain of rain spilling to the ground from the brim of his hat. He appeared to be embarrassed when he muttered, "I know I'm the boss, but it's taking some time to accustom myself." The corners of his mouth quirked up when he said, "Old habits die hard."

"*Sí.*"

"*Vengase,* Señor Ruíz, let's go inside. We're both drenched, and Pilar will have a hot pot of coffee waiting. You can dry out and visit with your daughter."

"*Gracias,* Felipe, but I want to see the progress you've made in the vineyard. I'll be in later. I would appreciate it if you would see that Oro is rubbed down and put in the stable." Ruíz handed the reins to Felipe.

Felipe accepted the stallion's reins and replied, "I'll make certain the stableboy rubs him dry and feeds him."

"*Muy bien.*"

"We'll wait supper for you. Julia is working in the vineyard, too. We couldn't stop her, although her mother worries she will take ill in the rain."

It was the first time Felipe had spoken of his daughter in Ruíz's presence since Julia had refused his proposal.

"I'll look for Julia. We'll come into supper together."

Felipe nodded and led Oro inside the hacienda compound.

He had tried to sound confident about bringing Julia to supper with him, but he knew there was a good chance he would fail. If he knew Julia, she would curse him and refuse to be seated at the same table.

Unfortunately, he couldn't blame her.

Chapter Fourteen

Looking for Julia in the downpour proved to be a difficult task. The workers were scattered throughout the vineyard, dressed in wide *sombreros* and shapeless, heavy *ponchos*. Most of them were bent double, digging trenches or snipping leaves from the vines.

Ranging through the vineyard, Ruíz checked the work in progress. Felipe's foresight to bring in extra workers was evident in the work that had already been accomplished. One-third of the vineyard had been drained and stripped of excess leaves. When he had made one complete tour, he gave up looking for Julia. Short of stopping and asking each worker their name, he didn't know how he would recognize her.

Ruíz found an extra shovel and joined a group of workers who were digging a long primary trench through one section of the vines to carry the run-off water from the smaller trenches. As he bent to his task, he tried to remember what it felt like to be dry. Despite his heavy *poncho,* he was soaked to the skin and rain had managed to seep into his boots, making him feel as if he were standing in a puddle of water.

Even though the first chill of autumn had dissipated after the rains came, it was thoroughly disagreeable and uncomfortable to be laboring in the constant downpour. He glanced at the leaden, dull gray sky. There was no sign of a let-up. He bent to his task again. Miserable, wet hours passed as the long afternoon wore on. He could readily understand Pilar's concern for her daughter. He hoped Julia had returned home.

Stepping backward, he drug his shovel through the muck, widening the trench he was working on. Because he wasn't watching where he was going, he bumped into another worker who was stripping the grape leaves.

"Perdóneme," he excused himself, and grabbed for the tottering worker before he fell face over in the mud. Steadying the worker, he was greeted by a loud sneeze. With his hands on the worker's shoulders, a current of awareness snaked through him. Staring closely at the partially obscured face, he recognized her.

"Julia!"

"Sí," she responded, and sneezed again.

Ruíz reached under his *poncho* and retrieved a sodden lump of cloth. It had originally been a handkerchief. Muttering under his breath about the damned rain, he returned the handkerchief to his pocket and shrugged.

"No help there, Julia, it's wet through."

She nodded and wiped her nose with an equally soaked corner of her *poncho*. When she tilted her head back, Ruíz noticed her dull eyes and red nose. Tentatively, he reached out and brushed his fingertips across her cheek. It was as he feared. Her skin was hot beneath the slick coating of rain.

"Madre de Dios, Julia. You're burning with a fever. I'm taking you home."

Julia gazed at him, but the brilliant emerald fire of her eyes was banked. They were glazed and lifeless. Handing his shovel to one of the other workers, he grasped her arm.

"*Vengase,* Julia."

She made a feeble gesture to pull free from him and muttered in a hoarse, cracked voice, "There's so much to be done, Ruíz. I'll go in at nightfall."

"You'll go *now.*"

Their eyes locked. Silently, their wills battled.

Brushing back a wet tendril of hair, she sighed. "You're right, Ruíz. I'll go, but I dread what *Mamá* will say. She warned me I'd get sick."

"Too late for regrets now. How long have you been working out here."

"This is the third day."

"When did you start feeling sick?"

"Just this morning."

"But you came out anyway?"

"*Sí.*"

She hasn't changed, Ruíz thought. *Same stubborn woman.*

Foregoing further discussion, he concentrated on getting them across the swampy vineyard, riddled with run-off trenches. She was doing her best to follow him, but after she stumbled for the fifth or sixth time, he stopped and lifted her into his arms.

Pushing her fists against his chest, she protested, "Ruíz, I can walk. You just need to be patient. I'm not accustomed to these boots."

He snorted. "Not used to your boots, that's a fine excuse, Julia. You're as weak as a kitten."

"Put me down, Ruíz," Julia demanded.

"No. Why are you so stubborn?"

She closed her eyes and shook her head. The ghost of a smile flitted across her face.

"I don't know, Ruíz. Forgive me, I realize you're only trying to help. I'll try not to be so stubborn." As if to verify her words, she relaxed against him and laced her arms around his neck.

He stifled a gasp. Her sweet capitulation and the soft bundle of her body affected him instantly. Beneath his soaked *poncho*, his manhood throbbed painfully. A warm coil started within him, banishing the rain-drenched chill.

Julia felt so good in his arms.

Silence stretched between them, filled by the thundering cascade of rain. While Ruíz threaded his way through the vines, their silence was pervaded by a heated awareness of each other, wrapping them together in a cocoon of warmth against the driving rain.

Even as he reveled in the sweet, silent communication of their flesh, he knew he owed her a spoken apology. With the vineyard behind him and the hacienda compound looming, he swallowed the bitter pill of his pride.

"Julia, I want to apologize for my behavior at the *quinceanera*. I had no right to interfere in your life. What I said to you was unforgivable. It shouldn't have—"

"Happened," she finished for him. "Why do you always say that, Ruíz? Why do you deny the existence of our feelings for each other?"

"I don't deny them, Julia." He detected the note of defensiveness in his own voice. "It's not the feelings . . . it's the behavior that—"

"But it really comes back to feelings, Ruíz," she interrupted him. "You're afraid of them because feelings are messy, and they cause scenes and make you do things you regret later. Isn't that it?"

"I suppose so," he admitted. Was he really afraid of his feelings? It was disturbing to think so. What kind of a coward did that make him?

She snuggled closer in his arms. "Feelings don't go away, Ruíz, no matter how you ignore or fear them. Believe me, I know.'' And as if in answer to the question he hadn't dared to ask, she added, ''I'm not going to marry David Treviño.''

After a few days of her mother's expert care, Julia's fever abated and her strength slowly returned. The rains had stopped, and the majority of the grape crop was untouched by mold. She was proud of her father and his timely efforts to save the vineyard.

But it wasn't her father that occupied Julia's thoughts while she was forced to remain in bed . . . it was Ruíz.

She vividly remembered the feel of his strong arms around her when he had carried her from the vineyard. Even if she had tried to forget, his presence would have reminded her. He stopped by to see her each day while she was convalescing.

Julia was surprised by his uncommon solicitude, and she wondered if he was still feeling guilty for the way he had treated her at Carmen Treviño's *quinceanera*. But she didn't ask.

Their conversations were guarded. They kept to careful subjects like the vineyard or the upcoming harvest. Their mutual attraction still sizzled between them, but its fires were carefully controlled. Their tumultuous relationship had become muted, played in a minor key. It was almost as if they'd returned to the innocence of their youth, talking and even laughing together with an ease she marveled at.

A subtle shift seemed to be taking place between them. A shift that filled Julia with spring-green hope again.

Ruíz seemed intent on exploring his feelings for her.

Ruíz paced the floor of his study. His stomach was tied in knots, and perspiration coated his brow, no matter how many times he wiped it dry. He felt like a callow youth, waiting to be with his first woman.

He had accepted Julia's implicit challenge and begun to explore what he really felt for her. Over the past few days, he had visited and talked with her, studying her reactions covertly. At the same time, he had been careful to keep his physical attraction for her in check because he didn't want it to cloud his judgment.

What he found had surprised him. He discovered the old Julia of his childhood. Despite her illness, her inherent vibrancy drew him to her like a moth to a flame. He enjoyed just being with her, talking and teasing, and sharing everyday concerns. She remained a strong-willed woman with firm opinions about most things, but he began to realize that her strength was tempered by fairness . . . and a loving heart.

How could he have forgotten what she was really like?

That was why their meeting today was so important. Felipe had taken a stand with regard to the harvest. Ruíz didn't agree with him, but Felipe was the boss now. Ruíz wouldn't try to overrule him, but he wanted to go over the figures with Julia and see what she thought.

Would she automatically side with her father or would she give his opinion fair consideration? He realized that, in some ways, it was a test of sorts and that it was probably a low tactic on his part. But he needed to know how she would react.

To make matters worse, he would be alone with her in the room where they had first made love. He had considered meeting with her somewhere else, but moving the meeting would have been awkward. His old study, in the deserted hacienda, contained all the records and ledgers for Los Montes Verdes.

When he had deeded the controlling interest to Felipe, Ruíz had asked him if he wanted to take the records to his home. Felipe had responded that he didn't have room in his *casa*. They had agreed the records would remain at the hacienda for the time being.

Ruíz heard Julia's footsteps echoing in the hallway before she appeared on the threshold.

Turning, he greeted her. *"Buenos días,* Julia. You're looking much better today." Even as he said the courteous words, he was aware of the changes that the illness had wrought upon her. The gray muslin dress hung on her frame, and her skin was pale. Her moss-green eyes appeared huge in her thin face.

He offered her a chair, murmuring, *"Por favor,* be seated. You mustn't squander your strength."

"Gracias, Ruíz. I do feel better, but I won't refuse a chair." She sat in the chair he held for her.

"Would you like some coffee or cocoa? I can ring José to bring us some."

"No, *gracias,* I've just had breakfast."

Ruíz cleared his throat. He felt incredibly tense, almost as if he were afraid to know how Julia would react. As if it would crush him to learn that she sided with her father. He silently chided himself. He was putting too much significance on her opinion. After all, it wasn't that important, he tried to tell himself.

But as tense as he felt, Julia appeared relaxed, sitting in the deep leather armchair with her legs crossed at the ankles. Her voice broke through his hesitation. "Should we start?"

"Of course." Ruíz leaned across the desk and picked up one of the heavy ledgers. Pulling another armchair next to hers, he balanced the ledger across the two adjoined arms of their chairs. Slipping underneath the open ledger, he seated himself, shoulder to shoulder with Julia.

It was the closest he had been to her since carrying her home from the vineyard. He caught the faintest trace of her gardenia perfume.

The scent haunted him, making him forget what he had set out to do. Instead, a vision of ebony tresses against naked golden skin assaulted him. Her perfect nude body lying on the crimson-and-indigo pattern of the very rug where they were sitting overwhelmed him.

Shutting his eyes, he breathed deeply and struggled for self-control. He was absurdly grateful that the open ledger hid his lap.

"Show me, Ruíz." Her voice was as soft as a caress.

With an effort of will, he held his hand steady as his finger skimmed a column of figures, coming to rest at the bottom of the page.

"This column shows the amount of cash for each item we'll need to harvest this year's crop. The bottom figure is the projected total expenditure for the harvest." Then he pointed to another figure on the next page and said, "This is the reserve we set aside for the harvest expenses. If you compare the two figures, you'll see we have more than enough to cover costs."

Next, he turned several pages and showed her yet another set of figures. "This is what the extra workers cost us to save the crop from the rain." His finger moved to another line and he explained, "This is the total expenditure for nine days of wages for the extra workers."

He lifted his head and their eyes met.

Julia nodded and said, "*Sí,* I'm following you."

"Do you agree with these figures?"

Julia's mouth curved into a smile. "Of course, they're mine, with the exception of the reserve. I believe you and my father mutually arrived at that figure."

"With input from you."

She nodded again and confirmed, "With my help."

"So you stand by these numbers?"

She laughed out loud, and her emerald eyes regained some of their old sparkle. The tone of her voice was teasing when she said, "I keep perfect books. You know that, Ruíz."

"*Sí,* you do."

She slanted her gaze at him, looking up provocatively from the corner of her eyes. Her head was tilted and her lips were parted. It took every last shred of his willpower to keep from kissing her.

Was she toying with him?

But it was Julia who diffused the intensity of the moment by lowering her head and returning her gaze to the open ledger.

"Since we've established that my bookkeeping is above reproach, what do you want to know?"

"It's not exactly something I want to *know*. I need your opinion."

"*¿Sí?*"

He took a deep breath. He had prepared the groundwork; there was nothing left to do but see what Julia thought.

"I want to keep the extra workers for the harvest. I believe we can afford them, and they would serve as a buffer if some of our workers fall sick. The ground is muddy, and several of our workers are still weak from the colds they caught . . . like you." He hesitated, purposely keeping his eyes from meeting hers. "What do you think?"

"I think your idea has merit. The cost should be minimal, and all of the temporary men are hard workers."

Ruíz released his breath slowly. It wasn't until that moment he realized he had been holding it, waiting for Julia's answer.

"I'm glad you agree with my idea. The only problem is, your father doesn't agree. He believes we shouldn't keep the extra workers because of the additional cost."

Julia lifted her head and their gazes snagged. He saw the swift knowledge in the depths of her eyes. If he thought to set her a test without her realizing it, he had sadly underestimated her intelligence and perceptiveness.

Silently, he cursed himself. Now he would never know how she really felt. She was bound to react bitterly to what she perceived as a manipulation of her.

But her next words were not what he had expected. They caught him completely off guard.

"Have you written your mother to tell her that you deeded the controlling interest of Los Montes Verdes to our family?"

Ruíz hesitated. Julia had recognized his test. Was she, in turn, testing him? After a moment's consideration, he knew it didn't matter. He was through with playing games. He'd been foolish to start. How could he have underestimated her?

"*Sí,* I wrote my mother weeks past. I wanted her to know of my decision and the reasons for it."

"And have you received a response from her?"

He nodded. "She wasn't happy with what I did. She said I was foolish and an ingrate . . . among other things. But considering how my mother is, she wasn't as upset as I had expected her to be. Her primary concern was that she would continue to receive her allowance. Since I had deeded away a portion of my interest in the vineyard, she cautioned me to spend even more of my energies on the Estrada *rancho.*" Ruíz shrugged.

"My mother has always thought my future was with the *rancho.* He paused and glanced away, confessing, "There was a time when I almost agreed with her, but you've helped to convince me differently, Julia. Los Montes Verdes will always be home . . . a part of me. The *rancho* belongs to Don Estéban's son and, through her mother, to Conchita. I'm only a caretaker."

"Feeling that way, it must have been difficult for you to deed the controlling interest of the vineyard to my father." She placed her hand over his, as if to comfort him.

"Not really. As I told you before, it was the honorable thing to do. And it neutralized my mother's power without hurting her interests. She hasn't mentioned selling her portion since I told her what I did."

Julia squeezed his hand. "As always, Ruíz, you've done your duty, putting everyone's needs above your own."

Ruíz studied her. Was she mocking him or did she really believe what she had said? Her expression was guileless, her dark-green eyes filled with concern. He had an overwhelming urge to take her into his arms.

"There was a time you made me feel as if *duty* was a dirty word."

Her face clouded, and she looked away. "There are some

things that should be done from a sense of duty . . . then there are other things that should only answer to your heart."

He wished he could sink into the floor. Why had he felt compelled to bring up the time he had rejected her love and obviously hurt her? He could kick himself for reminding her.

"I agree with you, Ruíz. We should keep the extra workers," she declared simply. "And I don't just agree in theory. I've always wanted what is best for Los Montes Verdes. You won't need to convince my father if you don't want to. I'll be glad to explain the figures and show him the wisdom of your idea."

The crush of people in Madame Plaisance's "parlor" was ferocious. A typical Saturday night, Lázaro thought, already bored from mixing with the customers. It was one of his little "chores," being in attendance on Saturday nights. When he became sole owner of the bordello, it was one of the first things he would change. There were much more interesting ways to spend his time, and he disliked the faint condescension most customers exhibited.

The customers were all hypocrites. They didn't mind frequenting such an establishment, but they seemed to feel superior to anyone who owned a "sporting" house.

Lázaro raised a glass of absinthe to his lips while scanning the crowd for someone of consequence to approach. His gaze snagged on a familiar face in the crowd. But the man who was standing next to the baby grand piano wasn't someone that he recognized from New Orleans. It was a face from home, David Treviño of San Antonio.

Maybe the evening wouldn't be a total loss after all, he thought. Any news he could glean about home might prove helpful with his plans.

Moving purposefully through the crowd, he approached Treviño and greeted him with an expansiveness he didn't feel.

"Mi amigo, David, it's good to see you here. *Bienvenida.* When did you get to New Orleans?" Lázaro held out his hand.

Treviño turned to face him. His eyes were narrowed and filled with an unspoken question, but he took Lázaro's hand and shook it. Several seconds ticked by as Treviño studied his face before his expression cleared. The light of recognition filled his eyes, only to be swiftly followed by a hint of distaste.

"Lázaro Estrada?"

"Sí." He bowed and murmured, "At your service, David."

He ignored Treviño's lukewarm greeting, realizing his youthful escapades had been frowned upon by the good citizens of San Antonio. He didn't care what they thought of him. They were all a bunch of backward dullards, living on the fringes of civilization.

Once he had the treasure in his possession, he planned to distance himself from the bordello and invest in "reputable" businesses. Then he would take his rightful place in the world, amidst the elite society of New Orleans, not a backwater town like San Antonio. No one would ever condescend to Lázaro Estrada again.

"You've been gone from home for a long time, Lázaro. Everyone wondered where you had settled. Do you live in New Orleans?" Treviño asked.

"Sí." He flashed his most winning smile and swept the room with his hand, declaring, "I'm part owner of this establishment. *Mi casa es su casa.* Let me personally take care of you, *mi amigo."*

Treviño's eyes widened at his declaration. His old childhood "friend" silently assessed the opulent room. When he returned his attention to Lázaro, he said, "You've done well, Lázaro. Very well indeed."

"Gracias, David, for your kind words, but I've been remiss as your host. I see that your glass is empty, *mi amigo.* What were you drinking?"

"Brandy."

Nodding, he snapped his fingers at his *mayordomo,* who was hovering nearby, instructing, "Pierre, bring my special guest our very best French brandy, compliments of the house."

Minutes later, Treviño's glass was refilled, and he regaled his "old friend" with bawdy stories about the "sporting" life. Under his careful flattery, Treviño's eyes lost their wary look, and he relaxed with his brandy.

David was obviously enjoying the titillating conversation, laughing out loud at Lázaro's jokes and anecdotes. After the third glass of brandy, he became expansive, bragging about his family's successful freight business.

Lázaro finished his one glass of absinthe while he listened attentively. Treviño paused and gulped the remainder of the brandy in his glass. His head came up, and he stared owlishly about him, expecting his glass to be refilled immediately. Lázaro obliged him, catching Pierre's watchful eye with the flick of a hand. Pierre, solicitous of his employer, also refilled his glass with absinthe.

Feeling the moment was ripe and that Treviño was sufficiently befuddled, he raised his glass and suggested, "A toast, *mi amigo,* to old friends and the beautiful city of San Antonio."

With an unsteady hand, Treviño clinked glasses with him and repeated, *"Por los amigos viejos y San Antonio."*

After their toast, David, who had evidently run low on conversation, sipped his drink and stared about the room. His glazed eyes rested with lascivious intent upon several of the whores.

"Speaking of San Antonio, what's the news from home?" Lázaro asked casually.

Swiveling his head, Treviño blinked at him. His voice was a slur, *"¿Qué?"* He narrowed his eyes, obviously trying to comprehend Lázaro's question through the fog of his inebriation.

"News from home? Is there any?" Lázaro prompted.

"Oh, ah, *sí.*" Realization dawned and a shadow passed over

Treviño's slack face. "Of course, your father . . . but you must know about your father. I was . . . ah . . . sorry to hear he was so ill. Will you be going home?"

"Probably." He already knew his father was gravely ill. He had hoped Treviño might have some other news to impart. "Anything else interesting?"

"Let's see." David frowned and wagged his head. After a moment, his head jerked up, bobbing loosely like a puppet's, as a thought occurred to him.

"Your sister was married to Ruíz Navarro, wasn't she?"

"*Sí.*"

"Ruíz is shipping wine to New Orleans," Treviño thumped his chest importantly, "on my freight wagons. His uncle is selling it for him. Do you know a merchant by the name of Montemayor in New Orleans? That's Ruíz's uncle."

Treviño nodded judiciously and appeared to be satisfied that he had fulfilled his duty as a conversationalist. His eyes slid away and canvassed the room again, resting with glassy-eyed anticipation on Madame Plaisance's finest girls.

Determined to squeeze the last drop of information from David before he passed out or went upstairs, he said, "I know Montemayor. Did you meet him when you took the wine to his establishment?"

"Of course, I met him at his shop. He's a nice enough fellow, and I saw someone else from home, too." Treviño giggled inanely and said, "This must be my lucky day. So many old friends from home."

Lázaro's interest was piqued. "Who else is here from San Antonio? If you see him again, send him to me." He winked. "I'll see he's treated right."

Treviño stared at him for a moment, his features contorting before he threw back his head and broke into gales of drunken laughter. Lázaro's eyes narrowed at the unexpected hilarity. What was he laughing at?

He felt a rush of warmth spread up his neck, and he glanced

around the room to see if other people were watching them. Rage pounded through his veins and he clenched his fists, wanting desperately to punch Treviño's silly face.

The stupid sot had better not be laughing at me, he thought darkly. People disappeared easily in New Orleans, only to be found floating in the Mississippi below the levee.

Wheezing, David stopped to catch his breath. Leaning over conspiratorially, he placed his hand on Lázaro's arm and hiccoughed. "I don't think it would be a good idea to send this old friend to you, *mi amigo.* He's a woman."

"*¿Qué?*"

"I saw Ruíz Navarro's sister, Teresa, at her uncle's shop. She and her mother are living here with Montemayor."

The stiffness in his body drained away. Treviño hadn't been laughing at him, only at the situation. His fury ebbed. He retreated into casual nonchalance once again.

"How interesting."

"I wouldn't go making no social calls, if I were you." Treviño wagged his finger at him. "The Navarros are snooty at best, but if they knew what your line of business was . . ."

Choosing to ignore the drunken man's insult, he could feel his features harden again. He had had enough of David's veiled innuendos. Turning away, he cast his gaze about the room, looking for a convenient excuse to abandon him.

Before he could murmur a farewell, Treviño threw his arm around Lázaro's shoulders and blubbered, "Didn't mean any offense, *mi amigo.* Besides, Teresa's taken. She's in love." He guffawed loudly and added, "To some poor *vaquero,* who just happens to work for your father. How's that for a coincidence?"

Lázaro was instantly interested again. Any information that involved both the Navarros and his father's *rancho* could prove to be extremely useful to him in the near future. Wanting to learn more, he turned back to face Treviño.

"How do you know Teresa is in love with the *vaquero?*"

"Got the proof right here." He withdrew a slim volume

from his coat pocket and showed it to him. "She gave me this volume of love poems to take to the *vaquero,* and she wrote "With love" inside." Treviño tried to look sly, failed in the attempt and admitted, "I peeked."

He stared at the seemingly innocuous book. His mind was churning with ideas. The volume of poetry just might provide him the key he had been searching for.

"Who's the lucky *vaquero?*"

"I don't remember his name." He thrust the book at Lázaro and offered, "Look for yourself."

His hand closed over the volume. He opened the cover and peered at the flowing script of Teresa Navarro's handwriting. The name leapt off the page . . . Allende Soto. Lázaro had never heard of him.

He wanted to keep the book, but he couldn't take the chance that David would remember his interest in the volume. There were other ways to obtain it without alerting him.

Returning the book to Treviño, he laughed and shook his head. "It's a good joke. The aristocratic Teresa Navarro with one of my father's *vaqueros.*"

Treviño accepted the book and returned it to his coat pocket. He smiled broadly, obviously glad he had mollified his host with some amusing gossip.

"Mi amigo, I've enjoyed our little talk, but . . ." He glanced over his shoulder in the direction of one of the whores and raised his eyebrows. "It's getting late and . . ."

Lázaro understood exactly what he wanted, and he was gratified to see that David was playing directly into his hands. He would have the book in his possession within the hour.

Clapping his "old friend" on the back, he offered, "Which one do you fancy? Any girl you want . . . with my compliments."

Treviño licked his lips, leaving a thin thread of spittle at the corner of his mouth. His glazed eyes managed to register pleased surprise laced with undisguised lust. Like a coy youth, he grasped Lázaro's shoulder and pulled him down close.

Nodding his head toward the opposite corner of the room, he whispered, "That one."

He raised his head and found the girl David had indicated. "The blond one?"

Treviño nodded.

"A wise choice, *mi amigo,* a wise choice," he murmured, hoping to stoke the fires of Treviño's anticipation. He caught the buxom whore's eye and made a slight gesture with his head. The girl rose to her feet and moved gracefully across the room.

"Her name's Angelique. She will give you many hours of the most exquisite pleasure." *Which you'll never stay conscious long enough to enjoy, you drunken fool,* he thought with cynical satisfaction.

David's slack face had turned the color of a tomato, and he licked his lips again. *"Muchas gracias,* Lázaro."

Angelique circled the two men and stopped behind Lázaro, obviously awaiting instructions from him. *"Con permiso,* David, just a discreet word so you'll be properly taken care of."

Nodding, Treviño's lust-filled eyes remained glued to Angelique.

Lázaro drew Angelique several paces away, his hand resting lightly on her satin-clad arm. Lowering his voice, he instructed, "Do whatever he wants. He won't last long and don't charge him." He dug his fingers into her arm. She jumped at the unexpected cruelty but was wise enough to not utter a sound.

Squeezing her arm harder for emphasis, he commanded, "Most importantly, steal the volume of poetry he has in his coat pocket and bring the book to me. Don't touch anything else, and don't *fail."*

Chapter Fifteen

Allende sat with his wounded arm propped upon the table in his cabin. Señora Flores had extricated the bullet and treated his wound. She had immobilized his arm in a sling so it would heal properly, but Allende had found the sling to be a nuisance. Even though it was his left shoulder and he was right-handed, there was precious little he could do with one hand.

The rain had been a blessing of sorts for him. Due to the inclement weather, it had been almost impossible to work with the horses. Taking advantage of the break in his round of duties, he had supervised the cleaning and repairing of all of the tack in the stables, but he still found himself with an abundance of free time.

Because he could manage to write with one hand, he was using the extra time to catch up on his correspondence with Teresa. He was reading each one of her letters and replying to them, in turn. Working through the packet, he reached the last one to be answered. The tallow candle flickered, and he strained his eyes to follow the words:

. . . There appears to be a lull in the constant round of parties in New Orleans. I welcome the relief. *Mamá* says it is because everyone is preparing for the holidays.

The brief hiatus has not affected *Mamá*. If anything, she is going out more, to public entertainments such as the opera, theater, and supper clubs. I have been staying at home and since *Mamá* is so busy, I have had more freedom but also a great deal of time on my hands.

I have taken to visiting my uncle at his mercantile establishment and begging him to let me work behind the counter. He refuses, saying it isn't a proper pursuit for a young lady. So, I sit useless, pining for you.

To return to *Mamá*, she is being courted by an older gentleman, a Creole merchant, who is a business acquaintance of my uncle. His family is not noble, but he is rumored to be extremely wealthy. His riches seem to be adequate compensation for his lack of blue blood . . . at least for my mother. She has conveniently discarded her mourning clothes already. When I think of my sweet *Papá*, it makes me very sad.

Allende, please don't think ill of me for being so cruel about my own mother, but I will never forgive her for separating us. I am counting the days, one by one, until we will be together again.

The weather is still very warm here and unbearably muggy. The heat is not like our dry Tejas heat. It saps . . .

A knock on the cabin door interrupted Allende's reading. Reluctantly, he abandoned Teresa's letter and rose. Moving toward the door, he wondered who would come to him at such a late hour.

When he opened the cabin door, he found Don Estrada's doctor standing there. Dr. Guerrero's hair was in disarray, and he was literally wringing his hands.

He wasn't completely surprised by the doctor's lack of composure, because he didn't hold a very high opinion of him. He knew Dr. Guerrero was more interested in his fee than curing people and that he didn't like to have his peaceful existence too taxed by his patients.

When Don Ruíz had offered to have Dr. Guerrero treat his bullet wound, he had politely refused, saying he would rather visit a traditional *curandera.*

Pilar Flores's skill was known far and wide, and he had confidence in her curative powers. Dr. Guerrero was another matter entirely.

"*Dónde está* Don Navarro?" the doctor demanded, forego-ing the usual greetings.

"He's at Los Montes Verdes. When did you arrive at the *rancho?*"

"This afternoon. Raul, *el mayordomo,* sent for me."

"Why do you need Don Navarro?"

"Because Don Estrada is dying." The doctor shrugged his shoulders. "Despite my best efforts, he's dying. He may not last the night, and Don Estrada is begging to see him."

The sound rattled the walls of the bedroom. A hoarse, choking sound, followed by a long wheezing gasp. The intensity and volume of Don Estéban's labored breathing seemed to suck the last wisp of air from the room, leaving an empty vacuum behind.

Ruíz instinctively clutched his own chest. The sound was so painful he felt as if he were suffocating, too. Pausing on the threshold, he closed his eyes and tried to force down the rising tide of his emotions. Gulping breath deep into his own lungs, he willed himself to remain calm in the face of such terrible suffering. He wanted to be able to comfort his father-in-law.

The strong smell of camphor assailed his nostrils and burned his eyes. Closing them, he rubbed them with his fists. There was a rustle of sound, distinct from the rhythmic, tortured breathing. Opening his eyes, his attention was drawn to the opposite side of the room. He noticed Dr. Guerrero's presence for the first time.

The doctor was a small man, made smaller by his stooped shoulders. The top of his head was bald, and, in his vanity, he combed the thinning strands of hair over his shiny pate. This morning, the pathetic remnants of his hair stood sticking up at crazy angles.

The doctor's red-rimmed, sleepless eyes met Ruíz's, and he whispered, "I've done all I can do. Raul sent for me yesterday when Don Estrada was unable to remain conscious for longer than a few moments. I've done all I can," he repeated. "Nothing helps him."

"What have you done?"

"I've burned camphor and given him laudanum."

"Doesn't the laudanum cause him to remain unconscious?"

The old doctor shrugged. Ruíz could almost hear the squeak of the man's stooped and rusty joints. "It eases his pain."

"Anything else?"

"I've purged him."

"You what?"

"I . . . ah . . . gave him a solution so he would . . . And to throw off the poisons and—"

"Has he been able to eat or drink?" Ruíz interrupted.

"No, he hasn't remained conscious long enough to eat."

"Then why would you rid the man of what little nourishment he already had? How can you expect him to battle for each breath if he has no strength left?" Ruíz realized his voice had lowered to a vicious growl, but he was frightened for Don Estéban . . . and angry.

Why wasn't the doctor doing more? Why wouldn't he try harder to alleviate his father-in-law's suffering? If only Don Estéban could be spared from the worst of the suffering while he died, Ruíz would feel better.

Don Estéban suddenly started coughing. A dry, hacking

sound that went on and on, spiraling out of control, as if being wrenched from the man's entrails. Ruíz rushed to the bedside and lifted his father-in-law in his arms.

Holding the sick man's lolling head and flaccid shoulders, he demanded, "His cough . . . what about his cough?"

Dr. Guerrero joined him at the bedside, shaking his head and muttering, "I gave him a dose of molasses and tincture of calomel but a few minutes before you came. There is nothing more . . ."

The coughing ebbed away, only to be replaced by a hideous gurgling sound and the gasping suck for air.

Listening to his father-in-law's tortured struggle, something snagged in the back of Ruíz's mind. A memory buried from weeks past . . . a vial of an herbal remedy that Julia's mother had given him. It had eased Don Estéban's coughing better than anything else his father-in-law had taken. Why hadn't he realized it before and gotten Don Estéban more of the medicine?

If Pilar and her herbal remedies could alleviate Don Estéban's symptoms during his final days, he would feel he had done everything humanly possible. He knew that there was no cure. He just wanted his father-in-law to die with the least amount of suffering.

"You are released from the case. I can't leave Don Estéban just now, so I would appreciate it if you would send Raul to me on your way out."

"I've done everything I know. You can't possibly blame me," Dr. Guerrero whined.

"I don't," Ruíz murmured, only half believing his words.

His arms felt like lead from holding the weight of his father-in-law's torso upright. But the discomfort was worth it. In this position, the sick man's coughing had ceased and his breathing seemed to have eased a fraction. It gave Ruíz hope.

"Hand me those pillows," Ruíz directed.

Dr. Guerrero complied, and Ruíz bunched the pillows beneath the sick man's shoulders. Slowly, Ruíz settled him against the pillows, using them as a prop to elevate his father-in-law's upper body so he could breathe easier. The pillows appeared to help. Don Estéban wasn't gasping quite as hard for each breath.

Triumphantly, Ruíz turned to the doctor and declared, *"Mira.* You haven't done *everything*. This position seems to help him—''

"I'm not a maid, Don Navarro, I'm a physician," the doctor's sneering voice cut him off. "I try to heal, not to—"

"Comfort suffering," he grated out. "You're relieved of your duties but don't fail to send Raul to me. *¿Entiende?''*

"If I'm to be dismissed, there's the question of my fee, Don Navarro. For the past six weeks, I've come here almost every day, forsaking my practice in San Antonio." Dr. Guerrero held out his hand, palm up. "I've done my best. Don Estéban is dying, and despite your dissatisfaction with my efforts, I must insist upon fair payment for my time."

Ruíz saw red at the doctor's greedy grasping while he was trying to help his dying father-in-law. Dr. Guerrero must have known his fee would be settled properly, but the physician obviously felt he had to have his money before he could leave.

If Ruíz hadn't been afraid that a scuffle might disturb Don Estéban, he would have cheerfully strangled the doctor to see how he liked to struggle for every breath of air. But this was neither the time nor the place to engage in a brawl.

"You're sorely trying my patience. I told you to leave and I meant it. You're just wasting the little time my father-in-law has left. Raul will pay you whatever you require from the household funds. Just ask him, but be quick about it. I want to see Raul within the next ten minutes."

The doctor scowled, opened his mouth to speak, and then shut it with a snap. Glaring at him, Dr. Guerrero sketched a hasty bow and retreated from the room without uttering another word.

Ruíz watched the doctor scurry away with a sense of relief.

He pulled a chair beside the bed. Before he sat down, he took a glass of water from the bedside table and raised it to Don Estéban's lips. Gently forcing his father-in-law's mouth open, he dribbled a few drops of liquid inside. The sick man greedily gulped the water and licked his lips.

Just as Ruíz had suspected, Don Estéban was starving for liquids. Carefully, Ruíz fed the sick man as much of the water as he would take. After he drained half of the glass, he turned his head to one side and moaned. Ruíz was uncertain whether he should try to force more water down his father-in-law's throat.

While he was considering what to do next, there was a light tap on the door and Raul entered.

"Dr. Guerrero said you wanted me."

"*Sí*, send Tomás to fetch Pilar Flores at Los Montes Verdes. She is a *curandera*. Have Tomás explain that Don Estéban is dying, and I need her to ease his suffering. It's not a request. I will pay her whatever she asks, and I want her to come today. And have Miguel come to me, too."

He would need to speak with Miguel personally, because he would be sending him on a much longer errand ... to New Orleans to notify Lázaro that his father was dying.

Pilar arrived a few hours later, and she brought Julia with her. Julia's appearance both surprised and secretly pleased Ruíz. He hadn't expected her to come with her mother. She wasn't a healer. Lupita, Julia's younger sister, had been trained as a *curandera*. He knew that blood and suffering disturbed Julia. And the harvest had begun at Los Montes Verdes. Knowing how important this harvest was to her, he was touched that she had come.

Explaining that her daughter's presence was necessary for practical reasons, Pilar told him she needed someone to sit beside Don Estéban while she rested. Julia was there to relieve her mother when Pilar grew weary.

Despite Pilar's explanation, Ruíz liked to think there was another reason for Julia's presence. He wanted to believe she had come because she still possessed feelings for him. He knew it was a selfish expectation on his part, considering his conflicted emotions about her, but he still found himself hoping that . . .

What did he hope?

He shook his head. Just what did he want from Julia? He wasn't certain anymore. He had explored his feelings for her . . . and the idea of their marriage didn't seem quite so daunting as before. Whether he could express the undying love she craved was another matter.

Of one thing he was certain. Watching Julia and her mother while they cared for his father-in-law, he knew he had made the right decision to send for Pilar. And their efficiency as a team couldn't be questioned, either. Pilar concocted hot mustard plasters, and Julia applied them to Don Estéban's chest. The plaster seemed to ease the sick man's breathing. Pilar brought her own special cough medicine, too. It soothed Don Estéban's hacking cough.

Their efforts didn't stop with plasters and cough medicine. Pilar plied Don Estéban with three different teas. One was made with shredded elecampane, an herb that helped to ease the patient's breathing. Another tea, made with ginger root, relieved his congestion, and, finally, there was the willow bark tea that cooled his fever.

Besides the herbal remedies that helped Don Estéban's symptoms, Pilar and Julia lavished him with every possible comfort. For hours, they patiently dribbled the medicinal teas down his throat. They also managed to coax an astonishing amount of beef broth into him, which gave the sick man some small bit of nourishment.

When the willow bark tea failed and his fever raged out of control, Raul showed Julia the springhouse outside the hacienda walls. The *adobe* structure backed up to a hill and housed a chill, artesian spring that bubbled to the surface. Julia would rush back and forth, countless times, to bring fresh, chilled cloths for Don Estéban's feverish brow.

After ten days of Pilar and Julia working themselves to the bone, day and night, Pilar brought the news to Ruíz.

"Don Estéban is awake. His breathing is easy, and he's asking for food," Pilar declared with satisfaction before adding, "he's asking for you, too, Ruíz. I don't know if there will be another . . ."

Ruíz understood what Pilar was hesitant to say. His father-in-law was dying and this might be his final opportunity to speak with him.

"*Gracias,* Pilar, for everything you've done . . . and Julia, too. You both have made such a difference. I don't know how . . ."

"There will be plenty of time for that," Pilar assured him.

But not plenty of time for Don Estéban, Ruíz realized.

"I'll go to see him now."

Don Estéban sat propped against his pillows. His eyes were clear, and his hands were folded neatly on his chest. His breathing was heavy but even.

Despite the improvement in his condition, Ruíz winced at the obvious toll the illness had exacted from the older man.

His father-in-law's once robust physique was skeletal, the flesh wasted away. His eyes were clear, but they were sunken in his face and rimmed with black circles. His usually bronzed complexion had become pasty with an unnatural greenish tint to it.

With a show of heartiness, his father-in-law greeted him, "*Mi hijo,* come sit beside me. We need to talk."

Ruíz was startled to hear Don Estéban call him his son. He had never uttered a term of intimacy before.

Pulling a ladder-back chair beside the bed, he murmured, "Don Estéban, it's good to see you're feeling better. I'm glad Señora Flores has been able to help you."

His father-in-law nodded. "She has powerful magic."

Again, Don Estéban's words took him by surprise. He was a practical man, or so Ruíz had always thought. He would have never guessed that Don Estéban subscribed to the old superstitious belief that the effectiveness of a *curandera* was based on the power of her magic.

What Pilar had done for his father-in-law had more to do with common sense and medicinal herbs than supernatural powers. But he didn't care what the older man believed, just as long as he was feeling better.

"You wanted to speak with me."

"*Sí.* Señora Flores's magic is strong, but even she cannot cheat the devil forever, eh? I'm dying, so I must speak of what will happen after I'm gone."

He paused, and Ruíz opened his mouth to protest the older man's bleak words, but his father-in-law forestalled him by raising his hand and saying, "Don't. I know I'm dying. That's why you must listen, Ruíz, and listen well.

"I had Señor Meredith prepare my will. Half of the *rancho* will be yours, and the other half will belong to Concepción."

Ruíz sucked in his breath in exasperation. He didn't want half of the *rancho* for himself, and he had explained his feelings to Don Estéban countless times. As his father-in-law had so bluntly pointed out, time was slipping away and he had made no attempt to reconcile with his only son.

"Don Estéban, I am honored you want to leave me half of your *rancho,* but I believe it should go to your son, Lázaro. I gratefully accept the half for my daughter, and I will safeguard it for her. But I cannot take what isn't mine." Leaning forward in his chair, he implored, "You should see Lázaro and try to put your bad feelings—"

"Pah!" Don Estéban bellowed. "I refuse to lay eyes on that

worthless whelp. *Sangre male,* he's got bad blood flowing in his veins.''

Ruíz sat back in his chair. He was disappointed his father-in-law wouldn't bend. It was the reason why he had waited to send for Lázaro. He had been concerned that Lázaro's arrival would further agitate Don Estéban's condition.

Maybe he shouldn't have waited so long. Lázaro wouldn't arrive in time to see his father alive. Maybe he should have summoned Lázaro sooner and made Don Estéban face his son.

"Sangre male," the dying man repeated, and wheezed. ''Just like his mother. I've never told this to anyone before but now that I'm dying . . .'' He shrugged. ''I caught my wife with a *vaquero*. She was a liar and a cheat, and her son is just like her.''

Astonished by the ugly revelation, Ruíz didn't know what to say or why his father-in-law had confided such a thing. After all, it must have happened long ago, and it was a private matter. He couldn't see how Lázaro possessed ''bad blood'' just because his mother had been unfaithful. If you used that line of reasoning, then Ruíz's late wife . . .

Remembering the docile Alicia, he couldn't stop himself from disagreeing with his father-in-law. ''You can't blame the children for their mother's sins. Alicia was a good wife to me.''

Don Estéban's lips twitched, and the semblance of a smirk played across his mouth. His eyes gleamed malevolently.

''Alicia was a good wife because she *feared*. I put the fear of *Dios* into her, and she learned her lesson. But Lázaro didn't . . . nor my wife. I tried to beat them into submission, to teach them the evil of their ways, but they defied me at every turn. They were nothing but liars and cheats.''

Ruíz recoiled in horror. All the old rumors were true. Don Estéban had brutalized his family, possibly killing his wife, but certainly driving his son away. He was suddenly reminded of the times Alicia had appeared fearful of her father. He had known that the older man possessed a cruel streak, but he had never guessed the depths of Don Estéban's brutality.

To such a man consumed by hate and cruelty, Ruíz felt he owed nothing. Despite what Don Estéban's will might say, he would do what he thought was honorable, and he wouldn't feel guilty about contradicting his father-in-law's wishes.

Don Estéban must have guessed some of Ruíz's feelings, because his eyes narrowed, and he observed, "You seem repulsed by what I had to do. But time and circumstances will harden you . . . or perhaps not. I had to claim this land with my blood and sweat. You've had everything given to you. The struggle is the important thing. It makes a man feel alive, full of power. And it teaches you, every lesson a harsh one. You learn not to suffer fools . . . or liars and cheats."

His father-in-law's eyes blazed, searing his flesh with the old man's righteous indignation. He heard the catch in Don Estéban's throat, followed by a strangled, gurgling sound. A coughing spasm overtook him, and Don Estéban clutched a fresh linen handkerchief to his mouth and coughed into it.

Knowing from past experience what needed to be done, Ruíz rose and poured a glass of water and uncorked the vial of Pilar's cough medicine. As soon as the spasm receded, Ruíz held the vial to Don Estéban's lips. The sick man swallowed some of the medicine and then drank the water.

Don Estéban collapsed against the pillows. The skin around his lips was blue. He threw the used handkerchief to the floor. Ruíz gazed at it. The snow-white linen was spotted with crimson blood.

"Bad, eh?" Don Estéban croaked. "I told you I didn't have much longer. I don't have the breath to argue with you about the *rancho*. You know my wishes.

"There's another matter I need to discuss with you. I've said I can't abide liars and cheats, but once I myself was a thief. I'm not proud of it, and I've paid for it all of my days." Don Estéban paused and reached for the glass. Ruíz handed it to him, and he took another sip of water. "My family was dirt poor, living in México. There were fifteen children, and I never owned a pair of shoes. Shoes, hah!"

He snorted, "We never had enough to eat, much less shoes. I left when I was sixteen with nothing but the ragged clothes on my back."

Despite his earlier revulsion at the older man's brutality, listening to his father-in-law's pitiful beginnings, he couldn't help but feel a measure of sympathy for what Don Estéban had survived.

"I don't want your pity, Ruíz, just your help to right an old wrong. When I'm finished, I want you to send for Padre Carrasco in San Antonio. It's probably too late, but send for him anyway. And I'm confessing this now, to you, because I can't tell the priest. After you hear the story, you'll know why."

Ruíz nodded in response.

"*Muy bien*. Where was I? I remember . . . I left my family and crossed several hundred miles on foot, alone. I was unbelievably lucky, but too young and ignorant to realize it. I had passed through the heart of Comanche country without seeing a single savage. Despite my good fortune, all I could think of was my empty belly. When I reached the Río Grande, I came upon a settlement."

Pausing, the dying man opened his mouth wide, as if trying to gulp the air necessary to finish his story.

"It was night, and if I noticed that the town seemed particularly quiet, I must have thought everyone was sleeping. Hoping to beg some food from the local priest, I went straight to the church on the square. It had been defiled, the altar torn apart, the saints' statues broken, and the benches scattered over the floor. In the nave of the church I found the priest with an arrow through his heart and his scalp missing. The Comanches had been there. Dazed, I left the dead priest where he lay and rummaged for some food. It was then I found the cupboard where the treasure of the church had been hidden. There was a wealth of gold and silver plates and many holy vessels studded with jewels.''

''You took them.'' It was not a question; Ruíz already knew the answer.

''I took them. Never had I seen such wealth, and I knew the church's treasure would provide me with a decent start. Without them, I would be just another ragged *peón,* begging for work. In the arrogance of my youth, I even convinced myself God meant for me to have his treasure.''

''I see.''

Don Estéban shook his head and contradicted Ruíz. ''You might think you understand my motives, Ruíz, but I doubt you do. Absolute poverty does things to a man, empties his belly and takes hold of his soul and . . .'' He stopped, and his eyes suddenly glazed over, as if he were staring at some far-off landscape. ''Have you ever noticed a live oak tree growing from a limestone cliff where the soil is thin and the rain flows away?''

''*Sí.*''

''Compare that tree with one growing in the rich loam beside a riverbank. What do you find?''

Ruíz thought that riddles were beside the point, but he shrugged and decided to humor the sick man.

''They are the same tree but quite different in appearance. The first tree on the cliff is usually stunted and has few branches. The tree growing beside the river is usually large with spreading branches and a dense canopy of leaves.''

Don Estéban nodded and said, ''So it is with a man . . . just the same. Poverty stunts and twists a man.''

Ruíz didn't respond. He understood his father-in-law's analogy, and he knew there was truth in it. But unlike trees, God had given men free will . . . the will to choose between what was right and wrong. The will to leave behind their poor start and begin again. Men didn't have to remain rooted to one place and become stunted and deformed.

Don Estéban didn't seem to notice Ruíz's silence; he was too engrossed in telling his story.

"So, I took the church treasure, and I came to San Antonio de Bexár. It was the only civilized area for leagues. I decided to settle here, but I was clever enough to melt down some of the silver and gold plates before I spent it. I purchased a grant of land from the Spanish government in México for practically nothing. They were desperate for Spanish citizens to colonize the area."

He stopped and coughed. "This was before the *gringo empresarios* brought people to Tejas. Many cattle and horses roamed wild on the plains. You just had to be clever enough to catch and tame them. Domesticated livestock could be bought cheaply, too, to improve the herds. As the colony grew, my *rancho* grew and prospered. I only needed a fraction of the treasure. I never touched the jeweled vessels, there was no way to disguise what they were. I've meant to return the items, but I feared to face the questions . . ."

"You could have left them in the cathedral in the middle of the night."

"I thought of that, but decided it was too risky. What if they fell into the wrong hands again?" He shook his head.

"No, Ruíz, it's up to you now. After I'm gone, you will do the honorable thing and my soul will be at peace."

"But wouldn't it be better if you confessed this to Padre Carrasco and gave him the treasure?"

At Ruíz's suggestion, Don Estéban's hand shot out, and he grasped Ruíz's arm.

"No! I fear the power of the treasure, and I don't dare tell a priest what I've done. It's sacrilege of the worst kind. I haven't laid eyes on it in years, but it has cursed my family. That's why my wife and son were . . . and then Alicia died." He licked his cracked lips and his eyes were full of fear.

It was the first time Ruíz had ever seen fear in his father-in-law's eyes, even when the older man spoke of his imminent death. Don Estéban's hand trembled, and he released Ruíz's arm.

"Only you can break the curse so it doesn't touch Concepción. I had a dream," Don Estéban mumbled and plucked nervously at the quilt on his bed. "Shortly after you came to live here, I had a dream. You are the one who will break the curse . . . It must be you."

More superstitious nonsense, he thought wearily. He couldn't understand why Don Estéban didn't want to return the treasure himself and absolve his soul, but what harm would it do to comply with this wish of his father-in-law? Only delay the return of a treasure that had been lost for years by a few days or weeks.

He knew better than to press Don Estéban to return the sacred objects himself; it wouldn't do any good. At least it was one promise he could keep, since he had no intention of honoring the dying man's will.

"I'll do as you ask, Don Estéban."

The fear drained from his father-in-law's eyes and he sighed. *"Muy bien.* The curse won't touch your child if you do as I say. *Mira,* listen carefully while I tell you how to find the treasure. My family knew of its existence, but I never told them where I hid it. I couldn't trust them . . . but I trust you."

His heart wrenched at his father-in-law's words. What bitterness and distrust there must have been in the Estrada family. And he wasn't completely worthy of the sick man's trust, either. It grieved him to be less than honest with Don Estéban, but, unfortunately, his father-in-law's hatred and obstinacy concerning Lázaro left him little choice.

"The treasure is hidden in a tunnel beneath this house. There is a niche in the tunnel with a statue of the Madonna in it. If you dig beneath the statue, you will find the treasure in an old trunk."

"How will I find the tunnel?"

"The easiest way is through my study. The tunnel can also

be reached from the springhouse beyond the hacienda walls, but that way is long and part of the tunnel may have collapsed. Do you remember the carved crucifixes on the mantel in my study?''

"Sí."

"The crucifix on the far right can be turned. It's a latch that unlocks a panel in the wall inside the fireplace. The opening leads into the tunnel. No one else knows about it. The workers who helped me build it are all dead. Keep this information a secret. Take the treasure, under heavy guard, to San Antonio."

"I will do it."

"Muy bien." Don Estéban's eyes fluttered shut. "I'm weary, *mi hijo,* and I've told you everything. Fight to keep the land, don't allow Señor Meredith to give up."

"I won't."

"Kiss Concepción for me . . . and . . . and tell her that . . . *I love her."*

"I will," Ruíz agreed quietly. Some deep instinct told him this was the first and last time Don Estéban had uttered words of love. What power they had, Ruíz thought to himself.

Julia craved to hear those same words of love from his lips, but in his confusion and pride, would he live as Don Estéban had, refusing to say the words until he was dying? Afraid the words would somehow diminish him and leave him vulnerable?

"Go now, Ruíz, I want to rest."

Ruíz knew, with an unshakable certainty, this was the last time he would see his father-in-law alive. As much as he deplored Don Estéban's cruelty and greed, he couldn't help but care about him, too. His father-in-law had been unfailingly generous and supportive of him, and any man who loved his granddaughter as much as he did, must have a spark of divine light buried deep within.

It was unfortunate that Don Estéban, after he'd found his own riverbank, hadn't opened himself to enjoy the rich new sustenance there. Instead, like the tree still growing from the cliff, he had hoarded the riches, both material and spiritual, not allowing them to transform him.

Rising from the chair, he bent over Don Estéban's sleeping form and murmured, *"Vaya con Dios."*

Chapter Sixteen

An unrelenting banging noise on his bedroom door roused Ruíz from a deep sleep. Fumbling for the tinder box on his bedside table, he lit the candle. By its flickering light, he draped a sheet around his loins to cover his nakedness. Grabbing the candle in one hand, he called out, *"Yo vengo."*

When he opened the door, Julia hurled herself into his arms, almost upsetting the candle in his hand.

"He's dead, Ruíz. He died in his sleep. I was sitting beside him, dozing, and then there was this awful silence." Julia gulped, and he felt her hot tears against the exposed flesh of his chest. "You know how the sound of his breathing filled the room. That's when I knew he had died . . . the silence . . . the terrible silence."

Ruíz placed the candle on the bureau beside the door and cradled Julia in his arms. Her grief and compassion for a cruel old man she barely knew struck a chord, deep within his heart. He wanted to tell her he loved her, but he couldn't find the words . . . those powerful words of love.

Instead, he asked, "Did he see the priest?"

"*Sí*, Padre Carrasco came this evening. I tried to find you, but no one knew where you were."

"I was helping Allende with one of the pedigreed mares that was foaling. Allende's left arm is still in a sling." Ruíz bent and kissed the top of her head. He smelled the unmistakable scent of her gardenia perfume in the dark, silken strands of her hair, and beneath his scant cover, he felt his loins tighten.

She was so warm and soft in his arms. Every curve of her body fit his like a glove. He trembled with the fury of wanting her. Retreating a pace, he held her at arm's length.

"*Gracias* for coming to me, but it wasn't necessary. I knew he was dying. We said everything to one another this morning."

Julia gazed up at him. One lone tear on her cheek caught the light from the candle, glistening with a crystalline radiance. He brought his thumb up and brushed it away.

"So you knew."

"*Sí.*"

"I guess I was the only foolish one. When he woke this morning and he seemed so much better, I had hoped he might get well. But *Mamá* explained after he . . . after he left us. She told me it's not uncommon for someone who is dying to seem as if they've recovered just before they pass away. I'm so stupid about these things, I didn't know. The cholera took Lupita so fast that . . ." She lowered her head.

He gently cupped her face in his hands, lifting it to meet his eyes. "Don't call yourself stupid, Julia. You're one of the most intelligent people I've ever known."

Gazing at the soft crimson curves of her lips, the urge to kiss her was so fierce he felt as if he would scream with the agony of his longing. But he steeled himself against his desire.

They had just begun to trust each other again. If he submitted to the powerful physical attraction between them without complete commitment, it would only cause her more pain. He knew what she needed from him, but he was still uncertain if he could live up to her expectations.

Grasping at anything to diffuse the magnetic pull of their desire, he asked, "So you told your mother he died?"

"*Sí*, I woke her before I came to you. She is with him, preparing the body." Julia shuddered and implored, "Hold me, Ruíz."

Ruíz did as she asked, pulling her against the length of his body. The ache in his groin worsened, and he felt his manhood stiffen and thrust against the barrier of his casually draped sheet.

Julia was fully dressed because she had been sitting up with Don Estéban, but the layer of her clothing didn't stop him from feeling the intensity of her arousal, too. Her nipples tightened, pushing against the cloth of her blouse, hard as new berries. The heat between her thighs warmed his legs, and he could smell the musky scent of her desire, intermingled with her gardenia perfume.

"Ruíz, his death . . . it hurts so. It reminds me of how I felt when Lupita died. I feel so alone . . . and I . . . I want to stay with you tonight . . ."

He sucked in his breath. He understood exactly how Julia was feeling. He had been thinking about Alicia's death all day, and the passing of their newborn son, and even his father's violent end. So much death surrounded them, making them want to reach out to the living.

And he understood Julia's need to be with him in an intimate sense, too. Death, he had learned, was a powerful aphrodisiac. It made you confront your own mortality. It fueled a compulsion to mate, to procreate, and begin a new generation.

He understood this and so much more. He knew Julia. They had grown up together. Again, it was on the tip of his tongue to tell her he loved her. But did he really love her or was he saying the words so he wouldn't face an end like Don Estéban had . . . alone and with no one? He couldn't use her to shore up his grief . . . not again. She was too good, too giving. She deserved his unconditional love. He refused to offer her a pale facsimile.

Instead of offering his love, he asked, "Will you marry me?"

"Do you love me, Ruíz?"

"I think I do, Julia. Will you marry me and let our love grow?"

"Why can't you . . . ?"

"I don't know. I have fears my love is selfish, or that your love will . . ."

"Smother you, dominate you? That you'll lose yourself, Ruíz?"

How well she knew him. It was almost frightening . . . as frightening as loving her without condition. He answered her honestly. *"Sí."*

She pulled back, breaking their embrace. Wrapping her arms around herself, her voice sounded small and hurt spilled from it. "That's the definition of love, Ruíz. You must lose yourself." She paused and then confessed, *"Por Dios,* I want you."

Reaching out, she caressed his cheek, stroking downward and lingering with her fingertips on his lips. "I shouldn't have asked to be with you. I was hurting. You were right to refuse me, Ruíz. I don't want to be with you again, not until . . . When you're willing to begin anew, knowing and needing each other, I'll be there."

She dropped her hand and turned. Before he could stop her, she had slipped through the door and shut it behind her.

He stared at the closed door. The words burned in his throat: *I love you.* Would he ever be able to say them?

Three days later, Don Estéban had been laid to rest on a hill above his *rancho.* It had been his wish, to be buried on his land rather than in the cemetery in San Antonio. The burial was a simple one, attended only by the *vaqueros* from the *rancho.*

Julia and her mother stayed behind to help Ruíz. As soon as the burial was over, Ruíz accompanied them home to Los Montes Verdes. They were all needed for the harvest. After the harvest, Ruíz would have Don Estéban's will read and see about returning the church treasure. For now, it was a relief to be leaving death behind and to join in the triumph of the harvest.

Riding past the vineyard, Ruíz was gratified to see the workers bent over the vines, filling baskets with the dark-red fruit. Ruíz, Pilar, and Julia found the old buckboard wagon on the top of a rise. It held baskets of food and barrels of water for the workers. Felipe was close by, directing the harvest.

The three of them dismounted. Julia and Ruíz hung back while Pilar embraced her husband. Felipe and Pilar spoke quietly for a few minutes and exchanged kisses.

Pilar returned to Julia and Ruíz, saying, "I'm going to the *casa.* A great deal of work has piled up during my absence, and I think my husband has sorely missed my cooking." She winked broadly and smiled.

"I'll come with you, *Mamita,* if you think you need me," Julia offered.

Pilar waved her hand in dismissal. "If I know my daughter, I expect you've had quite enough of being cooped up in a house all day and night. No, I'm certain your father has a more pressing need for you."

"*Gracias, Mamita.* I'll see you at supper."

Ruíz assisted Pilar to mount. Handing her the reins, he said, "I know I've said it before, but I want to say it again, Señora Flores. I'm deeply in your debt. You made Don Estéban's last few days so much easier for him. I cannot thank you and Julia enough."

"It was my pleasure to care for Don Estrada, but I appreciate your kind words, Señor Ruíz."

"Hug Conchita for me and tell her I'll see her tonight."

"I will," Pilar promised. "I can't wait to see her, too. Until supper." Pilar kneed her mount. Waving, she moved off at a fast trot.

Felipe approached Julia and gathered her into his arms, giving her a hug and admitting, "I missed you, *hija mía*. I'm glad you're home." Facing Ruíz, he said, "My sympathies for the loss of your father-in-law, Señor Ruíz. And I'm glad you've returned, too. I need you for the harvest."

"I'm happy to be home, Felipe. I hope you can forgive me for keeping your daughter and wife from you. I know you missed them both. I can't praise them enough. Their help was invaluable. I don't know what I would have done without them," he confessed.

Nodding, Felipe wiped his face with a colorful bandana. His eyes veered away, and Ruíz realized he didn't want to dwell on Don Estéban's illness and death. Ruíz guessed he was impatient to get on with the harvest, but Felipe's next words continued in a personal vein.

"Conchita has kept Luz busy. I fear Paco and I are too dull for her. She missed both Julia and my wife. And of course, she's been looking forward to seeing her *Papá*, too. She'll be delighted to have everyone back home. Although we'll all be a little more than busy over the next few weeks."

"I can't wait to see my daughter. I hope she hasn't driven Luz too crazy."

Felipe grinned. "You returned just in the nick of time. I think there's still hope for Luz."

Ruíz laughed and glanced around the vineyard. "I'm sorry I couldn't have come sooner, but you have my undivided support from now on . . . both for my daughter and the grapes. How is the harvest coming?"

"The work progresses. We've already gathered the white grapes. Some of the women have started to crush and clean them. Paco is overseeing the work." Felipe turned to his daughter and said, "Julia, I want you to assist the other women with the crushing and cleaning. Will you help?"

"*Sí, Papito*, I will help where you need me."

"*Muy bien.*"

"I see you've started picking the red grapes," Ruíz observed.

"Just yesterday. The grapes on the sunnier slopes are ready, but the ones in the hollows are not perfectly ripe." Felipe frowned, and his brow creased with frustration. "But I think we'll need to go ahead and pick the entire crop, even if we sacrifice a few days of maturity."

"*¿Por qué?*" Ruíz asked.

Felipe glanced at Julia and then at Ruíz. His brow was still creased with concern, and his voice held the faintest note of accusation when he replied, "Because of the extra workers you convinced me to keep, the harvest is proceeding faster than usual. We can't afford to have workers sitting idle, waiting for the grapes to ripen. Of course, we could let them go after these grapes are picked. Our own workers could finish."

Ruíz crossed his arms. Felipe was the boss now, but he still retained strong opinions about running the vineyard. He could sense a minor confrontation brewing.

"Didn't we promise the extra workers their jobs through the harvest?"

"*Sí*, but if we don't have work for them . . ." Felipe didn't finish his objection.

"There must be something that they could do," Ruíz declared.

Julia moved forward and touched her father's arm, offering, "*Papito*, I have an idea. The trenches we dug during the rains. They should be filled in before winter. Otherwise, the winter rains will run off, and the vines won't receive adequate moisture."

"That's a good idea, Julia," Ruíz agreed.

"Our own workers can do that later," Felipe grumbled.

"*Sí*." Ruíz admitted, but then added, "if they have the time.

They will be busy with the crushing and the other preparations for winter. The swine and cattle will need to be butchered, and the meat cured for winter provisions.

"Stores of firewood will have to be cut, and the holidays will be upon us. If we wait too long, we could lose a great deal of moisture before our workers can start on the trenches."

He studied the vineyard. It was literally honeycombed with ditches from their desperate efforts during the earlier torrential rains. "It's a big job."

"*Papito*, Ruíz is right. It's going to be a huge effort to fill those trenches. The extra workers could start the job while the grapes mature for a few more days. Later, our workers could finish the task."

Ruíz sought Julia's eyes, and he smiled at her. He appreciated her wisdom and foresight. Even more, he was thankful for her support. Lately, she had been agreeing with him far more than she had been arguing with him. It gave him a warm feeling, realizing she could see his point of view. After all, she had been the one who convinced Felipe to keep the extra workers. Thinking back, he also remembered the time she had acquiesced to his wishes concerning disciplining Conchita, too.

A sudden realization swept over him. Julia might be strong-willed and opinionated, but she was also fair and reasonable, unlike his domineering mother. And when she did fight for what she believed was right, her motivations weren't selfish. Usually, she fought for someone she cared about . . . Paco or Conchita or . . .

Studying her in this new light, he remembered their conversation the night Don Estéban had died. Losing himself to love her might not be so terrible. It might just prove to be the most wonderful thing he had ever done. Suddenly, he knew he wasn't afraid of losing himself anymore. On the contrary, he was beginning to realize he wouldn't be losing anything. Not losing, but gaining, something more precious than he had ever possessed.

Felipe's voice brought him back to the pressures of the harvest. "You've convinced me. The extra workers stay. As soon as the grapes on the slopes are picked, I want you to oversee the filling of the trenches, Ruíz."

His gaze locked with Felipe's. It was the first direct order Felipe had given his former *patrón*. He was gratified to see that the older man was finally comfortable being in command. Ruíz grinned at him in silent recognition of his authority, and Felipe grinned back. They clapped each other on the back.

"You can count on me, Felipe. We'll get those ditches filled."

Ruíz gazed at Julia over her father's head. Her emerald eyes flashed. She was so beautiful, so tender-hearted and loving. What a fool he'd been!

After refusing her love so many times, how could he convince her that he did love her . . . that he wasn't afraid of loving her and joining his life with hers? That he wanted her, not because of a sense of duty, but because he wanted her for herself.

It would take some doing, he realized. He would need to be very persuasive. He would need to pick his time and place.

Julia bent to the tedious task of removing stems and seeds and any other dross from the crushed white grapes. She was working shoulder to shoulder with the wives of the workers of Los Montes Verdes. After her vigil with Don Estéban and the subsequent funeral, it was comforting to be home again and among people she had known all of her life.

The women's light-hearted chatter ebbed and flowed around her, but she only listened with half her mind. Her thoughts, as usual, were centered on Ruíz. She couldn't help but recall every detail of his enigmatic smile from the day before when they had argued with her father . . . and the look in his eyes after her father agreed. His eyes had held the sudden awareness of a man awakening from a long and deep sleep. She shivered, remembering the intensity of his gaze.

What had it meant?

He had come to their *casa,* last night after dark, to see Conchita for a few minutes before the little girl was put to bed. She had held her breath, hoping he would ask to speak with her. But he hadn't sought her out. Instead, he had politely refused her mother's offer of a late supper and pleaded fatigue. He had looked exhausted, she remembered. But it had taken all of her willpower not to run after him to the hacienda.

She shook her head angrily at herself. When would she ever learn . . . or quit hoping? She was reading more into his smile and gaze than he had meant. He had only been grateful for her support, nothing more.

The night Don Estéban died, he had refused to be intimate with her. He had asked her to marry him again but that had been the honorable thing to do, considering that she had offered her body to him. She blushed, remembering her brazen need that night.

She knew Ruíz desired her, too, and with a passion that equaled her own. But he still didn't love her . . . not the way she loved him.

Love might come in time to him. She realized it was difficult for him to trust, and she was miserable without him. What was she waiting for? He still wanted to marry her.

Her mother had advised her to follow her heart, and she intended to do just that. The next time Ruíz offered marriage, she would accept him . . . hoping love would come in time.

Pierre found Lázaro in the gaming rooms at the back of the bordello. Occasionally, he would join a private game, just to keep his hand in. He was proud of his gambling abilities. He was a shrewd competitor and a good judge of character. His gaming skill had won him his share in the bordello. When he was sole owner, he would have more time and resources to pursue his gambling interests.

Pierre leaned down beside him and whispered discreetly in his ear, "There are two men asking to see you."

"Who are they?"

"I believe one of them goes by the name of Chivato. I did not recognize the other man. He gave his name as Miguel Vega, and he said he's from your father's ranch."

"Have they seen one another?"

"I do not believe so, unless it was in passing. Chivato is in your office. The man calling himself Vega is waiting in the parlor."

"Good. Go and tell Chivato to wait in the kitchen. Give him a bottle of absinthe to keep him occupied. Bring Vega to my office."

Pierre bowed and exited the room. Lázaro watched him go, experiencing a flutter of pleasurable anticipation. The moment he had waited for was at hand. His father was dead. There was nothing more to fear. The future held only riches . . . and pleasure. The treasure would soon be his.

He didn't care about the *rancho*. He had slaved on that damned land, and he hated it. And he knew with complete certainty that his father had left the *rancho* to his granddaughter and Ruíz Navarro.

The old scars burned on his back. So many ugly memories, filled with hate. When he had been a young boy, he had worshipped his father, and as he matured, he had tried to please him. But nothing he had done had pleased the old man. His father had found fault with everything. And when his father started to beat him and his mother, Lázaro's love turned to hate. Then he did everything possible to enrage his father . . . and the beatings continued.

Once, his poor, sweet mother had tried to intervene . . . to stop his father from whipping him. His father had stopped, but the next morning his mother was found dead. She had hung herself in the stables.

He felt the bile rise to his throat, remembering. The green baize poker table seemed to tilt. He shook his head and closed his eyes. He had blamed himself. Stupid, stupid. He should have known the old goat drove her to it. Despite his mother's awful death, he had continued to hope that one day he would win his father's admiration . . . and love.

Until Ruíz Navarro married his sister and came to live with them.

His father had invited Ruíz to live on the *rancho,* ostensibly to teach him about the ranching business. His father had doted on Ruíz. It was as if his son-in-law could do no wrong. Watching them together, he realized this interloper was usurping his rightful place. All the praise was for Ruíz. Lázaro received nothing but criticism and brutality. Slowly, his resentment and hatred grew . . . and grew . . . turning into rage. He wanted to kill them both, the old *bastardo* and the too-perfect Ruíz.

Fear of his father and of being caught by the authorities had stopped him. Instead, he ran away to start a new life and to bide his time. Now, with his father dead, he could execute the revenge he had planned.

The child must die, too, he had decided. He had never laid eyes on his niece, but it was enough to know that the old fool had adored her. His father had never adored his own children.

Someone was asking him if he was still in the game. Returning his thoughts to the present, he glanced down at his cards and found them unpromising. He folded and told the banker to credit his account with the remaining chips. Rising from the chair, he bowed low, murmuring an apology to his fellow players and pleading urgent business.

Pierre was standing outside the office, awaiting further orders. The door to his office was ajar.

"Wait here until I call for you."

Pierre nodded.

When Lázaro entered the office, a scruffy-looking *vaquero* leapt to his feet. The man was covered in dust, and the stubble of a beard shadowed his face. His nostrils flared. The man stank.

Wanting to get the unpleasant interview over quickly, he stated, "I'm Lázaro Estrada. You were looking for me. How did you find me?"

The man clutched his wide *sombrero,* holding the hat in front of him like a shield. His eyes were wide, and he licked his blistered lips.

"My name is Miguel Vega. I work on your father's *rancho.* I was given the address of your living quarters. I went there, and your manservant directed me to come here." He licked his lips again. "Ruíz Navarro sent me to tell you that your father is . . . dying. It is likely he is dead by now. *Lo siento.*"

"Spare me your sentiments. Is that all?"

"I believe Don Navarro expected you to return to the *rancho.* It would be my pleasure to escort you, *señor.*"

"But not mine," Lázaro snapped. "Tell Ruíz I will return home in a few weeks. Since my father is already dead, there's no hurry. I've pressing business here," he purposely lied to the *vaquero.* He wanted Ruíz to believe he wouldn't be coming home any time soon.

"*Sí, señor,* I will give Don Navarro the message."

Lázaro didn't bother to dismiss the *vaquero* directly. Instead, he raised his voice and called, "Pierre."

The *mayordomo* appeared at the door.

"Pierre, show this man out and then bring my other appointment to me. After that, you may resume your normal duties."

Pierre bowed and Miguel bowed, too. Miguel opened his mouth to say something, but the *mayordomo* relentlessly guided him from the office.

Lázaro almost laughed out loud, watching Pierre maneuver

the witless *vaquero*. Pierre's head was carefully averted and the snobbish servant appeared to be holding his breath. He must have noticed Miguel's distinctive aroma, too.

Taking out a ring of keys, he unlocked one of the drawers of the desk. He withdrew some papers and the slim volume of poetry. Crossing the room, he opened a cupboard door and retrieved a pair of saddlebags. He stuffed the papers and poetry volume into the saddlebags.

There was a knock and Chivato stepped through the open doorway, greeting him with, *"Buenas noches,* Don Lázaro."

Slinging the saddlebags over the back of a chair, his gaze swept Chivato. The man's eyes were glassy, and his jaw was slack. Chivato had wasted no time with the absinthe bottle.

"What brings you here?" Lázaro asked.

Chivato dropped his eyes, and his voice changed to a pleading whine, "I've bad news."

"Dígame."

"My associate in Tejas has sent word that the family I hired to rustle livestock on your father's *rancho* has disappeared. Señor MacGregor hasn't contacted him for several weeks." Chivato paused and ran his finger inside the collar of his dingy shirt. His brow was beaded with perspiration. "I'm sorry, Don Lázaro. I did my best. Do you want me to return to Tejas to find someone else?"

He hesitated on purpose. He enjoyed watching Chivato squirm for a while. After he'd drawn out the moment, he broke the tense silence by declaring, *"Sí,* I want you to return to Tejas . . . with me and the men you found. You did find the men?"

"Sí, Don Lázaro," he assured him, nodding his head vigorously. "I found the men."

"Muy bien. Go and round them up and get my roan stallion."

He opened the strongbox and withdrew a bag of gold coins, handing the heavy bag to Chivato.

"You'll need this to pay the stable bill and buy some provisions. Allow each of the men a small incentive, but explain they will receive payment in full when the job is completed. Meet me at my quarters, with the men and my horse, at sunrise. We leave for Tejas tomorrow."

Chapter Seventeen

Peter Meredith set aside the thick parchment document and asked, "Is it what you expected?"

"Yes, exactly as I had thought," Ruíz confirmed. There had been no surprises in Don Estéban's will. Everything his late father-in-law owned: land, livestock, and cash in the bank had been split evenly between his son-in-law and granddaughter.

There had been a few minor gifts of monies to trusted servants, and the hacienda with its furnishings had been bequeathed to Conchita. Ruíz grinned ruefully to himself and wondered if he would ever have a home to call his own again.

The church treasure hadn't been mentioned in Don Estéban's will. But then, Ruíz hadn't expected it to be.

Peter steepled his slender fingers and inquired, "You've already sent for Lázaro, haven't you?"

"Yes, before Don Estéban died."

"You must know Lázaro has good cause to contest this will as it's written. If Don Estrada would have only recognized his son's existence in the document and left him a small sum,

Lázaro wouldn't have a case. I tried to explain that to your father-in-law, but he was adamant. He refused to mention Lázaro because, as far as he was concerned, his son was dead.'' Peter's thin lips turned downward into a frown and he grumbled, ''I don't know why people retain attorneys when they refuse to listen to their counsel.''

Ruíz grinned at Peter and observed, ''Because attorneys are a necessary evil.''

''I take that as an insult,'' Peter shot back. The corners of his mouth were creeping upward.

''And so you should, Peter, so you should . . . against attorneys in general. Nothing personal, you understand?''

''You might be able to ease my wounded pride if you offered to buy me a drink.'' Peter fished his gold pocket watch from his vest and peered at the time. ''I'm ready to call it a day.''

''I'd be honored to buy you a drink, but I'm not quite through with business.''

Peter had already half risen from his chair, but at Ruíz's words, he lowered himself into his seat with an air of quiet resignation. Ruíz almost laughed out loud at his friend's obvious disappointment.

As far as he was concerned, Peter was the best attorney in San Antonio. He was smart, well-versed in the law, and a hard worker. But Peter also liked to play hard when he wasn't working. Ruíz looked forward to relaxing with Peter over a drink. The last few weeks had been exhausting, both physically and emotionally. Unfortunately, there were still a great many loose ends he needed to tie up.

''You won't have to worry about Lázaro contesting the will. I plan on deeding my half over to him. I'll need you to draw up the papers.''

Peter's blue eyes widened and he gasped, ''You plan on doing what?''

''Giving Lázaro what rightfully belongs to him.''

"But . . . but," Peter sputtered. It was the first time he could remember his smooth-talking friend to be at a loss for words.

Peter recovered fast, though, and he voiced his objections. "You're going against Don Estrada's wishes? Why? You've worked yourself to the bone on that ranch. I've watched you sacrifice yourself. And might I also point out that, since you only retain one-fifth of the vineyard, I would think—"

"That greed would dictate," Ruíz interrupted him. "No thanks, I've seen what greed can do to men. I have enough, and all my hard work on the ranch is for my daughter's security. I don't want something that isn't mine." Ruíz pinned Peter with his eyes. "That's my final decision."

Peter emitted a low whistle and shook his head. "As your attorney who is dedicated to your interests, I don't agree. But I get the message, and you're the boss. Everything that Don Estrada left *you* reverts to Lázaro. Is that it?"

"Yes."

"I'll draw up the papers, but have you considered Lázaro might turn out to be a difficult partner?" Peter leaned forward as if to drive his point home. "After all, you'll still be overseeing your daughter's half of the ranch. In order for the two parts to run smoothly, you'll need to get along with Lázaro Estrada."

Peter paused and straightened the cuffs of his snow-white shirt. "I don't like to repeat gossip, but Lázaro is not well liked in San Antonio, and his activities in New Orleans are rumored to be unsavory. You may have your work cut out for you."

"I know it will be a difficult situation, Peter. If nothing else, what Don Estéban did to his son . . . cutting him from his will . . . ensures Lázaro's resentment. Unfortunately, I feel I have no choice but to try and get along with him."

Ruíz gathered the papers spread before him. He stuffed them into a leather satchel and confessed, "I hope Lázaro doesn't remain in San Antonio. If he'll return to New Orleans and let me run the ranch, I'll send him his share of the profits." Ruíz grinned and observed wryly, "Then I'll need to hire an armored wagon to send all that loot to New Orleans. First, my mother and now Lázaro . . . I can only hope.''

''You better *hope* he trusts you to run the ranch and send him a full accounting,'' Peter agreed.

''That may be the most difficult part, getting Lázaro to trust me.''

''If I can be of any assistance, just let me know. I want to help you,'' Peter offered.

''I know you do, Peter, and I appreciate your offer. I'll let you know if you can help. How's our land grant case progressing?''

''Slowly . . . very slowly''

''What do you think the outcome will be?''

''I think you'll hold on to the bulk of the ranch. Don Estéban's land grant is relatively new, compared to some of the antiquities I've seen lately. And the wording is clear with good fixed boundaries, but the ranch will probably lose about four or five hundred acres.''

''Why?''

''Because Don Estéban went beyond the original boundaries of his grant and encroached or ''squatted'' on some prime pieces of land on the fringes. No one challenged him, so the land has effectively been deemed his, but there's no paper to prove it, only prior possession. Our new government does recognize ''squatting,'' so if you want me to retain the rights to the additional acreage, I can make a strong case for you.''

At the mention of ''squatting,'' a vision of Allende's story about the MacGregor family flashed through Ruíz's mind. There were so many people who desperately needed land to support their families. The Estrada *rancho* was large enough without taking additional lands. He realized he might need to sell some livestock to adjust to the new size, but it never hurt to cull the herds.

There was another reason not to fight for the extra acres. A reason he didn't like to admit, but not acknowledging the underlying conflict didn't make it go away. There were strong feelings in Tejas against native Tejanos and any prosperity they might enjoy.

Ruíz didn't want to stir up ingrained animosities. Now that Tejas was free from México, Anglos were pouring into the new nation, and all of them were clamoring for land.

"Just press our case for the original land grant. I'll give up the rest of the land."

Peter's sandy-colored eyebrows rose, and his words echoed Ruíz's unspoken concern. "I hope Lázaro Estrada agrees with you and doesn't cause trouble. You have a good case to retain the additional acreage but pursuing it could get nasty, especially with the way sentiments are running."

"I know. The ranch is large enough. We don't need the extra acres, and I don't want to inflame old hatreds and distrust. This is a new nation we've forged, the Republic of Texas. We must all work together to make it strong."

"I wish everyone had your foresight, Ruíz."

Ruíz smiled and said, "It's because I rely upon your wise counsel, Peter."

His friend snorted and chuckled. "It's getting thick in here." Peter rose from his chair and reached for his hat. "I think it's time for that drink." He snapped his fingers as if he just had a brilliant idea. "Better yet, why don't you plan on staying the night? I've got a cot you can use. We can have dinner together."

Ruíz hated to turn down his friend's kind offer, but he had little enough time to spare.

"I can't stay the night, but I will have dinner with you. I need to visit the *rancho* to be certain everything is running smoothly. Then I will return to Los Montes Verdes. The harvest is over, but the crushing is underway and preparations for the harvest celebration have begun.

"You're welcome to come to our harvest celebration," Ruíz invited. "It should take place in a few days. I'll send word. It will be quite a *fiesta* with dancing all night. And naturally, all the wine you can drink."

"Sounds pretty good. I might just ride out."
"You're always welcome."

Julia wiped her forehead with the back of her hand and called out, *"Mamita,* we're running low on shredded pork to fill the *tamales."*

Pilar straightened from stirring a huge cauldron of bubbling pinto beans. "I'll tell the men to slaughter another hog and roast it."

Nodding, Julia returned to her task of stuffing corn shucks lined with *masa* that constituted the outer shell of the *tamales.* Frenetic activity surrounded her. Los Montes Verdes was preparing for the harvest celebration.

The grapes had been picked and then crushed, all except for one huge, open vat of red grapes, which would serve as the focal point of tomorrow night's *fiesta.* Everyone at Los Montes Verdes would take a traditional turn, with lifted skirts and rolled pant legs, treading the last of this year's harvest. And there would be dancing and drinking far into the night.

Pits had been dug to roast whole hogs and sheep. Several turning spits were laden with young goats, and one large grill had been erected over glowing coals to hold the butchered carcass of a cow. The cow's head, considered a delicacy, was being slowly cooked in a covered pit. Its entrails were simmering with peppers and spices to make a savory stew, called *menudo.* Huge cauldrons of beans and rice were being cooked to serve alongside the meat dishes. Stacks of a flat, sweet bread dessert, called *pan dulce,* were baking in ovens.

Long trestle tables had already been erected in the hacienda courtyard. The tables were heaped with mounds of chopped onions and peppers, both sweet and hot, along with wheels of cheese, waiting to be used in a variety of spicy dishes. A small army of women prepared the *tamales, enchiladas,* and *chiles rellenos.*

Julia worked companionably beside the other women, dreaming of tomorrow night and . . . Ruíz. During the remainder of the harvest, everyone had been so busy that she had only caught glimpses of him. But each time their eyes had met, she had read a smoldering promise in the depths of his chocolate-colored eyes.

Once the harvest was over, Ruíz had left Los Montes Verdes to have Don Estrada's will probated and to settle affairs at the *rancho*. Julia knew he would return for the harvest celebration, and she felt light-headed with giddy anticipation.

She had already decided what she would wear. Her clothing would be traditional, with an off-the-shoulder white cotton blouse, decorated with lace and ribbons, and a full, flounced crimson skirt that provocatively displayed her ankles.

She would entice and beguile Ruíz, just as she had done at the *fandango*. But this time would be different. This time, she wouldn't refuse him . . . anything.

Allende rubbed his stiff shoulder. His left arm was finally free of its sling, but he hadn't regained full use of it. At every opportunity, he stretched and exercised the shoulder, hoping to extend his range of motion.

Watching the setting sun from the porch of his cabin, he felt singularly lonely. The *rancho* was quieter than usual. Only a handful of men remained to care for the pedigreed stock. Even the hacienda was as good as deserted, with one man, Tomás, standing guard.

Ruíz had invited all of the servants and *vaqueros* from the *rancho* to join in the harvest celebration at Los Montes Verdes. The *vaqueros* had drawn lots to see who would go and who would remain behind.

Allende had turned down Ruíz's invitation, taking Señor Ramos's place as temporary foreman so Ramos and his family could go and enjoy the festivities. He didn't feel like celebrating; there was nothing to celebrate. His life loomed empty before him. He missed Teresa.

The enforced inactivity due to his wounded shoulder had given him plenty of time to think . . . too much time to think. And now, the long, lonely winter months lay before him. Would spring ever come?

Would Teresa return to him . . . with the spring?

He shook his head. Teresa was young and beautiful and of noble blood. He had been a fool to agree to her mother's plan. Every eligible bachelor in New Orleans was being thrown at her. And what did he have to offer her in comparison? He was just a poor, semi-illiterate *vaquero*. He should have eloped with her when she had begged him to. Now she might never return to him.

Madre de Dios, he didn't want to lose her!

With his eyes narrowed against the crimson stain in the western sky, he spotted a lone rider descending into the valley. He watched as the rider drew nearer and wondered who it might be. There was something vaguely familiar about the lanky form, topped by a yellow mop of hair.

He recognized the bay mare first, and then he knew who the rider was. It was the boy whose father he had shot . . . Obadiah MacGregor.

Obadiah halted his mount and raised one bony arm in greeting. "Hi, mister. I hope you don't mind me dropping by. I figgered I'd find you here at ranch headquarters."

Surprised Obadiah possessed the courage to come to the *rancho,* he didn't know how to greet him. After all, the boy's father had been caught stealing from the *rancho*. He hadn't expected to see the boy again, and he hoped the unexpected visit didn't mean there was going to be further trouble with the MacGregor clan.

"You don't even know my name." He had purposely withheld his identity from the boy on that fateful day. "How did you find me?"

"You didn't tell me your name, that's true, but you did say you worked for Don Estrada. It weren't hard to find you."

Allende sighed. The boy was right, he had mentioned his employer's name that day, trying to strike fear into the boy's father. With that knowledge, it was easy to find him.

"Now that you've found me, to what do I owe this visit?"

"I came to thank you agin, mister. I've staked a claim on that valley you sent us to and built Ma a cabin with a real chimney. Everybody's happy as a fat tick on a lean coon dog. Ma's even talking some now. I jist had to tell you."

The tension drained from him in the face of Obadiah's open pleasure. A twinge of some unidentifiable emotion suffused him. He had killed this boy's father and earned Obadiah's eternal gratitude. Sometimes life was a strange affair.

If he were honest with himself, he was happy to see the boy. Obadiah's unexpected visit couldn't have come at a better time. It helped to take his mind off how lonely he was. Stepping off the porch, he extended his right hand.

"It's time you knew my name. I'm Allende Soto, and I'm pleased everything has worked out for your family."

Obadiah vaulted from the bay's back, gangly arms and legs flapping. He straightened and clasped Allende's hand. "Happy to know you, sir. Looks like your shoulder has healed."

He lifted his stiff left shoulder with a grimace. "Almost."

Ducking his head, Obadiah gathered his mount's reins and said, "Well, I'm glad." He shrugged his own shoulders and touched one bony finger to the brim of his beat-up hat. "Jist wanted to drop by. Guess I'll be heading out."

"Wait," Allende surprised himself by blurting. He didn't want the boy to leave ... not yet. "You didn't come all this way just to stop by and see me, did you?"

"Naw, I was headed to San Antone for supplies."

"The stores will be closed when you get there, and riding alone at night isn't a good idea. Have you eaten supper?"

Obadiah shifted from one foot to another and finally admitted, "Nope, I ain't et since this morning."

"I thought not. Stay the night and have some supper. I've got beans and rice and *tortillas.*"

"I don't want to be no trouble."

"You won't be. You can sleep on the floor by the hearth and leave at first light. You can even do me a favor."

Obadiah's face brightened at Allende's mention of needing a favor, and the boy readily agreed, "Anythin', jist ask."

"Since you're going into San Antonio, I'd be obliged if you would check to see if the mail packet has arrived. I'm expecting some letters, and no one will be going to town for the next few days."

The boy glanced around the deserted ranch yard and ventured, "You're not here alone, are you? I expected more hands on such a big spread, but this place looks plumb lonesome."

"I'm not alone, but most of the *vaqueros* are at Los Montes Verdes." He pointed to the southeast. "It's a vineyard over that way. Don Estrada passed away a few weeks ago, and Ruíz Navarro is my boss now. Don Ruíz is holding a harvest celebration tonight at the vineyard. I stayed behind to watch the *rancho.* That's why I can't leave to get the mail."

"I'll be glad to check fer your mail."

"And bring it back to me?"

"Sure. If I leave in the morning, I can be back by tomorrow afternoon."

"That's fine. I appreciate your help. Unsaddle your mount and turn her loose in the corral. There's fodder in the corral. Bring your bedroll. I'll heat up supper, and you can tell me all about your family."

The haunting strains of "La Canción de la Luna," a sad melody of a lover serenading his unrequited love, filled the air. Colorful scraps of clothing whirled by, splintered bursts of bright hues, caught between the light and shadow of the flickering torches. The commingled aromas of a variety of succulent foods spiced the gentle autumn breeze.

Julia had never seen the central courtyard so thronged with people. Besides the permanent workers of Los Montes Verdes, Ruíz and her father had invited the temporary workers as well as the *vaqueros* from the Estrada *rancho*. Everyone was there . . . except Ruíz.

Taking a sip of the delicate, straw-colored wine that was her favorite, Julia disconsolately wove her way through the boisterous merry-makers. Her full skirt swished against her legs. The skirt was perfect for dancing, and she had expected to dance the night away with Ruíz. But as the hour grew later and later, her dreams of dancing in his arms faded.

How could he have stayed away? He had never missed a harvest celebration, even when he had been married to Alicia Estrada. And this celebration had to be special for him. Didn't it? He had worked so hard to make the harvest successful.

Swallowing the last mouthful of wine, she started toward the cask to get more. As disappointed as she was feeling tonight, she was tempted to do the unthinkable and drown her sorrows in the fruit of the grape.

Glancing around, she happened to see a hurrying form detach itself from the shadows of her family's *casa*. It was Luz. She guessed Luz had just returned from putting Conchita to bed. It was about that time. Most of the younger children were conspicuously absent.

Earlier in the evening, the children had been everywhere, darting between the adults' legs, racing about the courtyard, and shrieking at the tops of their lungs. A few had even fallen into the fountain, but that had been hours ago.

Since then, they had eaten their supper and destroyed several *piñatas,* scrabbling for the spilled treasures of candy and toys. Now, the children, at least the younger ones, had been bundled off to bed, either to sleep in the stables or in the workers' homes.

The absence of the children and the lateness of the hour pressed down on Julia, making her feel even more abandoned than before. She reached the wine cask and turned the spigot. Luz walked past her, looking particularly pretty that night, with her long, wavy hair piled in curls atop her head. Julia finished filling her glass and straightened. Curious, her gaze followed Luz's progress. Where or to . . . whom was Luz hurrying?

Conchita's nurse stopped a few feet away and seated herself on a low bench. She looked as if she were waiting for a suitor, and she didn't have long to wait. Paco came rumbling up beside Luz and took her hand in his.

Julia's eyes widened, and her hand flew to her mouth. Luz and her little brother? How could it be possible? As surprised as Julia was by their pairing, a half-remembered image flashed through her mind of Luz and Paco huddled together at Carmen Treviño's *quinceanera*. How long had they been courting, she wondered, and did her parents know about it?

Paco kissed Luz's hand, and then they bent their heads together, whispering and laughing. She spun around, not wanting to watch them any longer. Her cheeks flamed with shame. Was her own life so desolate she had to spy on her little brother?

Staring into her full wineglass, she shock her head. Her preoccupation with Ruíz had truly made her blind. Even with all of them living in the same house together, she hadn't suspected that Luz and Paco were courting. Had her infatuation for Ruíz blinded her in other ways? she wondered.

Not watching where she was going, Julia was brought up short against the broad expanse of a man's crisp, white linen shirt. Her wine sloshed and spilled over. Tottering, she took a step back and tried to steady herself.

Strong fingers caught her elbow and held her swaying form. Lifting her head, she gazed into the man's face. She didn't recognize him, but she thought she might have seen him in passing once or twice before. He had sandy-colored hair and a kind-looking, freckled face. Not too many Anglos mixed with Tejanos these days. She wondered who he might be.

As if she had spoken the question out loud, he introduced himself, explaining, "I'm Peter Meredith from San Antonio. I'm Ruíz Navarro's attorney, and he invited me to the harvest celebration."

His Spanish was halting but perfect. Julia understood English, too, but she didn't tell him. So few Anglos bothered to learn the native tongue of Tejas. She enjoyed listening to his unfamiliar accent.

"I'm Julia Flores. Ruíz has mentioned you. My apologies. You must forgive me for having stumbled into you. I hope I didn't spill wine on your clothing." She retreated a pace, and he released her elbow.

Brushing the front of his shirt with his hand, he replied, "No harm done. The wine missed me." He grinned easily, revealing white, even teeth. "I'm a stranger here, and I haven't been able to locate Ruíz in this crowd. I'm glad you ran into me. You've given me an excuse to make a new friend."

"I've been looking for Ruíz, too."

Peter cocked his head and inquired, "What did you say?"

She felt the color rise to her cheeks and thought better of admitting that she was waiting for Ruíz. Instead, she said, "*Gracias* for your kind understanding. I'm not usually so clumsy."

Peter Meredith's gaze swept her and his eyes told her he liked what he saw, but his demeanor was properly circumspect.

"You don't look clumsy to me. In fact, you look as if you should be dancing. May I have the honor?"

She hesitated, using the excuse to brush at her own skirt to see if she had stained it with wine. It appeared she had been lucky, the wine had only spilled on the ground. Without looking up, she knew Peter Meredith was watching her, patiently waiting for her response to his invitation. She must give him some kind of answer . . . but what would it be?

All night, she had been longing to dance, and she had faithfully waited for Ruíz. But the evening was slipping away. She still wanted to dance. What could one dance hurt? After all, he was Ruíz's friend. Her decision made, she placed her wineglass on the corner of a table.

"I'd love to dance, Señor Meredith."

He linked his arm with hers and offered, "Call me Peter. Your surname is Flores. It must be your family who owns the vineyard with Ruíz?"

"*Sí*, my father is Felipe Flores."

Peter pulled her into the thick of the whirling dancers and observed, "Ruíz has often spoken of your family. He holds all of the Floreses in the highest regard."

Julia forced herself to smile, but any polite words she might have said choked in her throat. Ruíz had spoken of her family. She knew he held her family in the highest regard . . . but how did he feel about her?

And where was he?

Ruíz spurred Oro into a gallop. Night had fallen at least two hours before, and a full harvest moon hung on the horizon. Traditionally, Los Montes Verdes held their harvest celebration on the night of the full moon following the harvest. In the past, the Navarros had hosted the *fiesta*. This year, Felipe was the host, and he had decided to honor the old tradition, even though the full moon fell late in the month of October.

But the moon wasn't the only thing that was late . . . Ruíz was, too.

Señor Hotchkiss had certainly taken his time, haggling with Ruíz over the price of the emerald ring. He had seen the ring in Hotchkiss's *casa de empeños* when he'd been in San Antonio meeting with Peter. The dazzling green fire of the ring had reminded him of Julia's eyes. He hoped the ring would be the perfect gift to assure her of the sincerity of his intentions.

He hadn't counted on how long it would take for him to fix the price with Hotchkiss. At least, he had been able to persuade the German pawnbroker to let him take the ring and pay off its purchase price over time. He wanted to propose and present the ring to Julia tonight.

Now he was late for the celebration . . . very late. He hoped Julia wouldn't be too angry with him. He had been so busy with the harvest and Don Estéban's affairs that there hadn't been time to approach her with his proposal and vows of . . . love.

And he had wanted to wait until the harvest celebration. Tonight was the culmination of all they had worked so hard for. It seemed like the right time and place . . . if only he weren't so late.

He heard the sounds of revelry coming from the hacienda compound before he could see the lights. His heart lifted, and the blood sang in his veins in joyous anticipation. He could barely contain his excitement, thinking about making Julia his forever.

Along with his joy came a sense of rightness. They shared a common background and knew each other well. Her strength of character no longer troubled him. He regarded it as an asset. It was gratifying to know she would be standing beside him for the remainder of his life, a strong and vital wife. And if they should disagree and argue, he smiled to himself . . . the making up would be delicious.

No other woman had ever fired his blood like Julia.

Circling the hacienda compound, he entered through the back gate by the stables. He located a lantern and lit it. Glancing around, he wasn't surprised to find there was no one in the stables to care for Oro. Everyone was at the *fiesta*, except for a few blanket-wrapped cherubs who had been bedded down for the night in a mound of fragrant hay.

Moving quietly so as to not disturb the sleeping children, he led Oro to an empty stall. He unsaddled and rubbed down the stallion before giving him a ration of oats. With a final pat on Oro's sleek, muscled neck, he tiptoed from the stables.

Despite the late hour, the hacienda courtyard was thronged with people. Most of the food was gone, and Ruíz realized he was hungry. Snatching a *tamale* from a platter, he unwrapped its outer corn shuck and bit into the succulent tube of pork and spices surrounded by *masa*.

Threading his way through the crowd while he ate, he searched for Julia. Many of the workers recognized him, and they all stopped to congratulate him on a successful harvest. Before he knew it, his hands were filled with a plate of *cabrito*, beans and rice, and accompanied by a glass of red wine.

Ruíz hadn't spotted Julia in the crowded throng, so he paused to eat the food and drink the wine. His gaze fell on the dancers, spinning to the lively tune of "Adelita." It was then he finally saw her. She was dancing with Peter Meredith, and they were laughing together.

Something hard and brittle invaded his heart. Memories of Julia dancing with David Treviño at the *fandango* and the *quinceanera* flashed through his mind. Of all the women at the *fiesta,* Peter had to pick Julia to dance with. He couldn't help but admit that Peter had excellent taste in women.

With an outward show of serenity he didn't feel inside, he set aside his half-finished plate and drained his wineglass. Carefully, he wiped his hands and mouth on a napkin.

When he turned again to watch the dancers, Julia was lost in the crowd. He stood staring at the dancers, but his eyes couldn't seem to focus on anything. Taking a deep breath, he clenched and unclenched his fists. Moisture beaded his brow with the effort of controlling the emotions simmering beneath his calm facade.

Julia was his!

Even as the words echoed in his mind, he realized he had

no right to be upset at Julia . . . no right to think of her as his possession. He had come late to the celebration. He shouldn't expect her to be waiting, like a wilted flower on the sidelines, just for him. Peter was his friend. Peter would never try to take her from him . . . even if he could.

And if he trusted in Peter's faithfulness to their friendship, then how much more should he trust in Julia's love for him? She had proved it in countless ways and proclaimed it, over and over. She had never married; instead, she had spent her life waiting for him. It was an act of faith that awed him. If he lived to be a thousand years old, he couldn't hope to equal her selfless devotion.

The tension ebbed from his body. He wiped the moisture from his brow, adjusted the cuffs of his frilled linen shirt and smoothed his tight *bolero* jacket. He wanted to look his best for her, and he wanted to make her happy. There would be no ghosts of unresolved feelings between them tonight, he vowed silently, only love . . . and commitment.

The music ended and Ruíz spotted Peter and Julia across the crowded space reserved for dancing. The wavering torchlight illuminated her, and he drank in her loveliness.

This night, she had loosed her hair, allowing the ink-black cascade to spill beyond her waist. She wore a traditional low-necked, off-the-shoulder white blouse that revealed the high, golden-tinted mounds of her breasts. The blouse narrowed into the tiny span of her waist and disappeared beneath the crimson folds of her full, flounced skirt. Delicate ankles and part of her shapely calves peeped from beneath the skirt.

Julia lifted her head and their gazes snagged. She held his eyes for one brief moment, and then she glanced at Peter. Withdrawing from her dancing partner, her eyes filled with something akin to apprehension. She dropped her head and stood, her body rigid, waiting for Ruíz to approach them.

When he reached her side, she lifted her head and smiled. Defiance glinted in her eyes, and her chin was thrust forward.

He almost laughed out loud at the challenge in her gaze. This was the Julia he knew, and he wouldn't want her to be any other way. She obviously remembered the times he had allowed his jealousy to run rampant. That had been her first reaction. But the strength of her character and the purity of her feelings had evoked a second response from her. As clearly as if she were speaking to him, he understood her reactions.

Julia had danced with his friend . . . nothing more . . . and she dared him to say anything about it.

Ruíz met her silent challenge with ease. He took her hand and bowed low over it, murmuring, "Julia, you look especially lovely tonight. My compliments."

She inclined her head and replied, "*Gracias*, Ruíz, I'm glad to see you."

The unspoken part of her words hovered between them. He knew, with absolute certainty, that only Peter's presence kept her from chastising him for arriving so late at the harvest celebration.

Turning to Peter, he bowed again, greeting him. "*Mi amigo*, I'm happy you decided to join our *fiesta*. Are you having a good time? I trust Julia has taken excellent care of you."

Her eyes sought Ruíz's and she smiled, a slow curve of her full, carmine-colored lips. He had purposely taunted her with his implied jealousy. But she was too wise to rise to his bait.

Instead, she offered innocently, "I've done my best to see that Señor Peter has had a good time . . . despite the fact he's a stranger among us and was searching for your familiar face."

Ruíz made a show of wincing at her well-placed barb and then he winked at her. She lifted one shapely, black-winged eyebrow and shrugged.

Peter must have felt uneasy at being the object of their veiled innuendos, and not understanding, he tried to smooth over the situation.

"I was somewhat at a loss when I first came, but I was lucky enough to stumble into Julia. After we introduced ourselves, I asked her to dance. As you can see, I've been in very capable hands, although I will admit I'm a trifle thirsty."

"I'll fetch you a glass of wine, Señor Peter," she volunteered. "Would you care for white or red?"

"White, if you have it."

"*Sí*, it's my favorite."

"*Gracias.*" Peter bowed and accepted.

Julia moved away, slipping between knots of people, to fetch the wine for Peter. As soon as she was gone, Peter took Ruíz's arm and propelled him several steps away from the crowd, finding a shadowed niche against the hacienda wall.

"Julia is very beautiful, and she loves your daughter dearly, Ruíz. That's what we talked about while we were dancing . . . your daughter. I hadn't realized Concepción was living with the Flores family. She related some of your daughter's more lively escapades; they were very entertaining. Almost made me want a family of my own," Peter admitted wistfully. "If you ever think of remarrying, Ruíz, I would—"

"You'll be my best man, Peter," Ruíz interrupted him.

Peter's light-blue eyes widened, and he half turned to gaze at Julia's retreating form. "So that's how it is?"

"That's how it is."

"Congratulations, *amigo*. I'm green with envy. But I didn't drag you away from the party just to talk about your personal plans. I want to speak privately with you before Julia returns."

"*Por favor*, speak plainly."

"Someone has been making inquiries about the contents of Don Estrada's will. Not directly to me, but to some of my colleagues."

Ruíz digested Peter's information and nodded. He could understand Peter's caution, because the will was irregular, omitting any reference to Don Estéban's only son, Lázaro. But Ruíz had no intention of following the will's stipulations and cheating Lázaro of what was rightfully his.

There should be nothing to worry about.

Chapter Eighteen

Julia carefully balanced the two glasses of wine as she made her way through the boisterous merry-makers. One glass for her and one glass for Peter. Ruíz could fetch his own wine. It would serve him right for his veiled teasing about her dancing with Peter . . . and for arriving so late.

As she approached the two men, she noticed they had stepped away from the crowd and had their heads close together, talking. Business, probably, she thought with a sigh. Even in the midst of a celebration, men always found time to speak of business.

Her father stepped suddenly into her path, looking as if he had being doing some serious celebrating. Placing his hand on her shoulder, he asked, "Where are you going with that wine?"

"Ruíz has finally arrived. His attorney and friend, Peter Meredith, is with him." Julia angled her head toward the two men, indicating where they were standing. "Would you care to meet Señor Peter? He's very nice. His Spanish is good but a trifle stilted. I'm certain he must have learned it from a book."

"I'd be honored to meet Señor Meredith."

Julia and Felipe approached Ruíz and Peter. Julia handed Peter one of the wineglasses and made the introductions. "This is my father, Felipe Flores. *Papito,* this is Peter Meredith."

Felipe clapped Peter on the back, almost upsetting his glass of wine as he greeted him heartily. *"Quién es amigo de Ruíz es también mi amigo."* Without further preamble, he launched into a concern that must have been weighing heavily on his mind.

"Julia tells me you're Ruíz's attorney, and I could use a good attorney. I'm worried about the new government of Tejas. They seem to be hostile toward native Tejanos with land grants from Spain. I haven't had any trouble yet, but I can't help but be worried."

"I've already told Ruíz your lands are probably safe because Ruíz and his father served under Sam Houston at San Jacinto. In fact, Don Federico could be considered a hero of the Republic since he . . ."

Peter's words were swallowed up as Ruíz guided Julia away from the two men. His hand on her arm was warm, but its mere touch raised gooseflesh on her skin, making her shiver with pure, undiluted pleasure. It had been such a long time since he'd touched her.

Once they had melted into the jostling mob of people, he turned to her and asked solemnly, "Would you honor me with this dance?"

The musicians were playing a *fandango.* Julia knew it was Ruíz's favorite dance, and she savored her sweet moment of triumph. He had purposely pulled her away from Peter and her father. He had passed up a golden opportunity to discuss business. He must want to be alone with her . . . to dance with her under the stars, fulfilling her dreams of this special night.

She smiled and replied simply, *"Sí."*

He lifted her wineglass to her lips and toasted, "To us." Obediently, she took a sip, and he wound his fingers around hers on the wineglass stem, raising the glass to his mouth at the very place her lips touched.

Gulping the remainder of the wine, he repeated, "To us and this night." And then he took her into his arms and spun her around in the dizzying, eddying flow of the *fandango*.

They twirled together, legs intertwined, caught up in the music . . . and the magic of each other's touch. The music flowed through them and they moved together effortlessly, united by the common melody of the song. The pulsating beat echoed their own pounding hearts, fanning the building conflagration in their blood, making them ache to be even . . . closer.

When the music finally stopped, Julia leaned into the muscled hardness of Ruíz's chest and brushed her breasts provocatively against the crisp linen of his shirt.

"Why were you so late tonight?"

"To make you wonder." His voice contained the teasing note she knew so well. "And I have a surprise."

"What surprise?" She knew she should protest his lateness with greater fervor, but she didn't want to spoil the moment. It was enough that he had come and that he wanted to be with her.

"I can't tell you about the surprise yet, Julia."

"When will you tell me?"

"When the time is right." He leaned down and kissed the crown of her head, but his eyes gazed beyond her . . . to something at the back of the courtyard. Turning, she followed his gaze and found he was staring at the one lone vat of grapes beside the winery.

"Have you trod the grapes tonight, Julia? It's tradition, you know."

Julia swished her pristine skirt and admitted, "No, I haven't."

"Shall we?"

Julia giggled and replied, "*Sí*, Ruíz, I would like that." She followed him willingly, and they left the noisy crowd behind.

The vat stood empty in the shadows, some hundred *varas* from the *fiesta*.

Ruíz led her to the ladder propped against the large, oak-ribbed vat. Stopping before the ladder, he pulled off his boots and rolled up his pants to the knees, baring muscled calves that were lightly dusted with dark-brown hair.

She followed suit by kicking off her sandals and hitching up her skirt, pulling the excess material through her legs, diaper-fashion, and tucking the end into her waistband. Her precautionary measure succeeded in lifting her skirt to keep it from dragging through the grapes, but it also exposed a great deal of her legs.

Ruíz's eyes traveled up and down the expanse of her exposed thighs and calves. The heat of his gaze scorched her flesh.

He took her hand in his calloused fingers, and his voice was husky when he urged, *"Vengase."* They climbed the ladder together, Ruíz helping Julia from behind, and then they paused on the wide lip of the vat.

Julia stared down at the sea of grapes. She had treaded the grapes at harvest time since she had been old enough to lift one foot in front of the other. But each year, she felt the same hesitation and unsettling anticipation when she first stared down at the grapes.

Getting into a grape vat was a bit like plunging into a deep, icy stream. The initial shock of sinking into the mushy and pungent morass was anything but pleasant. After a few minutes, though, the unusual sensation wore off, and she enjoyed the sensual slide of the grapes against her bare feet and legs.

Tonight, treading the grapes was secondary. At least a hundred pair of feet had already done that job admirably. She knew the real reason why Ruíz had invited her into the vat.

Memories flooded her as they descended with a soft plop into the pulverized mess. A gasp escaped her lips when she sank to her knees beside Ruíz, her hand still firmly enfolded in his. She closed her eyes.

Images of playing with Ruíz in the grapes when they were children flashed through her mind. Years before, after taking their turn at treading the grapes, she and Ruíz would emerge, covered from head to toe with the rich, sticky purple pulp. Her mother had despaired, each year, of being able to eradicate the purple stain from her skin and hair.

She wondered how Ruíz's parents had reacted to his equally deplorable appearance. She had never thought to ask when they were children. If his family's reaction was anything like her mother's, it must have been something to hear. She chuckled at the memory.

He squeezed her hand and asked, "Are you thinking what I am?"

Opening her eyes, she found him towering over her, limned by the full, harvest moon at his back.

"I was thinking of the times when we were children and—"

"We rolled in this stuff until our parents thought we would never be clean again." Even in the wan light, she spied the mischievous gleam in his eyes.

Her heart lifted at seeing him openly happy. Over the past few weeks, there had been precious little joy in his life . . . only hard work.

"*Sí*, I was remembering."

"I was remembering, too." He moved closer to her and whispered seductively in her ear, "We're not children any longer, Julia. We can't roll in the grapes like before. What would you suggest?" But his next action belied his words. Without warning, she felt his hand at the back of her blouse and then the slimy mass of pulverized grapes sliding down her back.

She jumped back and squirmed, shrieking, "Oh, you! How could you!"

He had already retreated a few steps, with his hands held out in front of him, palms up. Worst of all, he was laughing uproariously at her outraged reaction.

"Ohhh!" she gasped. "You . . . you . . ."

Grabbing a fistful of grape pulp, she slung it in his general direction. He dodged and lunged away, heading for the far side of the vat. Watching him run from her was comical, the quicksand of squashed grapes sucking at his forward progress.

Despite his ungainly headway, she didn't hesitate. Grabbing up two handfuls of the purplish mush, she plunged after him, throwing the grapes at his retreating back and yelling unkind names at him.

It was like living yesterday all over again, the precious, innocent memories. The poignant promise of their youth.

Laughing at her mostly ineffectual attempts at revenge, he dodged and twisted, managing to keep himself just one step beyond her grasp. With lithe grace, he evaded the brunt of her assaults, only getting slightly splattered by her desperate missiles. He didn't even try to retaliate, he seemed only too happy to lead her on a merry chase.

After several turns around the circular vat, she stopped, gasping for air. There was a stitch in her side, and she doubled over until the spasm passed. When she straightened, he was there, standing before her. The spasm faded, and she decided not to let the opportunity pass.

Bending her knees, she scooped up two fistfuls of grapes. Raising her arms, she bore down on him, gleeful she would finally be able to even the score.

He was too quick for her. His hands came up, and he caught each of her wrists in his strong grip. His hold on her was firm and purposeful as he brought her hands down to his mouth.

His gaze locked with hers. Nuzzling one of her clenched hands, he insinuated his tongue tip between her curled fingers. Involuntarily, she opened her hand, and he bent his head, using his tongue and lips to scour her outstretched fingers. He nibbled and sucked, his tongue snaking out, stroking over the sensitive flesh of her palm.

Julia shivered with pleasure. When he had licked her hand

clean, he turned his attention to her other hand. Slowly, one by one, she unfurled her fingers, savoring his sensuous onslaught. His tongue and mouth worked their magic again. The flesh of her palm was empty, stained and quivering, but empty.

Ruíz's eyes were dark with passion when he pulled her into his embrace. His warm breath feathered the hair at her ear. *"Te amo,* Julia."

She stiffened in his arms. Those words . . . the words she had waited a lifetime to hear from his lips. Had he really said them? Did he really mean them?

Her head came up, and she searched his eyes, silently pleading for the truth.

"I'm in love with you, Julia," he repeated. "I guess I always have been but was just too blind to realize it. You and I were children together . . . and you were several years younger. I thought of you as another little sister, like Teresa."

He paused and took a deep breath, admitting, "After my father died, I felt dead inside, as if nothing mattered except work. I hadn't even finished grieving for Alicia. Because I didn't love her, I felt guilty. So guilty, I couldn't properly mourn her. It was a vicious circle with no end in sight. And then all the responsibilities came, one after another. My daughter, my mother, my sister, Don Estéban, the vineyard, the *rancho,* the debts . . ." His voice faltered, and he buried his head in her hair.

"I'm not asking for your sympathy. I just wanted you to know what I was feeling at the time, so you might understand why I acted foolishly." Lifting her face to his, he hesitated over the next words, "At first, you seemed to be my adversary, just another obstacle to overcome. When you offered your love to me . . . I couldn't accept it. I saw you as another responsibility. At the same time, I was afraid of your strength, Julia. It reminded me of my mother's domineering . . ."

Raising her grape-stained fingers to his lips, she whispered, "Don't torture yourself, Ruíz. *Yo entiendo.*"

"*Sí,* you have always understood, always been there for me. And you know me, Julia, sometimes you know me so well it's frightening. You were right about my being afraid of my feelings. I knew feelings could hurt and that they carry the added baggage of duty." Ruíz's lips curved into a wry smile. "Duty . . . that word you hate.

"But while you've been so right about us, I've been so wrong. Loving you is not a duty, it's a joy. I love you, Julia, your beauty, your strength, and your tender heart. And I'm blessed, so blessed that you love me, too." He stopped, and Julia felt him grow tense in her arms. "You do still love me, Julia? I haven't lost you with my bumbling and . . ."

"Sssh, Ruíz, you will always have my love. My heart knows no other."

Drawing her closer, he murmured, "*Gracias a Dios, gracias a Dios.* Then you will marry me?"

"Of course."

"*¿Cuándo?*"

Julia giggled at the impatient note in his voice. She felt the turgid hardness of his immediate need pressed against her abdomen. She couldn't help but tease him.

"First, you'll need to speak to my father, and the rest of my family. *Mamá* and I will have to make plans. Padre Carrasco will need to be notified. I'll want to draw up a guest list, and my mother's wedding dress will—"

He growled low in his throat and covered her lips with his, effectively stopping her lengthy recital of wedding plans. When he raised his head, he admitted, "Julia, I can't wait."

"Then don't."

Grinning at her open invitation, he dipped his head. His full, warm mouth closed over hers, savoring and tasting. Gently, he eased her lips apart and thrust his tongue inside her mouth.

She trembled at his intimate exploration. His tongue was

warm and heady with the sweet taste of the grapes he had suckled from her fingertips. Tentatively, she touched her tongue to his. Heated and sensitive, their tongues met in sinuous play, dancing together in long-suppressed desire.

Echoing the twining of their tongues, Julia pressed herself into Ruíz's arms, reveling in the familiar, hard-muscled planes of his body. He returned her embrace by curling protectively around her and guiding her slowly toward the ladder at the side of the vat.

With her back to the ladder, Julia murmured against his lips, "Where should we go?"

His answer was a long groan, filled with desperate need, and one word: "Nowhere."

"But, Ruíz, we can't—"

Her protest was cut short when he invaded her mouth again and crushed her to him. His hands moved downward to cup the fullness of her unfettered breasts against the thin cotton of her blouse. He flicked his thumbs across her slumbering nipples, and they leapt awake, straining against his hands. Aching for more.

He caressed her breasts tenderly, wringing long, low moans of pleasure from her lips. Sending tongues of molten flame through her veins. Making her limbs feel as if her muscles had melted away, only to be replaced by liquid fire.

When he lowered her blouse to her waist, the cool night air caressed her skin, making her nipples pucker even harder into almost painful pebbles of desire. His warm mouth eased one of her responsive pleasure points, suckling and laving the tender bud with honeyed sweetness before he gave equal attention to her other pouting breast.

She arched her back, forcing her breast deeper into the tender adhesion of his mouth. The scent of him, heated male mixed with the starchy smell of his linen shirt, enticed her. A wine-rich languor flowed through her body, centering between her thighs and building . . . building into aching pleasure.

Ruíz's hands moved to the waistband of her skirt, and he freed the knot of fabric she had pulled between her legs. Her skirt billowed out, drifting down into the grapes and wrapping around Ruíz's legs.

With his mouth worshipping her breasts, he slowly slid the fabric of her skirt upward until it bunched about her waist. The sensual touch of his hands on her legs made her gasp with delight. She wriggled and bucked against him. The heated need of her silently crying for his touch.

He didn't disappoint her.

His fingertips moved in lazy arcs across the hot flesh of her thighs, sending scintillating spirals of ecstasy along the taut cordon of her nerves. And when his fingers moved higher, along the sensitive inner flesh of her thighs, she thrust her throbbing woman's mound against his hand.

He found the slit in her undergarment. Julia could feel the heat and slick dew of her desire there. Cupping her with his palm, his fingers stroked the intimate folds of her, lingering with particular care on the thickened nub of her passion. His fingers and hand played reverent homage to her need, teasing and enticing, cradling and exploring.

She strained against him. The magic of his mouth on her breasts melded into the tantalizing pressure of his hands. Glorying in the hot flood of sheer, wanton desire, she felt the aching pleasure spreading through her . . . striving and . . . building. Her body was suffused with ecstasy . . . straining toward that pinnacle of passionate wonder . . . and release.

She convulsed then, under his expert lovemaking, spinning away into that mindless vortex of primal passion. Even as she cried out for him to join her, she felt the scalding heat and turgid length of him enter her. The muscles of her woman's sheath welcomed him, contracting in glorious completion.

Drifting back to earth, she buried her head in his shoulder, whimpering her joyous fulfillment against his perspiration-slick shirt. Her hands curled around his neck, caressing the soft texture of his hair.

Ruíz moved slowly within her, stopping to murmur low words of love and to trail kisses across her breasts. Julia moved with him, feeling totally satiated and wanting only to pleasure him. Bracing herself against the ladder, she opened herself completely and clasped her legs around his waist.

The boldness of her action seated him deeply within her body and struck a primitive chord within her. She moaned with the exquisite pleasure of enfolding him so deeply within her body.

He was hers.

Her heart soared. Her spirit took wing. Ruíz belonged to her . . . finally and totally . . . hers. He loved her and wanted to spend his life with her. The dream of her lifetime had come true.

But the tantalizing rhythm of his body inside her, and the sensuous play of his hands and mouth upon her flesh pulled her back from contemplating things spiritual . . . to the sweet surcease of the flesh.

Feeling his mounting need, her body responded with a need of its own . . . and she answered in kind. Moving against him in the age-old ritual of mating, meeting him, thrust for thrust. In slow, spiraling steps, they mounted together, climbing ever higher toward the stars, pausing in playful dalliance at each plateau. Reveling in the heated, musk of their bodies . . . made into one.

Climbing and straining together with their flesh drenched in perspiration and ardor, they caught hold of the tail of a comet and sped into that almost painful, shattering bliss of oneness.

She relaxed in his strong arms. All of her will and strength had drained away, like the run-off grape juice from the vat. He captured her mouth in a kiss filled with promise, expressing the wonder of their ecstasy far better than mere words ever could.

But when he withdrew his body from hers, she clung to him and whispered, "It hurts so when you leave me. I wish we could be joined forever."

Cupping her face in his hands, he brushed his lips against her mouth before he agreed. "I know how you feel."

The music of the *fiesta,* which had provided a steady, throbbing backdrop to their lovemaking, abruptly stopped. They gazed into each other's eyes, and, without speaking, they both wondered how long they had been together.

The pale disk of the full moon still rode in the sky. It was late but not that late. The musicians must only be resting. The harvest celebration usually lasted until dawn.

While Julia smoothed down her skirt, he fumbled inside the pocket of his *bolero* jacket. Removing a small, tissue-wrapped package, he presented it to her, murmuring, "With this ring, you are my betrothed."

Julia's fingers were trembling when she accepted the tiny packet. Carefully, she unwrapped it. A square-cut gem mounted on a band of gold nestled in the folds of paper.

Gasping with delight, she slipped it on her finger. It fit her hand as if it had been fashioned just for her. Fanning her hand back and forth, she said, "Ruíz, it's lovely, but I never expected you would . . ."

"I wanted you to be sure of the seriousness of my intentions." He smiled and leaned forward to kiss her. "After what we shared tonight, I guess the ring is almost superfluous. It was my surprise . . . what kept me so late from coming to you. I wanted—"

His words were cut short as Julia threw her arms around him and hugged him with a fierce joy. "It's perfect, Ruíz. I love it."

"I'm glad you like it, but in this light, I doubt that you even know what it is."

"No, but it doesn't matter. What matters is that you gave it to me . . . that you were thinking of me and wanted me to know that . . .''

"That I love you . . . and never want to be parted from you again." His voice throbbed with emotion. "I selected this ring because it reminded me of you. It's an emerald, Julia, with a dark, green fire that matches your eyes."

"Oh!"

"Vengase, Julia. Let's go inside where you can see it."

"Do you think we should? It's late and my family—"

"Won't notice you're missing until morning," he reassured her. "I'll wake you before sunrise. We're betrothed now, Julia."

"I don't want to leave you," Julia breathed. "I don't think I can stand it."

He nodded and kissed her forehead. Taking her in his strong arms, he lifted her up the ladder and followed her from the vat of grapes.

After he retrieved his boots and her sandals, they slipped through the shadows, barefoot, and entered the deserted hacienda. He led her through the dark hallways to his bedroom and lit the candle beside his bed.

Sinking to the floor to keep her stained skirt from sullying the counterpane on his bed, she studied the ring. The emerald glowed a deep, forest green, lit from within by sparks of shimmering light from the lantern's glow. Ruíz had been right . . . it matched her eyes perfectly.

Bending, he cradled her in his arms and pulled her to her feet.

"Do you like it?"

"Like it? Ruíz, it's the most magnificent thing I've ever seen." She lifted her head and gazed into his eyes, admitting, "It's glorious, but not as glorious as we are together."

"Then you don't like it?"

"Silly, I love it."

"I'm glad." He clasped her tighter and quirked both his

eyebrows at her. "You were sitting on the floor because you were afraid your stained skirt would dirty my bed?"

"*Sí.*"

"I'll remedy that," and with those words, he tore off his jacket and shirt and stepped from his tight-fitting pants, flinging them on the bed.

Naked, his engorged manhood sprang forth, beckoning her, a tiny droplet of moisture glistening on its tip.

His voice was husky when he offered, "Let me help you with your clothes."

Lázaro lay stretched upon his stomach, absorbing the heat from the sun-baked limestone terrace while he held a spyglass to his eye. He and his men had arrived at his father's *rancho* a few days before. The limestone caves above the valley of his boyhood home had proven to be a fortuitous hiding place. He had been able to watch all that transpired below without being detected.

He remembered these old caves with a certain fondness. There had been many times in his youth when he had hidden here, sore of heart and sore of body. The caves had served him well in the past, as they served him today, except for the quarrelsome men with him.

He would be glad when the job was done. Then he could poison Chivato and the other men before they started back to New Orleans. It would be a relief to be rid of their pernicious influence. Their constant, drunken squabbling maddened him. Besides, he had decided long ago there would be no witnesses to what he planned to do. Leaving witnesses alive would be foolish indeed. They could blackmail him later.

Until his plans were complete, he had to admit his hired thugs served a purpose. He had been careful not to show his face in San Antonio where he might be recognized. Instead, he had sent the men to make discreet inquiries that had garnered him valuable information.

The first inquiry had been concerning his father's will. His father had done exactly what Lázaro had expected him to do . . . leaving his entire estate to Ruíz and Ruíz's daughter.

He had thought he was prepared for the inevitable outcome, but when he had learned the truth, he was seized by such a rage at his father's perfidy that he felt as if he were going to explode. Only a bottle of absinthe, brought all the way from New Orleans, had been able to console him.

When his rage cooled, he was gratified to learn there were no rumors of a sizable treasure in his father's will. He wasn't surprised his father and Ruíz had kept the treasure a secret. Ruíz would probably wait and spend the ill-gotten treasure a bit at a time, melting down the gold and selling the jewels for cash.

Other welcome news had centered around the harvest celebration Ruíz was planning at his vineyard. Lázaro had watched as the *rancho* emptied of its *vaqueros,* making his plan easy to execute.

And he had gathered one other crucial bit of information by having some of his men watch the Navarro hacienda. Ruíz's daughter and her nurse usually strolled along the Guadalupe River every afternoon following their *siesta.*

Everything had fallen into place, aiding his plans. Tonight, with most of the *vaqueros* absent from the *rancho,* was the perfect time to strike and take Allende captive.

He watched the setting sun, waiting for darkness to fall and cover his actions. But just before dark, a stranger rode up and joined Allende in his cabin, an Anglo stranger.

With this unexpected disruption to his plans, he debated whether to go down and take Allende and kill the stranger or not. With a bit of luck, the *gringo* would leave in the morning, and Allende would be alone again.

Lázaro remembered enough about the past harvest celebrations at the Navarro's winery to know the *fiesta* would last all night. The hung-over *vaqueros* wouldn't show themselves until tomorrow evening. That would leave him an entire day to get what he wanted.

He decided to wait and see if the stranger left in the morning. If the *gringo* visiting Allende wasn't gone by sunrise, he would make his move. His men would kill the stranger and take Allende captive while the *rancho* was still deserted.

Lázaro would prefer not to execute the stranger in front of Allende. Sometimes a show of force backfired, making a captive even more recalcitrant. Besides that, he had no desire to kill a *gringo*. In Tejas, the authorities wouldn't stop until they found the killer of an Anglo, hunting him down relentlessly.

But if he was left with no other choice, he wouldn't hesitate. The *gringo* would die, and any stubbornness Allende might exhibit would be handled. He had already planned for that possibility. There was precious little time to waste in torturing Allende into submission.

He didn't sleep much that night, anticipating the coming day. Before the eastern horizon began to grow light, he sent two of the men to wait outside the Navarro hacienda compound by the river. Lázaro, Chivato, and the remaining three men crept down to the *rancho* and hid in a barn near Allende's cabin. Lázaro waited anxiously, hoping the stranger would depart.

A stream of smoke rose from Allende's chimney in the pale dawn light. Not long afterward, he was relieved to see the *gringo* stranger emerge from the cabin and catch and saddle his horse. Allende exchanged a few words with the *gringo* before he rode off.

Lázaro wondered, fleetingly, why Allende would befriend a *gringo*. Dismissing the errant thought, he gathered his men to make a dash for Allende's cabin. In a matter of minutes, it wouldn't matter who Allende had befriended.

Chapter Nineteen

Allende reached for the coffeepot sitting in the coals of the hearth. The door to the cabin banged open behind him. Startled, but expecting to find that Obadiah had returned to fetch some forgotten item, he spun around.

It wasn't Obadiah.

The muzzles of five pistols were leveled at him. A tall man, whose features were remarkably familiar, growled at the others, "Get in and shut the door. We need privacy." The other men obeyed by shutting the door and standing along the wall of the cramped cabin.

He experienced a brief moment of panic at the unexpected, armed intrusion. With an effort of will, he fought to remain outwardly composed. He didn't know what these men wanted, but he knew it would be to his benefit to remain calm until he found out. To that end, he held his tongue and waited for the intruders to speak first and make their demands.

But while he waited, he used the time to study the five armed men. He couldn't remember having met the man who had spoken, despite his familiar features. He appeared to be the leader; his bearing was aristocratic and he was well groomed. The man to the leader's right was small and slight and looked out of place behind the massive flintlock pistol he pointed.

Allende didn't like the looks of the other three men to the left of the tall leader. They were massive men with stone-hard faces and cold eyes. Stubbled beard sprouted on their jaws. One of them bore a jagged knife scar on his face, another one was missing an ear, and the third one had the ugliest, blackest teeth Allende had ever seen.

Returning his gaze to the tall leader, he hoped to make some sense of their hostile intrusion. But when he looked closer at the man who had spoken, his blood suddenly went cold. In his astonishment at their abrupt entrance, he had been lulled by the man's familiar features and civilized appearance. He had missed the look in his eyes.

The leader returned his stare, and Allende recognized the slightly unfocused and agitated gaze of a madman . . . a man completely without a conscience. He had seen that look before . . . in the eyes of a man who had taken delight in torturing and killing little children.

He had spent his life trying to forget the long-ago day he had hidden in the root cellar and survived the madman's killing spree. All his brothers and sisters, along with his parents, had died that day.

Dread filled him, and his thoughts turned to Teresa. Would he ever see her again? Did these men know the *rancho* was almost deserted? Had they come to steal the pedigreed livestock and kill the few witnesses?

Their leader spoke. "I see you were about to have coffee. My men and I would welcome some coffee."

Ignoring the leader's request, he countered with, "Who are you and what do you want? If you just want coffee, I would oblige you without the show of firearms."

"I didn't think you would be so formal, Señor Soto, wanting

us to introduce ourselves.'' His voice dropped to a menacing snarl, ''Our weapons should be introduction enough, but I don't mind indulging your request, within reason.''

Executing a mocking bow, he stated, ''I'm Lázaro Estrada, at your service.'' Waving his pistol in casual dismissal, he declared, ''The names of my men are unimportant. You will address yourself solely to me, Señor Soto.''

Allende wasn't surprised to learn that the leader with the mad eyes was Don Estrada's estranged son. It explained the man's familiar features. But he was surprised to learn that Lázaro knew *his* name.

Now that he knew who the leader was, he surmised that Lázaro had come, with armed help, to demand his rightful portion of the *rancho*. Obviously, he had heard he had been omitted from his father's will, but what he didn't know was that Ruíz had every intention of giving Lázaro what belonged to him—without a fight.

Some of the tension drained from Allende. With a few carefully chosen words, he might be able to diffuse this ugly confrontation. But the last thing he wanted to do was to insult Lázaro's pride by speaking of his private matters in front of hired thugs.

''Señor Lázaro, if I could have a word alone with you.'' Allende inclined his head toward the far corner of the room.

Hesitating, Lázaro gaze scanned Allende as if he were searching for hidden weapons. ''Make it quick.'' He waited for Allende to go before him.

Allende led Lázaro to the corner of the room. They stood so close that Lázaro's pistol pressed against his side. And the other men hadn't relinquished their vigilance, either. All of their pistols were still pointed at Allende's back.

Lowering his voice to a whisper, Allende said, ''Señor Lázaro, I believe I can help you to clear up any misunderstanding. You don't need guns to reclaim your heritage. Despite the words of your father's will, Don Ruíz is willing to deed you his half of the *rancho.*"

Lázaro moved so fast Allende didn't even see the pistol before it slammed into his face. Recoiling from the blow, his face felt numb with shock for several seconds. Then the shock wore off, and he felt the searing pain. Blood spurted from his nose.

"I do not discuss my family's matters with a hired *peón.* You've overstepped yourself. And I won't forget Ruíz has bragged to you about his proposed munificence." He sneered. "I don't want Ruíz's pathetic charity, even if I believed he would do such a thing."

Allende wiped his bleeding nose with his shirtsleeve. Forgetting his earlier fear of this madman, rage poured through him. He ignored the loaded guns.

"Don't believe me, *bastardo.* But get out of here! I don't want to look at your greedy face."

Lázaro didn't flinch at his insulting words. Instead, he appeared to relish them. His mouth curved into a thin smile, and he ordered, *"Hombres,* teach the *peón* some respect."

Within the blink of an eye, the three massive thugs descended upon him. They started by burying their fists in his abdomen, and then they took turns slugging him in the face. He warded off and returned as many blows as he could, but it was three against one. Slowly, their blows overwhelmed him, and he crumpled to the floor.

He refused to beg for mercy, and he didn't receive any.

Once he was down, the three men viciously kicked him, aiming particularly at his midsection. Pain exploded within him. His ears rang and stars danced before his eyes. As if from a faraway place, he felt his ribs give . . . one by one. Darkness began to swallow him as he ineffectually turned and twisted on the floor, trying to protect his ribs against their brutal kicks.

"¡Bastante! I need him conscious and able to walk, you fools," Lázaro commanded.

The punishing kicks stopped but the pain went on, convulsing Allende into a mindless animal writhing on the floor. It hurt to breathe, to move, even to swallow. The only taste was the sweet, metallic flavor of his own blood filling his mouth.

"Now that you understand the kind of respect I can command, you'll do as you're told. *¿Sí?*" Lázaro leaned down, threatening him.

Allende spat out a mouthful of blood and fought against the vicious claws of agony tearing at him. If it meant taking his last breath to do so, he wouldn't help this rotten son of a bitch.

"No."

Lázaro smiled again. The malice in his crazy eyes was unmistakable. He grasped Allende by the hair of his head and said, "I knew such a stupid *peón* would be stubborn. You think you are brave enough to take the pain." He laughed, his twisted joy hideous to hear. "If I had the time, I promise you, I would make you cower and grovel before me. I understand pain . . . and the limits of the human body."

He yanked harder on Allende's hair, forcing his head back. It felt as if his hair was being torn from his scalp by the roots. His eyes watered from the blinding pain, combined with the other brutal agony suffusing his body, but he refused to cry out.

"Unfortunately, I don't have time to break you," Lázaro's voice held a note of disappointment. "Believe me, I would enjoy doing so. Time just doesn't permit."

Allende merely blinked; there was nothing for him to say.

Grunting, Lázaro abruptly released his hold on Allende's hair. Before he could stop it, his head fell forward, slamming into the floor. He heard a soft, crunching sound and knew his nose had broken. Lying in a pool of his own blood and trying to shut out the anguish of his body, he savored the brief respite.

But not for long.

Hands tugged at him, lifting him to his feet. His abdomen felt as if it were on fire. He was afraid to breathe or even lift his head. He stood swaying, held up by the strength of his tormenters' arms. Lázaro shoved a slim book in front of his face.

Grimacing with pain, he wondered what the book was for. Glancing at the title, he could see it was a book of poetry.

Opening the slim volume in front of Allende's bleary eyes, Lázaro commanded, "Read the inscription."

Focusing his eyes on the handwriting, Teresa's distinctive script leapt out at him. After reading and rereading her letters countless times, he would recognize her handwriting anywhere.

The inscription read: "For Allende, I hope you will enjoy this. With all my love, Teresa." The date was smeared.

His pain-numbed mind was bewildered. Why were they showing him a book from Teresa? What were they trying to do?

"We are holding her as a hostage in New Orleans. If you were privy to the personal conditions of my father's will, you must know I've lived in New Orleans for the past few years. My men have your 'lover' hidden where no one will find her. She's safe for now, but if you don't cooperate, she will die. I have a man waiting to leave for New Orleans and see that she is killed." Lázaro paused for emphasis, "I want your answer now."

Allende lowered his head. Steeling himself, he tried to thrust aside the terrible physical pain threatening to suck him down. He needed all of his wits about him. He wasn't sure if he believed Lázaro. He suspected the book was a trick. Somehow Lázaro had obtained it without Teresa's knowledge, he guessed.

He stared at the smudged date. If he could make it out, it might provide a clue. But as hard as he concentrated on the date, he couldn't read it.

"Why love words and poetry, Señor Lázaro, if Teresa is your captive? Wouldn't she send me a note begging for my help so you would release her?"

"Good try, my brave *amigo*," Lázaro mocked. "But I'm

too smart to carry such a damning piece of evidence across Louisiana and half of Tejas. That would be foolish. If you don't believe I have Teresa, then don't cooperate.'' He shrugged. ''It's as simple as that. But you'll die, knowing you sent your beloved to her death, too.''

Despite the bravado of the madman's words, deep inside, he had a feeling Lázaro was bluffing. He doubted Lázaro had made Teresa inscribe a book of poetry to prove she was his captive. It didn't make sense. He was certain it was a trick.

But what if it wasn't?

Shaking his head, he tried to clear it. There was no way for him to be certain that Lázaro was tricking him. As long as there was the slightest possibility they held her captive, he couldn't afford to take the risk. Teresa's life might be forfeit.

He felt he had no choice. He must cooperate with Lázaro to ensure Teresa's safety. Even if he did help Lázaro, there was no guarantee Lázaro would honor his side of the bargain and not hurt Teresa.

He was trapped.

''I'll do what you ask. But if you harm Teresa, I swear I will exact my revenge.'' He stared directly at Lázaro and vowed, ''Even if I have to rise from my grave to do it.''

Lázaro laughed at Allende's vow and demanded, ''I want you to get us past the guard in the hacienda. But before that, I want you to write a note to Ruíz, telling him to join you in the hacienda. Make up some reason for needing him to come immediately. *¿Entiende?*''

''*Sí,*'' he muttered, hating himself for agreeing. Lázaro had obviously be watching the *rancho* and knew there was only one guard. He had planned well.

Cradling his broken ribs with his arm, he moved slowly to the table where he kept his writing materials. The same ones he used to correspond with Teresa. Within moments, he had scrawled a note to Ruíz. Lázaro snatched it from him, blew on the paper to dry the ink and folded it over.

Allende slumped against the table, not wanting to go through with Lázaro's demands. By getting them inside the hacienda and sending for Ruíz, he was leading his employer into a trap. Every nerve in his body vibrated in protest against betraying him.

I should continue to resist, he thought. The other *vaqueros* will return soon. The torture doesn't matter. He could withstand it.

Then he remembered Lázaro's threat. He glanced down at the volume of poetry. What if they really were holding Teresa captive? She was Ruíz's sister. Ruíz couldn't fault him for trying to save her life.

Lázaro sent the man with the blackened teeth to Los Montes Verdes with the note for Ruíz. The two remaining burly henchmen half carried, half dragged him to the compound.

At Allende's word, Tomás opened the gates readily for them. The scar-faced man lost no time in knocking Tomás unconscious, tying him up and gagging him. He hid Tomás in one of the outbuildings. The gates closed behind them. The man without an ear lowered the heavy wooden beam across the gates.

The front door of the hacienda was unlocked. Lázaro's two men propelled him inside. The plan was in motion . . . there was no turning back. He shuddered to think what awaited him and Ruíz.

He clung to one thin thread of hope. The note he had written had appeared, on the surface, to be exactly what Lázaro demanded. But the reason he had given to summon Ruíz was completely out of character for him. He prayed his desperate ruse would make Ruíz suspicious, and he would come prepared for trouble.

* * *

A bright shaft of sunlight pierced Julia's sleep. Groggy, she stretched and yawned. Green fire winked from her finger, catching the rays of the early-morning sun.

The breath caught in her chest as she stopped to admire the beauty of her emerald betrothal ring. Splaying her fingers and turning her hand, she watched in fascination as the light shimmered and reflected the deep brilliance in the gemstone.

Last night hadn't been a dream. She had the ring to prove it.

Realization swept over her . . . she wasn't at home. She was still in Ruíz's bed. He had forgotten to awaken her before daylight! Her family might already be searching for her!

Ruíz stirred in his sleep beside her, and she grabbed his shoulder, shaking him awake. She could hear the rising panic in her own voice, "Ruíz, it's daylight. You didn't awaken me!"

Bolting upright, he rubbed his eyes. Glancing out the window at the brightening day, he apologized, *"Por favor,* forgive me. I guess I stayed up too late last night," he admitted, and grinned wickedly at her. His gaze lingered on her naked breasts. "I hate to say this, but you need to hurry and dress. There might still be a chance that—"

"I doubt it," Julia cut him off. But she rose from the bed anyway and wrapped the sheet around herself, toga fashion. Stooping down, she retrieved her scattered, grape-stained clothing. When she straightened up and gazed at the bed, the breath caught in her chest again, and she gasped.

Ruíz lay sprawled, completely naked, in the bed. The raw masculine power of him, viewed in the full daylight, made her heart slam against her ribs. Her throat went dry, and she licked her lips.

Propping himself on one elbow, he gave her a slow, seductive smile. Patting the bed beside him, he offered, "If you believe all is lost anyway, come back to bed with me." His unruly brown hair slanted across his forehead, and she longed to smooth it back, but she knew if she got within arm's length of him, all would be lost.

"Te amo, Julia.*"*

She felt the warmth fan her neck at his blatant invitation. His words of love almost undid her resolve, but she shook her head. She opened her mouth to chastise him for trying to entice her to return to his bed. But the words never had a chance to leave her mouth. They were lost in the deafening crash of the bedroom door being thrown open.

Julia's father stood on the threshold. Felipe swung his head back and forth like an angry bull. First, his gaze pinned her for one brief second and then it raked over Ruíz's blatantly naked form. Her father's eyebrows flew up, like two startled raven's wings, and his features resembled an angry thundercloud.

Momentarily incapable of coherent speech or movement, she watched as her father's face turned red, went mottled, and then deepened into a brilliant purple. She could see his throat working, but no words were forthcoming.

Distracted from her father's rage by a rustle from the bed, she realized Ruíz had risen to pull on his discarded pants. Expelling her breath in a rush, she clutched the sheet tighter to cover her own nudity.

Her father finally found his voice and managed to croak, "What's the meaning of this?"

Despite her terror and embarrassment at being discovered in such a compromised state, she felt a hysterical bubble rise in her throat. She bit her lip to keep from laughing. Surely her father could have thought of something more original to say.

Ruíz surprised her by closing the distance between them in two swift strides and pulling her into the protection of his arms. With his arms wrapped around her, she sensed he was sending her father an unspoken message. She belonged to Ruíz now, and he wouldn't let her father's anger hurt her.

When Ruíz did speak, his voice was calm, the tone carefully neutral, "We were celebrating our betrothal. We planned on telling you—"

"Putting the cart ahead of the horse, aren't you?" Felipe interrupted, his voice quivering with indignation.

"*Sí*, we felt we couldn't wait," Ruíz countered.

"Seems you've already waited too long . . . to be married. Ruíz, you asked for Julia's hand several weeks ago, but then the betrothal was broken off. There will be no turning back this time," Felipe declared emphatically.

"No turning back," Ruíz agreed.

Hoping to help smooth over the awkward situation, Julia extended her left hand and proudly displayed the square-cut emerald ring. "*Mira, Papito.* Ruíz gave me this betrothal ring as a token of his seriousness."

Her father glanced at the ring for one brief second, and then his gaze bore down upon her.

"No mere stone is worth the priceless gift of your virginity."

She blanched at her father's damning response. Snatching her hand back, she retreated into the comforting shelter of Ruíz's arms.

Squeezing her waist reassuringly, he brazenly admitted, "I seduced her, Felipe. It's my fault. Your daughter was pure and innocent when she came to me. I allowed my passions to rule my reason. If you must blame someone, blame me, not your daughter. It was because of her great love for me that she compromised herself. If you seek further reparations, beyond our marriage, I'll willingly submit to anything you decide."

Lifting her eyes to Ruíz, she gazed at him with open adoration. He had taken all of the responsibility upon himself and even stretched the truth to protect her. It was true she had come to him out of love . . . and she had been pure and innocent. But that had been weeks ago.

Felipe's features softened at Ruíz's humble offering. He

gazed at the two of them standing together and seemed to be at a loss for words.

Finally, he stabbed his finger at both of them, emphasizing his ultimatum, "There will be no waiting this time to be married. Finding a proper house can come later."

Ruíz nodded. "No waiting."

"Muy bien. I'll fetch the magistrate from San Antonio. You'll be married tonight. *¿Entiende?"*

Ruíz started to nod in agreement again, but Julia grasped his arm and cried out, "But Ruíz," and then she turned to her father, "and *Papito,* I want a church wedding. I want to wear the dress *Mamá* wore when she married you. *Por favor,* I—"

"Your father is right, Julia," Ruíz interrupted her, "even though I can understand your desires. I'm sorry to have ruined the wedding for you, but your father is only trying to protect you. If something were to happen to me and you were with child—"

"Don't say it," Julia cut him off and covered her ears with her hands. "I don't want to think about anything happening to you . . . ever." A frisson of fear crept through her body. To think that something might happen to him after they had finally come together in love was . . . unthinkable.

Ruíz gently removed her hands from her ears. "You may not want to hear this, Julia, but I agree with your father. We should marry as soon as possible."

"Your future husband speaks wisely." Felipe stroked his jaw and added, "But I might know of a way to safeguard your future, *mi hija,* as well as fulfill your desires."

She raised her eyes hopefully. *"¿Sí, Papito?"*

"You will be married as soon as I can bring the magistrate from San Antonio. I want the ceremony to take place quietly at Los Montes Verdes to forestall wagging tongues. The magistrate will be sworn to secrecy. If he says anything, he will answer to me. In the meantime, Julia, you and your mother will decide on a wedding date for your church ceremony. Take the time you need to alter your mother's dress and arrange for a proper wedding celebration. Does this plan agree with you?"

Feeling as if a heavy burden had been lifted from her heart, she took a step forward, wanting to embrace him for understanding her feelings.

But Felipe must have seen the obvious joy on her face, because he stopped her quick agreement by lifting one hand and cautioning, "There is one condition, Julia. And Ruíz must agree to it, too."

"Sí, Papito?"

"You and Ruíz will not live together as husband and wife until after the church ceremony. That should give Ruíz ample time to find a suitable home for you."

"¡Papito!"

"Don't try to change my mind, Julia. Even though Ruíz has honorably taken the blame for your, ah . . . indiscretion upon his shoulders, I know my daughter. I know how strong-willed you are. You would never allow yourself to be seduced without your willing consent."

Felipe paused and pulled his hand through his hair in obvious agitation. He frowned at Julia.

"Your mother and I raised you to withstand temptation and abide by the laws of the Church. Waiting until after the church ceremony to be truly joined is the penitence I expect for you to redeem yourself. Can you agree to this?"

Julia lowered her eyes in the face of her father's unbending moral stance, but she refused to feel any shame for what she and Ruíz had done. What they had shared transcended the petty conventions of society. And she didn't believe God would condemn them, knowing the love they felt for each other.

On the other hand, she understood her father's disappointment with her. After all, in his eyes, she had blatantly disobeyed his moral strictures and disregarded her religious upbringing.

She tried to picture herself as a parent who had labored for long years to instill certain values in her children. What would she do if she caught her daughter . . . or son in such a compromising situation? She shook her head. It was hard to envision, but she thought she could imagine her own shocked outrage.

Lifting her eyes, she faced Ruíz. With an effort, she swallowed the lump in her throat and asked, "Do you agree with my father?"

Ruíz took her hand and squeezed it. "It seems an honorable solution for everyone."

"You and your sacred honor," she muttered under her breath.

Ruíz grinned at her and Julia scowled back. Why wasn't he fighting to be with her? Surely, the waiting would be as difficult for him as it was for her?

"The days will pass swiftly while you plan the wedding. Your father's, ah . . . honor has been offended. It's a small enough price to pay for his blessing."

Julia's shoulders slumped. She knew when she was beaten. *"Sí,* I agree."

But in her heart of hearts, she didn't really agree. People and their feelings should always come before such cold and empty ideals as honor and duty. Shouldn't they?

As much as she loved Ruíz and her father, she would never completely understand men . . . not if she lived to be one hundred years old.

Her father's stance relaxed. He opened his arms and said, *"Muy bien.* Let me be the first to congratulate you."

Julia and Ruíz joined Felipe in the traditional *abrazo* of congratulations. Felipe kissed his daughter's cheek and hugged Ruíz warmly, clapping him on the back. "Welcome to our family, *mi hijo.*"

"Gracias, Felipe." Ruíz returned the embrace and said, "I'm honored to be a part of your family. And I want you to know I will take good care of your daughter for all of her life."

"Muy bien," Felipe responded, his voice gruff with emotion. He ducked his head, but not quickly enough for Julia to miss the glistening hint of moisture in his eyes.

Her heart squeezed at seeing her father so affected by their impending marriage. Knowing they had pleased him beyond what words could express, she reconciled herself to waiting a few weeks longer to be Ruíz's wife ... in all ways. After all, she reasoned to herself, if she had returned home before dawn, they would have waited several weeks to be married in the church.

"Julia, I'll stand outside the door while you make yourself presentable. We will tell your mother, and then I'll find the magistrate. Don't take too long dressing," Felipe admonished her before he turned and started for the door.

Before he'd taken more than a step or two, he turned back and addressed Ruíz. "I had forgotten the original reason why I came to find you. A man brought me an urgent message for you, just after daybreak." Felipe retrieved a folded piece of paper from his waistband and handed it to Ruíz.

Ruíz accepted the folded note and asked, "Did one of the *vaqueros* bring it? Most of them were here for the celebration."

"I didn't recognize the man. Have you hired any new *vaqueros?*"

"Not lately, but you probably don't know all of the men." Ruíz scanned the note and said, "It's from Allende. I would recognize his scrawl anywhere. He wants me to come immediately to the hacienda. He says there are some records we need to go over today." Ruíz frowned. "That part doesn't sound like him. I could understand if he was concerned about a pedigree mare who was foaling ... but *records?* He hates paperwork."

Julia felt the icy finger of fear touch her again. She wanted to tell him not to go, but she felt silly, letting her emotions run away with her. Just because her father had cautioned them to marry in case something should happen, she was overreacting to the situation. Ruíz was always being summoned to the *rancho* for any number of reasons.

But Ruíz must have sensed her uneasiness, because he bent

and brushed her lips with his, reassuring her, "Don't worry, Julia. I'll be back in plenty of time for the magistrate. I promise."

Felipe cleared his throat and said, "I'll wait outside."

"I had wondered what brought you to my room at such an early hour, Felipe, especially after a long night of celebrating," Ruíz observed drily.

"The messenger woke me from a sound sleep. He said he had tried knocking on the hacienda door, but no one answered his summons. He tried my house next."

"I'm not surprised he was unable to rouse anyone here. Old José is growing deaf, and I don't keep any other servants now." His lips twitched, and the mischievous gleam she knew so well glinted in his eyes. "So, the urgency of the message was why you came storming into my room without knocking?" Ruíz tapped his chin with the folded note and waited.

Felipe looked abashed for a moment but recovered himself quickly, admitting, "I had intended to knock at your door, but when I heard my daughter's voice from within, I lost my head."

Ruíz's lips curved into a grin, and he concurred, "I would do the same if I ever hear Conchita's voice in a man's bedroom before she marries."

Chapter Twenty

Ruíz arrived at the Estrada *rancho* just past midday. The place looked deserted. The *vaqueros* who had gone to the harvest celebration were obviously taking their time returning, sleeping off the effects of the night before. He couldn't begrudge them. If Allende hadn't sent him a note and Felipe hadn't stormed into his bedroom, Ruíz would have done the same.

When he thought about being joined with Julia that night in a civil ceremony, his heart expanded with joy. Even if it was only a ceremony to safeguard Julia and the possible outcome of their intimacy, she would be irrevocably his. No turning back. No second thoughts.

He had never felt so right about anything in his life.

The vision of his future with Julia as his wife rose before him, filled with such beauty and harmony it made him feel like a giddy youth . . . starting all over again. The warmth of their love, the fire of their passion, the belonging to a family . . . all of these blessings lay before him. And Conchita would have a proper home. *Dios* willing, she would have many brothers and sisters, too.

Julia, his Julia. The playmate of his childhood, the help-mate of his work, the siren of his passion, the mother of his children . . . and the keeper of his heart.

Tonight, he would join with her forever. The waiting for the church-sanctioned ceremony would be difficult. He had understood Julia's dismay and silently agreed with her. But he had decided to put his own desires aside. He understood Felipe's stance as a father, even though he wasn't ashamed of what Julia and he had found in each other's arms. If ever two people were meant to be together, they were.

With difficulty, he put his thoughts of her aside and tried to concentrate on the matter at hand. He wanted to meet with Allende, conclude their business, and return as quickly as possible. The urgent business Allende had mentioned in his note had better prove to be truly urgent or Ruíz would have Allende's head on a platter.

Ruíz had lived most of his life shouldering immense responsibilities. He had thrived on the constant round of work and duty. But now that the slow time at the *rancho* was beginning and the harvest was over at Los Montes Verdes, he wanted to put aside his responsibilities for a time. He wanted to savor life . . . to spend time with Julia and Conchita.

This new awareness of the small joys of living had crept up on him, like a cat on stealthy feet. Julia had been the agent of his awareness, and he wanted to share with her his newfound joy in living.

Pulling Oro up before Allende's cabin, he dismounted. Finding it hard to believe Allende would be waiting for him at the hacienda, he decided to check the cabin first. When he lifted his hand to knock on the door, it swung open. He stepped inside and glanced around. The two-room cabin was empty.

Shaking his head to himself and wondering why Allende was suddenly concerned about the records of the *rancho*, he crossed to the hacienda gates. Raising his fist, he pounded loudly on the stout, oaken planks and tried to remember who had been left behind as guard.

After a moment's thought, he remembered and called out, "Tomás, *abré el portón. Es* Ruíz Navarro."

No answer. Nothing moved. The midday heat bore down upon him. There wasn't a breath of air, and it was very warm for late October.

Ruíz felt the perspiration trickle down the middle of his back. Uncomfortable and exasperated, he called out again, "Tomás, *vengase.* Open up. It's Ruíz Navarro."

Raising his fist to strike the oak gate again, it swung open, just like Allende's cabin door, the gate swung open, seemingly by itself, with a groaning squeak of its hinges. The opening was small, but big enough to slip through.

Where was Tomás? Ruíz wondered. And why wasn't the gate bolted? Even more perplexing was the fact the gate had appeared to be bolted when he had first knocked, but now it opened as if pushed by an invisible hand.

He stepped inside. As soon as he set foot within the compound, he intuitively knew something was wrong. The short hairs at the nape of his neck stood on end. He wished he had come armed, but his carbine was on Oro in front of Allende's cabin.

Before he could react to his intuition, the cold steel barrel of a pistol jabbed him, and a muscled arm encircled his throat, snapping his head back.

"Keep quiet or I'll shoot you."

Ruíz went limp in his captor's grasp. By not offering a struggle, he hoped to both lull his captor into a false sense of security as well as buy time to study the situation.

His first thought was of Allende. Had he willingly led him into this trap? And if so . . . Realization flared in his mind. The note!

The reason Allende had given for his urgent summons, to

go over records, was the key. He had wondered about Allende's unusual request—but not hard enough. Had Allende been trying to send him a warning?

His captor grunted and drug him back a few steps. He felt the muzzle point pulled away, but his captor kept a strong arm around his throat. Ruíz heard the latch of the *hacienda* gates click shut and the heavy beam shoved into place.

His throat was released and the round eye of the pistol returned, poking him from behind. He stumbled for a few steps and then got his bearings. His captor was urging him forward, through the open door of the hacienda and toward the study, with a single-minded relentlessness.

When they crossed the threshold of the study, it took his eyes a few minutes to adjust to the darkened room. Whoever was waiting for him had closed the shutters and thrown the room into premature twilight.

"Is he unarmed?" A voice barked from the shadows.

The man holding the pistol at Ruíz's back shifted slightly, and he experienced the degrading slide of the man's hand move over his body, searching for a concealed weapon. All he found was Ruíz's hunting knife, tucked inside his boot.

His captor removed the knife and replied, "Just this knife, nothing else."

A form advanced from the shadows. This man, too, had a pistol cocked and primed in his hand. His voice was low. "Remember me, Ruíz?"

Ruíz strained his eyes, studying the man's partially shadowed features. After a moment, recognition flooded his senses, and he ventured, "Lázaro?"

The man took another step forward. "So you do remember me. I'm honored." Lázaro's voice held a mocking note, "I thought you were too busy impressing the old *bastardo* to notice Alicia's insignificant younger brother."

"I think you've got that wrong, Lázaro. I've never forgotten you. I sent Miguel Vega to fetch you when your father died.

But Miguel returned, saying you had business that detained you in New Orleans.''

"*Sí*, that's what I told your messenger boy. Why should I rush home to mourn a father who made my life a misery and left me without a *peso?*''

At Lázaro's revealing words, some of the tension drained from him. So that was what the show of force was about. Lázaro had finally returned home to take what he considered to be rightfully his. It was a bad way to start a partnership, and he wished Lázaro wasn't so bitter and hostile.

"Lázaro, I understand your feelings. I didn't just send for you to mourn your father's passing, I sent for you to settle the inheritance between us. I don't agree with your father's excluding you from his will. My attorney in San Antonio has already drawn up the papers to deed you half of everything. That's only right. My daughter will retain the other half, and I'll supervise her holdings. That will make us partners. Can't we put this bad start behind us and find a way to work together?'' Ruíz extended his hand.

Lázaro ignored the outstretched hand and sneered, ''I don't want to work with you, Ruíz, and I certainly don't want your charity. Do you really expect me to believe your pathetic lies? A man facing cocked pistols will say anything to save his own skin.''

"I'm not lying to save my skin.'' He dropped his hand to his side. ''If you don't believe me, send someone to Peter Meredith, my attorney in San Antonio. Peter can verify—''

"*¡Bastante!* I'm not interested in any legal arrangements you have made . . . even if they do exist. I don't want half of this cursed land. Growing up, I sweated blood for this land . . . and for my father.'' Lázaro hawked and spat on the tile floor. ''It never got me anything, particularly my father's regard. But you, dear brother-in-law, waltzed right in and won my father's affection. How will you give me back half of that?''

Stunned by Lázaro's painful revelation, he wasn't completely surprised. He had never agreed with Don Estéban's callous disregard for his only son. And the brutal truths his father-in-law had revealed on his deathbed about the way he had treated his son sickened Ruíz. But he hadn't thought Lázaro would hold him responsible for his estrangement from his father. The man's twisted reasoning alarmed him.

He wanted to argue with him, but when he studied the malevolent gleam in Lázaro's black eyes, he realized further argument would probably prove fruitless.

Ruíz saw something else there, too, something even more alarming. Lázaro reminded him of the two men who had gone crazy while serving under Sam Houston in the Tejas war of independence. He would never forget the feral but glassy stare in those men's eyes. His brother-in-law's eyes held that same alarming combination . . . as if the soul had departed, leaving only the animal behind.

His heartbeat accelerated, and his stomach clenched in dread.

"*¿Dónde está,* Allende? What have you done with him? He wrote the note that brought me here." Ruíz licked his dry lips. "Allende should have no part in this. Where is he?"

"Your tender concern for your employee touches me. But then, he's not just your employee, is he? He fancies himself unofficially betrothed to your sister. Doesn't he?"

He was surprised Lázaro knew of Allende's connection to his family. Had Lázaro beaten that information out of Allende?

"Where is he?"

Lázaro jerked his head in the direction of the far corner of the room. Raising his hands above his head, Ruíz turned slowly so the man with the pistol embedded in his back wouldn't mistake his movement.

In the dim room, he could just make out two other strangers lounging in chairs with pistols in their hands. One of the men was slight and drab. The other man was burly and missing an ear. At their feet lay a crumpled form . . . Allende.

"May I speak with him?" Ruíz asked.

"Why not? But make it quick. We've other business to discuss, my dear brother-in-law."

Crossing the room, he ignored the two men on either side of Allende. Kneeling beside his prostrate form, he discovered they had tied Allende's hands and feet. His arms were brutally twisted behind his back and bound. Ruíz winced, realizing what the unnatural position must be doing to his newly healed shoulder.

Allende's eyes were open but there was a gag in his mouth, and he had obviously been pistol-whipped. An angry purple welt covered the right side of his face. His nose had been broken, too. It was swollen almost beyond recognition. Dried blood covered his face.

Ruíz wondered what other injuries Lázaro's thugs had inflicted upon him, injuries that weren't readily obvious.

"May I remove the gag?" Ruíz asked.

He sensed the unspoken command that passed from Lázaro, who was behind him, to the small man perched on one of the study's chairs. The man reached down and untied the gag around Allende's mouth.

"*¿Cómo está, mi amigo?*" Ruíz inquired.

"I'm fine, Don Ruíz, don't worry about me. Forgive me for sending the note to bring you into their trap . . . but I had to. Lázaro told me he is holding Teresa captive in New Orleans. If I didn't cooperate, he would have her killed." Moisture glinted in Allende's pain-filled eyes, and he begged again, "Forgive me, Don Ruíz."

Ruíz wanted to ask him if he had tried to send a warning by including the unusual summons in his note, but he didn't dare mention it. If Lázaro knew Allende had tried to trick him, he feared Allende would be subjected to another brutal beating.

"I don't blame you, Allende."

But while he was trying to remain calm and reassuring, his mind was working. Teresa was being held captive in New

Orleans? Lázaro had threatened to kill her to secure Allende's compliance?

His brother-in-law was a monster, but Ruíz was no longer afraid of him. Fury pounded at him, making his head throb and his hands itch. He wanted to tear Lázaro into tiny pieces. It took all of his raw willpower not to launch himself at Lázaro's throat.

Rising to his feet, he spun around and faced his adversary. Two pistols stabbed him from behind, silently warning him against sudden movements.

Ignoring the deadly muzzles at his back, he demanded, "Lázaro, is what Allende said true? Are you holding my sister captive?"

"No, I don't have your sister as a hostage." He grinned smugly and added, "But it was a good trick. It convinced Allende to send for you. I obtained a volume of poetry from a very drunk David Treviño. Your sister had sent the book with Treviño to deliver to Allende." Lázaro's voice took on a bragging note, "Very clever, don't you think? It fooled him completely."

Ruíz heard Allende groan behind him and mumble some unintelligible words. Then there was the awful sound of metal hitting flesh and bone. Allende was silent again.

Lunging for Lázaro in a blind rage, Ruíz anticipated the thought of digging his fingers into the soft flesh of his brother-in-law's throat. He forgot that four pistols were aimed at him. All he felt was a raw need to wipe the smirk from Lázaro's face.

Lázaro understood Ruíz's murderous intent, because he shrieked, "Hold him."

His captor from outside, a scar-faced man, and the hefty giant who sported only one ear, leapt to do Lázaro's bidding. He felt his arms cruelly jerked behind him, and his feet were lifted from the floor, halting his forward progress.

Lázaro nodded and said, "That's better. You can release

him now. I think he understands the hopelessness of his situation. You'll behave yourself, won't you?''

"You may have the upper hand now, Lázaro, but you better have a small army to back you," Ruíz replied defiantly. "My *vaqueros* will be returning soon, and you can't hold us here forever."

He had another thought, too. He had left Oro standing outside Allende's cabin. When his *vaqueros* did return, they were sure to investigate . . . and the hacienda would be the first place they would look.

"Don't worry. Our business will be concluded before that." Lázaro waved his hand in airy dismissal. "Enough of the social amenities. As you so cleverly pointed out, dear Ruíz, time is wasting." He lifted one eyebrow and favored Ruíz with his smug smile again.

"Before you get too cocky, I want you to know the compound is locked up, and I have another guard outside. He's already taken the precaution of hiding your mount. It could be a long time before your *vaqueros* realize something is amiss."

Ruíz's confidence ebbed at Lázaro's clever handling of the situation, but he refused to show it. Instead, he countered with, "My men will come to relieve Tomás soon." And then an awful realization struck him, and he demanded, "What have you done to Tomás?"

Lázaro laughed, and the sound of his laughter was ugly, mirthless and filled with malice.

"Tomás is safely out of the way, but he'll have a vicious headache when he awakens."

"Perdición take you, Lázaro! Why are you doing this? Allende and Tomás have never harmed you. This is between you and me, the others are innocent." Ruíz knew as soon as the words left his mouth that goading this madman would probably only worsen the situation, but he couldn't stop himself.

His brother-in-law's features twisted in rage, and he lashed out, "Don't presume to tell me what I can or can't do! You're in my power, Ruíz. *¿Comprehende?*" His face had turned purple, and his eyes bulged with fury. "*¡Bastante!* Enough of your prattling. You will answer my questions only. No more puling demands about the welfare of your employees. Your whining makes me sick."

"*Por Dios,* what do you want, Lázaro?"

Lázaro's hand shot out, and he slapped Ruíz on the face. "I'll ask the questions, damn you! *¡Silencio!*"

His face burned where he had been struck, but not just from Lázaro's blow, from his own embarrassment as well. He felt so helpless to stop this madman, and Lázaro had already hurt both Allende and Tomás.

Perversely, he would have felt better if Lázaro had pistol-whipped him as he had done to Allende. A slap on the face was demeaning, as if Lázaro were chastising a child.

He chose to ignore Lázaro's insulting blow. Clenching his jaw, he ground his teeth together . . . and waited. Let Lázaro take the lead as he had demanded. The sooner Ruíz knew what he wanted, the sooner he could formulate a plan to stop his brother-in-law.

"I want to know where the treasure is," Lázaro stated flatly.

Ruíz struggled to keep his features composed, despite his initial shock at the unexpected demand. In the sweet realization of his love for Julia and the tumult of the harvest, he had completely forgotten about the treasure.

Don Estéban had been wise to keep the secret of the treasure's location from his family. And Lázaro had been clever enough to guess his father would reveal where the treasure was to Ruíz. Lázaro must have been planning to take the treasure for himself for months . . . or maybe even years. It was obvious his greed for the treasure knew no bounds. He didn't care who he hurt . . . or worse . . . in order to get his hands on it.

And Ruíz was no fool.

The insanity in Lázaro's eyes, coupled with the man's long-buried resentment toward him, wiped out the hope that he would be allowed to live after he revealed the location of the treasure. Allende would probably die, too, because he knew too much. To turn over the treasure would mean sudden death for them both. Beyond that, Ruíz felt a personal repugnance at giving the treasure to his mad brother-in-law. The treasure belonged to the Catholic Church.

Unarmed and surrounded by determined and deadly men, he had only one option to keep himself and Allende alive. He must find a way to withstand Lázaro's demand and play for time, hoping someone would realize the hacienda compound had been taken over by armed intruders.

Surely his foreman, Ramos, would check the compound when he returned from the harvest celebration. Even if Ramos did realize something was wrong and tried to break in with the *vaqueros,* Ruíz was pragmatic enough to know Lázaro could kill them before they were rescued.

Unfortunately, he had no other choice or plan at his disposal. All he could do was try to delay Lázaro for as long as possible and pray for a miracle.

"What treasure is that?" Ruíz tried to sound bewildered. "You're welcome to all the cash in the bank since you don't want any part of the *rancho.* There's fifty thousand *pesos* in the San Antonio Republic Bank."

Lázaro's eyes narrowed, and Ruíz could see the gleam of greed in them. "How do I withdraw the money from the bank without taking you to San Antonio?"

"Simple, I write a draft authorizing you to take out the money. Everyone knows you're Don Estéban's son."

"Sí, and everyone seems to know I was excluded from his will, too," Lázaro observed caustically.

"With my signature and personal instructions, there should be no problem," Ruíz insisted.

"Then do it."

Ruíz walked slowly to the desk. He took his time, sifting through the contents of the desk drawers as if he were searching for bank drafts. He knew exactly where they were, but the minutes ticked by before he made a great show of finding them. Then he had to find a new nib for the quill pen, and he wrote for a long time, giving the bank president very specific instructions. Finally, his dawdling at an end, he glanced up.

Lázaro loomed over him, his black eyes like twin burning coals. Snatching the paper from his hand, he scanned the bank draft and the attached instructions. He folded the papers and tucked them into his vest pocket.

"Took you long enough. And don't think I don't know what you're trying to do. It won't work, Ruíz. There will be no more digressions." Lázaro leaned forward, his voice full of menace. "Where is the treasure?"

"What treasure?"

He caught hold of Ruíz's shirt and yanked the man's face to within a mere breath of his own. "If you won't tell me, there are ways to beat the information out of you."

Ruíz didn't flinch. He stared back into Lázaro's crazed eyes.

"I don't know what you're talking about. As you pointed out earlier, I'm completely in your power. If I don't know about any treasure, I can't tell you and escape a beating."

"Just as I thought. You've decided to be obstinate. I had hoped you would show some spine, my dear brother-in-law." Lázaro released his shirt. "It will be my pleasure to show you the torment I endured at my father's hands." Spittle had formed at the corners of Lázaro's lips, and his face was filled with hideous joy.

Stepping away from the desk, Lázaro snapped his fingers, ordering, "Bring the manacles and chains."

Ruíz felt his blood run cold at Lázaro's command. He had expected to be beaten like they had done to Allende, but he couldn't have guessed Lázaro would have designed such an elaborate scheme to exact his revenge. Manacles and chains and using Ruíz as a live example of how Don Estéban used to beat Lázaro. He shut his eyes for one brief second; it was as if he had been plunged into a nightmare. His brother-in-law was completely insane, twisted and cruel.

The two heavyset henchmen scurried to a saddlebag thrown over a chair. Opening the bag, they extracted two iron spikes, a hammer, and two short chains attached to manacles.

Lázaro indicated two marked spots on the unadorned stucco wall to the left of the fireplace. The marks were taller than Lázaro and approximately the width of his outstretched arms. Ruíz realized that Lázaro had measured the places ahead of time, in anticipation of his cruel demonstration.

The two thugs took turns swinging the hammer until they had driven the spikes deep into the wall. They attached the chains to the spikes, hammering the open loop at each end of the chain closed. The manacles dangled from the other end of the chains . . . waiting.

Ruíz was amazed at the precision of their workmanship. The ugly iron manacles were perfectly placed—high enough to strain the person chained to them and wide enough to spread-eagle a man so his back was completely exposed. Lázaro hadn't missed a detail.

He stared at the menacing manacles. They struck a spark of fear within him, and he mouthed a silent prayer that he had the strength to withstand the pain.

"Care to change your mind about the treasure?" Lázaro taunted him.

Allende must have regained consciousness, because suddenly he cried out, "If you know where the treasure is, Don Ruíz, tell him and save yourself."

Ruíz ignored Allende's plea, but Lázaro said, "Gag him again. He's welcome to watch, but I don't want to listen to his whining." Lázaro glared at Ruíz and asked, "Where is the treasure?"

"I don't know."

"*Muy bien. Hombres,* fetch the whip. I'll wield it myself

until I grow tired, then everyone can take a turn and have some fun,'' Lázaro observed as mildly as if he were ordering dinner.

The guard who was missing his ear returned to the saddlebags and withdrew a coiled bullwhip. Cold drops of sweat suddenly beaded on Ruíz's forehead as he studied the instrument of torture.

At least the ends weren't beaded with metal. It was a simple leather bullwhip. If the rawhide lashes had ended in metal beads, Ruíz knew such a whip was capable of cutting through muscle and severely injuring a man . . . sometimes fatally. The leather bullwhip, on the other hand, had sufficient cutting power to shred every ounce of flesh from a man's back and leave him incapacitated for days.

As if he could divine Ruíz's thoughts, Lázaro pointed out with diabolical precision, ''You see, I'm not trying to cripple you, dear brother-in-law.'' He wagged his finger playfully at Ruíz. ''No, it's authenticity I'm striving for. This is precisely the type of whip my dear departed *Papá* used on me. Of course, he didn't choose the leather whip because of his innate kindness. Oh, no, he used it because he was crafty. He always made certain he administered just enough lashes to torture me without affecting my ability to work. Clever, wasn't he?''

Uncoiling the whip, he expertly cracked it with a flip of his wrist. His lips twitched and his voice was low, almost caressing, ''You, Ruíz, on the other hand, are the master of your own fate. It is *you* who will pick the number of lashes by stopping me when you're ready to tell me where the treasure is.''

Ruíz couldn't quite hide the tremor that shook him at Lázaro's statement. He realized Lázaro saw his shudder and was gratified to see him so fearful, but it wasn't just fear that had moved him. It was his horror at seeing the monster Don Estéban had fashioned from his own son. It was no wonder Doña Estrada had chosen to kill herself.

The legacy of brutality never died . . . it just passed from one generation to the next.

"Prepare him, men," Lázaro commanded.

The two burly henchmen grabbed him and literally tore the shirt from his back. They marched him to the wall and stretched his arms above his head, snapping the manacles shut around his wrists.

He purposely let his mind float free, trying to ignore what was being done to him. With every ounce of willpower he possessed, he concentrated on thinking of other things: Julia's face, how tall Conchita had grown in the past few months, the debts he needed to pay . . . anything but what was happening to him.

The shriek of the whip tore the air, and he felt the first hot sear of the lash. It wasn't too bad, he reassured himself. He could endure it. He wished he had something he could bite into, to keep from screaming. The last thing he wanted to do was augment Lázaro's perverse pleasure by screaming in pain.

After the first fifteen lashes, he began to doubt how much longer he could hang on. The cuts of the whip were crisscrossing each other, the lash singeing already raw and open flesh. His entire back felt as if it were covered with a thousand fire ants, all stinging him at the same time. Tears of agony streamed down his face, and he sagged against the cruel manacles, their sharp edges gouging the flesh of his wrists.

But he hadn't cried out. Yet.

After twenty lashes, he began to feel dizzy. His power of concentration had deserted him, and only sheer obstinacy kept him from begging for mercy. All of his thoughts, such as they were, centered around the torture being inflicted upon him. Since he could think of nothing else but the exploding agony, he had made a game of counting the seconds between blows in his head. Silently, he promised himself the few seconds of respite after each time the whip bit into his lacerated flesh.

When he had exhausted his few brief seconds of relief, and the lash failed to fall again as he expected, Ruíz twisted partway around, as far as the short chains would allow him, to see what was delaying his tormenters.

Lázaro's grotesque laughter greeted Ruíz's desperate movement.

"Miss it? Maybe I picked the wrong form of torture for you, Ruíz. You seem to enjoy the whip. Some people like to be hurt. We keep special girls at my place in New Orleans to service the peculiar men who enjoy being beaten."

He didn't need to be told what kind of business his brother-in-law was engaged in. He could guess. But Lázaro's obscene mockery was less than the angry buzzing of a fly in his ear. His attentions were drawn elsewhere.

The prolonged respite was turning into its own brand of agony. Without the numbing blows of the whip descending, it was as if every mutilated piece of his back was coming alive with its own fiendish agony. White-hot, searing pain shot through him, sucking the very breath from his lungs. And with the blinding anguish came the first doubts he would survive.

To lose his life, and Julia, just when he had found her, was the cruelest blow of all, a fate worse than a hundred lashings. To be brutally murdered on his wedding day was a hideous irony. And to be deprived of watching Conchita grow up was like dying twice. In his desperation, thinking of everything that he would lose, a groan escaped his lips.

As soon as he uttered the sound, Lázaro pounced on it with malicious glee. "No, I don't think you're enjoying the pain, dear Ruíz. You just have more stamina than I gave you credit for. Care to tell me where the treasure is?"

Trying to move his savaged lips, he tasted his own blood. His lips were stiff and shredded from his biting into them, trying to keep from crying out. He managed to force out one word. "No."

"Very well, it's your body, Ruíz. Let's have a change of pace. I'll let one of my men have a turn. I warn you he will be more heavy-handed than I've been."

Ruíz's flesh quivered with its own silent answer.

Lázaro was right.

His new tormenter began to apply the lash with such force he felt as if he were being pummeled as well as whipped. The blows pounded against him, driving him cringing into the wall. After only a few strokes, he began to slip in and out of consciousness.

He embraced the welcoming blanket of oblivion. If he was unconscious, the pain couldn't reach him. The blackness rolled over him, plunging him deeper and deeper . . . driving him under . . .

The splash of something wet and cold stung him, stripping away his beloved blackness, bringing each brutalized piece of flesh into burning life. A hand grasped his hair and jerked his head back, adding another inconceivable torment to his mounting agony. Lázaro leaned close to Ruíz's ear. His breath was warm on Ruíz's neck, almost like the caress of a lover.

"That is sufficient play, Ruíz. It's no fun when you leave us."

Lázaro released his hair, and his head sagged forward, limp as a rag doll. Drops of water streamed from his face, but he could still feel the returning suck of oblivion . . . and he strained toward it.

"Don't worry, my dear brother-in-law, where the whip has failed, I have another surprise for you . . . and it won't fail to loosen your tongue."

Chapter
Twenty-one

The sun stood at eye level when Obadiah returned with Allende's letters. Pulling the bay mare to a stop in front of the cabin, he was mildly surprised Allende wasn't there to greet him. He dismounted and found the door to the cabin half open.

Calling out for Allende, he stepped inside and found the place deserted. He noticed the coffee cup he had used in the morning was still sitting in the same place, half full of the coffee he hadn't finished.

He couldn't understand why Allende wasn't home. He knew how much Allende had been looking forward to the letters. Pulling the letters from his shirt pocket, he placed them on the table. But he wasn't satisfied. He wanted to personally deliver them to Allende.

Scooping up the letters and returning them to his pocket, he left the cabin with the intention of asking around to see if anyone knew where Allende was. When he stepped onto the porch, he walked straight into a tall, older man.

The man recoiled a step and demanded sharply, "Who are you? What were you doing in Señor Soto's cabin?"

Obadiah gazed at the man. The older man stared back, suspicion stamped upon his features. At least he had spoken English, Obadiah thought. He knew he needed to explain his presence and gain the man's cooperation.

"I'm Obadiah MacGregor, a friend of Allende's. Who might you be?"

"You're trespassing on Estrada land," the man responded, accusation making his voice harsh. "I don't need to tell you who I am, but I will. My name is Ramos and I'm the foreman of this *rancho.*"

Offering his hand, he wanted to allay the man's mistrust. Using his most polite manners, he said, "Allende has spoken of you, Señor Ramos. I'm glad to meet you."

With obvious reluctance, Señor Ramos took his outstretched hand and shook it. "You say you're a friend of Allende's. Is this a social call?"

"Partly. I spent the night with him last night. Most of you fellers were gone to some big *fiesta,*" He retrieved the letters, for a second time, and showed them to Ramos. "I was going into San Antone for a few supplies, so Allende asked if I'd fetch 'em for him."

Señor Ramos studied the letters in Obadiah's hand. The suspicion faded from his eyes.

"I'm glad you came. Maybe you can help me. I've been looking for Allende since I arrived at midday. When did you last see him?"

"At dawn . . . and its pretty peculiar, Mr. Ramos, because the coffee cup I used is still sitting in the same place I left it. Allende must have left the cabin right after me."

Señor Ramos's eyebrows drew together into a straight line, and he stroked his jaw. "I wonder what would have called him away so quickly?"

"Could his boss, this Navarro feller, have sent for him? Could he have gone over there?"

"It's possible, but with the rest of us already at Los Montes Verdes . . ."

"And you're sure he's not here?" Obadiah asked.

"We've checked the barns and stables and outbuildings. His usual mount is still in the corral."

"Then he probably didn't go to his boss," he observed, more to himself than to Ramos. He didn't like the way things were looking. The *rancho* had been almost deserted at dawn. He pushed the first flutters of alarm away. He didn't want to think that something could have happened to one of the few friends he had.

"What about the hacienda compound?" he inquired.

Ramos frowned and hesitated, as if he wasn't certain how much information he felt comfortable giving him. Then he shrugged and admitted, "That's another problem. One of the men, Tomás, was left to guard the compound, but he didn't answer when I sent a man to relieve him. He might have gotten drunk to console himself because he couldn't attend the *fiesta*. He may be inside sleeping it off, but I don't dare break into the compound without orders from Don Navarro. It's unlikely that Allende would be inside."

"Yeah, all of this is pretty unlikely. I think someone should fetch your boss and let him know Allende's missing. I'll go if you'll jist point the way."

"Perhaps you're right." Turning around on the porch, he faced away from the cabin. Lifting his arm, he pointed and said, "Go southeast for ten miles until you reach the Guadalupe. Cross the river and climb the bluff. The vineyard is on the top of the bluff." Ramos gestured toward the bay mare and offered, "Your horse is burdened with supplies and has traveled all day. Let me get you a fresh mount."

"That would be right neighborly of you."

Within a few moments, Obadiah was remounted on a spirited

gelding. Staring down at the worried face of Ramos, he tried to reassure the older man. "I'll get there and back as fast as I can."

Ramos patted Obadiah's mount on the rump and muttered, "*Vaya con Dios.*"

Spurring the fresh horse into a gallop, he didn't slow his pace until he reached the river. While he was searching for a likely crossing place, he heard two shots ring out. Without thinking, he urged the gelding into the river and started to swim across, heading in the general direction from where the shots had come.

Wanting to save his carbine from getting wet and thinking he might need it, he jerked it from his saddleboot and held it above the water. At least he had had the presence of mind to bring it with him, and he also carried his pa's old pistol tucked into his belt.

Once the echo of the two shots died away, the waning day was eerily quiet around him. He reached the opposite side of the riverbank and rode for about a mile without finding a sign of anyone. He had almost decided to give up the search and climb the bluff to the Navarro vineyard when his eye caught a glimpse of something white lying beneath a huge, gnarled live oak.

He urged his horse forward, his heart thudding in his chest. He hoped he wasn't riding into a trap. When he reached the live oak, he realized what had caught his eye. It was the white blouse of a woman, and she was lying on the ground in a crumpled heap.

Swearing under his breath, he vaulted from his mount and raced to her side. She was lying on her back, and her left temple was matted with blood. She was young and pretty and he fervently hoped she wasn't dead.

Crouching down beside her, he dropped his carbine to the ground and gently pushed the black hair away from her temple. Examining the wound on her forehead, it looked as if a bullet had grazed her. Checking for a pulse in her throat, he was thankful to find she was still alive. If he could get help for her, she might live. The Navarro place had to be just over the rise. It was probably her home.

Awkwardly, he lifted her into his arms and struggled to rise to his feet with his burden. Luckily, she was a tiny thing, and he had built up some strength over the past few months while building the cabin for his mother and wrestling the steers Allende had given him.

Even as careful as he tried to be with her, the sudden movement jolted her awake. Her eyes flew open and filled with fear. She groaned some Spanish words while she scanned his face. She must have realized he wasn't her assailant because the fear left her eyes, only to be replaced by a look of frenzied agitation. Wriggling in his arms, she struggled to point toward the northeast, the way he had just come. The tone of her voice sounded frantic, as if she were begging for something.

"La niña, la niña la niña . . ."

Obadiah wished he could speak Spanish, and he strained to understand her, wanting to help. Before he could make out what she was trying to tell him, the agitation that had gripped her must have drained her frail strength, and she lapsed into unconsciousness again.

Julia floated through the day, her feet never touching the floor, her heart bursting with joy. She didn't even flinch when her father had uncompromisingly explained the situation to her mother and left to fetch the magistrate.

And she didn't care if she and Ruíz had to wait for a few weeks to be husband and wife. All that mattered, all that had ever mattered, was that Ruíz loved her and wanted to spend his life with her. At the thought of all the joy that lay ahead, she hugged herself and danced around the room.

When she twirled past her mother, she couldn't help but ask,

"Were you and father, you know, were you . . . ever intimate before you married?"

Pilar straightened slowly from rummaging through an old trunk in search of her wedding dress. She turned around and crossed her arms over her chest. Her dark eyes crackled with indignation, but the suspicion of a smile hovered at the corners of her mouth.

"Do you think that's a proper question to ask your mother, Julia?"

"Probably not, but I would like to know."

"Liking to know isn't enough. What's between your father and me is our personal business."

Julia nodded, knowing she had stepped over an invisible line between mother and daughter. But she couldn't completely contain her exuberance or her curiosity.

"Does father's touch . . . well, ah . . . does it . . ." Julia sighed and blurted out, "Does *Papá* take you to the stars each time . . . you know?"

The corners of her mother's eyes crinkled, and Pilar laughed out loud, shaking her head.

"You're incorrigible, Julia. But I will answer that question. *Sí* and *sí,* and that's how it should be. Didn't I tell you not to give up . . . to follow your heart?"

"*Sí, Mamita,* you did . . . and you were so right!" Julia flew into her mother's arms and they embraced. Tears of joy streaked both their faces.

The remainder of the morning passed in a glorious haze of activities. Julia and her mother planned the wedding, the celebration afterward and picked several tentative wedding dates. Julia tried on her mother's wedding dress, and they discussed the necessary alterations and the new lace they would add.

They ate a late, cold lunch with Luz and Conchita. Paco ate at the winery; he was busy overseeing the final straining of the grapes. Julia was bursting with her happy news, but she refrained from telling it. Her foremost consideration was Conchita and how the child should be informed. She felt it was only right for Ruíz to be with her so they could tell his child together.

Luz noticed Julia's frenzied gaiety and asked several pointed questions, but Julia put her off. Ruíz would be returning soon as well as her father with the magistrate. When they were all together, she and Ruíz would tell everyone and they would have their simple ceremony.

Besides, once her own news was out, she meant to ask Luz a few pointed questions of her own. She remembered seeing Luz and Paco together at both the *quinceanera* and the *fiesta* last night. She wanted to know if they were courting? Did Paco have serious intentions?

She had always hoped Paco would fall in love. Despite his light-hearted bravado, she knew he usually avoided women. She had often worried that he was afraid of rejection. But gentle Luz would be perfect for him, and she prayed they would marry.

As was customary, Julia lay down in her darkened bedroom to take her afternoon *siesta*. She was certain she wouldn't fall asleep. She was far too excited to sleep, she told herself. But the last thing she remembered was straining her ears to hear approaching hoofbeats . . . listening for Ruíz returning to her.

Two hours later, she awakened to Conchita's shrill laughter, and the little girl energetically bouncing up and down on the foot of Julia's bed.

Surprised she had fallen asleep, she rolled over. Thinking about the long hours of passion she had spent in Ruíz's arms the night before, a secret smile curved her lips. No wonder she had fallen asleep . . . she had been exhausted.

Julia turned her attention to the live jack-in-the-box who was making her bed shake. Conchita knew that she was forbidden from jumping on the beds, but the child had obviously either forgotten or decided the temptation was too great. And it wasn't in Julia's heart to chastise the little girl on this day when the world was so perfect.

Instead, she grabbed the bouncing child and held her wriggling form close, glorying in the knowledge she would no longer merely be Conchita's *tía*. After today, she would be the child's mother. And years from now, Julia would rejoice with Conchita when she planned her own wedding day.

Hugging the little girl, Julia murmured, "I love you, *mi niña.*"

"I love you, too, *Tía* Julia." Conchita wrapped her soft arms around Julia's neck and pleaded prettily, *"Por favor,* come with Luz and me to the river."

Julia hesitated. She wished she could say yes, but this was one day she wanted to stay close to home. She felt as if she were sitting on pins and needles, waiting for Ruíz and her father to return. For all she knew, they might have already come back while she was sleeping. And she wanted to look beautiful for the wedding tonight. She needed to take a bath and wash her hair and decide what to wear and . . .

"I can't today, *mi niña*. Perhaps tomorrow. I've a great deal to do. I hope you understand."

Conchita's full bottom lip protruded, a sure sign of her disappointment, but she had the grace to acquiesce, *"Sí,* but you promise—*mañana.*"

Laughing at the child's tenacity, she gave Conchita a squeeze.

"I didn't say I promised, but I will try very hard." She kissed the child's round cheek and urged, "Run along with Luz."

"Sí, Tía Julia," Conchita said, and scooted off the bed. With a final wave, the little girl ran skipping from Julia's bedroom.

Julia rose and began searching through her dresses, wanting to pick one that would be appropriate for her wedding tonight. She settled on an ecru-colored, lace-flounced dress. It needed pressing, so she went into the main room to fetch the flatiron and start heating it.

Her mother was already up and cooking. By utilizing some of the food left from the *fiesta* along with a pair of freshly butchered and plucked chickens, Julia could see that her mother was planning a festive dinner to follow the wedding ceremony. Judging by the amount of food already roasting over the hearth and bubbling in pots, she realized her mother must have foregone her usual *siesta* to prepare for the impromptu nuptials.

Feeling a surge of love for her mother's unselfish gesture that was laced with a pang of guilt, she offered, "As soon as I press my dress, I'll help you with the food."

"No, you won't. It's your wedding day . . . or should I say, one of your wedding days," Pilar teased.

"Have they gone?"

"You mean Luz and Conchita? *Sí,* they've gone fishing."

"Luz suspects."

"Sí, and this feast following on the heels of the *fiesta* last night is hard to explain. I put Luz off," Pilar sighed, "but I can't fool her much longer."

"I didn't want her to let it slip to Conchita."

"I understand and respect your wishes. You and Ruíz should tell the child together."

"Does Paco know?"

"Sí, he came home during *siesta* and I told him. He's sworn to secrecy, though, until you're ready to make the announcement."

"What did Paco say?"

Pilar laughed again. "I think his exact words were: 'It's about time.' "

"Sounds like my brother." She paused, knowing the answer before she asked the question, but she had to ask it anyway. "And Ruíz, has he returned yet?"

"No."

"Nor *Papá*?"

Her mother frowned and shook her head. "But I expect your father soon. He's had plenty of time."

She nodded woodenly, trying to ignore the awful sinking sensation in the pit of her stomach. She wasn't too worried about her father. He had probably been detained, waiting for the magistrate to finish his other duties.

But Ruíz ... she remembered the fear she had felt this morning when he had received the unusual summons from Allende. How could she have forgotten? In her newfound joy, she had hidden the feeling away ... but now it resurfaced and filled her with foreboding.

Fighting down her apprehension, she tried to lose herself in the mundane tasks facing her. She found the flatiron and placed it on the coals to heat. She got out the board used for pressing and balanced it between two chairs. But she couldn't quite dismiss her worries about Ruíz.

She wanted to fly to him, but she realized how foolish that would look. Shutting her eyes, she swayed back and forth, tremors running through her body. How could she possibly explain her unsubstantiated forebodings to her mother ... or her father? They would never understand.

Trying to put her worries aside, she managed to press the dress. When she was finished, she noticed the lengthening shadows outside. Darkness came early at this time of year, and with the darkness, her apprehension grew.

Her nerves were strung taut, like the vibrating strings of a guitar. She gasped, suddenly feeling as if she couldn't draw enough air into her lungs ... as if she were about to suffocate. The walls of the *casa* seemed to be closing in around her. She suddenly realized she couldn't stay between the four walls for one moment longer.

"It's getting awfully late. Luz and Conchita should have returned by now."

Pilar lifted her head from the rice pudding she was stirring and agreed. *"Sí,* it is late. I'm beginning to wonder where everyone is."

"I'm going down to the river to check on Luz and Conchita."

"Julia, I know you're nervous with all of this waiting, but shouldn't you continue to get ready? I've already started heating the water for your bath. I understand how you must feel, but—"

"Mamita, por favor, I have to get out of the house. I won't be long."

"Go, and come back quickly."

"Sí, Mamita."

Julia ran from the house and the hacienda compound. Once she was outside, her steps slowed and she took several deep breaths of fresh air, trying to calm the awful tumult of her emotions. Her eyes scanned the horizon, praying for Ruíz to appear on his palomino stallion.

There was no sign of him on the horizon.

Topping the bluff, she gazed down at Conchita's favorite fishing place by the old live oak. But what she saw escalated her forebodings to sheer, raw terror. The earth tilted and spun, and she feared she was going to be violently sick. Doubling over, she fought desperately for control. Her heart pounded like a death knell sounding in her ears, and a clammy sweat slicked her body.

Straightening with difficulty, she fought the spiraling plunge into panic and managed to call out, "What are you doing with her?"

The yellow-haired youth who was holding Luz's limp form in his arms stopped in his tracks and stared up at her. She could read the surprise on his features, even from the distance separating them.

His voice called back in English, "I don't know if you can understand me, but she's hurt."

She nodded, and tears began to stream down her face. In her distraught state, she was unaccountably grateful she was able to understand the Anglo stranger. All those long months spent pounding the rudiments of English into her head hadn't been wasted.

Sprinting down the hill, she stopped within a few steps of the stranger. Studying his youthful features up close, the knot in her stomach loosened slightly, and something told her she didn't need to fear this young man. He held Luz in his arms as if she were a fragile piece of china, and his face mirrored her own concern.

In her astonishment at finding Luz hurt and being held by a stranger, she suddenly realized she had forgotten about Conchita. Glancing frantically along the riverbank, she saw no sign of the child. The terrible panic returned.

"What happened?"

The tense look on the youth's face eased a fraction when he heard her respond in his native tongue.

"I was coming to the Navarro place. I heard two shots. Found this young lady lying here. A bullet must have grazed her head. Might not be too serious. Are you from the Navarro vineyard?"

"Yes. Did you see a child?" Julia held her breath, waiting for his answer.

"No, ma'am, I didn't see no child. Jist this lady." He paused, and Julia could read the swift realization that lit his light-blue eyes. "But maybe that's what this lady was crying about before she blacked out. She kept pointing back to the Estrada spread and calling . . . Let me see if I can—"

"*La niña?*"

"Them's the words." He bobbed his head.

"And she pointed toward the Estrada ranch?"

"Yes, and that's where I came from, looking for the boss man, Navarro."

"Why?"

"I went to the Estrada ranch to see Allende Soto. He's my friend, and he was expectin' some letters I brung him from

San Antone. But he weren't around and Señor Ramos, the foreman, couldn't find him neither. The only thing we could figger was to come here and see if Navarro knew—"

"Did you look inside the Estrada hacienda?"

"No, ma'am, it were bolted from the inside, and Señor Ramos said he didn't dare to force it without Navarro's orders."

"I understand." And she did understand . . . only too well. The unformed portents that had haunted her all day coalesced into a meaningful pattern and made sense to her. Ruíz, Allende, and now Conchita were being held captive inside the Estrada hacienda.

The horrible fears that had hounded her were all too real. With that realization, Julia calmed and found strength. Knowing was power. But there wasn't a moment to waste. And Luz needed attention, too. She made her decision without conscious thought.

"Give me your pistol," she demanded. "Do you have a carbine? I need it, too, and any ammunition you have. I also need your horse."

Astonishment spread across the youth's features, and he sputtered, "Ma'am, I . . . I don't know. What do you mean . . . my guns . . . my horse? What about this lady?"

"There's no time to waste. Your friend, Allende, is in grave danger, as is his boss and the child. They're in the hacienda compound. Don't ask me to explain how I know, it will take too long. There's a way to get inside the compound that won't be guarded. I have to go to them."

"But, ma'am—"

"You need to take this lady, Luz, to my mother," she interrupted his startled protest. "My mother's a healer. You seem to be a strong man. The Navarro compound isn't far, just over the bluff. Use my name, Julia Flores, to gain entrance. The guard at the gate will direct you to my mother's house. Her name is Pilar Flores. She will care for Luz. Please, I know it's a great deal to ask, but you must trust me, Mr. . . . "

"Obadiah MacGregor's my name, ma'am."

"Good, Obadiah, do you understand?"

"Yes, but Miss Flores, I think you should wait and let some men go—"

"After you take Luz to my mother, ask for my father, Felipe Flores," Julia cut him off again. "Tell my father he will need to gather some men to break into the Estrada compound. Tell him to come armed and that it will be dangerous. If my father isn't at home, tell my mother to send some men to Señor Ramos."

"But you shouldn't go on ahead, Miss Flores, if it's as dangerous as you say it is."

Ignoring him again, she demanded, "Your pistol, Obadiah." She held out her hand.

Shaking his mop of yellow-bright hair, he shifted Luz in his arms and thrust the pistol at her. Julia took the weapon and checked it to be certain that it was loaded and primed.

"Your carbine?"

Obadiah jerked his head downward, and Julia spied the carbine lying on the ground. She retrieved it and returned to him. "Your ammunition?"

"In my saddlebag. But I doubt you know how to load them."

"I may not," Julia snapped, "but someone else might."

He nodded, his young face a battleground of warring emotions. "I'll see that this lady . . . Luz . . . gets good care. May God protect you, Miss Flores."

Chapter
Twenty-two

Ruíz felt the unwelcome slap of the water again. With waking, pain reverberated through him, making it difficult to think or even breathe. His first realization was that he was no longer chained to the wall. He was lying facedown on the floor with the cold tile pressing against his bare chest. The next thing he realized didn't make sense. He heard the sobs, soft and high, of a child.

Who was crying? His mind was blurry, barely able to function, but he couldn't shake the feeling that he had heard those childish sobs before . . . that they were somehow familiar. Straining, he tried to—''

He jerked upright off the hard floor. Agonizing pain shot through him.

Conchita!

Lázaro chuckled. He leaned close to Ruíz and whispered, "This is the little surprise I had planned for you, Ruíz. You might withstand the lash . . . but your daughter's sobs . . . ?''

He couldn't believe what he was hearing: Conchita. They

had taken Conchita. *Madre de Dios,* would the nightmare never end? He struggled to form his thoughts. Where was his daughter? Was she in the room with him?

"Por favor, give me something to cover myself with. I don't want her to see me . . . like this. It will frighten her,'' Ruíz gasped.

His brother-in-law didn't answer. Instead, someone grabbed him by the armpits and hauled him to his feet. He almost blacked out again from the agony. Swaying on his feet, he stared down, trying to concentrate on the pattern in the tile floor. Anything to keep his mind from the weakness and anguish permeating his body.

"A shirt.'' Lázaro snapped his fingers and directed, "Put it on him.''

Ruíz clenched his jaw and dug his fingers into his hands, forming fists as the pain ricocheted through him, while Lázaro's thugs forced the shirt over his mutilated torso. Once the shirt was in place and buttoned, he stood swaying. It took every last ounce of his strength to keep from falling on his face.

"Why don't you sit down, Ruíz, to greet your daughter,'' Lázaro offered.

A chair was shoved at him and he sat.

"Muy bien. You've finally learned to follow orders. It's a beginning. And now, before I bring your daughter to you, I have one final request. Where is the treasure?''

His weary head jerked up. Despite the twisting agony devouring his body, his mind suddenly cleared. This was Lázaro's final ultimatum. He understood without being told. His daughter or the treasure.

There was no decision to be made.

Awkwardly, he slid to the floor and onto his knees. Facing the madman, he clasped his hands in front of him as if he were praying and bent his head. He didn't know how to beg any more effectively. He only prayed his complete submission would convince his insane brother-in-law.

"You will have your treasure, Don Lázaro, I will lead you to it. Take my worthless life in retribution if you must, but I beg you, don't harm my child. She's only a baby. After . . ." His voice faltered, knowing death was near.

Knowing he would never hold Julia in his arms again. Knowing Conchita would grow up without a father. He took iron control of his emotions and forced himself to finish, "You will have your treasure and your revenge. But let my child go, *por favor*. She's too young to be a threat to you."

Lázaro bowed formally, his countenance grave for once, not mocking. Ruíz drew confidence from the seriousness of his expression, hope sparking within him that Lázaro would spare his daughter.

"Of course, Ruíz. I wouldn't harm a child," Lázaro reassured him. And in the same breath, he ordered, "Bring in the girl."

The study door opened and another man Ruíz had never seen before entered, carrying his crying daughter. The ugly henchman was bald and possessed no eyebrows. The complete lack of hair made him look like a malformed egg.

Lázaro nodded, and the bald man knelt, releasing his small charge. Conchita, sobbing and sniffling, looked about her in bewildered dismay. Her gaze skittered over Ruíz and then returned. Her face suddenly lit up as she recognized him, and she ran forward.

"*¡Papito, Papito!*" Flinging herself into Ruíz's arms, she cried out, "Oh, *Papito,* I was so afraid. They hurt Luz and took me away. I was so afraid, *Papito!*"

He embraced his daughter and held her close, savoring these last, poignant moments with his child. He made his voice low and gentle. "I'm here, little one, and everything will be fine. Don't worry about Luz," Ruíz lied, trying to hide his fury at the knowledge that they had harmed her, too. "This is just an adventure. We'll tell everyone the story tomorrow."

Conchita raised her tear-streaked face and stared around her, blinking owlishly. "Just a story, *Papito?*"

"Sí."

"I like stories, *Papito*."

Before Ruíz could further reassure his daughter, Lázaro's voice, filled with impatience, rasped out, "I've allowed you sufficient time with her. Where's the treasure?" He gestured, and the bald man snatched Conchita from Ruíz's arms.

Rising with difficulty, he faced Lázaro. "My daughter will be safe if I show you?"

"Sí, you have my word." Lázaro promised.

Nodding, he shuffled painfully to the fireplace. He placed his hand on the carved wooden crucifix at the far right side of the mantel. Then he had a sudden awful thought. He had never bothered to look for the treasure after Don Estéban died. It hadn't been important at the time.

What if Don Estéban had told him incorrectly or what if the latch didn't work or the tunnel? Cold sweat broke out on his forehead, and his stomach churned. His daughter's life hung in the balance. He crossed himself and prayed.

Grasping the crucifix, he tugged hard. It turned! There was a groaning sound of hinges and the wall inside the cold hearth swung open. *Madre de Dios,* it had worked! He went limp with relief.

He heard Lázaro's satisfied grunt behind him. Triumph making his voice shrill, Lázaro commanded, *"¡Vámonos, hombres!* Bring the prisoners with us."

Ruíz was pulled along, and he glanced back to see a dazed Allende following, too. Lázaro's henchmen had removed the bonds from his hands and feet, but Allende slouched forward, moving slowly, bent over at the waist and clutching his abdomen, confirming Ruíz's earlier fears. Lázaro and his men had hurt Allende far more than was readily evident.

He wasn't surprised. His own body was so brutalized it barely responded to his simplest commands. He could feel the blood from his back already soaking through the fresh shirt. He tried to twist around, hoping Conchita couldn't see the crimson streaks staining the white shirt, but he was prodded forward by a pistol at his back.

Lázaro ordered lanterns brought to descend into the tunnel. Crawling through the opening, one by one, with Lázaro in the lead, they discovered crude stone steps leading downward.

When they reached the bottom of the steps, they moved forward in the dank darkness. The lantern light caught the image of a statue. It was the Virgin Mary.

Ruíz pointed. "Stop. This is where the treasure is buried."

Lázaro's evil face loomed from the shadows. "Are you certain?"

Lifting his head, he gazed about him. The bald man who had his daughter was missing from their unholy group. That gave Ruíz hope. Conchita was too young to be a coherent witness, and she was Lázaro's niece. Lázaro may have hated his father, but he had seemed to care for Alicia. Surely he would keep his word and let Conchita go.

Lázaro had brought along the scar-faced man, the man missing his ear, and the small, drab man. Four against two ... bad odds. But Lázaro and his henchmen had holstered their weapons, obviously lulled into a false sense of security because they believed he and Allende were sufficiently crippled by the beatings.

Even with his battered body, Ruíz would have tried to best them ... even with his last breath. Lázaro must have guessed he would fight to the end, because he had used the life of Conchita to bring him to his knees. For Conchita, he would sacrifice his own life. And if they had taken Julia, he would have done the same.

It was a bitter irony that once he had found love and looked forward to having a family, his life was to be prematurely snuffed out. This tunnel would be his and Allende's grave. He was certain of it. But he had no choice ... his life was forfeit already. He only wanted to save his daughter. *Gracias a Dios*, Lázaro didn't know about Julia, too. At least she was safe.

"Where is the treasure buried?" Lázaro demanded.

"Beneath the statue."

"I might have known. My father always had a macabre sense of humor. It would suit him to bury church treasure underneath a statue of the Virgin Mary."

Glancing down, Ruíz tried to judge how deep the niche was and how far they would need to dig. He noticed two old rusty tools lying on the floor of the tunnel, a pick and shovel.

Lázaro followed his gaze and commented, "How convenient. I won't have to send for tools. Ruíz, you and your *amigo,* Allende, can do the digging. We'll watch."

He wasn't surprised by Lázaro's decision. He and Allende were both in obvious pain. It suited his brother-in-law's twisted cruelty to submit them to further degradation and agony before he killed them . . . while his able-bodied thugs stood by.

With difficulty, they picked up the tools and bent to their tasks. Slowly, painfully, they started hacking at the wall of dirt beneath the statue. When the ground shifted beneath the platform of the saint, Allende reached out and caught the tottering Virgin. Reverently, he placed her on the ground to one side.

"Forget the damned statue. Keep digging," Lázaro's impatient voice commanded.

They obeyed, Ruíz hacking at the dirt with his pick while Allende shoveled away the crumbling earth. When Ruíz's pick grazed something hard and he guessed it was the trunk that held the treasure, he heard a whimper.

Glancing up, he was horrified to find that the bald man had joined them in the tunnel. The whimper he had heard came from Conchita.

An awful realization swept over him. Lázaro wouldn't have brought his daughter into the tunnel if he didn't mean to kill her. There could be no other possible reason for her presence. Her small body was going to join his and Allende's in this impromptu grave.

His insane brother-in-law was going to kill an innocent child!

There was nothing left to lose. He exchanged a pointed glance with Allende, hoping the man would understand and help him with his last desperate attempt to save his daughter. He thought he saw Allende bend his head, almost imperceptibly, in a nod of acknowledgment. At least, Ruíz reasoned, he and Allende had crude weapons in their hands while their complacent captors had put away their pistols.

But it was Conchita, herself, who provided the catalyst, squirming and crying in her captor's arms. The ugly bald man suddenly released her and shrieked in disgust, "The brat pissed on me!" He stared down at his wet shirt with horror stamped on his features.

Before Lázaro could react, Ruíz nodded to Allende and grabbed a handful of dirt, flinging it into Lázaro's eyes.

Julia dug her heels into Obadiah's gelding and forced the horse to swim across the river. The horse struggled beneath her, first swimming and then lurching forward on the unsure footing of the opposite riverbank. Once the gelding had found his feet, Julia urged him forward at a full gallop.

She seldom rode, and horses tended to frighten her. But she put her fears aside and clung to her flying mount, praying that she wouldn't fall or be thrown.

When she reached the valley that held the Estrada *rancho* headquarters, Julia circled around to the back of the hacienda. She knew her decision to come alone must have appeared foolish to the young stranger, Obadiah. But as soon as she had realized that Ruíz, Conchita, and Allende were being held prisoner in the Estrada hacienda, she had also feared that a direct assault might get them killed.

If she could sneak inside and assess the situation or secretly help the prisoners, she might be able to save them. And she knew just the way to gain access. She had accidentally found what she believed was an underground entrance to the compound when she was helping her mother nurse Don Estéban. It was in the springhouse where she had been sent to fetch cool water for the dying man's feverish brow.

The springhouse, built around a bubbling, artesian spring, lay outside the compound. But there was a tunnel leading from the springhouse toward the compound. Julia guessed the tunnel was there so the inhabitants would always have a source of fresh water, even if the compound was under siege. On one of her trips to the springhouse, she had explored the tunnel for a few steps, wondering if her theory was correct. Not possessing a lantern at the time, she had turned back. She was still convinced that the tunnel led to the hacienda.

She prayed she was right.

Dismounting outside the *adobe,* cone-shaped structure, which served as the springhouse, Julia tied the borrowed gelding to a tree. She untied the saddlebag holding the extra ammunition and slung it over her shoulder, secured the pistol in her waistband, and cradled the carbine in her right arm.

The thick, *adobe* walls of the springhouse had been built to keep the coolness within. Only four narrow slits at the top of the cone provided ventilation and light. Julia entered the springhouse through a wooden door, and then paused, letting her eyes adjust to the dimness inside.

The springhouse was just as she remembered it, with a crystal-clear spring gurgling to the surface, surrounded by moss and delicate ferns that thrived in the dim sunlight. Against the walls of the structure were crates of wine and foodstuffs that had been stored there to take advantage of the cool humidity.

The black mouth of the tunnel yawned at the opposite side. Again, she didn't have a lantern with her. There had been no time to fetch one. Even if she *had* brought a lantern, she wouldn't have used it. She didn't know exactly where the tunnel ended, and she couldn't take the chance the light might be seen by whoever was holding the prisoners.

Taking a deep breath, she entered the tunnel. Based on her memory, the tunnel angled sharply only a few steps past its entrance, blocking out even the pale light from the springhouse. Knowing this, she backed up slowly until she touched the cold, moist earth of the tunnel wall. Using the wall as her guide, she moved forward slowly, taking one step at a time and trying to keep her progress as quiet as possible.

Within only a few steps, complete blackness surrounded her, entombing her deeply inside the earth. She couldn't even discern the shape of her own hand when she held it in front of her face, the darkness was so complete. For a moment, she stood still, trembling involuntarily, feeling out of her element and overwhelmed by the black void she had entered. Shaking off her nameless fears, she forged ahead again, being careful to not lose contact with the tunnel wall.

With her vision useless, her other senses seemed to take over. Her feet registered each hole and pebble, and her fingertips became intimately acquainted with the earthen wall. The tunnel wall was far from smooth, it possessed its own peculiar land-marks: scooped-out pockets of earth, jagged fissures, and brief stretches of rock face. Her sense of smell sharpened, too. Her nostrils flared, taking in the rotting, fetid smell of damp earth. She especially strained her ears, searching for any indication she was nearing the hacienda.

At first, all Julia heard was the drip, drip of water. As she cautiously moved forward, step by step, other more compelling sounds reached her ears. She heard thudding noises, sounding as if someone or something was steadily hitting the sides of the tunnel. She stopped and held her breath, trying to make sense of what she was hearing, but the sound was alien . . . unidentifiable.

Summoning her courage, she began moving forward again, but before she had taken more than half a dozen steps, her alert ears picked up another sound . . . one she could identify.

It was the distinct murmur of voices!

Startled, she stopped again and crouched against the wall. What could the voices possibly mean? She didn't think she had come far enough to be under the hacienda, but if she wasn't directly under it, how could she be hearing voices?

The thudding noise grew louder. Concentrating, she tried to envision what it could be. She heard a rhythmic pounding, interspersed by a scraping noise. It was as if . . . as if . . . someone were digging in the tunnel.

At the sudden realization, her heart felt as if were going to leap from her chest. Her breath strangled in her throat. Never, in her wildest imaginings, had she expected to find someone in the tunnel with her . . . digging.

She had to know why. Her first thought wasn't encouraging, bringing back her earlier fears. Terror clawed at her, making her heart pound even harder. Despite the dank chill of the tunnel, perspiration covered her body.

Could someone be digging graves in the tunnel?

She buried her face in her hands, and her body shook uncontrollably. The blackness enfolded her, pulling her down, sucking the very breath from her lungs . . . encasing her like a tomb . . .

Gritting her teeth, she lifted her head and cocked the carbine. She drew the pistol from the waistband of her skirt and cocked it, too. Commanding her numb feet to move forward, she crept toward the awful sounds.

She had to know.

The tunnel wall angled again, coming to a sharp outcropping of stone, and on the other side, she caught a glimpse of light.

Julia melted into the jagged rock point. Bit by bit, with her face pressed against the filthy wall, she scooted forward until she could peer into the pocket of light.

What she saw astonished her.

The light was coming from a place in the tunnel that widened into a small, earthen chamber. Within it were Ruíz and Allende, digging into the side of the dirt wall. Incongruously, a statue of the Virgin Mary lay at their feet. Blood seeped through the shirt of Ruíz's straining back, and Allende worked, doubled over, clutching his abdomen.

It was as she had feared . . . they were hurt.

And surrounded by four . . . no five men . . . watching them dig.

One tall man looked vaguely familiar to her. Another was small and possessed the features of a rodent. There was a man with only one ear and another man who had a hideous scar marring his face. The fifth man was difficult to make out; he stood in the shadows at the far side of the tunnel.

She thought it strange that none of them had their weapons drawn. Except perhaps the man in the shadows, who appeared to be holding something in his arms. Whatever it was that he was holding looked as if it were too large to be a weapon. What could it be?

Julia strained her eyes to see what he was holding, and the bulky form in his arms suddenly shifted, wriggling and whimpering. She caught a glimpse of a small, pale face in the shadows.

It was Conchita!

She had been right. Ruíz, Conchita, and Allende were being held prisoner. It didn't matter that their captors didn't have their weapons drawn. It was obvious these five unknown men had already brutalized both Ruíz and Allende. Even in the dim light, Julia could make out the wide, frightened eyes of Conchita. The taut silence of the tableau before her was broken only by the sounds of digging, which carried its own unspoken menace. She sensed the evil and danger in the close confines of the tunnel.

Forcing herself to concentrate, she cast about for some way to help her loved ones. The five men all had pistols in their belts. Ruíz and Allende were unarmed except for the rusty tools in their hands. Julia had two cocked and primed weapons, but that would only give her two shots against five men . . . even if she succeeded in hitting both targets. And Julia knew she was no marksman, especially with her limbs trembling like they were. What if her efforts to help only got them all killed?

Then there was Conchita. What if she got hurt . . . or worse . . . in the cross fire?

Julia bit her lip savagely, praying for guidance.

The answer came—and it all happened so fast she didn't have time to think or to be afraid. She only had time to react.

The man holding Conchita released her suddenly and screamed, "The brat pissed on me!"

Ruíz flung dirt into the tall man's eyes, and he staggered back, rubbing his eyes and cursing furiously.

Allende savagely swung his shovel and cracked the head of the man who had been holding Conchita. Blood spurted from his bald brow, and he fell to the earthen floor, leaving the tunnel opening leading back to the hacienda unguarded.

"Conchita, run back to the steps!" Ruíz ordered loudly.

The little girl didn't question her father's abrupt order; she bravely scurried away into the darkness.

Emerging from her hiding place, Julia shouted, "Ruíz, catch!" She tossed the pistol to him, and he caught it.

Standing on the opposite side of Ruíz, Allende was too far for her to throw him the carbine, so she lifted it herself and leveled it at the other three men, warning, "Don't touch your weapons."

The rodent-faced man dropped to his knees and raised his hands above his head, blubbering, "Don't shoot, don't shoot." Allende, who was standing closest to him, took advantage of the man's fear and snatched the pistol from his belt.

Cursing obscenely, it was obvious the other two men didn't like having the tables turned on them. Julia stood opposite the scar-faced man and the man missing an ear. All of her concentration was on them.

Allende was behind the two men, and he prodded them. "Drop your weapons." With obvious reluctance, they did as they were told, letting their pistols fall to the hard-packed earth of the tunnel. He grabbed their weapons and stuck them in his belt.

Ruíz was positioned to the left side of Julia and standing directly across from the tall man whom he had pelted with dirt.

With lightning speed the tall man reached for the pistol in his belt and snarled, "Damn you, Ruíz, I won't surrender. You'll go to hell with me!"

Two shots rang out in the close confines of the tunnel walls. A smoky haze from the discharged gunpowder filled the small space.

"Ruíz!" Julia cried.

In the confusion, the scar-faced man lunged for Allende. Allende shot him point blank, and he sank to the floor, grasping the gaping hole in his chest.

Julia fought the raw, animal fear clutching her. Was Ruíz hurt or dead? *Dios mío,* she prayed, clinging desperately to the carbine, afraid to shoot for fear of hitting Ruíz or Allende by mistake, until the awful discharge of powder cleared.

Seconds ticked by . . . an eternity of time.

Slowly, very slowly, the tall man began to collapse, but even in his death throes, his hatred was so palpable she could feel it blanketing her, suffocating her with evil. As he doubled over and began to sink to the floor, she saw him draw another smaller pistol from his vest pocket.

Without hesitation, she shot him in the head.

He struck the dirt, face first.

Ruíz lunged forward and grabbed the tall man's second pistol. Ruíz and Allende possessed the only loaded weapons. The worst was over.

"Conchita, *hijita mía,* come to *Papá!*" Ruíz called out.

They heard her sobs before they saw her emerge from the darkness. Tentatively, Conchita edged into the light, hugging the tunnel wall, keeping as far as possible from the two remaining, unarmed thugs.

"Go to Julia, Conchita," Ruíz urged.

Julia, who was trembling uncontrollably from the bloody confrontation, dropped her useless carbine and snatched the frightened child into her arms. Conchita encircled Julia's neck with her arms and sobbed desperately into her shoulder. She held the little girl close with a fierce protectiveness.

Gently, Ruíz lifted the saddlebag from Julia's shoulder and stooped to retrieve the carbine. His voice was soft when he said, "Julia, *por favor,* if you can carry Conchita and follow us."

Allende bent to check for a pulse in the bald man's throat. Solemnly, he straightened and declared, "He's dead."

Ruíz and Allende prodded the two remaining men before them, herding them back to the hacienda and carrying the lanterns to light their way.

Julia followed on wobbly legs, clutching Conchita to her.

They ascended the steps leading from the tunnel and emerged into the study. Julia saw the manacles dangling from the wall. Blanching, she stared at Ruíz's shirt, crimson stained with the blood of his torture.

Before she could go to him, the staccato sound of shots and the splintering sound of wood breaking came from the compound.

Forcing their two captives to lie down on the floor, spread-eagled, Ruíz retrieved the ammunition and powder from the saddlebags. Quickly, he refilled the weapons and gave Julia a pistol to defend herself with. Then he pulled Julia and Conchita down behind a horsehair couch. Ruíz and Allende moved into place, crouched on either side of the study door, waiting.

More shots rang out, followed by an awful silence. Then Julia heard the tramp of heavy boots outside the door. Ruíz and Allende leaned forward, pistols aimed at the door . . . ready to shoot.

Felipe's voice called out, "Ruíz, Julia, are you in there?"

When Julia heard the blessed sound of her father's voice, she slumped forward and hugged Conchita tightly, giving prayerful thanks for their deliverance.

"*Sí*, we're in here, and we're glad to hear your voice," Ruíz responded.

Felipe and Señor Ramos burst into the room, followed by a dozen *vaqueros* and Obadiah.

Julia rushed into her father's arms, and he stroked her hair, murmuring, "*Hija mía*, you're safe. I was so afraid that . . ." His voice choked, and he couldn't finish the awful thought. Instead, he muttered, "The men outside are dead. It is over."

She left her father's arms to go to Ruíz's welcoming embrace. They hugged Conchita between them.

"Julia, *mi preciosa*, what you did was very brave . . . but very foolish. Conchita, Allende, and I owe our lives to you, but if I ever catch you putting yourself in such danger again, I'll . . ."

"You'll what?"

He shook his head and sighed, "My strong, brave Julia. What will I do with you?"

Held in the comforting protection of Ruíz's arms, Julia watched as the two remaining thugs were bound, hand and foot, to be taken to the authorities in San Antonio. Before the two men were led away, Obadiah surprised everyone by stepping forward and identifying the rodent-faced man as the one who had paid his father to rustle livestock from the Estrada *rancho*.

Whining and begging for mercy, the small man admitted his guilt and told everyone how Lázaro had paid him to find men to rustle livestock from the Estrada *rancho* to harass Don Estrada.

Listening to the man's explanation, Julia frowned. She turned to Ruíz, questions crowding her throat.

He must have understood her perplexed look, because he responded by piecing together the insane plan of revenge Lázaro had perpetrated: starting with the livestock rustling and ending

with Lázaro's ultimate greedy goal . . . the secret church treasure hidden in the tunnel.

The men murmured among themselves at the elaborate
revenge plan Lázaro had fashioned. Julia had heard enough. It
was difficult for her to believe so much cruelty and evil could
exist in the world. Now that it was over, all she cared about
was that Lázaro was dead. Ruíz and Conchita were alive, as
well as Allende.

But Ruíz was hurt, badly hurt. He sagged against her. And
Allende needed help as well. He was standing, just barely,
clutching his abdomen.

"I must get you and Allende home, so my mother can tend
to your wounds," Julia said.

Ruíz captured her gaze, and he quirked one eyebrow at
her. "I won't say no to your mother's help, but first, there's
something more important. I believe you and I have a date with
the magistrate."

Epilogue

December 1836

"Who knocks on my door, so late in the night?

We are pilgrims, without shelter, and we need a place to sleep.

Go somewhere else and do not disturb me again.

But the night is dark and cold. We have come from afar, and we are very tired.

But who are you? I know you not.

I am Joseph of Nazareth, a poor carpenter, and with me is my wife, Mary, who will be the mother of the Son of God.

Then come into my humble abode, and welcome! And may the Lord give shelter to my soul when I leave this world!"

Ruíz and Julia listened to the familiar words of the *posada* of the Christ Child. The procession, with paper decorated lanterns, entered the house on the San Antonio River and kneeled, murmuring prayers.

They watched from the arched stone bridge over the river. The same bridge where, in what seemed like a lifetime ago, Ruíz had experienced his first passion for Julia. Remembering, he hugged her close.

It was the last night of the *posada, Noche Buena.* The symbolism of the *posada* touched him deeply this year. The miraculous birth of Jesus and his wedding would be celebrated tomorrow.

He and Julia were to be married in San Fernando Cathedral. It was to be a double ceremony. Allende and Teresa would be married with them. Padre Carrasco, who had been amazed to receive the long-lost church treasure, would perform the ceremony.

When Ruíz had written his mother about Allende's bravery, Doña Eugenia had surprised him by relenting and sending Teresa home to be wed to Allende. Ruíz had also asked to purchase the hacienda at Los Montes Verdes from his mother so Julia would have a proper home. His mother had surprised him again and given him the hacienda as a wedding present.

Doña Eugenia had obviously mellowed. She was planning her own wedding to a wealthy Creole merchant. Reading between the lines of her letters, she wasn't just pleased with her newfound wealth and status. It appeared she loved the man as well. If his mother felt only half of the joy he had found, he could understand the drastic change in her.

Pilar had expertly nursed him and Allende back to health, making certain their wounds healed properly. Luz's head wound had proven more difficult, and she had remained in bed for several weeks. Paco had been crazed until she was well and as soon as she recovered, he proposed marriage. Luz had accepted, and their marriage was planned for the spring.

Conchita was filled with delight that her beloved *Tía* Julia would be her new *mamá,* and she couldn't wait to serve as their flower girl tomorrow. By last count, she had tried on her new lace-flounced dress seventeen times.

Ruíz bent and placed a gentle kiss on Julia's silky, midnight tresses. His heart was bursting with joy, and he could barely contain himself, dreaming of their wedding night to come.

While he and Julia would live at Los Montes Verdes, Allende and Teresa would reside at the Estrada *rancho*. The profits on their first shipment of wines to his uncle had been substantial, and the future was looking bright for the vineyard. The original land grant for the *rancho* had been cleared by the new government of Tejas, and he had given Teresa half of his share in the *rancho* as her dowry.

He sighed to himself. Life was good. There was nothing more he could want. God had blessed him . . . and his loved ones.

Julia swayed beside him and clutched his arm with her left hand. She lifted her other hand to her forehead and shook her head. Startled, Ruíz encircled her with his arms and asked, "What's wrong?"

"Just a dizzy spell. It will pass."

"I know you're nervous about tomorrow, but you should have eaten more at supper tonight," Ruíz softly chided her.

She straightened and released his arm. With a swift nudge of her elbow to his side, she muttered, "I'm not nervous. Speak for yourself." Turning her face to him, she smiled. "It's not nerves, Ruíz." Her emerald eyes sparkled when she admitted, "I'm glad *Papá* forced you to make an honest woman of me two months ago."

Stunned, he gasped and gazed down at her. Her grin was infectious, and he couldn't help but return it. "Is it what I think?"

"*Sí*, it is the fruit of our private harvest celebration. Conchita will have a new baby brother or sister in a few months."

"Julia," he murmured, "you've made me very happy."

"Te amo, mi esposo, te amo." Rising up on tiptoe, she curled her arms around his neck.

"Te amo, mi preciosa," he responded and captured her lips, reveling in her sweet gift and the unbroken harmony of life . . . beginning anew.

FROM ROSANNE BITTNER:
ZEBRA SAVAGE DESTINY ROMANCE!

PASSIONATE ROMANCE
FROM BETINA KRAHN!

LOVE'S BRAZEN FIRE   (0-8217-5691-5, $5.99/$7.50)
1794 marked the Whiskey Rebellion and the love that arose between the free-spirited Whitney Daniels and the reserved Major Garner Townsend. Their unlikely love thrives despite the fact that she is the leader of the very rebellion he is under orders to demolish.

MIDNIGHT MAGIC   (0-8217-4994-3, $4.99/$5.99)
Rane Austen was falling all over Charity Standing . . . literally. Struck by a bullet, Rane lies at Charity's feet and she is left to nurse him back to health. These luckless individuals finally get lucky in love.

PASSION'S RANSOM   (0-8217-5130-1, $5.99/$6.99)
Blythe Woolrich single-handedly runs Woolrich Mercantile and sometimes hopes to get away from all the responsibilities and from Philadelphia. Raider Prescott promises to take her away, only he does so by kidnapping her. He's the captain of a pirate ship who is using her for ransom. He certainly didn't expect to be charmed by her and lose his heart.

REBEL PASSION   (0-8217-5526-9, $5.99/$7.50)
Aria Dunning was against her Royalist father's support of the British King, but she was outraged by his plan to marry her to an English earl. When she meets Tyran Rutland she is surprised at her fluttering heart. Both are equally surprised at the surrender of his loyalty and his heart.

Available wherever paperbacks are sold, or order direct from the Publisher. Send cover price plus 50¢ per copy for mailing and handling to Kensington Publishing Corp., Consumer Orders, or call (toll free) 888-345-BOOK, to place your order using Mastercard or Visa. Residents of New York and Tennessee must include sales tax. DO NOT SEND CASH.